GREAT LIVES

Exploration

Exploration

GREAT LIVES

Milton Lomask

Charles Scribner's Sons · New York

Charles Scribner's Sons Books for Young Readers
Macmillan Publishing Company · 866 Third Avenue, New York, NY 10022
Collier Macmillan Canada, Inc.

Printed in the United States of America
First Edition   10 9 8 7 6 5 4 3 2 1
Cover illustration copyright © 1988 by Stephen Marchesi. All rights reserved.

Library of Congress Cataloging-in-Publication Data
Lomask, Milton.   Great lives: Exploration.
  Bibliography: p. 247   Includes index.
  Summary: Presents biographical sketches of twenty-five significant individuals in the history of world exploration, arranged alphabetically from Roald Amundsen to Amerigo Vespucci.
  1. Explorers—Biography—Juvenile literature.   [1. Explorers] I. Title.
G200.L66 1988 910'.922 [B] [920]   88–15744   ISBN 0–684–18511–3

Contents

Foreword

Three or four thousand years ago an Asiatic king decided to go out and conquer some of the nations around him. North and south and east and west he marched at the head of his big army, raiding and plundering and grabbing other people's real estate. Then one day he saw ahead a very tall mountain. Unable to see anything whatsoever on the far side of it, he concluded that he had reached the end of the world, turned his army around, and marched back home.

That king may have been a great warrior. But he was no explorer. "An explorer," the travel writer Alan Moorehead has noted, "is one of those people who cannot bear not to go see what's on the other side of the next hill."

The pages that follow offer brief life stories of twenty-five of the men and women who by looking over the hills have helped create those geographical marvels of our times—maps that show the whereabouts of practically every rill and creek, every river and lake, every bay and sea, every mountain and valley, and every atoll, island, and continent on the *surface* of the earth. I emphasize the word "surface" for the purpose of showing the limitations of this book. Today a new breed of explorers is looking up—into space—and down—into the interior of the earth and to the bottoms of the seas—but these investigators are not covered here. This book deals only with what we think of as geographical explorers—the adventurers who little by little, down through the centuries, have given us our present knowledge of the surface of the planet we inhabit.

As hundreds of people have contributed to this mammoth effort, alert readers may wonder why I have chosen the twenty-five individuals sketched in this book instead of others equally enterprising and courageous.

I'll try to answer that question.

The known history of exploration points to several extended searches carried out by scores of people. The 300-year search for the Northwest Passage is an instance of this. The 300-year search for the Northeast Passage is another. For these two continuing investigations it seemed only fair to select the men who completed them: in the case of the Northwest Passage, Roald Amundsen; and in the case of the Northeast Passage, Erik Nordenskiöld. On the other hand, choosing among the many explorers who in the nineteenth century opened up the interior of Africa called for guidelines less simple and more subjective in nature. It was John Hanning Speke who during this period completed the 1,500-year search for the source of the main channel of the Nile River. But there was a blandness about Speke that made him a weak candidate for a book entitled *Great Lives*. More suitable by far, I decided, were the three fascinating persons chosen here to represent the opening of the dark continent: Sir Richard Francis Burton, Mary Henrietta Kingsley, and David Livingstone. As for the others on the list—their accomplishments, I believe, explain their inclusion.

Accompanying the biographical sketches is a list of some of the important dates in the long history of geographical exploration. My main purpose in including this chronology is to underscore the meaning of the word "discovery." Discovery is a function of perception, of point of view. To say that a person found a new corner of the world is to say that he found a place new to him and to the people living in the part of the world from which he came. Those islands Christopher Columbus encountered in the Caribbean Sea in 1492 were new to him and to the people of the country that sent him on his voyage. They were not new, of course, to the people already living there and whose ancestors may or may not have been their original discoverers.

The importance of a discovery can be measured only by its consequences. Columbus was by no means the first human being to stand on the soil of the New World. Still, his was the important discovery, or if you prefer, the important rediscovery. It changed the course of history.

To some extent the same can be said of the labors of the twenty-five persons whose careers and personalities are examined in these pages. Few if any of them can be described as having lived perfect lives, for exploration is the work not of angels but of human beings. But all of them can be described as having lived great lives.

The Explorers' World

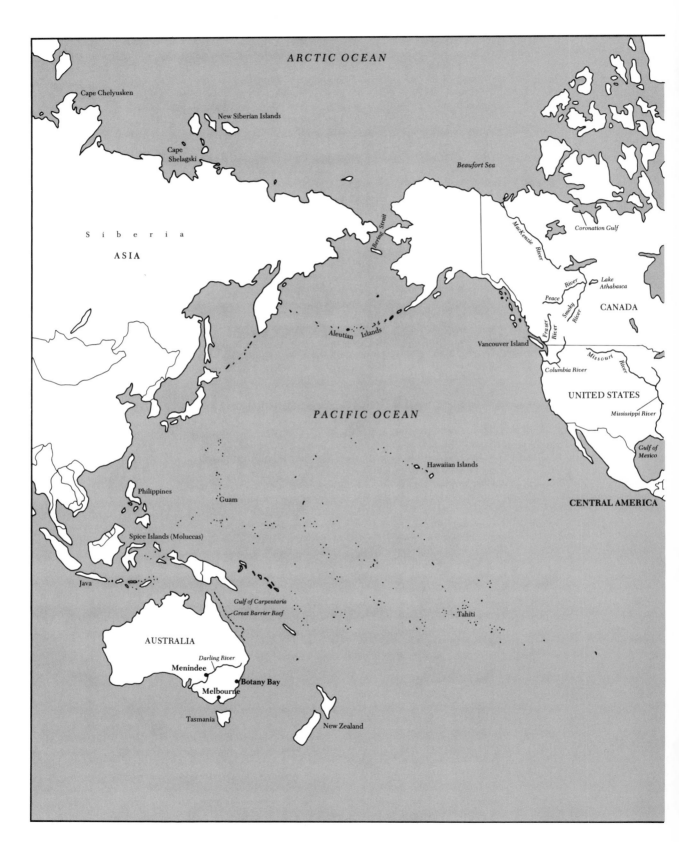

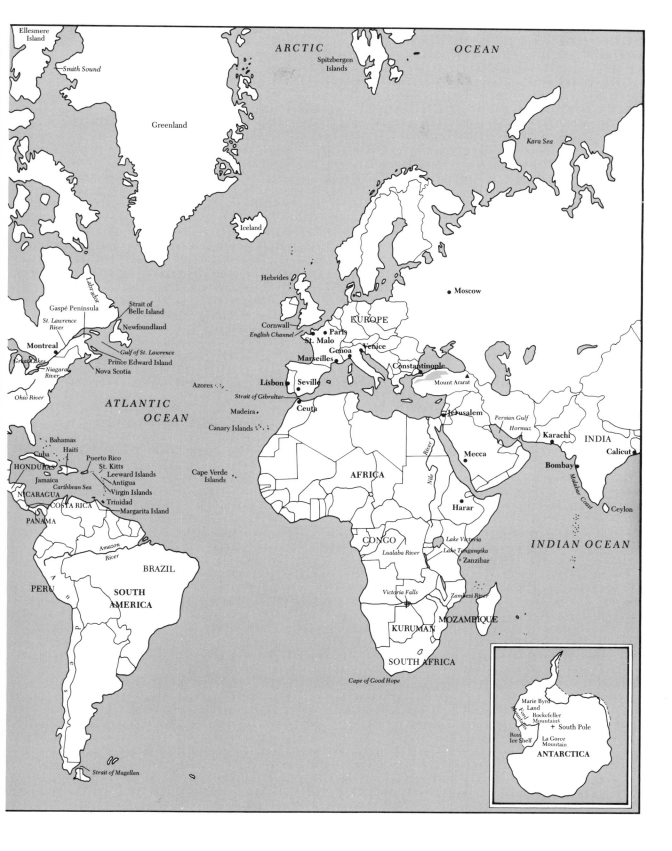

GREAT LIVES

Exploration

Roald Engebreth Gravning Amundsen

1872–1928   Norwegian polar explorer. Discoverer of the South Pole and the first person to reach both poles. Commander of the first expedition to sail through the Northwest Passage. Member of the first group of scientists and others to winter in the Antarctic.

Roald Amundsen was born on July 16, 1872, at Hividsten, a family estate in southeast Norway. His father, Jens Engebreth Amundsen, had accumulated a fortune as a ship skipper and, at the time of the birth of his fourth and last son, owned with his brothers thirty of the one hundred and eighty-five vessels registered at the port town of Sarpsborg across the Glamma river from Hividsten. His mother, Hanna Henrikke Gustava Sahlquist, was the daughter of a government worker. As such, she had grown up surrounded by refinements of the sort that a rough-spoken seafaring community could not provide. Three months after Roald's birth—at her urging and with her husband's reluctant assent—the Jens Engebreth Amund-

sens moved to Christiania (now known as Oslo), the capital of Norway.

Here, in a two-story villa on the forested outskirts of town, Roald and his brothers grew up. Theirs was a typical Norwegian childhood. They played in the woods with the other children of the neighborhood. They knocked off the top hats of passing gentlemen with maliciously aimed snowballs. At the moment each child could toddle he was put on skis—clumsy, homemade planks with toe-loop bindings fashioned from willow twigs. Skis especially made for children were available, but Jens Engebreth would have none of them. His boys "must learn the hard way for the sake of their characters." They were a feisty lot, fond of fist fights. "No fights!"

their father commanded, quickly adding, "But if you must, get in the first blow—and see that it's enough."

As the smallest of the neighborhood gang, Roald was the object of considerable teasing. He endured it, but only up to a point: Displaying a side of his nature that would surface from time to time in the years ahead, he ducked into the woodshed, then out—an uplifted ax in his hand and bloodcurdling warnings on his lips. We have the assurance of a family friend, Borchgrevink, who witnessed the incident, that thereafter the youngest of the Amundsens was treated with respect.

In 1886 Roald's father died, and a few months later his brothers left home to begin their adult careers, leaving him with his mother. Their relationship was a strained one, for Gustava Amundsen had plans for her son's future—plans wholly at odds with those he was already shaping for himself.

In his fifteenth year he came across two books by the English explorer, Sir John Franklin. During two overland expeditions, Franklin and his assistant had examined the North American coast along the Arctic Ocean. The tales related in the books were of men overcoming the rigors of the frozen North, of what an American novelist later called "grace under pressure," in frequent brushes with death. What heightened Roald's admiration for Franklin was the tragedy that terminated the Englishman's career. During Franklin's third expedition, this time in Arctic waters, his vessel became frozen in ice and Franklin died. Unable to free the ship, his surviving companions struggled to return to civilization on foot, only to die of starvation en route. Writing later of his first reading of Franklin's books, Roald described himself as filled at the time with a longing "to suffer for a cause," as Franklin had, "not in a burning desert but in the frosty North." His words point out the young Amundsen's fondness for martyrdom, which in the passing years would be tempered but never altogether eliminated.

In his mind, he was still braving the perils of the Arctic with Franklin when word reached Norway that one of its own citizens, the redoubtable Fridtjof Nansen, had done something that many others had only attempted. With a party of five, Nansen had crossed the ice cap that covers most of the island of Greenland, traversing more than five hundred miles with the aid of skis and dog-drawn sledges. When on May 30, 1889, Nansen came home, seventeen-year-old Roald was part of the crowd cheering from the docks of Christiania as the ship, bearing Norway's greatest hero since the days of the Vikings, sailed through the fjord. At that moment, Roald revealed later, he knew what he was going to do with his life. He was going to walk in the footsteps of Nansen and Franklin.

Did he mention these ambitions to his mother? If he did, she dismissed them as the daydreams of a teenager. During the fourteen years of Gustava Amundsen's marriage, her seagoing husband had been away from home more often than not. She wanted no more wandering males in her life. We are told that on the whole she was an indulgent parent, given to pampering her youngest son. But she could be stern. Roald, she announced in terms no seventeen-year-old of those times would dream of contradicting, was to become a physician.

Obediently, he enrolled at Christiania University. After all, she was his mother and, more to the point, she controlled the family purse strings. Obediently, he studied medicine, but his heart was not in it. Roald Amundsen had a kind of temperament often found in successful individuals. He would work any hours and suffer any drudgery to learn about things that interested him, but no one could compel him to spend his energies on things that did not.

The published reports of the world's polar explorers received more of his at-tention than his medical books. He read and reread newspaper accounts of Fridtjof Nansen's proposals for another polar expedition. Nansen was a marine biologist and this trip was to be a scientific survey of the waters encircling the North Pole. It was to be carried out from the decks of a specially built vessel called *Fram*, the Norwegian word for "forwards," and was to be conducted in a manner no man had even thought of before. Nansen's plan was to let the *Fram* freeze into the pack ice of the Arctic Ocean and then let it move with the currents across that vast Polar basin. Roald had watched his idol's return from his traverse of Greenland. He was on the docks of Christiania again when in the summer of 1893 Nansen departed for the three-year adventure that would become known as "the drift of the *Fram.*"

When in June of that year Roald came up for his final medical examinations, he flunked. He never told his mother of this, and when two months later she died, he left the university, free at last to begin preparing himself for the life of an explorer in the cold regions at the ends of the world.

He was twenty-one at this time, a striking-looking man with a long, lean face and intense blue eyes. His mother had called him "The Last of the Vikings." Indeed, his most prominent feature, a strong and hawklike nose, is one we associate with those daring rovers of the sea who, fanning out from Norway's countless fjords a thousand years ago, discovered first Iceland and then Greenland and finally the shores of North America.

By and large, the folks who knew Roald in his early years found him pleasant enough company, not much of a talker but a good listener and invariably courteous. Some, to be sure, saw in him a vein of prudery, the spinsterish sense of propriety of a man who blanched and sometimes walked away when the conversation turned to sex. He paid little attention to the young women around him, except a pretty cousin with whom, it was thought, he was for a time in love. One thing everyone noticed was his single-mindedness. Travel, the wasteland of the Arctic— these were the magnets that drew him; and once he quit the university, he set out to master the skills a polar explorer must acquire.

He practiced skiing in the mountains of western Norway. He studied astronomy, map reading, and surveying. To learn the art of navigation he shipped as a common sailor on a variety of vessels, and he earned his Mate's and then Master's certificates. Every time he heard that someone was planning an excursion in the direction of one of the

poles he tried to join it. But not until 1897 did he obtain a berth as an officer on an old fishing bark called the *Belgica* that Lieutenant Adrien De Gerlache, a Belgian naval officer, was refurbishing for a scientific look at Antarctica.

The *Belgica* set sail from Sandefjord on June 26, 1897, and Amundsen joined her in Antwerp.

After a long journey via Rio de Janeiro and Cape Horn, the scientists and sailors glimpsed on January 19, 1898, the western shore of Antarctica along that portion of the frozen continent known as Graham Land in the South Shetlands. To a man as eager to see this part of the world as Amundsen, it was an awesome sight, a boundless wilderness of whiteness broken here and there by outcroppings of black rock where the peaks of mountains rose above the snow. Moving westward, the *Belgica* encountered the pack ice found in all polar waters. To a person who had not seen this spectacle before it was a startling sight—a vast and glassy encrustation, its overlapping and slow-moving floes filling the air with an eerie droning sound that a French explorer described as "like the distant murmur of a great city at the bottom of a valley."

De Gerlache originally intended to encamp with his scientists on the mainland of Cape Adare and then send his vessel to winter in Australia. But these plans proved impossible. In the Bellings-hausen Sea, off the western coasts of Antarctica, the *Belgica* was caught in the ice, and all hands were forced to remain aboard while their ship, like Nansen's *Fram*, drifted slowly south-ward.

For most of them it was a miserable experience. On May 17, 1898, the sun disappeared and for the next seventy days, jammed together in a small and weather-beaten bark, they lived in the perpetual night of the Antarctic wilds. The unbroken darkness, the fear of some that they would perish in this des-olate gloom, the monotony of living side by side, day after day, with the same people, the lack of interesting activity, the numbing temperatures—all these factors took their toll. Some became sick, some died, some went insane.

Amundsen was one of the few who never lost heart. On the contrary, he enjoyed himself. After all, this was what he had come south for—to learn how to live under polar conditions. He kept busy. He and a shipmate constructed a new kind of tent, aerodynamically de-signed to diminish wind resistance dur-ing fierce Antarctic storms.

Spring came, and with it the release of the *Belgica* from its glistening prison. In May 1899, when Amundsen got back to Norway, his head was bursting with ideas for what was to be the first of

his own expeditions—the crossing of the Northwest Passage. The Northwest Passage! Few names have resounded so frequently in the long story of geo-graphical exploration. Its history dates back to the years following Christopher Columbus's great voyages when the people of Europe realized that what he had discovered was not an outlying sec-tion of Asia, as he himself thought, but a whole new continent. "The Barrier," they called it, for it stood between them and the spice- and silk-rich lands of the Orient with which they wished to trade. Surely there must be some waterway through the barrier, some shortcut to Cathay, meaning China and the islands in its vicinity.

Ferdinand Magellan, leading the first expedition to circle the globe, was the first to locate such a shortcut—the strait that now bears his name below the mainland of South America. But for a waterborne trader, going by the Strait of Magellan was a time-consuming un-dertaking; and for centuries the seadogs of half a dozen European nations prod-ded every inlet along the Atlantic shores of the New World in search of a more convenient route. Little by little, thanks to these efforts, it became clear that if such a channel existed, it lay across the top of North America.

But was there even a passage there? Though no one had yet laid eyes on

From 1903 to 1906, Amundsen commanded this modest vessel, the *Gjøa*, in the first successful navigation of the Northwest Passage. *Neg. 2A7042, Courtesy of Department Library Services, American Museum of Natural History.*

it, explorers and mapmakers were certain that there was, and in the eighteenth and nineteenth centuries events showed them to be right.

First, a Danish explorer in the employ of Russia discovered the waterway at the top of the Pacific Ocean that divides Alaska from Asia—a strait that would turn out to be the western entrance to the passage. Then a Briton, poking about in the upper Atlantic, discovered Lancaster Sound, the eastern entrance. Then two other Englishmen, acting at separate times, succeeded in penetrating the waterway as far as Viscount Melville Sound north of Canada. One of them reached it from the west, the other from the east; and the existence of the Northwest Passage was proved.

This was in 1854, and in the minds of explorers only one thing remained to be done about the Northwest Passage: Someone must sail through it. By the time Amundsen returned home from his ordeal on the *Belgica*, he had decided that the someone was going to be him.

It took him four years to organize and finance the enterprise. He used his patrimony, the inheritance from his mother, to buy the ship he needed. It was a small twenty-nine-year-old sloop called the *Gjøa*. The boat had seen service to a herring fishery and still smelled

of it. One of his first steps was to call on Fridtjof Nansen, for no Norwegian could expect to conduct a successful polar investigation without the great man's blessing. Amundsen got it. Indeed, Nansen helped him in every way he could, and on the night of June 16, 1903, the *Gjøa* pulled away quietly from the waterfront of Christiania to begin what was to be a memorable journey.

The crew reflected one of Amundsen's most firmly held principles. A big job, he believed, is best done by the smallest number of people. Sir John Franklin had taken one-hundred and twenty-eight men on the voyage that had cost him his life. Amundsen's party consisted of six.

In mid-August their bulky square-sterned sloop, its sail power abetted by a "hot bulb" kerosene motor—making it one of the earliest motor-driven vessels—chugged through Lancaster Sound. Winter arrived, and on October 3 the *Gjøa* became frozen into the ice and Amundsen and his companions encamped on the coast of King William Island at a place that appears on today's maps of Canada as Gjøahavn.

Here they stayed for almost two years. They could have pushed on in the spring of 1904, but Amundsen chose to linger for a variety of reasons. One was that before leaving Norway he had promised to seek the answer to a question that students of the polar regions had been pondering for eighty years. At each end of the great magnet that is the earth, there is not just one pole. There are two: the geographical pole and the magnetic pole. Back in 1831 the British explorer Sir James Clark Ross had determined the position of the North Magnetic Pole on the Boothia Peninsula of Canada, one of the land masses bordering the Northwest Passage. At once a question arose: Did the magnetic pole stay in one place as did the geographical pole—or did it from time to time move around?

There was only one way to solve this scientific puzzle. Someone must return to where Ross had found the North Magnetic Pole and see if it was still there. This is what Amundsen and his followers did, traveling overland to the Boothia Peninsula to learn from their instruments that the magnetic pole had moved—a discovery that ended the long argument forever.

Another of Amundsen's reasons for spending two winters at Gjøahavn was to him, as a polar explorer, even more compelling. Shortly after he and his party arrived there, the members of an Eskimo tribe called the Netsiliks appeared on the scene. Here, Amundsen realized, was a chance to learn from the people who knew best how to travel and work in the frozen North.

Under the guidance of the Netsiliks,

he and his men learned how to erect an igloo in three and a half hours. They learned what food to eat and what clothes to wear for survival in freezing temperatures. They learned how to manage the Eskimo dog.

The Eskimo dog is one of the most amazing beasts on earth: half tame, half wild, intelligent, frisky, ornery at times, capable of pulling heavy loads over terrains where other animals can barely propel themselves. But even these wonderful creatures have their limits. The huge emptiness of the polar wilds with the snow flying in the air makes them a world of mist and mystery. Every step is a step into the unknown, and the Eskimo dog, brave though he is, is often reluctant to move forward into what seems to be an unending nothingness. What was the answer to this problem?

Put one of your men up front ahead of the teams, the Netsiliks advised Amundsen. Pick a man the dogs like. Let him act as a forerunner, striding at the front of the caravan. The dogs will follow—steadily, even eagerly.

Skis and the runners of dog-drawn sledges tended to stick in certain kinds of snow. What was the remedy for that? Ice them, the Eskimos told Amundsen, and showed him how it was done.

On August 13, 1905, the travelers left Gjøahavn to forge westward through the treacherous and uncharted waters of Simpson Strait, then through Victoria Strait, Deane Strait, and Coronation Gulf into the Beaufort Sea. At 8:00 A.M. August 26, Amundsen's second in command crashed into his cabin. "Vessel in sight!" he shouted. Bearing down on them, flying the Stars and Stripes, was the whaler *Charles Hansen* out of San Francisco.

Her captain was James McKenna. "Are you Captain Amundsen?" were his first words when he boarded the *Gjøa*. "How surprised was I not," Amundsen wrote in his diary, "when Captain McKenna wrapped his fist around mine and congratulated me on a brilliant success."

He and his companions had conquered the Northwest Passage.

Back in Norway, in the fall of 1906, he began to work on another expedition. So far no one had reached the North Pole. That was to be his next project. Again he plunged into preparations that would require years of labor. Again he called on Fridtjof Nansen.

This time it was to make a request. Amundsen had decided that for the endeavor he now had in mind the only proper ship was the *Fram*, the vessel on which Nansen had executed his famous drift across the Arctic Ocean.

On a September morning in 1907 Amundsen stood in the high-ceilinged hallway on the bottom floor of Nansen's castlelike house near Christiania, waiting for the older man to come down from his study in the tower above. Nansen was not the owner of *Fram*. It belonged to the state, but as Norway's greatest man he controlled it and could convey that control to someone else.

Nansen had done no exploring since the drift of the *Fram*, nor would he do any in the future. Recently Norway had obtained its independence after centuries of living under the rule of neighboring states. Nansen was now his country's ambassador to Great Britain, with little time for other activities.

There was a touch of sadness visible in his strong features as he descended the grand stairway at the back of the big reception hall. He knew why Amundsen had come. Months before, during a scientific gathering in London, the two of them had discussed the matter.

Toward the bottom of the stairs, Nansen halted, his piercing eyes fixed on the younger man below. "You shall have *Fram*," he said.

It was a big moment for Amundsen. Nansen was giving him more than a ship; he was anointing him. It was as if the king of polar exploration had said: Henceforth *you* shall occupy the throne.

Two years later, with Amundsen's preparations nearing completion, the Norwegian newspapers were publishing a startling tale: Another man, Robert Edwin Peary, the American explorer, had reached the North Pole.

To Amundsen this was a disturbing development. He had no desire to do something someone else had done, and by the end of September 1909 he had changed his plans. Several explorers had tried to reach the South Pole; so far none had succeeded. Instead of going to the Arctic, Amundsen would go to the Antarctic and look for the South Pole.

He revealed this decision to only a few close associates. He did not even tell Nansen. Nansen had given him the *Fram* with the understanding that his destination was the North Pole. Were he to learn otherwise before the *Fram* left Norway, he might ask for it back. On August 9, 1910, when Amundsen started his journey with nineteen associates and about a hundred Eskimo dogs, the world was still under the impression that he was en route to the Arctic by way of the Pacific Ocean.

On September 6 the *Fram* dropped anchor off the Madeira Islands, west of Africa. From here Amundsen sent letters to Nansen and others, stating the true goal of his enterprise. Here too he told the men with him. Since they had signed on for a trip to the Arctic, he noted, they were free to leave him at this point if they wished. He

hoped, however, that they would stay. They did, and the *Fram* sailed on.

Word that Amundsen was going not north but south gave the newspapers of the world an exciting story. For years the British explorer, Robert Falcon Scott, had been making preparations for an expedition to search for the South Pole. Now Scott was heading for Antarctica with sixty-five companions in a ship called the *Terra Nova*. In the dramatic language of journalism, the hunt for the South Pole had become "a race": Amundsen the Norwegian versus Scott the Englishman. Who would get there first?

In mid-January 1911 the *Fram* closed in on Antarctica. Ahead lay the Great Ice Barrier, its outer edges rising some two hundred feet above the sea. Extending four hundred miles from east to west and two hundred miles from north to south, the Barrier is unlike any other natural phenomenon in the world. A mammoth shelf of solid ice, it fills much of the large inlet shown on the maps of Antarctica as the Ross Sea.

Here, on the Barrier itself, Amundsen and nine of his men set up a base camp to be known as Framheim. Meanwhile, at the far eastern end of the ice shelf, Scott and nineteen members of his group had established their base, Cape Evans.

Roald Amundsen and his party were the first men to reach the South Pole. They took this photograph a day or two after their arrival on December 15, 1911. *Neg. 270390, Courtesy of Department Library Services, American Museum of Natural History.*

On October 15, Amundsen and five of his men left Framheim to begin the fourteen-hundred mile trek to the bottom of the world. Their route took them over the Barrier, up the slopes of two mountain ranges, and across the great central plateau of Antarctica.

Amundsen had planned this trip with great care. Dogs pulled the heavily laden sledges. His men traveled on specially designed skis. And at seven sites along the way they erected depots— places where supplies could be stored, to be used upon their return to Framheim.

Scott and sixteen of his associates left

Cape Evans to start their journey to the Pole on October 24. Scott tended to leave things to chance, and such plans as he had made reflected a considerable ignorance of what would or would not work under polar conditions. He brought along only a few dogs, and neither he nor his associates knew much about handling them. His original idea was to rely on three motorized and tractorlike sledges and twenty-one ponies. One sledge sank into the seas as it was being unloaded from the *Terra Nova*. The others broke down on the trail. As for the ponies, they suffered horribly. Dogs can curl up in the snow and keep warm; ponies can't. Shortly after the trip began, all twenty-one had died or been killed.

Amundsen's party reached the South Pole at 3:00 P.M., December 15, 1911. Scott arrived at the Pole a month later, on January 17, 1912. Amundsen and his company returned to Framheim quickly and in good health. Most of Scott's men also got back to their base — but Scott did not.

Like Amundsen, he sited depots along the way, but he had marked them poorly, and in the uninhabited Arctic, where every place looks like every other place, such things are hard to see. Cut off from the others in late March, Scott and two of his companions, sick and out of food and fuel, perished in the snow.

Although Amundsen returned to Norway a world famous figure, the years that followed were not happy ones for him. The discovery of the South Pole, his crowning achievement, lay behind him, and never again was he able to mount an undertaking as challenging as that one.

In 1913 he witnessed the flight of an airplane for the first time and realized that the day of the dog-drawn sledge was waning. Future travelers to the cold tips of the world would do their exploring from the sky.

Sure enough, in 1926 the American aviator Richard Evelyn Byrd announced that he and his copilot Floyd Bennett were the first persons to fly to the North Pole. A short time later, riding in an airship built and piloted by the Italian aeronautical engineer Umberto Nobile, Amundsen repeated this journey to become the first person to have reached both poles.

Afterward he quarreled with Nobile, charging that the Italian was claiming more credit for this feat than he deserved. Still, when in 1928 the news broke that Nobile, piloting another dirigible, had crashed into the Arctic waters, Amundsen set out in an effort to locate and rescue him. At 4:00 P.M. on June 18, the flying boat carrying Amundsen and two other men on this mission took off from the upper shores of Norway. A few minutes later, a fisherman saw their craft heading into a bank of fog along the northwestern horizon— after which it was seen no more.

Exactly where Roald Amundsen died remains unknown. We know only that it was in the frosty North, of which he had dreamed as a youth and where he had accomplished so much.

Vasco Nuñez de Balboa

1475–1519   Spanish explorer and conquistador. Discoverer of the Pacific Ocean.

Who hasn't read the sonnet in which John Keats describes how "stout Cortés," standing "silent, upon a peak in Darien," became the first European to gaze on the waters of the Pacific?

We smile as we read Keats's glowing words, bearing in mind that their author was a poet, not a historian. His "stout Cortés," of course, was Hernán Cortés, the Spanish conquistador who in the years 1519–1521 seized the country of Mexico for his king. The man who only a few years earlier discovered the Pacific was Vasco Nuñez de Balboa—and few stories of Spanish conquest in the New World offer more instances of derring-do than his.

Balboa is believed to have been born in 1475 at Jerez de los Caballeros, a Spanish town of 14,000 people near the border of Portugal. His father was an impoverished *hidalgo* (nobleman) and at an early age Vasco Nuñez took employment as a fencing master in the household of a more prosperous *hidalgo*. Our knowledge of the young Balboa is skimpy, but we know that he was a strapping blond, good-looking, good-natured, attentive to the ladies, and fond of fun.

Given his passion for adventure, he could not have grown up at a better time or in a better place. All Spain was talking of but one thing: the discoveries by Christopher Columbus of many hitherto unheard of places in the Caribbean Sea at the far western rim of the Atlantic Ocean. Everywhere Spanish soldiers and merchants were organizing expeditions westward—the soldiers hoping to find new lands to conquer; the merchants, new sources of trade and profit. The frenzy to cross the Atlantic increased in 1498 when Columbus, on his third voyage, found on the northern shores of South America a region so rich in precious stones that later explorers called it *la Costa de las Perlas* (the Coast of Pearls).

In 1500 a wealthy Spanish official named Rodrigo de Bastidas obtained permission from the rulers of Spain, King Ferdinand and Queen Isabella, to sail west in search of "gold, silver, lead, tin, serpents, fishes, birds, and monsters." To this end, Bastidas fitted out two ships, and when these vessels left Spain in October 1500 Balboa was a member of the crew. He would never see his native land again. Henceforth he would live in what the people of Europe, having first believed Columbus's discoveries to be a part of Asia, had just begun to realize was a vast New World, waiting to be explored and exploited.

Once in the Caribbean Sea, Bastidas passed up the Coast of Pearls. Already, other fortune hunters had drained that area of its valuables. Instead, he instructed his chief pilot, Juan de la Cosa, to steer westward along the shores of what are now Venezuela and Colombia, stopping at Indian villages to exchange cheap European trinkets for gold and pearls. March 1501 brought the travelers into the Gulf of Urabá, where they disembarked at a village on the soil of the Darien or eastern half of the isthmus of Panama.

It was here that Balboa began to display one of the traits that in time would make him an unusually competent leader. He mingled with the natives. He asked them countless questions. By the time the expedition sailed out of the Gulf of Urabá, he had acquired an ample stock of information, not only about the Indians of Darien but about the tribes dwelling elsewhere on the isthmus of Panama.

From Urabá the Spaniards sailed further westward, along the Caribbean shores of Panama. Bastidas would have liked to have extended these explorations, but within a few days he learned that a wood-eating sea worm called *broma* was playing havoc with his ships. Turning away from Panama, pilot Juan de la Cosa set a course for Spain—only to find the ships leaking so badly that he had to put into a port on the southern coast of the island Hispaniola, now Haiti. There both vessels went down, their hulls shredded by the *broma*. Because the shores of Hispaniola were near, all the travelers survived. Most of them took ship for home as soon as they could, but Balboa remained.

He now found himself living on the

first of the islands discovered by Columbus to be settled by the Spaniards. Impressed by the knowledge of the New World that Balboa had acquired during his travels, Nicolas de Ovando, the recently appointed governor of Hispaniola, provided him with a plot of land and a gang of enslaved Indians to till it.

The acres put at his disposal were fertile and well-watered, excellent for raising stock and for growing maize (Indian corn), melons, and peppers. Had Balboa been content to settle for the easy life of a planter, he could have become wealthy. But farm life was not for him. He longed to see more of what the Spaniards then called "the Main" or *Tierra Firma*, meaning the mainland of South and Central America. Instead of waxing rich during his seven years on Hispaniola, he only half-cultivated his land, and he lived on money borrowed from his more diligent neighbors.

Then in 1509 came a chance to return to *Tierra Firma*. King Ferdinand had presented to two of his subjects, Alonso de Ojeda and Rodrigo de Nicuesa, a joint license to travel to *Tierra Firma*, where Ojeda was to take possession of New Andalusia, a stretch of land lying to the east of the Gulf of Urabá, and Nicuesa the bulk of present-day Panama lying to the west of that line. When one of the brigantines of Ojeda's fleet

put in at Santo Domingo, the main port and capital of Hispaniola, to pick up men and supplies, Balboa tried to join the crew—only to be informed by the governor of the island, Christopher Columbus's son, Diego Colon, that he could not do so. The problem was all that money he had borrowed from his neighbors. Under the laws of Hispaniola no debtor could leave the area until he paid his debts.

Unable to pay, Balboa hit upon a risky scheme. He arranged to sell the grain grown on his farm to Martin Fernandez de Encisco, the lawyer in command of the mainland-bound brigantines that were being manned and loaded in the harbor of Santo Domingo. At the last moment, Balboa saw to it that one of the large casks holding the grain was left empty, slipped into it, and in this manner was carried aboard Encisco's vessel.

That night he wriggled out of his hiding place and wrapped himself in one of the ship's sails. There he remained until the brigantine was well at sea. At this point he emerged and presented himself to Encisco who, seeing before him a well-set-up young man, shrugged and put him to work.

Encisco's mission was to carry provisions to Ojeda who, months earlier, had taken over as governor of New Andalusia and founded a settlement called San

Sebastian on the eastern shores of the Gulf of Urabá. In January 1510, when Encisco reached the South American mainland at the site of present-day Cartagena in Colombia, he was startled to find one of Governor Ojeda's brigantines standing in the bay and to learn that everything had gone wrong in San Sebastian. The Indians in that area were fiercely unfriendly. They were also unconquerable, due to their practice of dipping their arrows into a poison extracted from a local shrub. Ojeda had departed in fright, traveling on one of his two brigantines, and most of the settlers, abandoned by their leader, had fled to Cartagena in the other one.

Encisco was appalled. He had invested money in Ojeda's expedition, and the thought of losing the fortress and the thirty huts that he now learned the governor had erected at San Sebastian was more than he could bear. He announced his intention of continuing his journey as planned and insisted that the fleeing settlers come along—but found, when the two ships reached San Sebastian, there was no longer anything there. The Indians had burned down the fort and the thirty huts.

What to do? Food was almost gone on both ships. To go ashore at San Sebastian was to face the poisoned arrows of the natives. Encisco was a lawyer by profession, having little experience

as a navigator and less as a soldier. He assembled his crews and asked for advice.

Most of the men favored a retreat to Hispaniola. Not Balboa. Stepping forward from the group, he delivered a brief speech. He reminded his listeners that they had come to the New World to make their fortunes and begged them not to give up now. He told them that he had been in these parts before, that on the opposite side of the Gulf of Urabá was a country named Darien. He assured them that the inhabitants were a quiet people. They owned much gold. They cultivated sweeping fields of grain. But most important of all, they did not "put the herb [the poison] on their arrows." He urged the despondent settlers to follow him to Darien.

They did so. A few days later the Spaniards were marching into the principal village of that part of Panama. On its outskirts they encountered a body of natives who were frightened at the appearance of almost two hundred white men, clad in armor and brandishing steel swords. But the Indians' unpoisoned arrows were no match for the Spaniards' fire-belching harquebuses, and as soon as the brief encounter ended, Balboa sought out the local *cacique* (chief), a genial Indian named Cemaco. Balboa knew how to talk to the

This 1540 map of the New World combines the discoveries of Balboa with some fanciful superstitions. The mapmaker has labeled parts of the southern continent "land of the giants" and "cannibals." *Courtesy of the National Maritime Museum, the MacPherson Collection.*

natives, and in no time he convinced Cemaco that his people and the invaders could live together in peace.

Balboa's biographers tell us that his methods were different from those of most conquistadors. It was his policy, wherever he went, to gain the friendship of the natives. If that failed, he did not hesitate to use crossbows and flaming guns. Nor did he hesitate to follow the custom of his day, which was

to make slaves of those he defeated in battle. But never did Balboa subject the original inhabitants of America to the cruelties so frequently practiced by other Spanish conquistadors in the southern half of the New World.

The success of his methods was not lost on those who had followed him to Darien. At what has been described as the first town meeting on American soil, the Spaniards took two steps. First, at Balboa's urging, they named the town where they now found themselves Santa Maria de la Antigua del Darien. Then, unanimously, they proclaimed Balboa their captain and governor.

Encisco was outraged at these proceedings. When the first Spanish ship arrived at Antigua to pick up gold and to deposit provisions and additional settlers for the new colony, Encisco departed with it. Eventually he got back to Spain, where he complained to the king and queen that Balboa had robbed him of his rights and property in the New World.

He was not the last man to carry tales to the ears of their majesties. Balboa knew well that Antigua stood on that section of the isthmus of Panama that King Ferdinand had given to Rodrigo de Nicuesa and that Nicuesa had long since founded a colony in the northern reaches of the isthmus. One morning Nicuesa showed up in Antigua with some of his followers and Balboa clapped him in jail. Then he summoned another town meeting and persuaded its members to banish Nicuesa from the colony. Back in Spain, Nicuesa pronounced Balboa a villain and a scoundrel. He claimed that instead of sending the king his share of the gold gathered in Darien, Balboa was keeping practically all of it for himself.

This was a lie. Balboa could be rough and ready, but he was honest. Besides, he had not come to the New World to enrich himself. He had come to explore and to make discoveries.

Frequently he sallied forth from Antigua, accompanied by an army, to visit the *caciques* of neighboring tribes. Some welcomed him; some didn't. And when they didn't, there were bloody battles which Balboa usually won.

In the fall of 1512 five of the neighboring chiefs stopped fighting one another long enough to confer together. Their plan was to combine their armies, attack and destroy Antigua, and kill Balboa. Their plot might have succeeded had it not been for a pretty Indian girl named Fulvia, whom Balboa had captured and who now lived in his household as a servant.

It so happened that one of Fulvia's brothers belonged to one of the scheming tribes. He told his sister of the impending attack, a revelation that put Fulvia to some troubled thinking, for she had fallen in love with her handsome master. At first she was torn between the need to be loyal to her brother and his people and her passion for Balboa. In the end, love won. Forewarned by his sweetheart, Balboa marched out of Antigua at the head of a well-armed force, encountered the approaching Indians along the way, and sent them fleeing back to their tribal homelands. Like all conquistadors, Balboa had with him a number of priests, and these men had succeeded in bringing large numbers of natives to Christianity. One of the most prominent of these converts was Cacique Comogre, ruler of a province located a hundred and fifty miles west of Antigua. Chief Comogre's oldest son, Panquiaco, had also embraced Christianity, but he was critical of the warlike ways of the Spanish colonists. Once, when Balboa and some of his followers were visiting the Comogre, Panquiaco rebuked them for fussing over the division of some gold that his father had given them.

Panquiaco stood up in the throne room of his father's palace to make this speech. Most of the Spaniards, he charged, came to the New World talking of God but thinking of gold. "Christians!" he said to Balboa and his party. "What means this? Why quarrel over such trifles?"

Balboa may have found these words less than interesting, but presently he was listening hard to the young orator. "If you so love gold," Panquiaco continued, "that to secure it you forsake your homes and with so many fatigues and dangers come here to disturb the peaceful people of these lands, I will show you a province where you will be able to gratify your desire."

At this point Panquiaco lifted his arm and pointed south. Over there, he announced, lay a land abounding in gold and called by the Indians Biru or Peru. And how could the Spaniards get to that land? They could go there by ship, for on the far side of the mountains called the Sierras lay an *otra mar* (another sea), at least as large as the Caribbean and perhaps even as large as the mighty Atlantic itself.

This was the first Balboa had heard of the existence of Peru and of the ocean that would come to be known as the Pacific. At once he resolved to organize an expedition and search for both places.

But on his return to Antigua he found himself faced with a variety of difficulties. Some of the Spanish settlers were angry at the high-handed manner with which Balboa governed the colony. It took time to repress this brief but vigorous rebellion. Months earlier Balboa had sent two of his associates to Spain to tell King Ferdinand that the criticisms of him that Encisco and Nicuesa had spread in that country were untrue. One of these emissaries had turned out to be a secret enemy. Instead of defending Balboa to the king, he had attacked him vehemently.

It was to counteract these strictures that Balboa, on January 20, 1513, wrote a letter to his "Most Christian and Most Mighty Lord." He assured King Ferdi-

On September 25, 1513, Balboa first glimpsed the Pacific Ocean from the shores of Panama. *Neg. 103686, Courtesy of Department Library Services, American Museum of Natural History.*

nand that since "we came to this land I have sought so much [in] the service of Your Royal Highness that never by night nor day do I think of anything but how to place in safety these few [Spanish] people that God cast here." He informed the king that "above all, I have striven that . . . the Indians . . . be well treated, [and consequently] I have learned very great secrets from them and things whereby one can secure very great riches and [a] large quantity of gold, with which Your Royal Highness will be very much served."

It was in this letter—the longest and earliest of its author's writings to come to light—that Balboa told King Ferdinand why most of the settlers in the colony founded by Nicuesa in northwest Panama had perished, either at the hands of hostile Indians or because of the rigors of the climate. He informed the king that Nicuesa had tried to live in the wilds of Panama in the same way wealthy *hidalgos* lived in civilized Spain. Instead of getting up early and getting to his work, Balboa wrote, Nicuesa lingered in his sleeping quarters, attended by numerous slaves. In the New World, Balboa advised His Highness, you could not run a colony "from the bed."

Not until September 1513 was Balboa able to leave Antigua and begin his hunt for the Pacific and Peru. In the often dangerous crossing of the isthmus of Panama, he was accompanied by 150 Spanish soldiers, almost 800 Indians, and a pack of dogs trained to fight. The leader of these animals was Leoncico, Balboa's pet dog. We are told that Leoncico went everywhere with his master, that he was in the arms of Balboa when he stowed away on Encisco's brigantine to begin the voyage that had ended at Antigua.

In the early morning hours of September 25, 1513, one of the Indian guides informed Balboa that the steep hill they were approaching marked the end of their search. Balboa promptly ordered his followers to stay where they were. Then he trudged up the hill, Leoncico beside him.

At 10:00 A.M. he stood on that peak in Darien, looking down on the Gulf of San Miguel on the southwestern shores of Panama, with the waves of the Pacific rolling away beyond it. He let a few minutes pass before signaling his soldiers to join him. They came scrambling up the hill, crying "The sea! The sea!" Balboa nodded as they gathered around him. "There you see, friends and companions," he said, "the object of your desires and the reward of your many labors. As the notices of another sea given us by the son of Comogre have turned out to be true, so will the words of Panquiaco be fulfilled concerning the great riches of the lands to the south [Peru]."

Then, taking twenty-seven of his men with him, Balboa descended the hill, waded into the waters of the Gulf of San Miguel, lifted his sword, and took possession of the Pacific in the name of his king.

The rest of Balboa's story is short and sad. By the close of 1516 King Ferdinand had died, Queen Isabella having long since preceded him in death. The new occupant of the throne of Spain was Ferdinand's grandson, known to history both as Charles I, King of Spain, and Charles V, Emperor of the Holy Roman Empire. Charles had heard of the existence of Peru, and one of his first official acts was to send to the New World a mammoth expedition, headed by an elderly soldier named Pedrarias, to look for that gold-rich land. The king's orders to Pedrarias were to leave Balboa in charge as governor of Antigua and to take into his own hands all of Panama and certain adjoining lands in South America with the title of viceroy.

Pedrarias, an ambitious man, was profoundly envious of Balboa because of the glory that now was his as the discoverer of the Pacific. On his arrival in the New World, however, Pedrarias took care to hide these feelings behind a mask of polished civility. He even went so far as to offer to betroth the oldest of his daughters to the Governor of Antigua—an offer that Balboa, although he already had a couple of Indian wives, politely accepted.

In the opening months of 1517 Balboa, acting on orders from Pedrarias, began building ships on the shores of the Pacific with the idea of sailing south in search of Peru. Meanwhile Pedrarias had established his capital on the banks of the Atrato (now the Darien River) in a town called Acla that Balboa himself had founded some years earlier.

At Acla, Pedrarias was surrounded by advisers who warned him daily to keep an eye on the Governor of Antigua. Their guess was that when the ships were ready, Balboa would simply sail off and grab Peru for himself.

Aroused by these accusations and at least half believing them, Pedrarias decided that Balboa must die. It was easily done. He sent a message commanding Balboa to come to Acla to confer on royal business. Balboa left at once, only to be taken into custody when he reached the little town on the Atrato, where he was put on trial and charged with treason—which is to say, with plotting to steal the king's ships and go exploring on his own.

The judge in charge was one of Pedririas's closest advisers. Nothing Balboa could say, nothing his many friends could say, availed. In the opening weeks of 1519—most authorities give the date as January 12—the discoverer of the Pacific was beheaded on the orders of a high official of the kingdom he had served so well.

Robert O'Hara Burke

1820–1861   Irish-born soldier, police officer, and explorer. Leader of the first expedition to cross the continent of Australia.

Born in 1820 into a land-owning family at St. Cleram in County Galway, Ireland, Robert Burke was educated at military academies in England and Belgium and in his twentieth year joined the Austrian army. In 1848, when his regiment was disbanded, he returned to his native land, worked for five years in the Royal Irish Constabulary, and then emigrated to Australia, Great Britain's newest and largest colony.

Reaching the island continent "down under" in 1853, he resided briefly on the island of Tasmania before crossing the Bass Strait to begin his work as a police inspector in Melbourne, capital of the recently organized colony of Victoria at the eastern end of the southern coast of Australia.

At the time of his arrival in Melbourne, the colony of Victoria was only three years old, but its considerably older capital already had taken on the hustle and clamor of a medium-size city back home. Gold had been discovered in the vicinity and numerous ships, packed to their gunwales with prospectors, were reaching Melbourne daily. A traveling author, sojourning there in the early 1850s, found the place "a modern Babel—a little hell on earth—a city of rioters, gamblers and drunkards . . . speculators, crime, excitement and disorder. . . ." There was plenty for Inspector Burke to do. Obviously he did it well, for by 1855 he had been sent out to Castlemaine, one of the most populous of the gold-mining districts, as superintendent of police.

In the 1850s the settled portion of

Australia consisted mainly of a line of coastal towns straggling southward from Sydney in the east around to Melbourne and nearby Adelaide in the south. Fifty miles inland civilization ended, except for a few outlying sheep stations. So little was known of the unmeasured realm beyond these points that people spoke of it as the "Ghastly Blank." What was out there? Everywhere in Melbourne that question was being asked, especially by those prominent enough to belong to The Philosophical Institute (soon to be chartered by the Queen of England and renamed The Royal Society of Victoria), a private club devoted to scientific studies.

"Inland exploration!" More and more that expression was being heard in the meeting rooms of the Royal Society on one of Melbourne's principal thoroughfares. Surely the time had come for someone to take a look at the Ghastly Blank. Already a few intrepid individuals had ventured inland. Among them was the learned and immensely capable Charles Sturt of Sydney. In 1845 Sturt had pushed almost to the center of the continent.

The reports he'd brought back ranged from alarming to promising, with the alarming tending to predominate. It was an article of faith among Australians that at the heart of the Ghastly Blank lay a great inland sea like Russia's Cas-

Burke had great daring but may have lacked the scientific temperament essential for successful exploration. *Courtesy of the Trustees of the Public Library of Victoria [Australia].*

pian Sea, spreading its life-giving waters. But Sturt found no such body. He found shallow salt lakes, deserts baking in the tropical sun, and forbidding mountains rising sheer from desolate plains. He'd seen other things as well: prairies ranging to the horizon where sheep and other domestic animals could be grazed, forests thick with valuable hardwoods, and broad, gently flowing rivers down which the products obtainable on their banks could be shipped to market.

In 1857 the Royal Society formed a

Committee of Exploration to "fit out" an expedition to examine the "bush," as the almost entirely unknown back-country was called. Funds were raised and an advertisement inserted in the Melbourne newspapers asking men familiar with the bush to apply for the post of leader of the enterprise. Burke applied and was accepted. For the second most important position on the inland exploration team, that of surveyor, the committee selected a scholarly young scientist named William John Wills, with the result that the ensuing penetration of the Ghastly Blank would come to be known as the Burke-Wills Expedition.

Why Robert Burke was chosen to lead it would seem to be anybody's guess. He had none of the qualifications stressed by the Royal Society's Committee of Exploration. His experience in the bush was negligible and he possessed no scientific skills. "Exploration," the travel writer Alan Moorehead has noted, "seems to require slow, unhurried tenacity and persistence, great patience and tact, a scientific rather than emotional approach, a willingness to reject the flamboyant thing and to accept the middle of the road."

Those were not Burke's qualities. He was brave. But it was the flamboyant bravery of a man who to achieve his goals would push himself beyond the limits of his ability, seemingly under the impression that he had no such limits. He pursued his police work steadily and responsibly. But off the job he lived in a manner that can be described as eccentric, even Bohemian. He was given to galloping his horse through forest and swamp with such wildness that some of his associates considered him "not quite sane." He built a pool in his backyard and there, we are told, he often sat "naked in the open with his helmet on his head, reading a book." It delighted him to annoy a certain magistrate who was known to fall into a rage whenever anyone swung on his garden gate. On more than one occasion Burke rode thirty miles out of his way just to swing on it. He fell in love with a singer-actress named Julia Matthews. When she spurned his offer of marriage, he bought a piano, hired someone to teach him to play, and spent hours pounding out the songs that Julia featured in her theatrical appearances.

Perhaps it was his Irish charm that won him the leadership of the expedition. Perhaps it was his daredevilish behavior, for no doubt in the eyes of the staid and chair-loving members of the Royal Society that was exactly how an explorer should conduct himself.

On the assumption that the inland-exploration team would encounter immense stretches of sand, the planners of the expedition provided it with a contingent of camels. Six of these ungainly beasts were obtained from a touring vaudeville show, and a member of the team hastened to India to purchase the others and to hire some experienced camel handlers known as sepoys. When at 4:00 P.M. on August 21, 1860, the caravan took off from Royal Park in Melbourne, it consisted of ten white men, three Indian sepoys, two wagons, twenty-three horses, and twenty-seven camels. A band played and a great crowd cheered the adventurers off.

The Royal Society left the choice of a route to Burke, and his decision was to try to cross the continent from Melbourne on the south to the Gulf of Carpentaria on the north, a trek of almost 2,000 miles, most of it through unknown country.

By early October the caravan had reached Menindie (now spelled Menindee), an outpost on the Darling River, consisting of a pub housed in a shanty and a handful of shacks and generally regarded as the jumping-off place into the interior. Already some of the many troubles that were to beset the expedition had begun. The supply wagons were bogged down in thick mud. One reason for stopping at Menindie was to wait for them to catch up. Five men, worn out by the rigors of the journey, had left the group, and a newly hired

replacement was threatening to leave. Burke and his chief assistant, George Landells, were quarreling. The problem between them arose because of Landells's conviction that the camels could survive only if their food was laced with rum. Sheepshearers who lived along this route had broken into some of the rum casks. As the wagons were overloaded, Burke had announced his intention of abandoning the remaining casks. Landells objected vehemently, arguing that without rum the camels would die of scurvy. Burke stuck to his decision, Landells walked off, and the surveyor Wills took over as second-in-command.

At Menindie Burke established a depot and planned the march to his next major objective, a little stream called Cooper's Creek 400 miles to the north. The largely unexplored terrain lying between Menindie and Cooper's Creek was believed to be almost totally without water. Burke's solution to this problem was to split his company in two. A small advance party, lightly laden enough to move fast and led by himself, would press on to Cooper's Creek. The others would stay at Menindie to sort out supplies and rest those animals that had fallen ill during the tramp from Melbourne.

Guiding Burke and his party when they headed north on October 19 was

William Wright, a newly recruited member of the group. A onetime sheep-station manager, Wright had lived and traveled for years in the bush. He knew it well. At Torowoto Swamp, 200 miles short of Cooper's Creek, he left the advance party. His instructions from Burke were to return to Menindie, collect the salt, food, and other supplies and bring them up to Cooper's Creek as fast as possible.

But to William Wright "as fast as possible" turned out to mean never. His story, voiced later, was that upon his arrival at the Menindie depot, he found the supplies he'd agreed to carry north to Burke still in disorder. They were scattered all over the place. The ailing animals were still ailing and half of the men left at the depot to recuperate were even sicker. Still worse was the discovery that the Royal Society was not honoring the expedition's checks. To Wright this was a crucial problem. If the Royal Society was no longer financing the enterprise, was he still on the payroll? Uncertain as to the status of his job, he took off for his home in the vicinity, leaving his ailing companions to struggle with the scorching heat and biting centipedes and flies of Menindie.

"One rather wonders about all this," writes Moorehead in *Cooper's Creek,* his lively account of the Burke-Wills expedition. "Wright, of course, should

never have been employed by Burke . . . not at any rate as an officer of the expedition: he was too slow, too limited, too venal, one of the kind whose horizons are no higher than their salaries. But how hard did the others push him to move? . . . It might have been that they were quite ready to shuffle off the responsibility upon Wright, and when he did nothing, they succumbed to the general inertia of that hot, fly-ridden, leaderless camp on the Darling."

While Wright dallied on the banks of the Darling River, Burke and his followers slogged on toward Cooper's Creek, reaching that waterhole on the sun-parched plains of upper Australia on November 11. A week passed, two weeks, three, four. Still there was no sign of Wright and the desperately needed food and other stores he'd promised to bring north. It never occurred to Burke that Wright was not coming at all. He assumed that the one-time sheep-station boss had been delayed, either by the hazards common to travel in the bleak region or by the occasionally hostile actions of roaming bands of aborigines, as Australia's natives were called. He was in a hurry to move on, in a hurry to reach his goal, the Gulf of Carpentaria, 700 miles to the north.

Here was a situation where calamities

might have been avoided had Burke possessed the patience that Moorehead has called one of the requisite attributes of an explorer.

But of patience Burke had none. By the opening of December he'd decided not to wait for Wright. Again he split his small band, leaving half of it at Cooper's Creek with his third-in-command, William Brahe, in charge. Brahe's orders were to create a living and storage compound to be known as Depot LXV and to wait for Wright.

Accompanying Burke when he left Cooper's Creek on December 16 were young Wills, Charles Gray, and John King. Both Gray and King had courage, and King was bright and personable. The temperature stood at 109 degrees in the shade and far higher readings lay ahead. The Australian summer had set in and on January 19, 1861, at the site of the present town of Cloncurry, they entered the subequatorial tropics.

For fifty-seven days they struggled across gritty deserts and over rugged mountains, bashed at intervals by cyclonic storms and streaming rains. At last, on February 11, they reached the Flinders River where one of its several outlets pours into the Gulf of Carpentaria. They had attained their goal, but it was a goal none of them would ever see. Ahead of them stretched an impassable mangrove swamp. Nor was there

in the vicinity so much as a knoll from which they could view the rolling waters of the sea they had traveled so far to reach.

Backward they turned, in the direction of Cooper's Creek and Depot LXV. Food dwindled to a few ounces per man per day. Gray died quietly in the night. The others found him in his bedroll when he failed to appear in the morning and they went to wake him. The three survivors straggled on, throwing even thinner and more angular shadows on the hot floor of the plains. By the night of Gray's death on April 17, they had been traveling for seventy-three days with still almost a hundred miles to go.

And now occurred an incident destined to be etched on the collective memory of the Australian people for generations to come. At Depot LXV on Cooper's Creek William Brahe was trying to make a difficult decision. Prior to his departure, Burke appears to have said that if by the end of three months he and his party had not returned, Brahe was to assume either that they were lost or that they had made their way to settled places on the east coast of Australia. At that time Brahe was to leave Depot LXV and move southward to Menindie. By April 17, Burke and his party had been gone for almost four months. Confronting Brahe was the question of how much longer he and his companions could hold out where they were. Owing to the failure of Wright to arrive with the stores left at Menindie, food and other supplies were running low. One of Brahe's men was seriously ill. The others were beginning to break under the strain of long and boring hours in the midst of a dreary, empty, and unchanging landscape. On April 20, Brahe decided that the time had come to head south.

That day, or perhaps that night, he and his men dug a hole and placed in it a camel box filled with rations. Alongside this they inserted a letter from Brahe to Burke, stuffing it into a bottle. They took these actions against the unlikely possibility that Burke and his companions might still manage to reach Cooper's Creek. On a nearby coolibah tree, Brahe indicated the whereabouts of the canned food, cutting into its bark the following message:

DIG
3 FT NW
April 21, 1861

Early the next morning he and his men took off.

At 7:30 that evening the three emaciated figures of Burke, Wills, and King stumbled into Depot LXV to find its wooden stockade unmanned, its tents gone, its campfires out, and no human beings in sight! They found the buried food. They found the letter that Brahe had written to Burke. It was from this that they learned the bitter news—less than ten hours earlier Brahe and his men had abandoned Depot LXV and were now moving in the direction of Menindie, 400 miles to the south.

Burke and his companions briefly considered trying to catch up with them, only to conclude that in their present exhausted condition they would never be able to do so. They decided that their only chance for survival was to work their way up Cooper's Creek in the hope of reaching a settled area 150 miles to the west in the vicinity of Mount Hopeless.

They did not make it. Wills was the first to perish on the trail, and so weak were Burke and King that it took them hours to scratch out a shallow grave for him. This was on or about June 28, 1861. Burke died two or three days later, and King survived only because a band of wandering aborigines found him collapsed on the banks of Cooper's Creek. They fed and nursed him and carried him seven miles upstream to an encampment, where a rescue party sent out from Melbourne to search for the missing explorers found him in September.

For the next few months, stories of

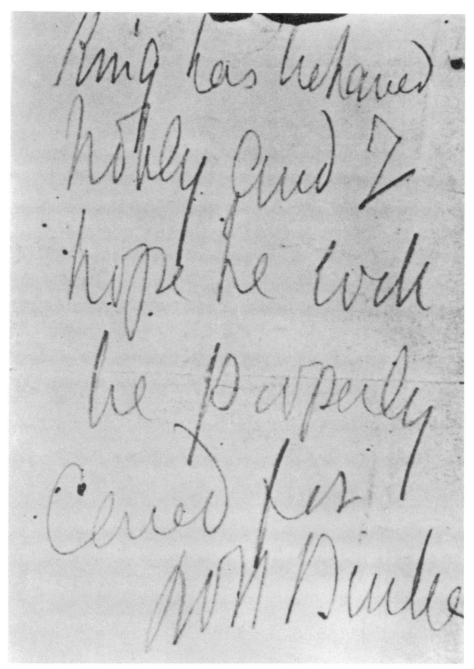

As Burke lay dying near Cooper's Creek, he wrote a last letter to commend his fellow explorer, John King: "King has behaved nobly and I hope he will be properly cared for." *Courtesy of the Trustees of the Public Library of Victoria.*

the expedition crowded the columns of the Melbourne press. In November the colonial government set up a Royal Commission of Inquiry. The task assigned to its investigators was to determine the blame for the misfortunes that had befallen the expedition. Their report, issued in January 1862, was notably balanced. Though Burke was given high marks for having reached his goal, his obvious contribution to the tragic outcome of the enterprise was not ignored.

"Mr. Burke," the investigators asserted, "evinced a far greater amount of zeal than prudence in . . . departing from Cooper's Creek before the party [William Wright and his associates] had arrived from Mendinie . . . in undertaking so extended a journey with insufficient supply of provisions, Mr. Burke was forced into the necessity of overtaxing the powers of his party, whose continuous and unremitting exertions resulted in . . . the prostration of himself and his companions from fatigue and severe privation."

Nor did the Royal Society's Committee of Exploration escape censure. Its members, the Commission of Inquiry noted, knew of Wright's failure to carry to Cooper's Creek the supplies so sorely needed there. Why had they not seen to it that Wright carried out his orders from Burke?

As for Wright himself, no basis for criminal proceedings against him was found but, as Moorehead writes, he was "publicly condemned as the man upon whom the guilt chiefly lay, and that was a reputation he was unlikely to live down."

In 1863 the bones of Burke and Wills were brought to Melbourne for a funeral procession witnessed by forty thousand people. At their joint grave in Melbourne Cemetery a thirty-four-ton monolith of undressed Harcourt stone, erected a short time later, carried this inscription:

In memory of Robert O'Hara Burke and Willam John Wills . . . comrades in great achievement, companions in death, and associates in renown.

Sir Richard Francis Burton

1821–1890   English soldier, poet, ethnologist, archaeologist, swordsman, linguist, translator, and explorer. One of the few non-Muslims to enter Mecca in Arabia, sacred city of the religion of Islam, and the first to enter Harar in Africa, another Muslim shrine. Discoverer of Lake Tanganyika, explorer of other sections of Africa, and one of the seekers of the source of the Nile River.

Shortly after the birth of Richard Burton on March 19, 1821, at the port of Torquay on the English Channel, his parents, Colonel Joseph Netterville and Martha Baker Burton, hastened northward to spend a few months at Barhan House, the home of Mrs. Burton's family in Hertfordshire.

Colonel Burton, recently retired from the British army, was looking forward to a life of leisure, supported by the income from his wife's inheritance. The colonel liked to go boar hunting. He enjoyed dabbling in chemistry. Nothing pleased him more, at the close of a day filled with these pleasures, than to share a glass of wine with congenial friends in the cool of the evening. What he did not like was work, and Fawn M. Brodie, one of Richard's many biographers, reads into the younger Burton's lifelong industriousness a determination, at an early age, to be as unlike his father as possible. "Where his father frittered away both time and money, giving himself wholly to sloth in the end," Mrs. Brodie has written, "the son worked as if pursued by a demon. . . ."

The colonel's problem in 1821 was that though his wife's fortune was adequate, it was not large; hence his decision, toward the end of Richard's first year, to leave expensive England for France where he could indulge himself cheaply.

They settled first at Tours. Here they occupied a small chateau on the banks of the Loire River, and here Richard's sister and his brother Edward were born. Jotting down some reminiscences of these times long afterward, Richard was at a loss to explain why, after the pleasant years at Tours, his parents elected to go elsewhere. Indeed, at this point the Burtons became wanderers on the face of Europe, living in France, in Italy, and moving a total of fourteen times over a period of ten years.

It would appear from Richard's published memories that those endless hops from here to there were hard on the children. Such education as they secured was irregular. Their father, preoccupied by his hobbies, ignored them for days on end, then suddenly set about punishing them for their misdeeds, occasionally resorting to the rod. Their mother alternately neglected and pampered them. Neither parent, according to Richard, ever addressed them as intelligent human beings; and, as the years moved on, both parents became full-time invalids, everlastingly complaining and looking for cures for what were often imaginary ailments. Small wonder, writes biographer Brodie, that among Richard's numerous pursuits as an adult was a serious study of the medical sciences.

He was in his twentieth year when the colonel announced that both sons were to become clergymen. He sent them to England, where Richard was enrolled at Trinity College, Oxford, and

Edward at Cambridge University.

At Oxford, Richard was popular with his fellow students. They liked his high spirits, his flare for imaginative pranks that outraged the authorities, his capacity for liquor, and his impressive skills as a fencer and boxer. "Ruffian Dick," they called him, admiringly, and for years thereafter the nickname stuck.

He arrived at Oxford sporting a flamboyant moustache. It was the envy of his clean-shaven companions, who gloried in his refusal to remove it in the face of a university rule forbidding such hirsute adornments. All his life Burton considered himself ugly, but no one familiar with existing portraits would be likely to endorse that judgment. He was a big man, almost six-feet tall with enormous shoulders and a well-muscled body. In a roomful of people there was something about him—his black hair, his fierce black eyes ("panther eyes," observers called them), his gaunt features, his virile manner—that made the other men present seem insignificant.

But if Ruffian Dick made lasting friends among the students, he made virulent enemies among the faculty, and within a few months he concluded that Oxford was not for him. For one thing, he disapproved of its educational methods, having long ago created ones for himself that he considered superior. For another, he had no intention of becoming a clergyman, having already found himself out of touch with the teachings of Christianity. When he learned from his friends that there were great opportunities for a young man in the British army in India, he knew what he was going to do. Nor did it take him long—a few more pranks, a few flagrant acts of disobedience—to persuade the university to ask him to leave at the end of his first academic year. This was in 1841 and on October 28, 1842, he landed in Bombay, to begin a nineteen-year military career that would carry him from cadet to captain.

In India he began at once learning the native language. He had already acquired a proficiency in Latin and Greek—both ancient and modern—in several of the languages of modern Europe, and in Arabic. Now he began adding to the list. He had a natural bent for languages. More to the point, he worked hard at them, devising a system that enabled him to master a new tongue in two months. In time he could speak twenty-nine different languages and a sufficient number of dialects to bring the total to forty.

He did not study languages merely for the purpose of becoming a regimental interpreter, an office he held for several years, but because he saw in them the key to the philosophies of the East. Contemptuous as he was of the religions of his own world, he could never learn enough about those of the mysterious Orient. He learned Arabic so that he could read and understand the Koran, the sacred book that stands at the center of the Muslim religion, just as the Bible stands at the center of Judaism and Christianity. A mastery of Persian opened up to him the mystic doctrines of Sufism, a philosophical system of mysticism practiced principally by followers of the founder of Islam, the prophet Mohammed, who call themselves Shiites.

It was while he was at or in the vicinity of Karachi in what is now Pakistan that he began his intensive study of Indian life. Unlike other British students of it, he did not confine himself to observations from a distance. He stained his face with henna and donned native garb. Then, wearing a false beard and long hair, he frequented the bazaars of Karachi and other cities of the area, posing as a merchant dealing in linens, calicoes, and muslins. He discussed religion with the priests, played chess with the theological students, and smoked opium with the addicts. In short, he learned the life of the region by living with the natives. These methods of investigation enabled him to write books containing the most vivid accounts of Oriental culture ever published. But they did not set well with

Disguised as a pilgrim, Burton traveled to the holy Islamic shrine at Mecca. This picture of male and female pilgrims appeared in his 1855 book, *Personal Narrative of a Pilgrimage to El-Medina and Mecca*, and, like that book, is perhaps a little too imaginative. Muslim men and women did not travel together, and while women were constrained to cover their faces, they resorted not to masks but to silk veils. *Courtesy of the New York Public Library.*

his fellow officers. Some of them were heard complaining that Ruffian Dick had become a "white nigger." It was disapproval in high circles of his practice of "going native," we are told, that prevented Burton from advancing beyond the rank of captain. He had been in India for seven years when the sand storms common to the desert area around him damaged his eyes. He suffered from a case of ophthalmia so severe that he was put on sick leave and sent home for an extended period.

In England he stayed with relatives and perfected plans for the most dangerous of his exploits—his penetration of Mecca, birthplace of the prophet Mohammed in southwestern Arabia and holiest of the shrines of Islam. Under Islamic law, Mecca was closed to nonbelievers, and a number of Christians and Jews, visiting there, had paid with their lives for their curiosity. Every year saw thousands of believers making the pilgrimage to Mecca, and to Burton, smitten as he was with the exotic and forbidden, a desire to join one of these treks to observe the sacred city from the inside had long since become an obsession.

When he left England in April 1853, he was dressed in the Arabic manner, head shaven, beard long, skin darkened by walnut juice. To the outside world he was now no longer Richard Burton.

He was Mirza Abdulla, a Persian dervish (wanderer) and a faithful follower of Islam. At prolonged stops along the way, at Cairo in Egypt and elsewhere, he posed as a doctor, hanging out his shingle and soliciting patients. One of his purposes for doing this was to test his disguise, for those who came to him were Muslims. Another was his wish to enlarge his knowledge of family life in the Muslim world.

On the first day of September, traveling with a caravan of camel-borne pilgrims, he reached Mecca and at once hastened to the Kaaba—the cube-shaped building in the courtyard of the great Mosque that is the heart of Muslimism and the site of the Black Stone, the most venerated of all Islamic objects. Once inside this hallowed chamber, Burton was all eyes, ascertaining among other things that the Black Stone was a meteorite, a rock that had fallen to earth from space. To be seen taking notes on what he witnessed in Mecca would have cost him his life. Still, when he left the sacred city six days later his garments and luggage were stuffed with pieces of paper covered with his crabbed handwriting.

Mecca was not the only Muslim shrine to come under Burton's scrutiny. The fall of 1854 found him at Harar, in what is now Ethiopia, another city sacred to Islam and barred to nonbeliev-ers. Again he traveled disguised as a devout Muslim, but in this place he revealed his true identity to the Amir, the local ruler, hoping that the Amir's desire for the friendship of powerful Britain would protect him, which it did. By this time he had published his three-volume *Personal Narratives of a Pilgrimage to El-Medinah and Mecca,* one of the most popular of his forty-eight books. He was now a famous man, and The Royal Geographical Society and other influential bodies in London were happy to finance what was to be the most ambitious of his explorations—his search for the source of the Nile, the north-moving river that makes the desert bloom in North Africa and flows into the Mediterranean Sea at Alexandria, Egypt.

But where in the heart of Africa did this mighty stream arise? That, for over a thousand years, had been one of the burning questions of geographical exploration. Everlasting renown awaited the man who could answer it, and in 1851 Burton assumed the leadership of the first expedition to make a serious effort to do so. This, his first attempt to penetrate Central Africa, where it was assumed the great river began, ended in disaster at the East-African town of Berbera. Here, on a rocky ridge overlooking the Red Sea, the some forty-five members of the expedition

An attack by Somali tribesmen in East Africa left Burton scarred but in no way daunted his adventurous spirit. *Courtesy of the New York Public Library, Division of Prints and Photographs.*

halted for a spell to prepare for their plunge into the interior of the continent. And here on an April night in 1855 their camp was overrun by Somali tribesmen, wielding pistols and other weapons. One of Burton's British co-leaders was slain. Another was injured. Burton himself was severely wounded. A javelin slashed his right cheek to produce in time the scar that for years contributed so noticeably to the Satanlike ferocity of his features. Ordered home

to England to recover, he had no choice but to put the search for the headwaters of the Nile out of his mind for the time being.

The Crimean War was under way: Britain and her allies versus Russia, chiefly for control of sections of southeastern Europe. As soon as he was well, Burton volunteered to spend five months at the Dardanelles, where he commanded a cavalry unit. Back in England in December 1855, he began preparations for another expedition to explore the center of Africa, then a blank on the map to most Europeans, and to seek the source of the Nile.

One of the first persons to hear of these plans was twenty-five-year old Isabel Arundel, member of an old and aristocratic Catholic family. Isabel and Burton had met for the first time at Boulogne in France. This was in 1850, and during the intervening years the slender but strongly built Burton with his "straight Arab features" and his "fierce, proud, melancholy expression" had been constantly in Isabel's thoughts. In London, during the summer of 1856, they met again. Soon they were walking together daily in the Botanical Gardens, and in August they were engaged.

Isabel's mother was horrified. Save for a small inheritance from his mother, who had died recently, Burton had nothing. Besides, Mrs. Arundel complained, he was not only not a Catholic, he was known to be scornful of all Western religions. She reminded her daughter that there were many far more suitable young men about.

"Let them marry somebody else," Isabel replied. Her heart was fixed on Burton. If she could not be his wife, she would be nobody's wife. "I would not live like a vegetable . . . with a good and portly husband," she wrote in her diary. "A dry crust, privations, pain, danger with him I love would be better." She was aware of the stories making the rounds—exaggerated tales, no doubt, but not wholly inaccurate, of Burton's affairs with native women in Muslim countries, of his wild nights in Eastern brothels and drinking spots. She knew, at least to a degree, what she was letting herself in for, that Burton was a difficult man.

How difficult, she soon had reason to understand more fully. In October, when he left England to put his expedition in training, he did not even drop by to say good-bye. He sent a note to her sister Blanche, asking Blanche to break the news gently. Isabel wept, prayed for his welfare, and waited for him to return. It was an ordeal she would endure often in the years ahead.

As second in command of his expedition, Burton had chosen a young lieu-

tenant in Britain's East Indian Army named John Hanning Speke. Six years younger than Burton, tall and slender with blue eyes and fair hair, Speke had accompanied Burton on his first unsuccessful attempt to invade the African wilds. He too had served in Crimea and had reached England shortly after Burton's return there. Meeting in London, the two men sailed first to Bombay, where Burton arranged for Speke to receive a leave of absence from his military duties. They then moved on to the island of Zanzibar off the shores of East Africa. Here they spent the next six months laying in supplies and equipment for a two-year expedition and assembling a small army of porters and beasts of burden.

By mid-June 1857, when they left Zanzibar for the African mainland, Burton had begun to realize that in selecting John Hanning Speke as his companion he had made a mistake. The two men were utterly dissimilar. Burton drank hard, played hard, and gave no thought to his personal health. Speke drank little, played even less, and watched over his health as if he were his own mother. Burton was not given to planning ahead; he threw himself joyously into an adventure and hoped for the best. Speke set goals and moved toward them soberly and systematically. Speke loved hunting; he would shoot at anything that moved. Back in India, Burton had hunted a little, only to give it up for obvious reasons. His father enjoyed hunting, and whatever the father enjoyed the son was resolved to hate. In only one respect were Speke and Burton alike—and this similarity was probably the major cause of their mutual dislike. Speke was as ambitious as Burton, as determined to distinguish himself. As travel writer Alan Moorehead notes, for this expedition into the depths of Africa, "Burton needed a disciple but what he got was a rival."

As the expedition forged westward, the tropical heat, the insects, the hard-to-climb mountains, the steaming jungles—all had an enervating effect on the two men. Both fell ill. Burton was half blind and compelled by a temporary paralysis to ride in a hammock, slung on poles and carried by eight natives. On February 13, 1858, they rounded the top of a steep hill and looked down on the bright waters of Lake Tanganyika, the longest of the lakes of central Africa. For the two Europeans it was the first significant discovery of their hazardous venture—and for Burton the last.

Could these rippling waters be the source of the Nile? Was there a northbound stream flowing out of Tanganyika? Burton put these questions to the people living in Ujiji, a village on the eastern banks of the lake. Yes, the villagers answered; at the northern tip of the lake a large stream called the Rusizi flowed out of it. Overjoyed, Burton and Speke rounded up canoes and paddled up the lake, looking for the river they now assumed to be the Nile.

But it wasn't. Either the villagers did not know whereof they spoke or they were lying. As Burton and Speke glided northward, they met bands of roving natives—men and women who said they had seen the Rusizi many times. According to these travelers, that river flowed southward into the lake and therefore could not be the Nile.

Profoundly disappointed, angry at one group of natives for lying to them and at the other group for telling them the truth, the two Englishmen and their entourage turned away from Tanganyika to begin the eight-hundred mile trudge back to their starting point on the island of Zanzibar.

The eighteenth of June brought them to Arab-occupied Kazeh, now Tabora in central Tanzania, where they stopped so that Burton, still very ill, could rest. It was during their stay here that Speke voiced a proposal that was to make him the discoverer of the source of the Nile—and Burton made a decision that he would regret for the rest of his life.

The natives and the Arab slave dealers had spoken of a lake seemingly even larger than Tanganyika, lying to the northwest of where they now were. Speke suggested that he and Burton have a look at it. Still half-blind and unable to walk, Burton shook his head. He told Speke to go look at it on his own. Speke did so, returning six weeks later with two startling announcements. One was that he had found what is now known as Lake Victoria. The other was his conviction that somewhere along the northern borders of that mammoth body of water was the beginning of the Nile. Burton asked the logical question: Had Speke actually seen a stream flowing northward out of Victoria? Speke said he had not, an admission that until he could return and further explore the area he would not be in a position to say that he had located the source of the Nile.

Thus this matter stood when on September 6 the explorers moved on, reaching Zanzibar in February 1859. From Zanzibar, having quickly disbanded the expedition, they took passage on a clipper ship to Aden at the foot of the Arabian Peninsula, where they parted company. Burton, recovering from his ailments but not yet well, decided to rest where he was for a few days. Speke arranged to take ship for England. His parting words to Burton, as they said their good-byes on the docks of Aden on May 9, was that he would not reveal the discovery of Lake Victoria until Burton could join him in London, where they would announce it and their other findings together.

But this promise was not kept. When on May 21 Burton arrived in London, he was dismayed to learn that not only had Speke reported the discovery of Lake Victoria to the Royal Geographical Society but that he had persuaded that organization to finance another expedition to Africa, to be led by himself, to locate exactly where on the northern shores of Victoria the Nile began.

At this point the long-standing feud between Burton and Speke became a matter of public knowledge. For several months Burton himself issued no public utterances. When he finally did so, it was simply to assert that he did not think the Nile started at Lake Victoria—a position with which some other English explorers, including the famous Dr. David Livingstone, agreed. Speke, on the other hand, went public at once. In the press and on the lecture platform he charged that Burton would have abandoned their expedition before they even reached Tanganyika had not he—Speke—insisted that they go on. What Speke was saying, in effect, was that he and he alone was the true discoverer not only of Lake Victoria but of Lake Tanganyika as well.

Appalled by Speke's exaggerated

claims, Burton busied himself with other matters. He tended to some family affairs. He visited his sister, now married to a well-known general and living in Dover. He pursued his courtship of Isabel Arundel, albeit with a lack of enthusiasm which shows that he was not yet ready for marriage. He completed another of his many books.

This chore behind him, he journeyed to the United States. He spent most of his nine months there examining the beliefs and practices of the Mormons in Salt Lake City. Strange how this man who described himself as averse to religion devoted so much of his time to studying it. Indeed, one perceives in his actions, as distinct from his words, an affirmation of a statement from the pen of England's famous woman explorer, Mary Kingsley: "The final objective of all human desire is a knowledge of the nature of God." Having learned what the Mormons thought about the Deity, Burton returned to England to marry Isabel on January 22, 1862, in a Catholic chapel in London. He was forty, she thirty.

By this time Speke had returned to Africa, where, on July 28, 1862, he found on the northern rim of Lake Victoria a break in the shoreline that he named Ripon Falls and through which the waters of the lake poured out to form the Nile. When in June 1863 he returned to London to report this discovery, the old argument broke out anew.

Speke had not gone around the lake. How then could he be sure that Ripon Falls was the only place where a northward-moving stream exited from its waters? Perhaps Lake Victoria was not one huge lake as Speke contended, but a series of smaller lakes linked by one or more rivers. Perhaps, as Burton and other students of Africa asserted, the Nile began one hundred miles or more to the south of Lake Victoria.

This issue had become a clamorous controversy, with Speke defending his position in the press and elsewhere, and Burton and others attacking it. Finally, in September 1864, the British Association for the Advancement of Science sponsored at Bath, Speke's home town, a gathering of leading geographers and explorers who were to read papers and deliver talks about the matter. The highlight of this meeting was to be a debate, scheduled for September 16, between Speke and Burton.

From the pen of Isabel Burton we have an enchanting explanation of why her husband agreed to appear in public with a man to whom he had not spoken so much as a word since the two of them parted company many years earlier at Aden. Sometime before the meeting, Isabel wrote, a friend "conveyed to Richard that Speke had said that if Burton appeared on the platform at Bath . . . he would kick him. I remember Richard's answer: 'Well, that settles it! My God, he *shall* kick me.'"

On September 15, the day before the great debate, Richard and Isabel, attending one of the evening sessions of the conference, spotted Speke at the far side of a crowded auditorium. The two men made a point of ignoring each other. Burton saw that someone was beckoning to Speke and that the latter had risen from his chair. Hurrying from the room, he was heard to say in a loud voice, "I can't stand this any longer."

Next morning the members of the conference gathered early for the eagerly awaited debate. The hall was full when Burton, standing alone on the platform, noticed that a note was being handed from person to person. Minutes passed before he learned that on the previous afternoon Speke, hunting partridge on the estate of a cousin, had climbed onto a two-foot stone wall, holding the muzzle of his breech-loading gun close to his body. The gun had no safety catch. Somehow one of its barrels discharged, tearing a gaping wound in Speke's chest. Fifteen minutes later he was dead.

The news jolted Burton. He was seen sinking into his chair, exclaiming, "My God, he's killed himself!" We have Isa-

bel's word for it that when she and her husband got back to their lodging at Bath Richard "wept long and bitterly, and I was for many a day trying to comfort him."

Burton's biographers interpret his reaction to Speke's death in various ways. A strong possibility certainly is that he was weeping not so much for an enemy who had once been a friend as for his folly in not having gone with Speke to Lake Victoria so that the two of them could have discovered the source of the Nile together.

For the Nile does indeed begin at Ripon Falls at the northern end of Lake Victoria. And when in 1875 the Welsh-born journalist and explorer Henry Morton Stanley proved this to be the case, Burton immediately delivered a speech, admitting that he had been wrong and that Speke had been right.

After 1864 Burton traveled from time to time to strange regions, but none of these explorations was on the grand scale of his earlier expeditions. Books continued to pour from his writing desk—wonderful books, some of them, and most of them both scholarly and readable. Among them was his monumental translation of the *Arabian Nights,* those ancient Oriental tales of fabulous adventurers such as Aladdin, Ali Baba and the forty thieves, and Sinbad the Sailor.

He continued, as Isabel had anticipated, to be a difficult husband, often taking off on long trips without warning, leaving his utterly devoted wife to weep and pray and hope for his safe return. She, on her side, spent money lavishly—money that they did not have—hosting large and extravagant parties and surrounding herself with expensive horses.

But these were merely the quirks of what was on balance a good marriage. Richard's parents were gone; his brother had become mentally ill; his sister was not always around—and as the years rolled on Isabel became the core of his existence, the anchor on which he relied. She was quick to defend him against malicious gossip—an uphill battle, for Richard was fond of relating outrageous stories of his misdeeds in the fabled Orient: the men he had slain in cold blood and the beautiful young women he had stolen from the harems of turbaned potentates. Those who knew him intimately smiled at these tales; those who didn't shuddered and spread them abroad.

Soon after his marriage in 1861 he quit the army to enter the country's civilian foreign service, acting as consul in sundry parts of the world. He and Isabel were living in Trieste at the head of the Adriatic Sea when, on the morning of October 21, 1890, after a long struggle with gout, Richard Burton died.

It is a revealing commentary on this flawed, reckless, and gifted man that it was precisely those who knew him best who admired him most. They saw him as witty, honest, generous, good company, and a good friend. For all his flamboyance, he was singularly unpretentious. He talked little of himself, wrote even less. The nearest he ever came to bragging was to describe his life as a "blaze of light without a focus." If by that he meant that he had done many things but accomplished little, he was as usual underrating himself. As biographer Brodie points out, Burton made his mark in at least three worthwhile fields of endeavor: He was a distinguished writer, he was one of the few great linguists of his time, and he was one of his country's top-ranking explorers.

Richard Evelyn Byrd

1888–1957 American pioneer aviator and polar explorer. Navigator of the first airplane to reach the North and South poles. Leader of the expeditions that, by mapping much of the interior and large sections of the coastlines of Antarctica, brought that continent into the consciousness of the world.

The little city of Winchester, Virginia, in the Shenandoah Valley, where on October 25, 1888, Richard Evelyn Byrd, Jr., was born into the first of the First Families of Virginia, never saw much of the undersized boy who would grow into one of his country's most celebrated airmen and explorers.

He was twelve when he received a letter from one of his father's friends, Adam C. Carson, a judge on the United States Circuit Court in the Philippine Islands. The Judge wanted "Dickie" to pay him a visit, and Dickie at once decided to do so. Mounting his bicycle, he spent the afternoon visiting friends in the neighborhood, informing them of his imminent departure for distant climes. Then he pedaled home and showed the letter to his parents.

Their immediate reaction was unfavorable. His lawyer father, Richard Evelyn Byrd, Sr., was fond of Judge Carson but disturbed at the thought of his small son traveling halfway around the world by himself. His mother, Eleanor Flood Byrd, pointed to the newspapers. The year was 1900. With the guerrilla forces of a native rebel chieftain battling the occupying forces of the U.S. Army in the Philippines, those islands at the far end of the Pacific were not the safest places in the world.

But Dickie knew how to handle his folks. Assuming the ingratiating demeanor that in later years moved large scientific organizations and corporate presidents to support his explorations, he won their consent. His mother took him to Washington, D.C., bought him a ticket, allowed herself a few tears, and put him on the train to San Francisco.

From there he sailed across the Pacific. He spent the better part of a year in the Philippines. Then, sailing for the United States by way of the Indian and Atlantic oceans, he saw the half of the world he had not yet traversed.

The Dickie Byrd who came home from these adventures, his biographer Edwin P. Hoyt tells us, was no longer a boy. He was a young man who had circumnavigated the globe and "whom Winchester could no longer contain." Apparently his parents were impressed.

At any rate, they sent him away to school, first to the Shenandoah Military Academy in Winchester and then to the Virginia Military Institute in Lexington, Virginia. Hoyt suspects that his father found Dickie's absence from the family circle not only bearable but pleasant. The senior Richard considered his namesake "erratic and impatient" and was happier in the company of his other sons, sobersided Harry, who was to become a governor of Virginia and United States Senator, and high-spirited Tom, headed for a successful career in the growing and marketing of apples. Dickie was studying at a third institution, the University of Virginia in Charlottesville, when on a

spring day in 1908 he received the long-hoped-for appointment to the Naval Academy at Annapolis, Maryland.

At Annapolis his behavior was characterized by traits that he kept throughout life. He got along well with his fellow students, but there seems to have been little or no depth to these relationships. He showed a marked ability for planning and organizing activities and for seeing to it that they were carried out. He tended to be polite, friendly—and aloof. "Most of the time," a student publication said, "Dick wanders about with a faraway look in his eyes."

We know now what he was dreaming of: the polar regions. The many attempts of explorers to uncover the secrets of the frozen North were a staple of the newspapers of his time. In the same year that saw him off to the Philippines he had resolved, and so written in his diary, that some day he would do what no other person had done— he would go to the North Pole. The news during his first year at the Academy that someone else had done so extinguished that dream, but it was quickly replaced by other dreams of a similar nature.

At the Academy he went in for sports, determined to strengthen a body that was deficient in both size and muscularity. His football career ended in his third year when, during a game with

Princeton, he broke his right foot. His career as a gymnast, a brilliant one, ended in his last year when in the course of an intricate stunt on the rings, his hands slipped and he fell thirteen feet, landing on the already damaged foot. Commissioned an ensign upon his graduation in 1912, he was serving as a signal officer aboard the warship *Washington* when he fell through an open hatchway and injured the right foot for the third time. On this occasion the operating surgeons had to fasten the weakened bone with a galvanized pin. It would remain with him from then on, along with a noticeable limp.

For two years his ship operated in the Caribbean. During this period he was twice decorated for saving the lives of drowning seamen. He was still in the Caribbean when in the summer of 1911 he enjoyed his first trip in an airplane and wrote his parents that he had discovered his life work. He was going to be an aviator. The announcement left his mother unperturbed, probably because the dangers common to the early years of flight were beyond her comprehension. It was otherwise with his father. An old-fashioned southern squire, scornful of the multiplying products of modern technology, he let it be known that he had as good as lost a son. In lawyer Byrd's mind it was a foregone conclusion that in the near fu-

ture Dickie would perish in one of those silly flying gadgets.

In the autumn of 1914 Ensign Byrd was assigned to a new post, that of aide to Josephus Daniels, President Wilson's Secretary of the Navy. This transfer put the young man in the Washington, D.C. area, aboard the U.S.S. *Dolphin*, the secretary's yacht, and a few months later, on January 21, 1915, he married his childhood sweetheart, Marie D. Ames of Boston and Winchester.

At this point Byrd was giving thought to the troubled status of his career. Other members of his Annapolis graduating class had already moved up in rank. He had received no promotions, nor did there seem to be any in the offing. At fault, he realized, was his game leg. In the eyes of the navy he was handicapped.

Behind these sober reflections one detects the concern of a twenty-two-year-old man suddenly confronted with the responsibilities of a marriage and the maintenance of a home in Boston where his four children would grow up. Obviously his navy career was going nowhere and the time had come to do something else. In March 1916 he requested and was granted retirement, but instead of seeking other employment he moped about for a few weeks. Biographer Hoyt pictures him at this juncture in his life as considering himself a failure, succumbing to feelings of self-pity wholly at odds with his normally confident and optimistic nature.

In May 1916 the navy came to his rescue, recalling him to active duty and promoting him to lieutenant junior grade with the proviso that he was not to serve at sea. Ordered to Rhode Island, he organized the state's naval militia, and when his country entered World War I he was brought back to Washington to establish the Navy Department Commission on Training Camps and to act as its secretary.

Though pleased to be busy, Lieutenant Byrd had no intention of spending the rest of his life "sailing a desk." He was determined, game leg notwithstanding, to achieve a more active role for himself. In 1917 he talked a medical board into letting him take flight training at the naval air station in Pensacola, Florida, and when he returned to Washington in April 1918 he was naval aviator 608. During the ensuing months he developed some of the navigational instruments that made possible the first crossing of the Atlantic by a naval flying boat and almost single-handedly persuaded the Congress of the United States to install a Bureau of Aeronautics in the Department of the Navy. It would be said later that had Byrd never flown to the Poles, his part in providing the navy with wings would have

ensured him a place in the history books.

His interest in the polar regions had never died. In 1925 when he heard that the famous Arctic explorer Donald B. MacMillan was planning an exploration of northern Greenland, he wangled a place on the expedition for a naval flying unit to be commanded by himself. MacMillan resisted this development. Byrd had long since acquired a well-deserved reputation as a man who, having joined a project, insisted on running it. MacMillan feared that the presence of the self-willed naval officer, now a lieutenant commander, would have the effect of diminishing MacMillan's authority as the originator of the enterprise. Byrd persisted. He knew the right people to see and what to say to them, and during the summer of 1925 his unit of three seaplanes explored 10,000 square miles of northern Greenland and nearby Ellesmere Island by air.

There were moments of strain between him and MacMillan, and Byrd returned to Washington convinced that MacMillan was right about one thing: No exploration could be expected to do first-rate work under divided authority. One expedition, one commander. That now became Byrd's motto, and the one commander, of course, must be himself.

When Seymour Millais Stone painted this portrait of Byrd in 1931, Byrd was already famous for his conquest of the North Pole and for having flown to the South Pole. *Courtesy of the National Portrait Gallery, Smithsonian Institution; transfer from the NMMA; gift of the artist, 1931.*

The fall of 1925 brought word that the great Norwegian explorer Roald Amundsen had for the time being given up a projected flight to the North Pole. At once, Byrd decided to make that attempt himself. As his sidekick in this ambitious endeavor, he selected thirty-five-year-old Floyd Bennett, one of the navy men who had accompanied him on the expedition to Greenland. This was a perfect partnership. Bennett was a chief machinist's mate with no apparent desire to be anything more. He was resourceful, brave, and a superb pilot. In Bennett's eyes graduates of the Naval Academy were superior beings, and he carried out Byrd's orders promptly and without question.

Months went into the preparation of an enterprise that required the raising of $140,000 to cover, among other things, the purchase of a plane, the recruitment of a fifty-person crew to service it, and the leasing of a ship to carry personnel and equipment to the Arctic. One of Byrd's first decisions was to make his try for the Pole in a trimotor airplane. Only two were on the market. One, available from the Atlantic Aircraft Corporation, was a large monoplane built by the famous Dutch designer Anthony Fokker. The other was a product of the Ford Motor Company. Byrd bought the Fokker, largely because it was the cheaper of the two.

Setting out to raise funds, he traveled to Detroit to call on Edsel Ford. It would not have surprised him had Ford said nothing doing, given the commander's choice of a plane obtained from the Ford Company's chief competitor in the emerging aviation industry. But Byrd was too bold a man to be deterred by such considerations and Edsel Ford too big a one to make anything of them. Ford listened attentively while Byrd outlined his project, stressing the vast areas of the Arctic waiting to be explored. Then he gave him $20,000, whereupon Byrd hastened to New York to collect additional money from John D. Rockefeller, Jr., and other wealthy individuals.

In the beginning he hoped that his project would be conducted under the auspices of the navy. But this was not to be. The navy gave him a pat on the back and a leave of absence to pursue his plans, but any further support it refused to provide. Byrd had enemies in the upper echelon of the service, admirals who regarded him as overly aggressive and given to doing things his way instead of the navy way. When on April 5, 1926, the commander and his crew departed from American shores on a wooden steamer called *Chantier*, they did so as the Byrd Expedition, a strictly private undertaking.

Their destination was Spitsbergen,

a Norwegian island in the Arctic Ocean, four-hundred miles north of the Norwegian mainland. Byrd's intent was to establish a base on this snow-covered area and from there try to fly to the North Pole in his Fokker plane, named *Josephine Ford* after Edsel Ford's daughter.

The members of the Byrd expedition reached Spitsbergen on May 1, to find Roald Amundsen already there. In recent months the Norwegian explorer had changed his mind. He too was now planning to attempt a flight to the Pole, using an Italian-made dirigible called *Norge*. Byrd and his crew were still putting the *Josephine Ford* in shape for its impending journey when on May 7 the *Norge* touched down on Spitsbergen.

We have conflicting stories as to what happened during the next few days. One story says that, following the arrival of the *Norge*, the effort to attain the Pole became a race between Byrd and Amundsen, with each man striving feverishly to be the first to take off. The other account says that though the *Norge* was ready to fly on the evening of the eighth, Amundsen deliberately held back a couple of days so that Byrd could go first. Given the fierce rivalry among explorers, can we believe that the Norwegian acted in this generous manner?

We can. Fifty-four-year-old Amund-

sen had long since won his laurels: first to reach the South Pole, first to sail a ship through the Northwest Passage, the waterway across the top of North America that links the Atlantic and Pacific oceans. Amundsen, moreover, was a kindly and large-minded man, quite capable of helping a new and younger explorer get his chance at fame.

The *Norge* was still in its hangar when shortly after 2:00 A.M. on May 9 the *Josephine Ford* took to the air with Byrd as commander and navigator and Bennett at the controls. The first people to view the vast expanse of the upper Arctic from the air, the American aviators soon found the answer to an age-old question. Was there or was there not a continent at the North Pole, similar to the one that surrounds the South Pole? For centuries many geographers and explorers had assumed there was. The observation of Byrd and Bennett as they winged steadily northward showed that there was none. The North Pole stands in the midst of an ice-filled sea.

They reached the Pole at 9:02 A.M., circled the area briefly, and then headed back to Spitsbergen, reaching the island at 4:30 P.M. They had traveled approximately 2,500 miles and had been airborne for fifteen hours and thirty minutes.

Presently those figures gave rise to

a charge—one that would surface again years later—that Byrd had not actually reached the Pole, that with a cruising speed estimated to be no more than seventy miles an hour, the *Josephine Ford* could not have flown from Spitsbergen to the Pole and back in fifteen hours and thirty minutes. The two countries in which these criticisms first appeared, Norway and Italy, wanted the Norwegian-commanded and Italian-built *Norge* to win the prize, so the charges were nearly everywhere else dismissed as sour grapes. On June 23, Byrd returned to the United States. He was hailed as a hero, treated to a ticker-tape parade in New York City, and lavishly honored by his government.

He was now his country's foremost pioneer aviator and on the way to becoming its foremost explorer. In late June, Byrd, Bennett, Norwegian-born Bernt Balchen, and others set out to demonstrate the feasibility of commercial flight across the Atlantic by ferrying eight hundred pounds of mail from New York to Paris. The venture was successful enough to make its point, but it was attended by misfortune. The plane used, a Fokker trimotor called *America*, crashed during a test flight. Byrd's arm was broken and Bennett so injured that he had to withdraw from the project. On the arrival of the *America* over Paris, adverse weather prevented it from

landing and pilot Balchen was forced to return to the coast where he put the plane down safely in the surf off Ver-sur-Mer.

The success of Byrd's Arctic expedition had whetted his appetite for polar adventure. By the end of 1937 he had begun preparations for an expedition to the Antarctic. His intent this time was to establish a base on the mammoth conformation along the coast of the frozen continent, originally known as the Ross Ice Barrier—a name that was changed to Ross Ice Shelf as explorers realized that it was not a barrier but a highway to Antarctica itself. From this base Byrd would conduct a scientific exploration of large portions of the adjoining landmass and attempt a flight to the South Pole.

Months of organizing and fundraising followed. The untimely death of Floyd Bennett on April 25 was a blow from which Byrd recovered with difficulty; but he kept on, gradually amassing substantial financial support. Some of it came from wealthy businessmen, some from scientific bodies, including the National Geographic Society, an organization with which Byrd would be intimately associated for the rest of his life.

The two ships of the Byrd Antarctic Expedition left American shores in October 1928, carrying forty-one men, four airplanes, ninety-four sledge dogs, and a quantity of scientific instruments. On the Ross Ice Shelf, reached in late December, the team erected a miscellany of buildings—living quarters, workshops, and laboratories—to be known as Little America.

Working out of this base, they photographed 150,000 square miles of territory and discovered a number of Antarctic landmarks, including the Rockefeller and Ford Mountain ranges, the 10,000-foot La Gorce Mountain, and the large area now known as Marie Byrd Land. In the early morning hours on Thanksgiving Day, November 28, 1929, Byrd and three companions began the flight for the South Pole, reaching it at 1:14 P.M. and returning to Little America shortly after 10:00 P.M. When in June 1930 the expedition returned to the United States, Byrd again found himself the subject of celebrations and honors. He received the Navy Cross for extraordinary heroism, and Congress promoted him to the rank of rear admiral.

In October 1933 he led another expedition southward. Getting to the Pole had been the major objective of the preceding voyage to Antarctica. This one was heavily scientific, including intensive studies of the biology and weather of the region and of the depth and composition of the nearby waters. The major finding, clearing up an old

geographic mystery, was that Antarctica was not, as some supposed, a collection of mountainous islands but a huge and self-contained continent.

Reaching the Ross Ice Shelf in January 1934, the members of the expedition set out to establish an advanced base for meterological observations a hundred miles south of Little America. There, in an opening dug into the 200-foot-thick ice, they erected a shack to shelter some of the scientists and their equipment. When the swift onset of the sunless Antarctic winter prevented them from storing supplies for more than one person, Byrd arranged to spend the winter there by himself. His subsequently published story of his experiences during the next few months, a book titled *Alone*, is one of the most vivid pictures we have of life on the frozen continent and of the endurance and courage of its author. So extreme were the temperatures at the advance base, ranging from forty to as low as eighty below zero, that Byrd found it impossible to take a complete bath at any one time. The best he could manage was to wash a third of his body each day.

On the last day of May 1934 he came close to dying when poisonous carbon monoxide fumes began escaping from the pipe of his cooking stove, the only source of heat in his small cabin. For weeks he was desperately ill. He was in touch with the other members of the expedition by two-way radio, but he said nothing of his plight in his daily reports to Little America. He feared that if he did so, Dr. Thomas Poulter, his second-in-command, and some of the others would endanger their own lives traveling across the ice in the winter darkness in an effort to rescue him.

The admiral never mastered the use of the radio. His messages to the home base were always somewhat garbled, but by mid-July they had become so markedly so that Poulter and his associates realized that something was wrong.

Their first attempt to rescue him was beaten back by temperatures of around eighty below, but a second trip succeeded. On August 11 Poulter and three other members of the project reached the advance base to find Byrd so weak that two months and four days passed before they were able to remove him to the relative comfort of Little America. By the time the expedition got back to the United States in May 1935, Byrd had become more than a hero to his countrymen. As biographer Hoyt writes, he was now a "national institution."

Hoyt calls his account of the Admiral *The Last Explorer*. His point would seem to be well taken. Byrd was indeed the last, or at any rate almost the last, of the so-called "classic explorers": men like Columbus and Magellan, Captain James Cook and Amundsen, who so dominated the expeditions they led that those activities became the lengthened shadows of themselves.

Today the thrust of exploration is away from the surface of the earth, up into space and down to the bottoms of the seas. These searches tend to be costly enterprises, conceived and directed, not by individuals, but by governments, and conducted by so large an array of scientists and engineers that their names flash by us and are forgotten.

The change took place during Byrd's lifetime. On the eve of World War II there was another expedition to Antarctica, and after it came two more. All were government sponsored, with one of them utilizing the skills of 4,000 persons. The newspapers called each of these endeavors a "Byrd expedition," but in fact his part in them was small. When he did show up at one of the several American bases in Antarctica, the bright young scientists and engineers doing the work gave him short shrift. In their eyes, he was an old fossil, hopelessly out of touch with the modern way of doing things.

Was the admiral hurt by this shabby treatment? If so, he gave no sign of

Byrd spent the winter of 1934 alone in this Antarctic camp, gathering scientific data and nearly dying in the process. *Neg. 296833, Courtesy of Department Library Services, American Museum of Natural History.*

it. His bout with death at the advance base in the Antarctic winter of 1934 had left him a changed man. Many who knew him noticed that he had lost the taste for glory that had shaped his earlier years. During World War II he conducted important secret missions that helped his country win the long, hard battle in the Pacific. Both before and after the conflict he participated in movements organized to discourage the recurrent armed conflicts and outbursts of hate that have so flawed the quality of life in the twentieth-century world.

He paid his fifth and last visit to Antarctica in late 1955 and early 1956. It was a short stay. He was not well, and when he returned to the United States it was to spend much of his time in his Boston home, an ample structure overlooking the Back Bay, where he died on March 11, 1957.

Byrd was a highly contradictory man, indeed something of a paradox. He was a superb public relations person, skillful at using the media of his day, the newspapers and the radio, to create interest in and support for his great explorations. On the other hand, he was an intensely private person, steadfastly refusing to share his thoughts and feelings with the public. He was known to have kept diaries, but to this day these and his other private papers are locked up in the family home in Boston, closed to the eyes of journalists and historians alike.

John Cabot

1450–1499   Born Giovanni Caboto in Genoa, Italy. Seafarer in the employ of England whose explorations of the coast of North America established England's claim to territory in the New World.

For reasons to be mentioned in the course of this sketch, our knowledge of John Cabot is regrettably meager.

Like his famous contemporary, Christopher Columbus, he began life in the mid-fifteenth century at the port of Genoa on the Italian shores of the Mediterranean Sea.

By 1476, however, he was no longer there. On March 28 of that year the rulers of Venice pronounced him a citizen of that Italian metropolis, and the document that tells us this also tells us that by then John Cabot had been living in Venice for at least fifteen years.

Doing what? Many things, it would seem.

He engaged in the buying and selling of products of some sort.

He married and became the father of three sons: Lewis, Sanctius, and Sebastian. Of Lewis and Sanctius almost nothing is known. As for Sebastian, he would follow in his father's footsteps, becoming a skillful mariner and mapmaker, an explorer on a limited scale, and the promoter of several ambitious exploratory expeditions.

During the Venetian years John Cabot also traveled a good deal. One of his business ventures took him to Mecca in Arabia—a journey which shows that he was not averse to taking risks. Mecca was the holy city of the religion of Islam, and Christians and Jews found within its confines were summarily expelled or summarily beheaded.

He studied the works of the geographers of his day. His biographer, Sir Charles Raymond Beazley, believes that he was deeply influenced by the teachings of the brilliant Italian astronomer Paolo dal Pozzo Toscanelli. In the late fifteenth century many of the nations of Europe were seeking sea routes by which their merchants could travel to the flourishing silk, spice, and gem markets of China, Japan, India, and the islands off the coasts of Asia. One of Toscanelli's theories was that since the world was round, those places could be reached just as readily by sailing west across the Atlantic as they could by sailing east around the bottom of Africa and across the Indian Ocean.

As we now know, it was to some extent Toscanelli's ideas that induced Christopher Columbus in the late 1480s to ask the kings of Portugal, Spain, France, and England to sponsor the voyages across the Atlantic that he would undertake in the succeeding decade. And during the same period that Columbus was laying before the crowned heads of Europe his Enterprise of the Indies, his plan for reaching the markets of the East by sailing west, Cabot was presenting a similar proposition to some of the same monarchs. Nothing came of Cabot's efforts, but they were still on his mind when in 1492 King Ferdinand and Queen Isabella, the rulers of Spain, finally agreed to send Columbus on the first of his historic journeys of discovery.

By this time Cabot was living in England. At first he resided in London, where he appears to have acted as a business agent for one of the trading firms in Venice. Later he moved to Bristol, the liveliest of England's seaports on the Atlantic and the center of England's oceangoing commerce. He was still working on Bristol's bustling docks when in 1493 Columbus completed his first voyage, and his discovery of islands in the Caribbean Sea at the western end of the Atlantic was the talk of Europe.

In this development John Cabot spotted an opportunity to try once more to acquire backing for his own exploratory schemes. His efforts to do so took time. Columbus was on his second voyage when in the spring of 1496 Cabot obtained a long-sought audience with Henry VII, king of England.

Several years earlier King Henry had rejected Columbus's Enterprise of the Indies, taking the position that the Genoa-born navigator's idea of trying to reach the East by sailing west was "a joke." Now Henry realized that he had made a mistake, and his mind was open to everything John Cabot had to say.

Indeed, from the standpoint of the commercially minded monarch, Cabot's suggestions were a marvel of logic and common sense. Like Columbus, he believed that the distant regions his fellow Italian had found were in the neighborhood of the spice- and gem-rich countries of Asia. There was wealth to be got in those parts, and it would never do to let Spain have it all. England should grab its share.

Cabot pointed out that Columbus, crossing the Atlantic far to the south, had reached one section of the fabulous Orient. He now proposed to cross the ocean along a more northerly latitude and thus reach another section of it. What did Henry Tudor, king of England, think of that idea?

Henry thought well of it. On March 5, 1496, he plunked down the royal seal on a long document that authorized "our well-beloved John Cabot" to go exploring in the Atlantic. And at this point we must attend to an ironic side-light on Cabot's first voyage of discovery in the summer of 1497.

In later years his son Sebastian contended that it was he, rather than his father, who conducted the 1497 venture. Indeed, on one occasion Sebastian said his father couldn't have commanded that expedition because by then he was already dead. Understandable, surely, is the statement by the explorer-historian Vilhjalmur Stefansson that one reason we know much about Columbus and little about John Cabot is that "Columbus was fortunate in having a learned and loyal son, Ferdi-

nand, who devoted himself to the preservation of his father's memory, while John Cabot was unfortunate in having a learned but self-centered son, Sebastian, who not merely failed to give his father due credit but did his best to make people believe . . . that he himself, and not his father, was the great voyager."

Obviously, the younger Cabot's proven abilities included a certain skill at manipulating the truth. On May 2, 1497, when a tiny vessel named *Matthew* carried the twenty members of the expedition into the waters of the Atlantic, John Cabot was not only very much alive but also very much in command. Steering his ship first north into the seas off Iceland, then in a generally southwest direction, he reached the rim of North America on or about June 24.

Because his own logbook has disappeared, the exact location of his landfall remains a guess. Some authorities think it was the shores of Newfoundland or Nova Scotia; some, the biographer Beazley among them, believe it was Cape Breton, one of the larger islands fringing the outer edge of the Gulf of St. Lawrence.

Wherever he was, Cabot promptly planted the flag of England and claimed the surrounding area of a million miles or so for King Henry. Then he and his companions explored sections of the

John Cabot sailed from Bristol, England, on exploratory expeditions to North America in 1497 and 1498, as shown in this painting from the City of Bristol Art Gallery. *Courtesy of Bridgeman/Art Resource, NY.*

Canadian mainland before setting the course for Bristol, where they arrived on August 6, 1497.

To reduce this adventure to a few black words on white paper is to make it all sound very simple and easy. Be assured, it was a tremendous accomplishment, and Henry VII was tremendously impressed.

On one score, however, his Majesty was a trifle disappointed. Cabot had brought home neither silks nor spices nor precious stones. Never mind, said Cabot, who by this time had learned how to soft-talk the king. He assured him that the islands and coasts he'd seen were very close to "the Land of the Grand Khan," meaning China. The thing to do now was to return to where he had been. Only this time he'd investigate the land mass he'd encountered until he found an opening in it—a waterway across which he could sail into the Sea of Japan and thus to the shores of "the Land of the Grand Khan."

Henry agreed to this procedure, and in May 1498 John Cabot left Bristol to begin his second voyage of discovery. This time he had more to work with: half a dozen ships as opposed to only one on the previous venture. Some of the ships, alas, went down in storms. But with the remaining vessel or vessels John Cabot explored the coast of North America at least as far south as Cape Hatteras and perhaps as far as Florida— far enough, at any rate, for England in the years to come to claim as its own those sections of the New World where the thirteen original American colonies would take form.

By the late fall of 1498 Cabot was back in England. Again he brought no silks, no spices, no gold or precious stones. Nor had he found a passage to China. This was much to the disappointment of his Majesty, but throughout the year of 1499 Cabot continued to receive the pension and other rewards that Henry VII had promised him.

After that, however, the record of his life goes blank, and for the next century or so historians tended to neglect him. Those who did write of him usually confused the events of his first with his second voyage or vice versa, and some accepted the mythical tales spread by Sebastian Cabot, that ungrateful pup.

Too bad! The story of "our well-beloved John Cabot" deserves a better and a fuller telling.

Jacques Cartier

1491–1557   French navigator whose discovery and exploration of the St. Lawrence River established France's claim to territory in the New World.

Jacques Cartier was born in 1491 at St. Malo, the ancient seaport that stands on a granite island in the English Channel near the northern shores of a scenic section of France called Brittany. Of this Breton's first forty-three years nothing is known save that he once shipped as a seaman on a Portuguese vessel bound for Brazil. Not until 1533 does the light of history fall on him with enough brightness to let us follow his movements.

On October 31, 1533, Francis I, the king of France, signed a document authorizing Captain Cartier to equip and man a couple of ships, cross the Atlantic to the vicinity of Newfoundland, and in the name of the king look for a break in the land, a waterway to Asia.

Francis was not the only European monarch eager to find what sixteenth-century Europeans spoke of as a "northwest passage to China." For at least sixty years after Christopher Columbus's voyages of discovery the people of Europe tended to regard the New World he'd found not as a richly endowed frontier to be settled and developed but as a wall, standing between them and the fabulous silk, spice, and gem markets of Asia with which their merchants wished to do business.

Even before Columbus reached the mainland of South America and began seeking a waterway through the landmass, England's John Cabot was poking at the shores of North America looking for an opening there. Columbus found no such channel. Neither did Cabot, but in 1520 Spain's Ferdinand Magellan discovered at the bottom of South America the strait that now bears his name and sailed through it to become the leader of the first group of Europeans to reach the Orient by way of the Pacific Ocean.

But to King Francis, Magellan's southwest passage to China was of no value. For one thing, it took too long to get from France to Magellan's strait and even longer to get from there to Asia. For another, that trade route belonged to Spain and what Francis wished to find was a northwest passage, one that the traders of his country could use without doing battle with Spanish men-of-war.

That King Francis chose Jacques Cartier for this mission tells us a couple of things about him. Obviously the Breton seadog enjoyed an enviable reputation as a navigator, for crossing the turbulent North Atlantic in the tiny vessels of his day was no easy task. Just as obviously he had a powerful friend at court, and his subsequent naming of an island after Philippe de Chabot, Admiral de Brion, suggests that it was that gentleman who persuaded the amiable but singularly indecisive king of France to send Cartier on the first of his three voyages.

Cartier began his preparations at St. Malo in March 1534, only to encounter trouble. During John Cabot's futile search for a northwest passage, he had discovered that the waters off Newfoundland and nearby Labrador teemed with salmon, herring, and codfish. In Catholic France, fish was in great demand, and in the spring of 1534 half the men of St. Malo were getting ready to spend the summer on the Grand Banks, the extensive fisheries along the coasts of Canada. None of them would sell Cartier the ships he needed nor provide him with the crews to run them.

Desperate to be off, the captain sought help from his Majesty. Presently a message was handed down, saying in effect, "Give the captain what he needs. By order of the king." On April 20, 1534, Cartier, with two vessels of sixty tons burthen each and a total of sixty-one men, was en route to the New World.

April was a good time to sail west, for then the Atlantic winds blow easterly. So rapidly did they blow the little ships across two thousand miles of ocean that by May 10 they were anchored in a little bay along the eastern shores of Newfoundland.

From here they steered first north and then west through the Strait of Belle Isle into an enormous spread of water that in the years ahead would become known as the Gulf of St. Lawrence. Churning seas, dark fogs, and

Jacques Cartier explored Canada in hopes of discovering a passage to the rich lands of the Orient. *Neg. 15106, Courtesy of Department Library Services, American Museum of Natural History.*

murky mists made the going difficult as Cartier felt his way southward along the western coasts of Newfoundland before turning west. Islands looming up in the gloom with threatening swiftness received the names of Catholic saints and French notables. A jagged spire of rock, now called Funk, became for the time being Bird Island, owing to the presence of thousands of sea gulls and petrels on its craggy heights. To the headland of a much larger island Cartier gave the name Cape Savage in commemoration of the lone Indian who stood there waving at the French as they approached, only to flee as their ships touched beach. Disembarking briefly on what is now Prince Edward Island, the visitors hung a couple of presents for the vanished brave on the limb of a tree: a steel knife and a wooden girdle.

July brought a striking change in the climate: a blazing sun overhead, unruffled waters below. Suddenly, to the west, framed by the headland of Prince Edward Island on the south and a higher promontory on the north, a seemingly boundless arm of the gulf came into view. Could this majestic basin be the entrance to the northwest passage? Members of the expedition dispatched in longboats to reconnoiter the area came back with dispiriting news. It was only an inlet. Cartier's

name for it, *Chaleur* (Bay of Heat), reflected the July weather and his internal annoyance.

Still its shores had to be explored. Anchoring his ships in a cove of the bay, Cartier climbed into a longboat and examined the surrounding land. He was impressed by the fertility of the grassy meadows to the south. Should France ever undertake to settle this beautiful country, thousands of farms could be carved out of those far-reaching acres. To the north rose what is now known as the Gaspé Peninsula. Many ship's masts could be made from the tall cedars and spruces growing on its densely forested slopes.

He was completing his survey, heading back for his ships, when suddenly the previously empty bay came alive with fifty Indian canoes rapidly surrounding him. Many of their occupants stood up, waving their arms as they did so and grinning ecstatically. Gestures of good will, Cartier surmised, but he preferred to take no chances. He ordered his sailors to fire the longboat's cannon over the heads of the encircling natives.

This put them to flight, but on the following morning a smaller group of them appeared. What happened next indicates that Cartier and his companions were not the first white men to enter Chaleur Bay, for these Indians knew exactly how to win the friendship of their helmeted and armor-clad visitors. They brought with them quantities of pelts, and this time the captain and his men made haste to procure these valuable furs in exchange for iron hatchets and other French-made instruments and trinkets.

By mid-July the fleet was anchored in a harbor at the northern end of the Gaspé Peninsula. Mounting to the heights above, Cartier planted a thirty-foot cross, bearing the fleur-de-lis of France on its wooden shaft, and took possession of the adjoining wilderness for his king. The sixty-one members of his company were not the only witnesses to this ceremony. At Gaspé, as at Chaleur Bay, the French found themselves in the midst of a band of Indians. These people too watched the raising of the cross, and Cartier, watching

In July 1534, Cartier planted a thirty-foot-high cross at the harbor of the Gaspé Peninsula, a scene commemorated by the painter Samuel Hawksett. *Courtesy of Musée du Séminaire de Québec.*

them, knew from the expressions on their bronzed faces that they comprehended what he was doing and that they did not like it.

Sure enough, no sooner did the French regain their vessels and start preparing them to sail on than the chief of the Indians came after them in a canoe, accompanied by some of his sons. The chief was an elderly man, grim-faced and stern-mannered. Halting his canoe a short distance from the ships, he shouted something obviously intended for the ears of Captain Cartier.

Cartier did not understand the old man's words, ground out in a strange, gutteral tongue. But he understood at once the gestures that followed. First, the chief, using two of his fingers, made a cross in the air. Then, pointing in the direction of the wooden cross atop the hill behind him, he shook his head vigorously. His meaning was clear. "You had no right to erect that cross without our permission. This land belongs to us!"

At that moment a scheme took form in Cartier's mind. To explore this bounteous country properly, he would have to learn the language of its inhabitants. He knew the names of two of the chief's sons, Taignoagny and Dom Agaya. He would persuade their father to let Taignoagny and Dom Agaya sail away with him. He could teach them French so that they could serve as interpreters. They in turn could help him learn their language.

He beckoned to the chief, urging him to come aboard. When the old man hesitated, Cartier held up a shining iron hatchet, indicating that he wished to give it to the chief.

That worked. The chief came aboard, bringing his sons. Cartier handed him the hatchet and plied him with other gifts. Using signs, he told the chief a whopping lie. He said the wooden cross on the hill had no significance. He had just put it there as a landmark so that he'd know where he was when he came back to this part of the world. Finally he announced his intention of taking Taignoagny and Dom Agaya with him when the fleet left the Gaspé Peninsula. The old man protested, but to no avail. Surrounded by sword-carrying Frenchmen, he had no choice, when he took his departure, but to leave his young sons behind.

Whereupon the fleet sailed away. Soon its two ships were working westward along the northern shores of an island in the Gulf of St. Lawrence now known as Anticosti. Ahead of them stretched a sheet of shimmering water that, like Chaleur Bay, seemed to have no end to it. What Cartier was looking at was the St. Lawrence, the 2,350-mile river that, tumbling out of the Great

Lakes, travels to the Atlantic Ocean across the lower reaches of Canada. But the captain had no way of knowing what he was seeing. He labeled it "the unknown sea" and his guess was that here, at last, was the passage to China he was seeking. As such, it would have to be explored.

But at the moment there was no time for that. Under the terms of his commission from King Francis, Cartier was to be back in France within the year—and the year was nearly gone. In mid-August he set his course for home, arriving at St. Malo on September 5, 1534.

King Francis didn't know what to think about Cartier's first voyage. Francis rarely knew what to think about anything. It irked him that his Breton sea captain brought home no valuables of any sort—no gold, no silks, no spices, no precious stones. Fortunately for Cartier, his friend at court, Admiral de Brion, not only knew what to think about the matter but also how to make the king think the same thing. The admiral pointed out that the "unknown sea" Cartier had sighted could indeed be a sea-lane to Asia. In any event, it should be looked into, and on October 31, 1534, Cartier received from the admiral a paper ordering him to return to the New World to investigate the "unknown sea" and its surroundings and to do everything in his power to

convert the natives to Christianity.

When on May 19, 1535, Cartier again set sail from St. Malo, it was with a larger fleet than before: three ships, a hundred sailors to manage them, a handful of French noblemen interested in seeing Canada, and the Indian brothers, Taignoagny and Dom Agaya. During their stay in France the brothers had become fluent in the language of that country. They were now in a position to act as Cartier's interpreters. In fact, by this time the captain himself was no longer wholly unacquainted with the language of the natives of Canada, most of whom belonged to the tribes of the Huron-Iroquois. During his previous voyage, Cartier had jotted down a number of Indian words in his logbook, the record of his journeys written in part by himself and in part by various members of his command. On his second visit to the New World he would add many words to this list.

Storms in both the Atlantic and in the Gulf of St. Lawrence impeded the three vessels, but by early August they were entering the "unknown sea"— only, of course, it was not a sea. As the fleet beat its way westward, Taignoagny and Dom Agaya recognized the country through which they were passing. It was they who informed Cartier that he was not traveling through a strait that divided the continent and linked the Atlantic and Pacific oceans. He was bucking the currents of a river so long that none of the dwellers on its banks had any idea of where it began. For many miles, to be sure, its waters were salty due to the coming and going of the tides from the Atlantic. But the day came when the sailors, dropping their buckets to test the water, found it to be fresh.

When Cartier learned that the channel beneath him did not go to the Pacific, he ordered some of his sailors to man a couple of longboats and go back to the Gulf of St. Lawrence. They were to examine the southern shores of what is now the Quebec section of Canada. Perhaps one of the streams flowing into the St. Lawrence along this previously unexplored stretch of land would turn out to be the northwest passage. But none of them did, and when the longboats returned from their fruitless search, the fleet continued westward.

Though Cartier was disappointed by his failure to locate a northwest passage, he was enchanted by the stream on which he now found himself and determined to explore it as far as possible. In his logbook, written to be read by the king of France, he wrote that as a result of "the present expedition . . . for the discovery of lands formerly unknown to you and to us, you will learn . . . of their fertility . . . and of the

richness of . . . the largest river that is known to have ever been seen."

Today we realize that the St. Lawrence is by no means the largest of the world's rivers. Still Cartier's description of it was not altogether in error. As Trudy Henmer writes in her book about it, when "the St. Lawrence . . . is considered along with the five Great Lakes [from which it flows] . . . it becomes one of the world's largest inland waterways. Together these lakes and this river span half the width of North America and drain an area of land equal in size to all of France and Great Britain."

On September 14 the fleet reached the St. Charles where that river flows southward into the St. Lawrence close by the towering cliffs that now support the city of Quebec. Here stood Stadacona, home village of the people—the Quebec Indians—to whom Taignoagny and Dom Agaya belonged. Here on the fringes of Stadacona, Cartier began the erection of a fortress to serve as the headquarters of his expedition. And here began the bizarre and at times disturbing events that were to dominate the remaining months of his second voyage.

Stadacona lay 800 miles to the west of the Atlantic Ocean. On an island in the St. Lawrence, some 150 miles upriver, according to the villagers, stood another and larger settlement called

Hochelaga. When Cartier expressed an interest in visiting that village, the inhabitants of Stadacona urged him not to. Donnacona, their chief, asserted that the captain would learn nothing of interest at Hochelaga. Pronouncing the St. Lawrence above Stadacona too dangerous to navigate, Taignoagny and Dom Agaya informed Cartier that they would never accompany him on such a trip.

The captain was hard put to understand the vehemence of this opposition to his plans. His guess, probably correct, was that the Stadacona people did not want the Hochelaga people to get any of the good things the French had brought with them: the hatchets and washbasins, the bells and other items that the Indians loved. On September 19 when he boarded the *Emerillon*, the smallest and liveliest of his ships, he had no knowledge of the waterway in front of him, nor did he have natives on deck to guide him through the river's twists and turns.

The 28th brought him to a section of the St. Lawrence now known as Lake St. Peter. Here the river widens enormously. Here, unable to find a channel deep enough for the *Emerillon*, Cartier transferred himself and his thirty some companions to the ship's two longboats. Thus the journey was completed, and the minute the captain's eyes fell on

the stockaded village that was his destination, he knew why its inhabitants called it Hochelaga. In their language the word meant "place where the river is obstructed," and on either side of the island where Hochelaga stood, the swift and rock-broken waters of the Lachine Rapids made travel farther up the St. Lawrence impossible.

Coming up the river, Cartier had met and talked with several Indians. Plainly word of his coming to Hochelaga had traveled fast. As the longboats approached the island, every man, woman, and child belonging to the village came running to the shoreline with shouts of joy.

Before leaving the longboat he donned his brightest suit of armor and hung a silver whistle about his neck. Once ashore, he was literally carried into the village by the exuberant Indians.

Apparently they regarded him as a god or a superior medicine man. They brought their sick people to him and for several hours he moved among them, letting the ill and the handicapped touch him and touching them in return. Then there was a feast that went on for several more hours. After that the men of the village escorted the captain to the highest elevation on the island. Cartier called it "Mount Royal," and many years later the French version of those words would give the name

"Montreal" to the huge city that now encircles this 900-foot hill.

From the top of Mount Royal, Cartier could see, in the far west and north, the Ottawa River and the tree-dark region known to the Indians as the Kingdom of Saguenay. If the French were looking for precious metals and fine furs, he was told, Saguenay was the place to go.

The second week of October brought Cartier back to his fortified headquarters near the village of Stadacona on the banks of the St. Charles River. The months that followed were trying ones. At mid-winter a "pestilence," as the French called it, swept the camp. Today we call this pestilence scurvy, a terrible illness caused by the lack of ascorbic acid in the diet of its victims. Before the disease ran its course among Cartier's followers, twenty-five of them were dead.

As the days grew colder, food supplies dwindled. Heavy snowfalls made hunting difficult and one of the ships showed signs of rot and had to be scrapped. Some of the inhabitants of Stadacona were still angry with Cartier for having gone up river to Hochelaga. From time to time bands of openly hostile natives could be seen lurking in the forests beyond the wooden walls of the French fort. Chief Donnacona, however, remained friendly, and one day Cartier was delighted to learn that Donnacona had spent time in the Kingdom of Saguenay, the distant land that the captain had sighted from the top of Mount Royal during his visit to Hochelaga. Was Saguenay, Cartier asked, as abounding in furs and precious metals as he had been led to believe? The chief's answer, yes, set the captain to thinking hard.

He had found no passage to China, and when he went back to France in the spring, he would have neither furs nor precious metals to give to King Francis. But one thing he could take home. He could take Chief Donnacona, and the chief could tell his Majesty about the riches of Saguenay.

It was easier to dream up this scheme than to put it into effect. Donnacona had no desire to travel to the faraway land of the king of France. In the end Cartier had to use force. As he was preparing his remaining vessels for the journey home, he lured the chief aboard one of them by a promise of many gifts. Donnacona had brought his warriors with him. They were lined up on the waterfront, but when the French threatened to fire their cannons, the Indians took to their heels. On July 6, 1536, when Cartier ended his second voyage at St. Malo, his passengers included not only Donnacona but ten other Indian men and an Indian girl.

Once in France, he was chagrined to learn that for the time being King Francis was too busy with other matters to consider the sea captain's request for a third voyage to explore Saguenay. In 1541 Cartier was permitted to travel again to the New World, but his efforts to establish a French colony there, in accordance with the king's instructions, proved unsuccessful. On his return to St. Malo in 1542 he resolved to go on no more journeys of discovery and exploration.

The closing years of his life—his death came September 1, 1557—were clouded by his feeling that France had forgotten about the beautiful country he had explored and claimed for it. Indeed, Jacques Cartier would be dead for almost fifty years before France awakened to the value of its possessions in what was to become Canada and began planting the settlements that would bring it far more wealth than it could have obtained in the golden cities of the Orient.

Christopher Columbus

(Italian name, Cristofo Colombo; Spanish name, Cristobal Colon)

1451–1506   Italian navigator in the employ of Spain and discoverer of America.

So numerous were the accomplishments of Christopher Columbus that practically every nation and nationality on earth has claimed him as its own. In the extensive literature about him he has been described as Spanish, Jewish, Portuguese, French, German, English, Greek, and Armenian. But in the opinion of Samuel Eliot Morison, the dean of Columbus's modern biographers, such efforts to make him something other than he was can be ignored as wishful thinking.

"As there was a good deal of moving about along the shores of the Mediterranean in the Middle Ages," Morison writes in his *Admiral of the Ocean Sea: A Life of Christopher Columbus*, "some of the Discoverer's remote ancestors doubtless belonged to other races than the Italian. His long face, tall stature, ruddy complexion and red hair suggest a considerable store of barbarian rather than Latin blood, but . . . he himself was conscious only of a Genoese origin. There is no more reason to doubt that Christopher Columbus was a Genoese-born Catholic Christian, steadfast in his faith and proud of his native city [the ancient seaport of Genoa on the Italian shores of the Mediterranean] than to doubt that George Washington was a Virginia-born Anglican of English race, proud of being an American."

Of Columbus's early life, from his birth in the autumn of 1451 to his permanent departure from Genoa in 1476, little is known. Indeed of his mother, Susanna Fontanarossa Colombo, nothing is known, and of his father, Domen-

73

ico Colombo, only a few facts.

Domenico was a woolen weaver, what the British called a master clothier, meaning that he owned his own looms, carried the products of them to market, and took on and trained a number of apprentices, Christopher and his brothers Bartholomew and Diego among them. Domenico was good at his work. Had he stuck to it consistently he might have become a wealthy man. But he was as venturesome in the paths of commerce as his son Christopher would be in those of the briny deep. Domenico Colombo was forever neglecting his looms to engage in get-rich-quick schemes but forever failing at these endeavors. Like the "Mr. Micawber" of Charles Dickens's novel *David Copperfield*, he was forever confident that tomorrow something would turn up and his fortune would be made. Several times Domenico would have gone broke had it not been for the resourcefulness and steadiness of his bright and enterprising sons.

Genoa was a town of seafarers and, as Morison writes, "every boy in it took all the sailing he could get." By Columbus's fourteenth year he was piloting "a little lateen-rigged packet" along the shores of Liguria, the region of which in his day Genoa was the chief city. Later he is believed to have gone on two longer voyages, one to the island of Chios in the Aegean Sea and the other across the Mediterranean to the city of Carthage on the northern shores of Africa.

Columbus was given to boasting, to indulging in what his friends called "little exaggerations." Writing of his youthful escapades long after he had become Spain's Admiral of the Ocean Sea, he identified himself as the captain of the caravel or carrack that took him to Carthage. But he was only twenty at the time, and Morison's guess is that he made that journey as a common sailor, working before the mast.

Such was his likely status when in the spring of 1476 he left Genoa with a fleet of five caravels, carrying goods to be sold along the European coasts of the Atlantic. The five ships cleared the Strait of Gibraltar and were pressing westward when on August 13, 1476, thirteen French and Portuguese men-of-war bore down on them. In the ensuing exchange of gunfire Columbus was wounded and his ship sunk. Leaping into the sea, he grabbed a floating sweep, and by alternately pushing the big oar ahead of himself and resting on it, he managed to swim the six miles to the southern shores of Portugal. Misfortune had thrown him into the arms of his destiny, for it was in Portugal during the next eight or nine years that he acquired the skills and the knowl-

Christopher Columbus may be the most famous explorer in history. *Anonymous portrait, from the Gioviana Collection, Florence; Courtesy of Giraudon/Art Resource, NY.*

edge that would enable him to cross the Atlantic and become the discoverer of a hitherto undreamed-of continent.

People gathering on the beach whereon he was washed ashore, exhausted and in pain, carried him to the nearby town of Lagos. Here they nursed him back to health, and he trudged northward to Lisbon on the banks of the Tagus where that river sweeps broadly into the Atlantic to form one of the finest harbors on earth.

For a young man dreaming of adventure on the high seas, Lisbon was the ideal place to be. In the late fifteenth century Portugal was the ocean-going center of the world, and Lisbon was the chief port and capital of Portugal. For many years Portuguese mariners had been pushing ever deeper into the South Atlantic, planting commercial towns on the coasts of Africa and discovering and settling the adjoining islands. "Every spring," Morison writes of the Lisbon Columbus knew, "fleets of lateen-rigged caravels [brought] . . . into the Tagus bags of Malagueta pepper, cords of elephant tusks, coffles of Negro slaves, and chests of gold dust. . . . along the quays and the narrow streets of the old town seamen from Scandinavia, England, and Flanders jostled Spaniards, Genoese, Moors, [and] Berbers."

At the time of Columbus's arrival on this colorful scene, he had enjoyed little or no formal education. Years later, he appears to have told one of his sons of time spent at the University of Pavia in northern Italy, but the well-preserved records of that ancient institution make no mention of him and it would seem that again we are in the presence of one of his "little exaggerations."

Still essentially illiterate at the age of twenty-two, Columbus now found himself among people who could teach him the many things he longed to learn: mathematics and astronomy, including the art of navigating by the stars; the languages of Portugal and Spain, so that he could converse with the sailors on Lisbon's clamorous docks; and enough Latin to let him read the Latin translations of Ptolemy, the second-century Greek scholar whose textbooks were everywhere regarded as the very last word in all things geographic.

Once on Lisbon's streets, he had no trouble locating friends and benefactors. Many families from Genoa had long since settled in the Portuguese capital. These people saw to it that he was fed and sheltered and that he gained employment. Soon he was traveling on a Portuguese caravel, a member of a partly commercial and partly exploratory expedition that ended its outward trek in the frozen waters north of Iceland. Soon, too, he and his brother Bartholomew, who had recently come to Lisbon, were operating a mapmaking shop on the banks of the Tagus.

Other and more rewarding business ventures followed. The summer of 1478 found Columbus commanding a ship engaged in the sugar trade, an undertaking that put a good deal of money in his purse. By 1478 he had become a man of substance in his adopted land, and the closing months of that year found him taking as his bride the twenty-five-year-old Felipa Moñiz de Perestrello, a member of a noble Portuguese family.

The only child of this union, a son named Diego, was born in the Madeira Islands where for a time in the early 1480s Columbus conducted a mercantile establishment. A few years later, after Felipa's untimely death, Columbus's relations with a Spanish peasant woman named Beatriz Enriques de Harana made him the father of a second son, known to us today as Ferdinand Columbus and best remembered as the author of the first biography of his famous father. Columbus's failure to marry Ferdinand's mother seems to have had nothing to do with his feelings for her. He seems to have been as devoted to her as he had been to his wife. But by the time he met Beatriz Enriques in 1488 Columbus had be-

come a frequent visitor at court, and under the customs and standards of his day no gentleman married to a woman of the lower classes could expect favors from any European king.

It is not known exactly when or even under what circumstances Columbus began planning the extraordinary expeditions that would bring the existence of a whole new world to the attention of the old. Some students of his life believe the idea for what he called the "Enterprise of the Indies" first came to him during his journey to the frozen waters beyond Iceland. It was during that voyage, they suspect, that Columbus learned that some four-hundred years earlier a boatload of Vikings had crossed the Atlantic and landed on the shores of a strange continent. Then and there, according to this interpretation, Columbus resolved to do likewise.

Other authorities doubt this theory. Morison, for one, found no evidence that Columbus ever so much as heard of the Vikings. Morison's conclusion is that Columbus and his brother Bartholomew planned the Enterprise of the Indies in their Lisbon mapmaking shop and that the ideas behind it were a natural outgrowth of the maritime interests prevailing in Portugal at that time.

It is certain that in the late fifteenth century most of the European nations fronting on the Atlantic were looking for sea-lanes by which their merchants could sail to the rich trading centers of the Indies, meaning not only India but also China, Japan, and the so-called Spice Islands off the southeastern heel of Asia. For Portugal this endeavor reached a high point in 1488 when one of that country's men rounded the Cape of Good Hope at the bottom of Africa, thus confirming the long-held belief that the Indies could be reached by sailing eastward around the world.

Note, please, the word "around." Long since proven false is the once widely credited story that Columbus had to convince the crowned heads of Europe that the world was round. In fact, for hundreds of years before his birth the universities of Europe had been teaching that the earth was a sphere. All educated people knew it was. So did all sailors, innocent of book-learning though most of them were. The sailors knew that as they approached an island with a mountain at its center, the first thing they saw was the top of that mountain. Only as they worked their way landward did the far nearer beaches of the island come into view. Obviously their ship was moving on a curve. Obviously the world was round.

And since it was round, it followed that one could get to the Indies by sailing either east or west. And the contention that one could get there quickly and easily by sailing west was the very heart, the alpha and omega, of Columbus's plan, his Enterprise of the Indies. The idea was not original with him. As Morison notes, the notion that the silk- and spice-rich East could be reached by sailing west had been in the air for at least eighteen years when in the second half of the 1480s Columbus laid his plan before Joao II, the King of Portugal. King Joao submitted the scheme to a commission of astronomers, mariners, and pilots. When these experts disapproved it, Columbus moved to Spain in the hopes of persuading King Ferdinand and Queen Isabella to send him across the Atlantic.

Columbus's first appearance at the court of Spain took place in the spring of 1486. In the beginning Ferdinand was only mildly interested in the Italian-born navigator's plans. Isabella liked them from the start, and in the years ahead the handsome, auburn-haired queen would prove a consistently loyal supporter of the red-haired voyager.

But in 1486 *los Reyes Catolicos* (the Catholic sovereigns) had another matter on their minds. The Moors still occupied the province of Spain known as Grenada. Until these old enemies could be chased out, *los Reyes Catolicos* had neither the time to study Columbus's plans nor money enough to put them under way. Like the King of Portugal, they put his request into the hands of a group of learned advisers, and for six-and-a-half years Columbus had no choice but to wait for their report.

Those six-and-a-half years were difficult ones for the future Admiral of the Ocean Sea. His efforts to interest the ruler of Portugal in his scheme had left him broke. From time to time Isabella saw to it that he was provided with funds, but the sums dispensed from the royal treasury were barely sufficient to support himself, his mistress, and his two sons, Ferdinand having been born soon after his father's removal to Spain. Frustrated and impatient, Columbus sent Bartholomew to England on the chance that King Henry VII might be persuaded to finance the Enterprise of the Indies. Henry consulted his aides, and when those gentleman pronounced the enterprise "a joke," Bartholomew moved on to France for an unsuccessful audience with King Charles VIII.

For Columbus there were no idle moments during these trying years. There were maps to be drawn for use with the proposals that he and his brother were submitting to the crowned heads of England, France, and Spain. There were books to be read. Columbus pored over the works of Ptolemy and those of other great geographers. He studied the Bible, taking note of those passages that have been interpreted as specifying the extent and nature of the globe on which we live.

We know now that these sources gave Columbus an erroneous idea of the size of the earth. Ptolemy, for example, pictured the world as having only three continents: Europe, Africa, and Asia. Moreover, according to Ptolemy, these land masses were very close to one another. Hence Columbus's insistence, during his talks with Ferdinand and Isabella, that the distance from Spain to Asia was only some three thousand miles instead of the at least twelve thousand miles it actually is.

Another book that Columbus read and reread was the account by the four-teenth-century Italian traveler, Marco Polo, of his journeys across Asia and of his long stays in the magnificent palaces of the Great Khan of China. Small wonder that when Columbus finally got to some islands on the far side of the Atlantic, he was baffled to find on them, not pearl-encrusted emperors dwelling under golden domes, but naked Indians living in huts made of mud and wood.

In the opening months of 1492 Columbus's long wait finally ended. On January 2 the Moors surrendered to a Spanish army, and in April Ferdinand and Isabella signed the arrangements that made Columbus an admiral, enabling him to obtain the ships, men,

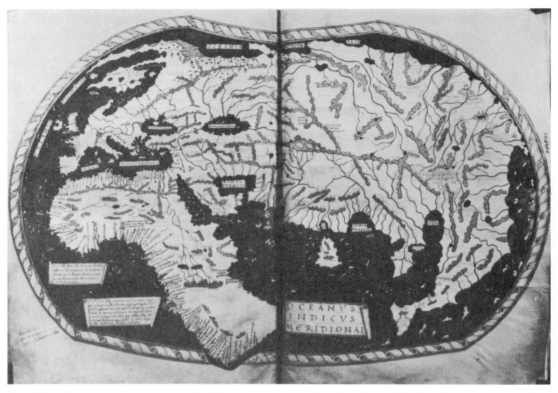

In 1492, the same year in which Columbus set out for the New World, Henricus Martellus drew this map of the world. The voyage of Columbus would forever alter the European conception of the world. *Courtesy of The British Museum.*

and supplies needed to begin the first of his four voyages across the Atlantic.

Voyage Number 1 began from the riverside town of Palos in the early morning hours of August 3. We all know the names of the tiny caravels that carried the ninety members of the expedition down river to the Atlantic: the *Santa Maria,* commanded by the admiral himself; the *Pinta,* by Martin Alonzo Pinzon; and the *Niña,* by Martin's brother, Vicente Yanez Pinzon. The little fleet did not descend the river alone.

The same king and queen, who were now enabling Columbus to give Europe a vast frontier, a refuge for the impoverished and the persecuted of the Old World, had only recently signed an order to expel the Jews from Spain. Accompanying Columbus's outgoing fleet that morning was another little vessel, bearing some of these unfortunate people into the uncertainties of exile.

On September 9, after a short stay in the Canary Islands, the three ships of the expedition lurched into the open sea. Of late years a few other Europeans, most of them English, had ventured for short distances into these unknown waters, only to be beaten back by unfavorable winds. Morison's answer to the question of why Columbus succeeded where others had failed is that he was a superior navigator. He took care to shape his course along latitudes where the winds were behind him.

Still there were touchy moments as the flotilla sailed westward under blissfully sunny skies. Since on October 1, according to the admiral's faulty calculations, the three vessels had traveled far enough to reach Japan, Columbus concluded that they had missed that country and were heading for the mainland of China. The tenth of October witnessed what some authorities call a "little mutiny." Some members of the expedition, frightened by what seemed to be an ocean without end, wanted to turn back, but the admiral insisted that they go on.

It's well he did. On October 12, at 2:00 A.M. the seaman manning the lookout on the forecastle of the *Niña* was heard shouting, *"Tierra! Tierra!"*

Precisely where this historic landfall occurred remains in dispute. Morison puts it on the Bahamian island now interchangeably known as Watling's or San Salvadore. Other students of the voyage place it on one of nine other islands in the Bahamas, and the latest study by the National Geographic Society puts it on a narrow slip of land called Samana, sixty-five miles southeast of San Salvador. Wherever it lay, it was inhabited by friendly people. Indians, Columbus called them, because he thought himself to be in the Indies. As the island offered neither golden domes nor pearls, the admiral, wishing to carry home something of value, took along a few Indians when he departed, thus making the first of his many contributions to the slave trade of the world.

Steering in a generally southeastern direction, Columbus discovered and explored first another of the Bahamian islands; then Cuba, which he mistakenly took to be a part of the mainland of Asia; and finally, a large island that the inhabitants called Ayte (Haiti), a name that it would bear again in later years and that the admiral called Hispaniola.

By December 5, when the fleet arrived at Hispaniola, one of its members had deserted. Cuba's inhabitants had said there were deposits of gold on nearby Babeque. A storm defeated Columbus's effort to locate this island, and in the confusion the commander of the *Pinta*, Martin Pinzon, hoping to get to the gold before the admiral did, sailed off on his own—only to learn upon

The landing of Columbus at Guanahani, West Indies, on October 12, 1492, is depicted by painter John Vanderlyn. Columbus, in the foreground, bears the large Spanish flag; the Pinzan brothers, who commanded the *Niña* and the *Pinta*, carry banners. *Courtesy of Library of Congress.*

reaching Babeque that there was no gold. Almost from the start of the journey, Martin Pinzon and Columbus had been at odds. Pinzon was convinced that it was his navigational skills rather than those of his superior that had carried the expedition to the landfall in the Bahamas. Already he was planning to say as much to their Catholic Majesties when the fleet returned to Spain.

Columbus was aware of Pinzon's schemes, but at Hispaniola he had troubles of another sort to think about.

While what remained of his flotilla explored the northern shores of that island, the *Santa Maria*, the flagship, slid onto a shelving reef of coral and all efforts to save it failed. The admiral shifted his flag to the *Niña* and pondered an unwelcome problem.

What was he to do with the crew of the wrecked flagship? Although the *Niña* was to prove the most seaworthy of all his vessels, it was too small to carry an additional forty men and boys. Columbus had not intended to establish colonies for Spain during this voyage, but now he decided to erect a fortified settlement, to be known as La Navidad, on a sheltered cove along the shores of Hispaniola. The crew of the abandoned *Santa Maria* would be left there.

On Hispaniola, as in the Bahamas and Cuba, the Indians were friendly. Columbus put to them the standard question of all Spanish explorers and conquerors of the New World: Was there gold in these parts? There was, he was told, a distant section of the island called Cibao that harbored a large mine of it. Time would prove Cibao to be as devoid of the precious metal as was Babeque, a circumstance that raises an interesting speculation. Were these congenial Indians lying? Behind their polite ways, did they hate and fear these white intruders and deliberately mislead them?

Once La Navidad was complete, Columbus considered leading an expedition to Cibao, only to change his mind. It occurred to him that by this time, late December, Martin Pinzon might be on his way to Spain, eager to whisper tales harmful to the admiral into the ears of King Ferdinand and Queen Isabella. Columbus's decision in early January 1493 was to leave Hispaniola at once in the hopes of reaching Spain before Pinzon could get there. But on January 8, in the waters to the east of

the island, he sighted the *Pinta* and signaled its commander to come aboard the *Niña*. Face to face with his enemy, Columbus pretended to accept Pinzon's story that he was compelled to leave the fleet by disabling winds and suggested that the two of them sail home together.

This arrangement was short-lived. In February a sudden and terrible storm parted the ships. Black clouds, riven by thunder and lightning, swallowed up the *Pinta*. Punishing winds blew the *Niña* into the harbor of Lisbon, and for four days Columbus was a guest of King Joao II of Portugal. The first of the monarchs to reject the Enterprise of the Indies, Joao listened to Columbus's tales of wondrous finds and clapped a hand to his forehead. "Oh, man of little comprehension!" the king scolded himself. "Why did I let slip an enterprise of so great importance?"

When on March 25, 1493, Columbus finally reached the shores of Spain he learned that Martin Pinzon had beaten him home. His rival's first action after the storm-battered *Pinta* entered Spanish waters was to dispatch a message to Ferdinand and Isabella, asking permission to come to court and acquaint them with what had happened. But their Majesties refused to see him, preferring to wait until they could hear a report of the voyage from the admiral himself. Crushed by this snub and worn out by his travels, Martin Pinzon walked to his country house on the outskirts of Palos, took to his bed, and died.

Columbus, on the other hand, was summoned to court at once, and was received there with pomp and pageantry. The king and queen were delighted with everything he had to tell them, especially with his description of the natives of Hispaniola as "so gentle and docile" that they could be rounded up by the hundreds and sold for good prices in the slave marts of Seville. So pleased were their majesties with the admiral's exploits that they urged him to begin preparations immediately for a second voyage, partly for the purpose of finding more lands for the crown, partly for the purpose of planting Spanish colonies in those he had already located. Had Columbus declined this offer and been willing to let others complete his Enterprise of the Indies, he might have spent the rest of his life in wealth and comfort. But if he had, chances are that he would never have been willing to endure the risks of an uncharted ocean in the first place. He chose to go on, and by so doing he put himself in harm's way, for he was famous now and fame raises enemies around a man.

When voyage Number 2 began at Cadiz on September 25, 1893, Columbus found himself in command of the largest nonmilitary armada ever to sail from Spain: seventeen ships and about 1,500 persons (most of whom were to become settlers of their country's new colonies). During this expedition that lasted nearly three years, Columbus's discoveries included the islands of St. Kitts and Puerto Rico, the Leeward Islands, and the Virgin Islands.

The troubles that were to plague him henceforth began with his arrival at Hispaniola, where he found that the "gentle and docile" Indians of the island had destroyed La Navidad, having reduced its buildings to ashes and killed the forty Spaniards the admiral had left there during his previous voyage.

To Columbus this was a blow from which he never fully rallied. From this point on, one detects in his behavior a bitterness, a harshness, and a tendency to be cruel to those who brooked him—traits not previously noticeable in his character. He promptly did what he had to do. He found another place along the northern coast of the island and put his colonists there. He named this place Isabella, after the queen.

Chosen in haste, Isabella proved to be an impossible location, and a few months later the admiral found a better site with a better harbor on the southern shores of Hispaniola. Here he established a town that for many years would be the capital of the Spanish Indies. He named it Santo Domingo in memory of his father, Domenico Colombo. When all efforts to find gold yielded only small amounts of inferior metal, Columbus sent four caravels of slaves to Spain. Into dank and vermin-infested holds he crammed hundreds of captured Indians, including nursing mothers with their infants.

Columbus knew how to handle a sailing ship, but like most seafaring explorers he was a poor manager of landlubbers. Most of the settlers of his colony were young *hidalgos* (gentlemen), accustomed to taking their ease while slaves did the work. They balked when the admiral put them to the menial tasks without which no newly founded settlement could survive. There were rebellions and mutinies in defiance of the admiral's authority, and in the fall of 1495 a member of the Spanish bureaucracy landed on Hispaniola with orders to investigate Columbus's administrative practices. When this gentleman began criticizing Columbus's methods, the admiral concluded that the time had come to present his version to their majesties, and by early June 1496 he was back in Spain.

This time there were no pomps and pageants for him at court. Not that Ferdinand and Isabella were unkind. After all, he was their admiral. He had

brought the crown much wealth. He had founded an overseas empire, where young *hidalgos* who owned no property in Spain could acquire land, where Spanish traders could seek new markets, and where some of the inmates of Spain's crowded prisons could be dumped. After two years of haggling over what the crown was to get from the expeditions and what Columbus was to get, their Catholic Majesties authorized the admiral to make another crossing of the Atlantic.

Voyage Number 3 began on May 30, 1498, at Sanlucar de Barrameda at the mouth of the Guadalquivir River: only six ships this time, and at the Canary Islands three of them left the fleet to explore on their own. In the eyes of the leaders of Spain, Columbus was no longer the towering figure he had once been. In part his fall from grace was an outgrowth of his own mistakes as a colonial administrator. In part it was an outgrowth of the steadily increasing effort by men envious of his achievements to belittle him, a movement that confirms Alexander von Humboldt's statement: "There are three stages in the popular attitude toward a great discovery: First men doubt its existence, next they deny its importance, and finally they give the credit to someone else." The number of individuals, both in Columbus's time and later, who have claimed that it was they, or at any rate someone other than Columbus, who discovered America could not begin to be counted on the fingers of one's hands.

On his third voyage Columbus discovered the island of Trinidad, and then, steering to the south and west, reached the mainland of South America. This was on August 5, 1498, and Morison believes that Columbus's landing spot was "a little round cove" called Ensanada Yacuna on the extreme northeastern corner of the Paria Peninsula. "I believe," the admiral wrote in his journal nine or ten days later, "that this is a very great continent, which until today has been unknown." Although Columbus realized, as he recorded in his log, that he had found an *otro mundo* (another world), he still thought himself to be somewhere in the East Indies, within striking distance of the golden cities of China and Japan.

Moving farther west, he came upon an island that he named Margarita. So beautiful was this spot of land off the coast of Venezuela and so temperate were the winds that bathed it that Columbus concluded that he had found the long-sought-for "terrestrial paradise," the Garden of Eden. He found some pearls in the vicinity, but he seems to have missed the extensive pearl fisheries that in later years would put large sums of money in Spanish pockets. Columbus did not linger at Margarita because, as Morison writes, "duty called." He was no longer just an admiral. He was now also Viceroy of the Spanish Indies, which is to say, governor of all of their majesties' possessions in the *Otro Mundo*. He was carrying in the holds of his ships provisions for Santo Domingo. These would spoil unless they were delivered soon, so northward he sped to his capital on the southern shore of Hispaniola.

Strife and upheaval awaited him. Again there were rebellions in the colony, outbreaks of discontent among men vying for whatever power and wealth this little outpost of Spanish civilization afforded. Soon, complaints about Columbus's handling of these troubles were on their way to Ferdinand and Isabella. The late summer of 1499 witnessed the arrival at Santo Domingo of Francisco de Bobadilla, a royal commissioner charged with putting matters right. Learning that Columbus was making a habit of hanging dissident colonists, Bobadilla put him in chains and sent him to Spain. There, following the arrival of his ship in December 1500, Columbus took lodgings at a monastery in Seville. But the sight of the Admiral of the Ocean Sea wearing the habit of a monk and laden with manacles and fetters angered the people of Seville and in December Columbus was summoned to court. In the eyes of Ferdinand and Isabella he was still their admiral, still a man who had done great things for the crown. On the seventeenth they relieved him of his chains and a short time later they asked him, once again, to go discover lands for Spain.

Voyage Number 4 began at Cadiz on May 9, 1502, and included four caravels and a hundred and forty-four men and boys, as well as Ferdinand Columbus, the admiral's fourteen-year-old son, and Bartholomew, the admiral's brother. Some historians dismiss this journey as unimportant because Columbus did not find what he was seeking, an opening in the American mainland, a waterway or strait through which he could float to the fabulous cities of China and Japan. Morison, on the other hand, treats voyage Number 4 as a remarkable feat of navigation, a saga of daring, of hardships endured and of dangers overcome.

Stopping at this or that island as he sailed westward, Columbus made his first landfall on the mainland on the shores of what is now the country of Honduras in Central America. From here he moved slowly south and then west along the coasts of Nicaragua, Costa Rica, and Panama, looking in vain for the strait that would carry him to the Orient—a search that ended at Limon Bay. Today we can savor the irony of this termination of a fruitless journey,

for Limon Bay is the Caribbean entrance to the manmade strait that cuts across the isthmus of Panama, known as the Panama Canal.

From Limon Bay the Admiral backtracked sixty-five miles to the mouth of the Belen River, where he founded the village of Santa Maria de Belen, the first European settlement to rise on the soil of continental America. No sooner were its fragile huts and fort in place than the settlers were called on to repulse a fierce Indian attack, during which twelve of them were slain.

None of the four vessels of the fleet had come across the sea in good condition. At Santa Maria de Belen, one of them, the *Gallega*, was scrapped as no longer seaworthy; and when on Easter night in 1503 the mariners of the expedition abandoned their settlement to sail into the Caribbean, the remaining caravels—the *Vizacaino*, the *Santiago*, and the *Capitana*—were dangerously riddled by teredos, wood-eating worms. The admiral set his course for Hispaniola, hoping that his leaking vessels could carry the expedition safely into the harbor of Santo Domingo.

But this was not to be. By the end of April the *Vizacaino* had gone down, and on June 24 Columbus had to run the *Santiago* and the *Capitana* into a cove on the northern shores of Jamaica. Here, on the rim of an inlet that appears on modern maps as St. Ann's Bay, the one hundred sixteen survivors of the expedition beached their sinking ships.

And here they remained. Fortunately, the Indians of the island were friendly. That, however, is more than can be said of most of Columbus's men. Within a few weeks more than half of them had deserted him and were living with the natives.

As neither the *Santiago* nor the *Capitana* could be repaired, two of the admiral's pilots constructed an Indian-style canoe and paddled northward to find help in Santo Domingo. Eight months passed before they returned with a rescue vessel that carried the admiral and the handful of men who were still loyal to Hispaniola. From there, accompanied by his son and brother, he embarked for home, reaching Spain on November 7, 1504, to complete the last of his great voyages.

On this return to Spain there were no summonses to court for Columbus. There was no word, kindly or otherwise, from their majesties—a circumstance that cut him to the quick, for he was proud and sensitive and fully aware of the importance of his efforts on behalf of the crown. When on November 26 Queen Isabella died, the admiral was not even invited to the funeral.

Ignored by those he had served so well, Columbus retired to a rented house in Seville and nursed his ailments. He was only fifty-four, but his long journeys on difficult waters had aged him before his time, and the bouts of arthritis that had plagued him for years had of late become a severe and crippling gout.

Despite numerous and sentimental tales to the contrary, Columbus was not poverty-stricken. Long before, the rulers of Spain had agreed to give him a percentage of the wealth produced by his travels. This promise had been kept, and at his home in Seville Columbus was looked after by servants and by medically trained attendants.

One promise the crown had not honored. He was to have been the Viceroy of the Spanish Indies for life, but because of his inept handling of the colony on Hispaniola this post had been taken from him. From his bed in Seville he dispatched letters to King Ferdinand, demanding it back.

Ferdinand ignored these pleas, but Columbus was not altogether out of touch with the court. His oldest son Diego was on the king's payroll, and in May 1505, his infirmities notwithstanding, the admiral traveled by mule back to the town of Segovia near Madrid where the royal court was in session.

Ferdinand welcomed him warmly. To Columbus's continuing demand for a return to him of the office of Viceroy, however, the king turned a deaf ear, although after Columbus's death he gave that post to Diego and also permitted him to inherit the title of admiral.

When the court moved, first to Salamanca and then to Valladolid, the gout-stricken old seadog went along. The waves still called to him. On at least one occasion, perhaps often, he begged Ferdinand to send him on another journey of exploration. The king politely but firmly refused.

On May 20, 1505, the admiral's condition suddenly and dramatically worsened. His sons and a few friends gathered at his bedside. A priest was called; a mass was said. The last sacrament was administered to the dying man, and "After the concluding prayer," Morison tells us, Columbus was heard to murmur, "*'In manus tuas, Domine, commendo spiritum meum.'**

---

*Into thy hands, Lord, I commend my spirit.

"Having said this, he died. So ended the life of the man who had done more to direct the course of history than any individual since Augustus Caesar."

So far as we know, the admiral died still under the impression that what he had found at the end of the Atlantic was simply an outlying segment of Asia. How often has the old quip been heard, the one that asserts that when he left Spain he didn't know where he was going, that when he got there he didn't know where he was, and that when he got back he didn't know where he had been?

That's a feeble joke, to be sure, but it's an excellent description of the true explorer that Columbus was: a man who dared uncharted seas to open to the world the great continent where now stand the United States, Canada, and the countries of South and Central America.

James Cook

1728–1779   English-born, the first European to explore the eastern coast of Australia, thus establishing England's claim to that continent. The first to cross the Antarctic Circle, he conjectured the existence of what was later discovered to be Antarctica and altered the perception of the whole of the South Pacific.

There was nothing out of the ordinary in James Cook's years of growing up, nothing certainly to indicate that at the age of forty he would embark on one of the most extraordinary careers in the history of exploration.

Morton-in-Cleveland, where he was born on October 27, 1728, was an obscure hamlet in a northeastern corner of the Yorkshire section of England, fifteen miles inland from the North Sea. His father, James Cook senior, was a Scottish-born agricultural laborer, and his mother, Grace Cook, a Yorkshire village woman. The younger James grew up in a succession of small clay-built cottages with thatched roofs belonging to the various yeoman-farmers for whom his father worked.

At age six he learned his "letters,"

the alphabet, from a neighbor lady, and soon thereafter he spent time at a charity school where he learned to read and do sums and made what seems to have been a mixed impression on his fellow scholars.

"It has been asserted by those who knew him at this early period of his life," the historian of the area wrote later, "that he had such an obstinate and sturdy way of his own as made him sometimes appear in an unpleasant light, notwithstanding which *there was something* in his deportment which attracted the reverence of his companions." We can call these remarks convenient hindsight, but we can also recognize the accuracy of them, for during Cook's three extensive voyages of discovery, he invariably enjoyed the respect though seldom the affection of those who traveled with him.

In his seventeenth year he got a job, measuring out raisins and ribbon in a combination grocery and clothing store. The work was not to his liking, and in his eighteenth year we find him at the little city of Whitby on the North Sea, starting a three-year apprenticeship to John Walker, a Quaker shipmaster and ship-owner engaged in transporting coal to ports along the coasts of England, through the Baltic and Mediterranean seas and to America.

"No man," said Samuel Johnson, the preeminent literary figure of Cook's England, "would be a sailor, who had contrivance enough to get himself into jail; for being in a ship is being in jail, with the chance of being drowned." In the years to come, James Cook would acquire an intimate acquaintance with the perils and discomforts of a sailor's life, but no sooner had he begun his labors under shipmaster Walker than he realized that he had found his world, that henceforth the sea would be his home.

In 1750 his apprenticeship ended and he joined the complement of a coal-bearing vessel, spending the next five years coming and going in British and Norwegian waters as an able seaman and teaching himself geography, mathematics, and astronomy. His great biog-

rapher, John C. Beaglehole, believes that he would have passed the remainder of his life in this fashion, had not world events dictated a change in direction.

In July 1755 the Seven Years War erupted, with England and France vying for domination in the New World. Cook joined the Royal Navy. By 1758 he had risen to master of the *Pembroke*, a sixty-four gun vessel and one of the nineteen ships of the line sent across the Atlantic with orders to attack the French strongholds of Louisburg and Quebec—an enterprise that ended with the fall of Quebec and shifted the control of Canada from French to British hands.

On the day after the fall of Louisburg in the summer of 1758 the *Pembroke* was moored in the nearby harbor, and Cook, strolling ashore, was struck by the behavior of a man in the uniform of an artillery officer. To quote from Beaglehole's story of the incident: "The man was carrying a small, square table, supported by a tripod. [Every so often he would] set the table down so that he could squint along the top in various directions, after which he would make notes in a pocket book."

Cook, curious, approached and questioned the man. His name? Samuel Holland. Dutch-born but now a military engineer with a British regiment. What

William Holl engraved this portrait of Captain James Cook after a painting by Nathaniel Dance. *Courtesy of the New York Public Library, Division of Prints and Photographs.*

was the equipment he was carrying about? A plane table. And what was he doing with it? He was "observing angles." In other words, he was "mapping the place and its encampments."

Cook insisted on being instructed in the use of the plane table. Holland was glad to oblige, and in a matter of months Cook had acquired sufficient mastery of the science of surveying to help chart the Gulf of the St. Lawrence River and the river itself. His encounter with Hol-

land was a major turning point in his life. The day was near when Cook's skills as a surveyor and mapmaker would attract the attention of influential men in London and pave the way for his great explorations.

For a short time after the war ended in December 1762, however, his actions were those of a man bent on trading the shifting life of a sailor for a settled existence on land. First he resigned from the navy, then he got married. Little is known of his bride, Elizabeth Batts, except that she was thirteen years younger than he and belonged to a respectable family living in the East End of London. Cook and his wife were occupying modest lodgings near the Thames and expecting the first of what were to be six children when in the opening months of 1763 the Lords of the Admiralty, the rulers of the Royal Navy, sent Cook back across the Atlantic to spend the next three years surveying the coasts of Newfoundland and some adjoining islands. So exact were Cook's charts of these areas that he received special recognition. In the spring of 1768 the Royal Society, England's foremost scientific body, was planning observations of the upcoming Transit of Venus—the passage of that planet across the face of the Sun—from the shores of the recently discovered island of Tahiti in the South Pacific, and the

Lords of the Admiralty recommended that Cook be put in charge of the investigation.

Thus began the first of his remarkable voyages of discovery. On July 25, 1768, the *Endeavor*, the 366-ton bark selected to transport the expedition, began the journey to Tahiti by way of Cape Horn at the bottom of South America. Among the ninety-five individuals aboard was a small group of scientists and their assistants, headed by the handsome, 25-year-old Joseph Banks, a botanist destined for fame as a collector of specimens from around the world and as a patron of the sciences.

No two men could have had more different backgrounds than Banks and Cook. Banks came from the elegant haunts of upper-class England, Cook from the humble environs of a Yorkshire farmer. Conflicts between two such men would not have been surprising, but there were none. Not only did Cook get along with Banks and the other scientists, he learned from them. Today his recorded impressions of the customs, beliefs, and surroundings of the Tahitians, now available in his published journals, are widely regarded as classics of ethnographical and geographical writing.

The congeniality prevailing between the self-educated Cook and the Oxford-educated Banks can be cited as but one of the many examples of the curious blend of qualities that the leader of the expedition had brought to his labors. Quick to anger, Cook ran a tight ship, demanding the immediate and unquestioned obedience to his orders that his own long experience before the mast had taught him was the first requisite of survival at sea. But he was fair. His punishments were even-handed and neatly tailored to the offense committed.

He showed concern for the well-being of his crew, far in excess of that shown by most ship commanders of his era. Few of his men, on this or his other voyages, suffered from scurvy, the debilitating and often fatal scourge of a sailor's life. In those days, before the discovery of vitamins, he saw to it that his men's diet was rich in fresh meat and fruits. *Endeavour* even carried a goat to supply milk for its passengers. Cleanliness of persons and places ranked high among Cook's requirements. The decks were scoured regularly with vinegar and, when the behavior of the winds permitted, the vessel was relieved of vermin by carefully controlled fires.

The Transit of Venus, on June 3, 1769, came and went, and was duly observed. But a month later, when Cook sailed from Tahiti, he did not immediately steer for home. Prior to his

Cook's ship journal of April 12, 1769, records his first glimpse of Tahiti ("King George's Island"). At noon, he wrote, "several of the natives of the island came out to us in their canoes and brought with them cocoanuts and a fruit very much like a large apple but did not eat not half so well." *Courtesy of The British Museum.*

departure from England two sets of orders had been handed to him, one of which would remain hidden from the world until 1928. These secret orders instructed him, once the scientific duties on Tahiti were completed, to roam the Pacific for a while and look for what the geographers of his day called *Terra Australis Incognita*, the unknown southern land.

For centuries many geographers had been of the opinion that there lay at the bottom of the world a large and as yet unsighted continent. Some went so far as to say that this land mass had to be there to balance the land masses they believed to exist at the other end of the globe. It was believed that without this balance the spinning sphere on which humanity dwelt would have wobbled out of orbit long since and disintegrated. One famous cartographer, the German-born Abraham Ortelius, was so sure this continent would be one day discovered that he included it on his 1570 map of the world and labeled it *Terra Australia Nondum Cognita* (the Not-*Yet*-Known Southern Land).

As a matter of fact, there was a not yet known southern land, the one we now know as Antarctica. But what the geographers of Cook's day had in mind was a far larger entity, one that filled practically the whole of the lower por-

tion of the world, beginning at or just below the southern tip of South America and extending westward at least as far as Australia and perhaps beyond. Whereas all Antarctica lies under ice and snow, much of the *Terra Australis* of their imaginings basked in a temperate zone where crops could be cultivated, animals grazed, and precious metals dug from the soil.

Now Cook was pursuing this geographical phantom. Early October brought him to New Zealand, already discovered but not yet explored. He explored it, found it to consist of two islands, and moved on.

His next landfall, on April 19, 1770, was the southeast corner of Australia, then called New Holland, a name bestowed by the Dutchmen who had ventured there half a century earlier. On April 28 Cook dropped anchor in an inlet to which he gave the name Botany Bay. He spent the next four months creeping northward, exploring the eastern coastline of the continent as far as the Cape York Peninsula, sailing with difficulty through the labyrinthine coral formations of the Great Barrier Reef. On August 21, at Cape York, he hoisted the Union Jack, the British flag, and in the name of King George III took possession of the almost two thousand miles of littoral he had examined, dubbing the area New South Wales, the

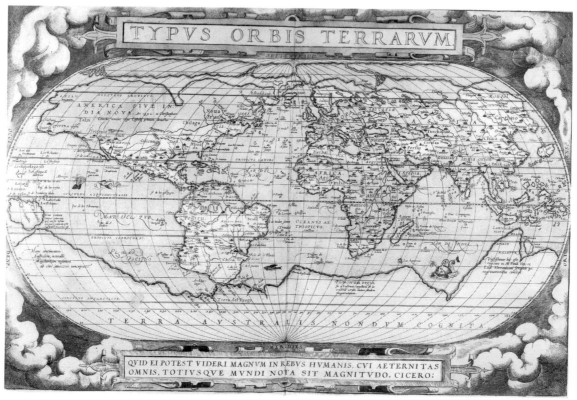

Abraham Ortelius's *Typus Orbis Terrarum,* a map made in 1570, displays a southern continent labeled "the not yet known southern [australis] land." Other captions reflect mysteries that would in time be solved by Cook: "Some believe Magellan sighted this southern land"; "No one is certain if newly discovered New Guinea is part of this southern land"; "Here [in Australia] are the extremely vast lands about which the traveler Marco Polo wrote." *Courtesy of the New York Public Library, Division of Rare Books.*

name the lower half of it still bears.

Then he set course for home by way of the Cape of Good Hope at the southern end of Africa, reaching England on July 17, 1771. He brought with him, for the edification of the Royal Society and the Admiralty, the charts of many hitherto unexplored lands, copious reports on the customs and languages of their occupants, more than a thousand species of dried plants, five hundred fish preserved in alcohol, five hundred bird skins, and thirteen hundred detailed drawings of the people and places encountered.

As for *Terra Australis Incognita,* all Cook could say was that in a sweep across the South Pacific he had seen no sign of it. His report did not discourage those who still believed that it was down there someplace. If it was not in the South Pacific, perhaps it was in the South Atlantic. Indeed, there was reason to think so, for as far back as 1739, a French explorer traveling in the waters south of the Cape of Good Hope had seen in the distance a high snow-covered bluff that he named Cape Circumcision. He believed it to be part of the unknown southern land.

On July 11, 1772, Cook left England on his second expedition, this time with two ships and a total complement of one hundred eighty-six men. His orders were to begin his exploration in the South Atlantic. He was to look for Cape Circumcision. If it proved to be a continent, he was to explore as much of it as possible. If it turned out to be only an island, he was to proceed southward in the hope of finding *Terra Australis Incognita*, somewhere between the Cape of Good Hope and the South Pole. These chores performed, he was to circumnavigate the globe, searching for new islands in the South Pacific and mapping those already discovered.

On December 10, 1772, Cook found himself for the first time in the presence of icebergs. "Islands of ice," the sailors called them. On January 3, having failed to locate Cape Circumcision, Cook inscribed in his journal the belief that if Cape Circumcision existed, it was "nothing but Mountains of Ice, sur-rounded by field ice," and that since it was "a general received opinion that ice is formed near land . . . there must be land in the neighborhood of this ice, that is either to the Southward or Westward." Investigations many years later would confirm both guesses. Cape Circumcision was the ice-sheathed mound of rock, about five miles square, that appears on present-day maps as Bouvet Island. A few hundred miles beyond the highest latitude—which is to say the latitude farthest south (71° 11′)—achieved by Cook during his second expedition, lay the continent of Antarctica.

Shortly before noon on January 17, 1773, the two ships of the expedition crossed the Antarctic Circle. They were the first European vessels to do so, though not necessarily the first vessels of any sort, for it is believed that Ui-te-Ranjiora, a chief from the Polynesian islands of the Pacific, brought his tiny boat into the pack ice of these dangerous seas as long ago as 650. On January 28 Cook yielded to the complaints of his crew that they could not manage their sails in this freezing region. Having made a half turn about, he sailed to the calmer reaches of the South Pacific. By the time Cook returned to England on July 30, 1775, he had long since written, "I have now done with the southern Pacific Ocean . . . and flatter

Sydney Parkinson, one of the artists who accompanied Cook on his expeditions, drew this exotic Maori man. *Courtesy of The British Museum.*

myself that no one will think I have left it unexplored," and the geographers of the world were erasing *Terra Australis Incognita* from their maps and minds.

He was now a famous man in his own country. London society pelted him with invitations. Even James Boswell sought him out. Destined for fame as the biographer of the great Samuel Johnson, Boswell asked Cook to take him on his next voyage and Cook said nothing doing. Chagrined though Boswell was by this put-down, he quoted with approval the statement of a contemporary that the explorer of the Pacific was "a plain sensible man with an attention to veracity." During the months following Cook's arrival home he was received at court, painted by a well-known portraitist, and elected to membership in the Royal Society. This attention he took in the unruffled manner of a singularly unselfconscious man who, during his rare sojourns on English soil, preferred to be with his wife and children at their home in the British capital's unfashionable East End.

On April 10, 1775, Cook was named Fourth Captain of the Greenwich Hospital for invalid sailors. From this date on he could have lazed through life, drawing good pay for doing no work, speaking before the Royal Society and other prestigious scientific groups, at-

tending parties, and basking in the approval of his countrymen. But as the developments of the succeeding months tell us, Captain Cook had no intention of passing the remainder of his days as a landlubber.

For two hundred years English sailors had been looking for what they called the Northwest Passage, a waterway supposedly lying across the top of North America that English traders could use to shorten their trips to the markets of the Orient. Most seekers of the Northwest Passage had sought it from the eastern or Atlantic side of the New World. Now, in the winter of 1775, the Royal Society was arranging for a hunt to be made from the western or Pacific side. In the beginning, the leaders of the Royal Society assumed that Captain Cook had done all the exploring he would ever wish to do. When, in February 1775, he volunteered to lead the forthcoming expedition, they were as delighted as they were surprised.

Thus it came about that, on July 12 of that year, Captain Cook sailed from England with two ships, the *Resolution* and the *Discoverer,* and one hundred ninety-two companions, to begin an expedition marked by finding new islands in the Pacific, by frustration in the ice-clogged waters of the Arctic Ocean, and by tragedy on the shores of a scenic bay in the tropics. The expedition headed for its ultimate destination, the waters to the west and north of Alaska, by way of the Indian and Pacific oceans. There were numerous stops in the Pacific at such places as the islands of Tasmania, New Zealand, Tongatabu, and Tahiti. At times, all along the way, Cook's conduct was that of a man who had undergone some sort of change in mind and spirit.

Years before, on the eve of his first voyage of discovery, the then president of the Royal Society, Douglas James, the Earl of Morton, had given him "hints" to guide him on his travels. One of Morton's suggestions was that Cook do no harm to the natives he encountered.

During his previous voyages, Cook had followed this instruction religiously. When hostile natives attacked, he told his marines to scare them off by firing over their heads. Now, on this third journey, his orders in such cases were to fire on them.

Thievery was endemic among the islanders. It was a game with them. Nothing more delighted a Tahitian, for example, than to slip a pair of field glasses or other valuables from the jacket pocket of an English officer and run off laughing. If chased and caught, he gave up the goods and went on his way. In the past Cook had let thieves

go. Not this time; this time he called for punishments—on most occasions flogging and once he saw to it that deep creases were slashed into the culprit's arms. Taking note of the uncharacteristic testiness displayed by the captain on his third voyage, Beaglehole writes that "We are troubled to see an unfamiliar Cook rising up by the side of the scrupulously humane Cook we have known."

What caused this change? Beaglehole attributes it to weariness. After two long and trying voyages, the Cook of the third voyage, he believes, was suffering from an "internal tiredness" that by depriving him of forbearance and alertness helped create the gruesome incident that was to take his life.

By mid-December 1777 the *Resolution* and the *Discoverer* were moving northward across the Equator. On the morning of January 18 they sighted lands that were not marked on any map. Cook called these newly found regions the Sandwich Islands after John Montague, Earl of Sandwich, the first Lord of the Admiralty. Today we know them as the Hawaiian Islands.

By late August the two ships had sailed through the Bering Strait, the body of water that divides North America from Siberia, off the northwestern shores of Alaska. Ahead lay an ice pack so formidable that they could not proceed. Was this frozen sea the entrance to the long-sought Northwest Passage? Perhaps so, perhaps not. All Cook knew was that at the time it could not be entered, and his decision was to spend the coming winter on one of the Sandwich Islands and return early the next summer to make another attempt to locate and traverse the Northwest Passage. On January 17, 1779, the ships of the expedition dropped anchor in Kealakekuia Bay on the western side of the island of Hawaii.

On their previous stop in the Sandwich Islands, Cook and his associates had failed to spot this island, the largest of them all. It was new to them, and although its numerous inhabitants were friendly and spoke a language similar to that of the Tahitians, their ways were strange.

On the afternoon of the expedition's arrival, Cook arranged to go ashore accompanied by some of his own people and a group of native priests. On a paved quadrangle, some twenty by forty yards in size and surrounded by a wooden railing adorned with human skulls, Cook became the center of a baffling religious ceremony. Apparently these people considered him a god. During the ensuing weeks the natives prostrated themselves when they saw him coming. The area where he and his scientists planted their tents for the making of geographical observations was put under taboo—that is, rendered sacred and barred to all the women of the island and to all the men except the most important priest.

On February 4 the ships of the expedition weighed anchor to begin the return trip to the Arctic, but a week later they ran into a violent gale. The foremast of the *Resolution* was sprung, forcing them to return to Kealakekuia Bay, where the damaged mast could be taken ashore and repaired.

In the dark hours of February 14 a cutter belonging to the *Discoverer* was stolen. When news of this theft reached Cook, his first reaction was to weigh what steps should be taken to recover the small ship-to-shore boat. Indeed, for a time he seemed to be his old self again, careful and restrained. But toward mid-morning anger took over. He armed himself, assembled an escort of musket-carrying marines, and hastened ashore. His plan was to seize Kalei'opu', a prominent chief, and hold him hostage until the cutter was returned.

A mob of natives accompanied Cook and his marines as they headed shoreward. As they neared the bay, a member of the mob threatened Cook with a dagger and a stone—seriously or in mere bravado, Beaglehole writes, "we cannot tell. Cook fired one barrel of his musket, loaded with small shot, at this person, and at that moment, when we must think, the strained cord of his temper snapped he lost the initiative." Because the man was wearing "his heavy war hat, the shot did no damage—except that it further enraged the Hawaiians."

By the time Cook reached the rim of the bay, the screaming natives were all around him. He was hit from behind by a club and stabbed in the neck by an iron dagger. These blows did not kill him, for he was a very strong man. But they sent him to the ground. He fell with his face in the water, and at once his assailants were on him, hacking him to death with their weapons.

It took the man who succeeded him as the commander of the expedition two days to persuade the Hawaiians to bring what remained of Cook's body to the ship. After that, the expedition returned to the Arctic in another futile attempt to find and enter the Northwest Passage. Then they headed home, reaching England on October 4, 1799.

The word of Cook's death stunned the nation. It was a rare Englishman who did not realize that his country had lost one of its greatest sons. The memory of the man and his accomplishments lingers on. Even now, to mention the Pacific Ocean is to think of the honest and plain-spoken Yorkshire farmer who opened up the secrets of that vast region of the world.

Leif Erikson

Late tenth and early eleventh centuries.   Icelandic-born Norwegian. Known as the first European to explore the coasts of North America.

Leif Erikson's adventures belong to what has come to be known as the Viking Age, an era that began in the summer of 793 when the people of Northumbria, one of the kingdoms into which England was then divided, were "sorely frightened by dire portents." First, according to an ancient history called the *Anglo-Saxon Chronicles*, there were "immense whirlwinds and flashes of lightning." Then, "fiery dragons were seen flying in the air." A famine ensued and on the eighth of June "heathen men," disembarking from longships with the heads of snarling animals on their prows, overran the island of Lindisfarne, a bastion of Christianity in the North Sea, plundering the cathedral and the monastery and killing or capturing those monks and nuns unable to escape.

The "heathen men" were Vikings, so named because they came from the *Viks*, the bays and fjords of Sweden, Denmark, and Norway. For the next two and a half centuries their presence was felt in every corner of Europe. They returned to England again and again, often for extended stays. They dotted the shores of Ireland with walled cities, Dublin among them. They created great trading centers in the heart of Russia. They founded in northwestern France the dukedom of Normandy, from whence a hundred and fifty years later one of their descendants, now remembered as William the Conqueror, crossed the Channel to seize control of England.

Southward and eastward the Vikings roamed; westward, too, into the open wastes of the Atlantic, where on Iceland

and other islands they established what soon became busy agricultural communities. "They went everywhere there was to go," scholar Magnus Magnusson has written of the Vikings. "They dared everything there was to dare, and they did it with a robust panache and audacity that has won the grudging admiration even of those who deplore their depredations."

Violence accompanied their wanderings, but this was not the whole of their record. They carried new ways of doing business to Russia and to the Byzantine Empire. They took new forms of art to the British Isles. There and elsewhere they installed new methods of administration and justice. The word "law" itself was their gift to the English language. The populations of their Scandinavian homelands were growing, and in those chill and mountainous regions tillable land was becoming increasingly scarce. Many a Viking pointed the prow of his ship into the North Atlantic with nothing more warlike in mind than a desire to find on some island a piece of ground where he could graze his livestock and grow grain and vegetables.

They introduced ships more technologically developed than any seen before—sleek and handsome vessels that they spoke of as "ocean-striding bison" or "surf-dragons" or "horses of the lobster's heath." We know something of the lineaments of these vessels thanks to the archaeologists of our own times. Since the remains of a Viking Age ship were extracted from a mound of blue clay in Norway in 1880, a dozen similar ships have been unearthed.

A typical Viking warship was about 76 feet from tip of prow to stern and 17 feet in the beam of the hull. It utilized both wind and manpower. A 35-foot mast, abaft of center, carried a large square sail, brightly decorated with multicolored stripes. On either side were 16 holes for the oars. The ships resurrected to date have no fixed seats, so one assumes that the rowers sat on their sea chests. The draft of this vessel was shallow, 3 feet on the average, so it needed no harbor in which to anchor. It could be run onto a beach and secured there. As Magmusson writes, "It was an oceangoing landing craft," ideal for calls on a foreign countries, especially if one intended to carry out raids.

Another Viking vessel, known as a *knorr*, was the one most commonly used on the open seas. It, too, boasted a sail and mast. Wider on the beam than the warship, but much like it in appearance, the knorr had half-decks fore and aft. Amidships was an open hold. A settler could store his provisions there and tether his cattle and horses, and a merchant could stow his goods.

This Viking ship, discovered in Oseberg, can help us to visualize the vessel used by Leif Erikson. This beautifully carved 1,000-year-old oak vessel is 66 feet long and 17 feet wide, with rowlocks for 30 oarsmen. *Courtesy of Universitetets Oldsaksamling, Oslo.*

Like the warship, the knorr was steered by a paddle rudder affixed to the starboard quarter of the stern.

We owe most of our knowledge of the Viking to the Icelandic sagas. The sagas, however, were not written at the time of the episodes they recount. The Viking Age had gone when historians and poets in various parts of the Scandinavian world began inscribing on calfskin the stories of the Vikings that their forebears had handed down from generation to generation by word of mouth. The sagas constitute some of the finest literature to come out of the Middle Ages, but as history they can be troublesome. Written long after the event, they mix fact and fancy to a degree that often leaves us uncertain as to where and when things happened, and sometimes as to whether they happened at all.

Where Leif Erikson is concerned, however, our sources of information are relatively trustworthy. They include detailed accounts of his deeds in two sagas, references to them in others, and, most reassuring of all, excavations in Canada by modern archaeologists show that almost five centuries before Christopher Columbus reached South America, one or more parties of Vikings set foot on the shores of North America.

Though Leif was a descendant of Norwegian kings, he was born in Iceland. Many years earlier his father, Erik the Red, participated in "some killings" in his native Norway and fled to Iceland to escape the wrath of his victims' kinfolk. In Iceland he married a cousin named Thyodhild and established a homestead on one of Iceland's fjords. Here Leif was born in the year 980 or thereabouts, and here his flaming-haired and flaming-tempered father got into trouble again.

First, some of Erik's slaves accidentally started a mountainside avalanche that crushed the roof of a nearby farmer's house. The owner of the damaged house and his slaves came to Erik spouting angry words, whereupon swords flashed and blood flowed. Then Erik and another neighbor quarreled over the ownership of a pair of boards. There was more sword play and more bloodletting. Finally, the judges of the local court ordered Erik to leave the country for three years.

Erik put his exile to good use. He sailed west, driven by old tales asserting that out there somewhere was an uninhabited island many times bigger than Iceland. He found the fabled place. Like Iceland, it was a land of glaciers and lava plains, permafrost and snow-topped mountains. But along its southwestern shores, on gently sloping hillsides above a network of fjords, stretched green and fertile pastures.

At once a scheme formed in Erik's mind. Here was a region waiting to be occupied. Here was a place where many people could create homesteads for themselves and where he, as the first settler, would be in charge. When his exile ended and he returned to Iceland, he went about telling everyone of the grand area he had discovered; and when they wanted to know what it was called, he said that he had named it Greenland, reasoning that that word would make it sound attractive.

It did indeed. When in the early summer of 986 Erik put himself, his family, and their belongings on a long ship and headed again for Greenland, twenty-five boatloads of settlers traveled with them.

In Greenland, at a place called Brattahild, Erik's son Leif grew up. We can be sure that the dreams of his youth were not unlike those of the warrior-poet Egil Skallagrimsson, who in one of the Sagas is described as writing these verses during his early years:

My mother once told me
She'd buy me a long ship,
A handsome-oared vessel
To go sailing with Vikings
To stand at the stern-post
And steer a fine warship,
Then head back for harbour
And hew down a foeman.

On attaining manhood, Leif requested a long ship so that he could go adventuring on the high seas as his father had done. Erik agreed that he should have it, but he laid down one condition: The young man must make his first journey to Norway. The settlers of Greenland needed many things that could be gotten only from there, and in recent years fewer and fewer merchants from the homeland had been bringing their trading vessels into the Greenland fjords. Once in Norway, Leif was to call on the king and beg him to send more traders to the settlement his father had founded.

The early summer of 999 found Leif

on his way, but instead of going directly to Norway he veered a few hundred miles off course and made his first landfall at the Hebrides, a scattering of islands in the Atlantic off the coast of Scotland.

It was a logical place to stop, for in those days the Hebrides were one of the great trading centers of the world. Leif's original plan was to stay only long enough to call on some of the local merchants, but soon after his arrival he fell in love with a young woman named Thorgunna and lingered on.

But Leif did not intend to marry. He gave Thorgunna a golden ring for her finger, a cloak of Greenland wool, and a belt made of walrus and ivory. Then he resumed his journey.

Reaching Norway in the fall, he hastened to the court of King Olaf Tryggvason. We have seen that his father was banished forever from one country because of "some killings" and temporarily from another because of blood feuds with neighbors. This same Erik the Red enticed settlers to Greenland by using methods we associate with real-estate promoters of our era. Now, in the behavior of his son in Norway, we can see the same mixture of daring and practicality.

The Norway to which Leif had come was astir with the beginnings of a new religion. For centuries the Scandinavians had worshipped those adventuresome deities we encounter in the old Norse and Germanic myths. Odin, considered to be the father of the Scandinavian gods, was said to have sacrificed one of his eyes to his search for knowledge and was usually portrayed as a one-eyed man disguised as a simple farmer. Close to Odin in power were Thor the Thunderer, the patron of seamen and farmers, and Frey, the fertility god.

King Olaf Tryggvason had abandoned these deities for the Christian Trinity. He had commanded his subjects to do the same or else—the "or else" ranging from having their homes burned down or their heads removed.

Leif was quick to measure the temper of the man he had traveled almost 2,000 miles to meet. Soon the two of them had struck a bargain, and King Olaf Tryggvason agreed to send more trading vessels to Greenland. In return, Leif was to see to it that the people of his father's settlement converted to the faith of Rome. Back home in the autumn of the year 1000, he set out at once to keep his promise. It is a gauge of Leif Erikson's power of persuasion that in a short time Greenland had become an outpost of Christianity in the far western waters of the North Atlantic.

This task accomplished, Leif turned to another matter. Often heard in Greenland was the story of the strange travels of one Bjarni Herjolfsson. For many years, as a merchant in Norway, Bjarni crossed the Atlantic each year to spend the summer with his aging father in Iceland. One summer, on his arrival there, he was startled to learn that his father had left Iceland and had gone with Erik the Red to live in a place called Greenland.

Bjarni did not even stop long enough in Iceland to unload his goods and sell them as he had planned to do. He moved on, determined to join his father. According to the Icelanders, he would reach Greenland by sailing due west along the sixty-fifth parallel, but once on the open sea he encountered a storm that threw him off course. When the storm abated, he found himself in the midst of a fog bank where for several days all he could do was furl his sail and still his oars and wait for the sun to reappear.

When it did, he saw over to his right a barren and rocky land. The Icelanders had told him that when he reached Greenland he would know he was there from the glaciers on its mountains. But here there were no glaciers. That, decided Bjarni, could not be Greenland, and he sailed on.

On the following day, again to his right, he spotted another land, densely forested with tall trees. That one, too, he told his crew, could not be Greenland. As he continued his voyage, his little ship reached still another land, a pleasant-looking region of grassy fields and green hills. Nor could that be Greenland, Bjarni decided.

By this time he realized that he was far south of where he ought to be. Coming about, he steered north and east and a few days later pushed into the very fjord along which his father lived. At this point—so the story concluded—Bjarni gave up his life as a trader to dwell thereafter on the farm of his father in Greenland.

Many of Bjarni's neighbors in Greenland were annoyed with him. How, they asked one another, could a man cast eyes on hitherto unknown lands and not go ashore to see what was there, even though in every case Bjarni's crew had implored him to do so? That, they scolded, was no way for a Viking to behave.

No one could ever accuse Leif Erikson of not acting like a Viking. He had fulfilled his agreement with his father. He had gone to Norway and had gotten favors for Greenland from the king. Now he was free to go where he wished, and, in the spring of 1001, he decided to find the three lands Bjarni had discovered and explore them.

His first stop was a visit to Bjarni himself to buy from him the ship on which he had traveled. It was thought

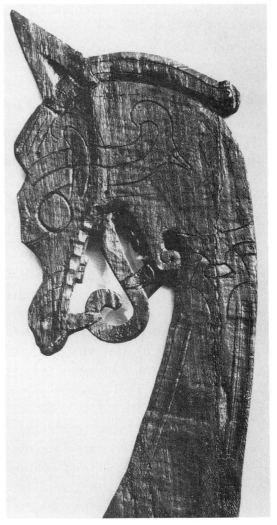

This decorative post was used to help support a tent for sleeping quarters aboard a Viking ship discovered at Gokstad. Built in the mid-ninth century, it is 76½ feet along the stern and 17½ feet across the beam. Leif Erikson's ship probably had a broader beam and sat deeper in the water but otherwise might have been quite similar. *Courtesy of Universitetets Oldsaksamling, Oslo.*

in Greenland that once a ship had gone somewhere, it could return there on its own, as a horse that has lost its rider can return home alone.

Be that as it may, in the spring of 1002 Leif sailed westward, taking with him thirty-five persons to work the rigging and man the oars of his vessel. He also took along some cattle, which suggests that he was planning to spend considerable time on one or more of the places he was seeking. Was he also, perhaps, thinking of establishing a settlement?

Two hundred and fifty miles beyond Greenland, Leif and his crew encountered the first of the three lands Bjarni had sighted and went ashore to look around. As Bjarni had reported, it was a forbidding region. Leif named it Helluland, meaning "Slab-Land," and we now assume from the descriptions of it in the sagas that it was Baffin Island, off the northeastern shores of Canada.

Onward they moved, soon coming to the second of the three unknown lands. This, too, they examined on foot. Leif called it Markland, meaning "Wood-Land." This would seem to have been the stretch of the North American mainland later known as Labrador.

After leaving Labrador, according to one of the Sagas, "they were at sea two days before catching sight of land. . . . Reaching an island which lay north of

it," and which we have reason to believe was Newfoundland.

They went ashore and looked about them. . . . After which they returned to their ship and sailed into the sound which lay between the island and the cape projecting north from the land itself [the Canadian mainland]. They made headway west around the cape. There were big shallows there at low water; their ship went aground, and it was a long way to look to get sight of the sea from the ship. But they were so curious to get ashore that they had no mind to wait for the tide to rise under their ship, but went hurrying off to land [in the ship's boat], where a river flowed out of a lake. Then, as soon as the tide rose under their ship, they rowed back to her, and brought her up the river, and so to the lake, where they cast anchor, carried their skin sleeping bags off board, and built themselves booths [turf and stone enclosures roofed with cloth awnings]. Later they decided to winter there and build a big house.

There was no lack of salmon there in river or lake. . . . The nature of the land was so choice it seemed to them that none of the cattle would require fodder for the winter. No frost came during the winter, and the grass was hardly withered.

Once they had finished their housebuilding Leif made an announcement . . . "I intend to have our company divided now in two, and get the land explored. Half our band shall remain here at the hall, and the other half reconnoitre the countryside . . . yet go no further

Was Leif Erikson, not Christopher Columbus, the first European to discover America? Per Krogh, painter of "Leiv Eiriksson Discovers America, A.D. 1000," thinks so. *Courtesy of Library of Congress; gift of Norwegian Friends of America through Dr. Alf Bjercke of Oslo, Norway.*

than they can get back home in the evening and not get separated." So for a while that is what they did, Leif going off with them or remaining in camp by turns. Leif was big and strong, of striking appearance, shrewd, and in every respect a temperate, fairdealing man.

Among his companions was a German named Tyrkir, who had been close to Leif's family for many years and had helped bring Leif up.

When one evening Tyrkir failed to appear at the end of his day's reconnaissance, the worried Leif assembled a party and went out in search of him.

They had gone only a short distance when they saw Tyrkir coming toward them, a big smile on his pinched and pleasantly ugly face.

"Why are you so late, foster-father," Leif demanded, "and parted this way from your companions?"

The saga tells us that Tyrkir talked for a time in German, "rolling his eyes all ways and pulling faces." Eventually he switched to a language they could understand.

"I went no great way further than

you," he said, "yet I have a real novelty to report. I have found vines and grapes."

"Is that the truth, foster-father?" Leif asked him.

"Of course it's the truth," he replied. "I was born where wine and grapes are no rarity."

At that moment Leif knew what he was going to call the country to which he and his friends had come. When in the spring they returned home, he went about, like his father before him, telling everybody what a fine place he had found and that he had named it Vinland. And as had happened to his father, the pleasant-sounding name he selected appealed to people and soon other Greenlanders were sailing for Vinland.

One group of them, sixty-nine men and five women accompanied by a cargo of livestock, established a settlement where a boy named Snorri seems to have become the first white child to be born in America. Their intention was to stay indefinitely, but at the close of their second winter they were forced to leave by hostile natives, Indians or Eskimos or both, whom the Vikings called *Skraelings*, meaning "savages" or "wretches."

But where was Vinland? For many years various historians have placed it in different places. Some put it as far south as Florida, some as far west as Minnesota. In 1960, archaeologists digging near the little fishing village of L'Anse aux Meadows, at the northern tip of Newfoundland, uncovered the incontrovertible evidence of the existence of an ancient Norse settlement.

But if we are to say that Vinland lay in that area, we must deal with those "vines and grapes." Today no grapes grow northward of Maine, but that in itself does not rule out the possibility that Vinland embraced Newfoundland and the adjoining mainland of Canada. In the 1530s Jacques Cartier of France, the discoverer of the St. Lawrence River, saw grapes growing on both sides of that stream, and studies of modern climatologists indicate that in Leif Erikson's time the southeastern shores of Canada were from two to four degrees warmer on the average than is the case today.

One thing we can say with certainty: Tenth- and eleventh-century Vikings, roaming the world in their beautiful ships, discovered and explored the New World and for varying intervals lived on its soil.

Vasco da Gama

1460?–1524   The Portuguese navigator who linked West to East by providing his country with a sea-lane to the Orient.

So clearly is Vasco da Gama one of the greatest of the explorers that it is disappointing to find that segments of his life, especially the first thirty-some years of it, come close to being a blank to us. He was the third son of Estavan da Gama, a nobleman and for a time the *alcaide-mor* (mayor or law-giver) of Sines, the seaport in the south of Portugal where Vasco grew up. Even the date of Vasco's birth at Sines is a matter of guesswork, probably 1460. We do know that in the mid-1480s he was old enough to be a member of the royal court where King John II, the so-called "John the Perfect," regarded him as one of his most capable assistants. The king was heard to remark that Gama was a person who knew how to get things done. He was also, according to John

the Perfect, a man who knew nearly everything there was to know about "affairs of the sea," and in the late fifteenth century the affairs of the sea were the major affairs of Portugal.

For many years the navigators of that country had been prowling southward along the Atlantic shores of Africa, braving wild currents and heavy weather in an effort to find a sea lane to India where one could purchase spices and other precious commodities desperately needed by the people of Portugal. When in 1488 Bartholomeu Dias rounded the Cape of Good Hope at the bottom of Africa, there was rejoicing at the court of King John. If one Portuguese vessel could get that close to the Indian Ocean, then other ships could cross that mammoth sea to Calicut and

A sixteenth-century manuscript depicts the fleet commanded by Da Gama in 1497. *Courtesy of Bibliothèque Nationale, Paris.*

to other trading cities along the eastern or Malabar Coast of India.

An expedition to do just that was being readied when John the Perfect died. This was in October 1495, and on a summer day two years later his successor, King Manuel I, presided at a solemn ceremony at his summer castle in the hills west of Lisbon, the Portuguese capital. Richly dressed priests, nobles, state officials, and courtiers crowded the great hall as Manuel announced that he was sending out a fleet to seek a passage to India.

The motive for this undertaking was twofold: to acquire the riches of the East and to spread the doctrines of Christianity. Those who made the journey, he said, would have no easy time of it. For months they would find themselves in waters previously unbroken by European prows. At many of their ports of call they would be in the presence of "Moors," the name the Portuguese gave to all believers in Mohammedanism, the religion of Islam, whose countless followers were implacable enemies of the Catholic faith. Finally the king announced that as the captain-major of this dangerous mission he had selected Vasco da Gama who, as Manuel's royal predecessor had said, understood the affairs of the sea and knew how to get things done.

On July 8, 1497, Gama left the docks of Lisbon; his fleet consisted of four vessels. Three of these were regular sailing ships. The other was a storeship loaded with supplies for what was to be the longest ocean voyage known to date. In the holds of the storeship were a number of stone pillars. These were to be set up wherever the voyagers landed, partly to show that Christian feet had trod these places, partly in anticipation of the day when Portugal might wish to add these territories to those parts of Africa it had already claimed as belonging to its king.

After two brief stops, one on the African mainland, the other at the Cape Verde islands, Gama bypassed the turbulent waters along the coast of central Africa by setting a course that took him westward across the Atlantic almost to South America and then in an southwestern direction back to Africa. On November 9 the fleet dropped anchor in the Bay of St. Helena, less than two hundred miles north of the Cape of Good Hope. Captain-major Gama and his one hundred seventy companions had spent ninety-six days in the open sea.

They swarmed ashore quickly, happy to feel solid ground under their feet. They were also happy to find that they were not alone. Living somewhere beyond the sand hills rimming the bay was a tawny-colored people known as

Hottentots. At first the natives hung back, frightened by these armor-clad intruders. But little by little they began coming down to where the Portuguese were gathering wood and other supplies for their vessels. The captain-major saw to it that they were given some small trinkets, and for several days all went well.

Then Fernao Velloso, one of the Portuguese men-at-arms, requested permission to accompany some of the Hottentots across the hills. Velloso wished to have a look at their Kraal, their stockaded village. The captain-major hesitated, fearful of losing his soldier. But in the end his brother Paul, captain of one of the vessels of the fleet, talked him into letting the young man go.

A few hours later Velloso came scrambling down the nearest hill, chased by a gang of natives armed with wooden spears. In the ensuing skirmish the captain-major suffered a leg wound. Only with difficulty was Velloso rowed out to his ship. He was a cheerful, devil-may-care sort. When one of his companions chided him for coming down the hill faster than he had gone up it, his eyes danced. "Of course," he said. "I suddenly realized that you fellows could never get along if anything bad happened to me."

On the following day, November 16, the four ships moved on. On the 22nd they rounded the Cape of Good Hope and on the 25th they anchored in Mosell Bay on the lower shores of what is now the country of South Africa. Here they remained for thirteen days, long enough to scuttle their storeship and transfer its contents to the other vessels. Here, as at the Bay of St. Helena, Hottentots descended upon them. From beginning to end, however, these natives were congenial. When the Portuguese made ready to depart, two hundred black men crowded onto the beach to serenade them off with flutes. Gama ordered his musicians to sound their trumpets, and both groups broke into a dance—the Hottentots onshore and the Portuguese on the decks of their ships.

On December 15 the voyagers passed the mouth of the Great Fish River. This was the farthest point reached by Bartholomeu Dias when nine years earlier he discovered the Cape of Good Hope. As the voyagers worked their way first eastward across the bottom of Africa, and then northward along the southern half of its eastern shores, they found themselves navigating unknown seas with occasional stops to investigate unknown lands. Wherever they disembarked, the natives, a mixture of Hottentots and Zulus, were ready to supply the visitors with food and water, animal skins and ivory, in exchange for caps and bells.

Then on March 2, 1498, as the Portuguese anchored in a roadstead off Mozambique, they saw that they had reached those regions of East Africa where Arab merchants had established great trading centers and where the inhabitants lived in handsome white-walled houses and went about fully clothed like the people back home in Portugal.

Now a strange thing happened. Seemingly unaware of the meaning of the huge crosses painted on the sails of Gama's ships, the sultan of Mozambique and his attendants assumed that, like themselves, their visitors were followers of the prophet Mohammed, founder of the religion of Islam. Gama and his officers had fallen into a similar error, believing that the people who came out from Mozambique to greet them were Christians.

Disillusionment came quickly. At Gama's request, the sultan had sent out a couple of Moorish pilots whose task it would be to guide the Portuguese to India through the Arabian Sea, the big northern arm of the Indian ocean. When the two pilots discovered that they were on a Christian vessel, they deserted. A few days later, having learned that the sultan was contemplating an attack on his fleet, Gama sailed on.

His hope was to obtain the pilots he needed at one of the other Arab ports along the shores of East Africa. But on April 7 at Mombasa the behavior of the local sultan and his cohorts was hostile from the beginning. Only after leveling portions of the waterfront with their bombards, their rock-throwing cannons, were the Portuguese free to resume their journey.

On Easter eve, April 14, they reached Melindi, the largest of the Arabs' East African ports. Apparently the sultan of Melindi had been told of the power of the Portuguese guns. He provided Gama with food and other supplies. In addition, he put the captain-major in touch with the elderly Ibn Majid whose long familiarity with the Arabian Sea made him the finest pilot in this part of the world.

It was Ibn Majid who guided the three Portuguese ships across the Arabian Sea, a journey that took twenty-three days and ended on May 20, 1498, in the waters off the city of Calicut on the Malabar Coast.

For Gama it was a moment when he could say to himself, "Mission accomplished." After a journey of 314 days he had opened to his country—and, by extension, to all of Europe—a passage to India.

But his troubles were not over. To the Zamorin, the Hindu king of Calicut, the appearance of men from a distant country was both an opportunity and a problem. On the one hand, he welcomed Gama's request that Calicut set

Vasco da Gama and his crews navigated the eastern coasts of Africa and opened up trading routes from Europe to India. *Courtesy of Bibliothèque Nationale, Paris.*

up trade relations with Portugal. On the other hand, he could not ignore the interests of the Arab merchants who had long since established themselves. The products of India were making the Moors wealthy, and they had no wish to share them with the subjects of a Christian king.

Some days the Zamorin listened to what Gama wanted him to hear. Other days he listened to the Arab merchants.

Gama identified himself as an envoy from the most powerful country on earth and gave the Zamorin a letter written and signed by King Manuel. The Arabs said anyone could have written that letter. They told the Zamorin that Gama was a pirate, trying to get his hands on the riches of Calicut by ingratiating himself with its ruler.

Twice the Zamorin invited Gama and his companions to the palace for elaborate festivities. Then, prodded by the Arabs, he threw the captain-major and thirteen of his men into prison—only to release them four days later, frightened by threats coming from Paul Gama and the other Portuguese ship captains.

Gama won this tug-of-war. On August 29, when he began his journey home, the holds of his vessels bulged with the products of India—cinnamon, cloves, ginger, nutmeg, pepper, and precious stones. His passenger list included a number of Indians, one of them sent by the Zamorin as Calicut's ambassador to Lisbon.

The return trip was long and arduous. They were sailing against the wind, and the crossing of the Arabian Sea took three months. As the fleet stood south in the Indian Ocean, an epidemic of scurvy, the dreaded disease of the sea, so reduced the crew that Gama had to sink one of his ships for lack of hands to run it. As the remaining two vessels moved up the Atlantic, storms separated them for several weeks and the captain-major lost his brother Paul to consumption.

Still, his arrival at Lisbon in late August or early September 1499 was an occasion for celebration throughout Portugal. King Manuel was delighted with the presence at his court of an ambassador from Calicut. He was even more delighted at the riches Gama had brought home. He plied the captain-major with financial rewards and probably danced at his wedding when a year or so later Gama took as his wife Catherine de Ataide, a lady from a good family. She would make him the father of six sons.

He had not seen the last of India. Never again, however, would he travel there as a peaceful envoy. On his next journey east in 1502, he went as a conquistador, as the Admiral of India, commanding ten warships and five caravels. This time his instructions were to take possession of Calicut and of the other trading centers along the Malabar Coast for Portugal—a mission he accomplished in a series of savage naval bombardments. By the time he returned to Lisbon in 1503, much of India was under Portuguese rule, a situation that would prevail until the seizure of these regions by the Dutch one hundred sixty years later.

Again, as in the aftermath of Gama's first voyage, he was the recipient of honors from a grateful king. Among these was a grant of land that in 1510 made him the count of Vidigueria and one of the richest men in the kingdom. His benefactor, Manuel I, was dead and had been succeeded by King John III when Gama undertook his last journey to the East in 1524.

He went this time as viceroy (governor) of his country's Indian lands. His job was to plan and put in place a number of badly needed administrative reforms. Gama was working at these tasks in the city of Cochin on the Malabar Coast at the time of his death at three o'clock Christmas morning. Burial was in the Franciscan monastery at Cochin until in 1535 his body was conveyed to Portugal to rest in the church at Vidigueria.

Henry, Prince of Portugal

1394–1460 Now remembered as "Prince Henry the Navigator." His sponsorship of numerous expeditions in the South Atlantic ushered in the Great Age of Exploration, during which time the waterways between Europe and the Orient were opened and America was discovered.

Born on March 4, 1394, at Oporto on the Atlantic coast of Portugal, Henry was the third son of King John I of Portugal. His mother, Philippa, was a daughter of England's powerful nobleman John of Gaunt. In Henry's behavior as an adult one can see the effect on him of his mother's iron will and high moral standards. It was Philippa who saw to it that the training of her sons was not confined to doing those noble deeds expected of the offspring of royalty. The English historian Edgar Prestage tells us that all five boys were equally well versed in mathematics, astronomy, the other sciences, and the liberal arts, with the result that they grew up to be "not only men of action but students as well."

Henry was sixteen when his father began making preparations for an assault on the city of Ceuta on the northern shores of Africa, opposite the Cape of Gibraltar. Ceuta belonged to Catholic Portugal's longtime enemies, the Moors, who were Muslims. The conquest of Ceuta, King John reasoned, would benefit his country in several ways. For one, it would end Moorish domination of the shipping lanes of the Mediterranean Sea. For another, it would discourage the frequent invasion and plundering of Portugal by Moorish warriors.

King John was a prudent man. He had no intention of carrying out his plans until he could learn exactly where the fort of Ceuta stood and how well it was manned. Gathering these facts took several years. He had to assess their strength in secret so that the Moors would not get wind of his intentions. With this in mind, the king sent some ambassadors to Sicily to demand the hand of its queen for one of his sons. King John knew that this request would be refused. He also knew that en route home from Sicily his envoys could make some excuse for disembarking at Ceuta long enough to spy on its defenses.

However, the ambassadors were so closely watched during their stay in the big African port city that they dared not draw a map. On their return they used a pile of sand and some beans to show the king a "picture" of Ceuta, indicating the whereabouts of its citadel and other strong points. Armed with this information, King John began assembling a fleet to take his soldiers to Africa. As there was no way of hiding this activity from the Moors, he let it be believed that he was angry at the Dutch, whose warships had been preying upon Portuguese ships. Secretly he dispatched a message to Holland, telling its ruler what his real aims were. On July 25, 1415, he sent his fleet of over 200 vessels and 45,000 men, not northward to Holland as everyone had been led to expect, but southward across the Strait of Gibraltar.

King John and his sons were aboard the lead caravels, and to twenty-one-year-old Prince Henry the arrival of the armada off the shores of Ceuta was the moment he had eagerly awaited. His mother had died recently, and one of her last wishes was that Henry and his brothers "bear themselves honorably" when they confronted the Moors in Africa. Henry was resolved to do this.

Like his brothers, Henry longed to enter what were called "the lists of chivalry" with the title of knight. More than once had King John offered Henry and his brothers this honor. They refused because they believed that it was all right for the sons of merchants to buy their way into knighthood by staging "fetes and games" for their monarch, but the sons of a king ought to earn their knighthood by performing some great service for their country.

When Henry landed on the beaches of Ceuta with a contingent of soldiers, the opportunity to do just that lay before him and he made the most of it. He led the attack on the citadel, the fort of the city. The battle was long and hard. For a couple of hours Henry and seventeen of his men were cut off from the rest and had to claw their way back to the main body. Henry was wounded. Eight of his followers were killed. But by the evening of August 16 the banner of St. Vincent—the flag of Lisbon, capital of Portugal—flew from the tower of the citadel. Within hours Henry had received his rewards from a grateful father: knighthood, dukedom, and the governorship of newly conquered Ceuta.

It is not known exactly when Prince Henry began dreaming of the grand enterprises that would make his career one of the most productive in the history of exploration. It is known that during his three years as governor of Ceuta he spent much time listening to the tradesmen and other travelers coming into that city from the interior of Africa.

These people brought with them exciting tales of a strange and varied land: mountains rich in gold and other precious minerals; tribesmen, eager to exchange the ivory so abundant in their regions for the products of Portugal's farms and factories; profitable trade in slaves, carried on by the Arabs who entered the dark continent from the east; mighty rivers bearing colorful names, among them the Nile, the Congo, the Senegal, and the Gambia; and beautiful offshore islands waiting to be occupied and cultivated.

Here, in short, was a bountiful world still practically unknown to Europeans. When Prince Henry was relieved of his duties in Ceuta and returned to Portugal in 1418, he knew what he was going to do for the remainder of his days. He was going to bring to his fellow Europeans a knowledge of the continent of Africa, of the many islands lying in the Atlantic off its coasts, and of the farther reaches of the Atlantic itself.

To his lifework Prince Henry brought two of the qualities that had been so prominent in his mother: a relentless determination in carrying out his objectives and a strict code of behavior. He never married and there were no women in his life. He took seriously the teachings of his church. He regarded chastity as a virtue to be cultivated and intimate relations with women outside of marriage to be a sin. Perhaps the most ingratiating of his qualities was his forbearance. Often the leaders of the expeditions he organized and sent out returned to confess that they had been unable to accomplish the hard tasks he had asked of them. On these occasions no frown darkened his strong features and no words passed his lips except a quiet "Try again." With Prince Henry we would seem to be in the presence of Geoffrey Chaucer's "varray parfit gentil knight."

Like his father, he was patient and systematic in the selection and pursuit of his goals. He read and reread the works of Ptolemy and other ancient geographers and mapmakers. According to these classic scholars, the islands lying close to Africa were as far west as any sailor need or dare go. Beyond them were no more bodies of land, only

Prince Henry the Navigator (in large dark hat) is shown to the right of the patron saint of Portugal in the center panel of an altarpiece by Nuno Gonçalves, now in the Museum of Ancient Art, Lisbon. The future King John II is to the right of Henry, and the king and queen of Portugal kneel in the foreground. *Courtesy of Giraudon/Art Resource, NY.*

churning waters brimming with who knew what terrors: whirlpools, capable of wrecking a vessel, monsters capable of eating it up.

Henry respected the authors and believed they could be right. However, they could also be wrong. And the scientist in him believed that there was only one way to find out. Someone must sail out there and have a look. So he dispatched several expeditions, telling their leaders to push as far out as they could. When these explorers did so, they found that there were no disastrous whirlpools and no monsters except mammoth but harmless whales.

They also discovered that there were more islands in the far reaches of the Atlantic. They called them the Azores, and on their return to Portugal they told Prince Henry a fascinating story about one of them. On the far tip of one island, they said, stood the tall stone figure of a man with his arm raised and pointing ever westward as if to say, "There's more out there." Years later, as we now know, Christopher Columbus found out what that "more" was, and Amerigo Vespucci, another great navigator, gave it the name "America."

Among the other islands found by the explorers sent forth by Henry were the Madeiras. Following the discovery of this fertile and picturesque archipelago in 1418 and 1419, Henry sent out

several groups to colonize it, and by 1455 there were five settlements and 800 inhabitants.

To be sure, the effort to colonize one of the islands of the archipelago was the victim of biological miscalculation. One of the would-be settlers brought along a couple of families of rabbits. Rabbits multiply fast, he noted. While he and his fellow settlers were raising their first crops, they would survive on rabbit stew. Alas, the rabbits outdid themselves. Within a few months their progeny were consuming every freshly grown stick of sugar cane, every blade of grass, every fruit-bearing shrub—and the settlers were forced to move to an adjoining island.

According to Ptolemy and the other ancient geographers, no ship sailing down the Atlantic coast of Africa dared go beyond Cape Bojador. To venture South of Bojador, the classic writers taught, one entered the Tropics or the Sea of Darkness, a stretch of the South Atlantic where white men would turn black and perish with their vessels. Again, Prince Henry told himself that maybe it was true and maybe not. Again, the scientist in him concluded that the only way to find out was to have a look.

Year after year, beginning in 1421, he sent his explorers down the coast of Africa with orders to sail as far below

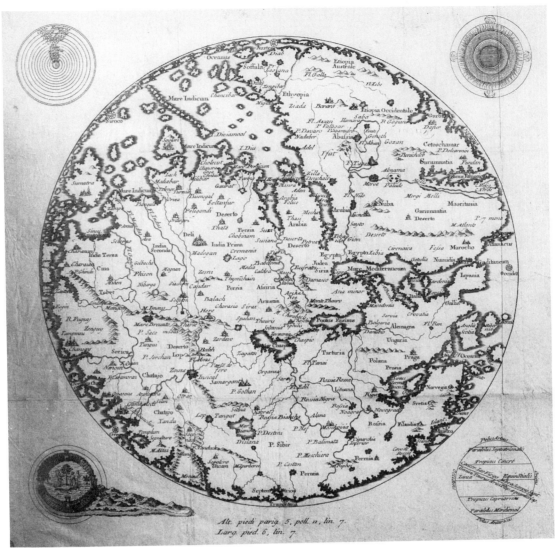

Fra Mauro of Venice made this map of the world for Henry. It now belongs to the Biblioteca Marciana, Venice. *Courtesy of SEF/Art Resource, NY.*

Cape Bojador as possible. By 1446 they had reached points in the Atlantic 1,300 miles below Bojador and 2,000 miles of previously unknown coastline had been added to the navigational charts of the world. By 1457 they were at the Cape Verde Islands, thus proving that the Tropics were navigable and raising the hope that someday European vessels would reach what is now known as the Cape of Good Hope on the southernmost tip of Africa. Meanwhile, many of Henry's explorers had moved inland along the Gambia and other rivers, and at newly built trading centers along the African coast Portuguese traders were doing a lively business in gold dust, ivory, and slaves.

Prince Henry supervised these activities from a collection of buildings on Cape St. Vincent that had become known as *Villa do Infante* (Village of the Prince). Here he immersed himself in the study of nautical matters and surrounded himself with some of the finest mathematicians, astronomers, and mapmakers in Europe. Here he established a school for seamen. Here, except for occasional absences to fight with the armies of his country, he passed his days. And here, on November 13, 1460, he died.

Prince Henry had accomplished more than probably even he realized. He himself never went out on a voyage of discovery, but the innumerable mariners he sent on such ventures laid a foundation on which future exploration would be built.

In 1488 Bartholomeu Dias, the Portuguese navigator, pushed past the Cape Verde Islands to attain the Cape of Good Hope.

About ten years later another Portuguese navigator, Vasco da Gama, rounded the Cape and crossed the Indian Ocean to India.

And in 1492 Italian-born Columbus, sailing for Spain, pushed beyond the islands Prince Henry's men had sighted—the Azores—to discover the New World.

Hoei-shin

Fifth century   Chinese Buddhist monk. Believed to have been one of the first Asians to find and explore portions of North and Central America.

We all know that Columbus discovered America, but we also know that he was not the first person to cross an ocean and stand on the soil of what we think of as the New World. Five hundred years before Columbus touched the northeastern shores of South America, a band of Vikings landed on the northeastern shores of North America. And five hundred years earlier a Chinese Buddhist monk whose religious name was Hoei-shin, meaning Universal Compassion, crossed the Pacific and landed on the western shores of North America.

According to present-day scholars, our main evidence for Hoei-shin's historic voyage is a report of it by Hoei-shin himself—an account that first appeared in one of the annals or re-cords-of-events maintained by the emperors of ancient China. Writing in one of these annals in the year 499, Hoei-shin reported that he had recently returned from a visit to a distant country called Fusang.

He does not indicate exactly where Fusang was. He does say that it lay some five thousand miles east of China, and today scholars interpret that statement in various ways. Some believe Fusang to have been in Alaska or in British Columbia, Canada. Others place it in California, or even Peru, but most believe Fusang to have been in Mexico.

Hoei-shin called the country Fusang because of the presence of "many Fusang trees." It is not clear what sort of trees these were, but it is plain that they were important to the area's economy. They yielded many useful products, including paper, cloth, and wood. There was no iron in Fusang, but copper, gold, and silver were plentiful.

Hoei-shin's description of the customs and manners of the place suggest the existence of a well-ordered and fairly advanced civilization. The people lived in houses "built of wooden beams." They erected "no fortified or walled places," forged no weapons, never went to war, and had a written language.

There was a king and three classes of nobles. Hoei-shin notes that the "name of the king is pronounced Ichi," a statement that has led some modern historians to believe that the citizens of Fusang were forerunners of the Incas, the highly civilized people whom the Spanish conquistadors encountered a thousand years later in Peru. "When the King goes forth," the monk-explorer informs us, "he is accompanied by horns and trumpets. The color of his clothes changes with the different years. In the two first of the ten-year cycles they are blue; in the two next, red; in the two following, yellow; in the two next, red; and in the last two, black."

One gathers that crime was not prevalent. At any rate the people of Fusang built only two prisons. "Trifling offenders," we are told, "were lodged in the southern prison; . . . those confined for greater offenses in the northern. . . . men and women imprisoned for life were allowed to marry" and the children of these unions were "sold as slaves. If a man of any note was found guilty of crimes, an assembly was held . . . in an excavated place. There they strewed ashes over him and bade him farewell."

The domestic animals available in Fusang consisted chiefly of oxen and reindeer. "Stags are used here," writes Hoei-shin, "as cattle are in [China]. . . . and from the milk of the hind they make butter."

In Fusang, according to the monk, "marriage is determined upon in the following manner. The suitor builds himself a hut before the door of the house where the one longed for dwells, and waters and cleans the ground every morning and evening. When a year has passed, if the maiden is not inclined to marry him, he departs; should she be willing, it is completed."

To all this Hoei-shin adds a statement which suggests that he may not have been the first Asian to visit the country of the Fusang trees. "In earlier times," he writes, "these people [in Fusang] lived not according to the laws of Buddha [then the religion practiced throughout China]. But it happened that in the second year-naming Great

Light of Song [A.D. 458], five beggar-monks from the kingdom of Kipin [a part of China] went to this land, extended over it the religion of Buddha, and with it his holy writings and images. They instructed people in the principles of monastic life, and so changed their manners."

Hoei-shin had been dead for over a thousand years when in the late 1740s the story of his trip to Fusang was brought to the attention of modern scholars by Joseph de Guignes, a distinguished French student of Chinese History. De Guignes believed the story, but in the beginning some of the other men and women working in his field did not, one of them contending that the Buddhist storyteller had made it all up and was "a humbug and a liar."

There were others, however, who found the tale fascinating and looked into it. Some went to China to see what they could learn about Hoei-shin in old Chinese texts. Some examined the western coasts of North and Central America, hunting for relics that would substantiate the presence of fifth-century Chinese in the land of the New World.

Those who traveled to China found in its literature many stories inspired by Hoei-shin's report of his voyage to Fusang. Some of these were obviously fables, but others had the ring of truth.

The scholars who traveled to sections of North and Central America were also lucky. One of them, inspecting the coast of California, unearthed some small statues of Buddha, perhaps the very images that Hoei-shin tells us his fellow monks carried to Fusang.

The late eighteenth century saw the appearance of two scholarly books, written by American experts on China, dealing with the Chinese discovery of America: *Fusang* by Charles G. Leland, published in 1875, and *An Inglorious Columbus* by Edward F. Vining, published in 1885. Within the pages of these volumes one finds answers to the two big questions raised by Hoei-shin's narrative of his voyage to Fusang.

Question one: Were the Chinese of Hoei-shin's day interested in exploring other lands?

Most were not. They called their country the Celestial Empire. In their view all that was worthwhile in the world resided within its borders. The people beyond those borders were considered dogs and animals; there was no point in visiting them because there was nothing to be learned from them.

But one group of Chinese did travel frequently beyond the borders of their country: the Buddhist monks. To be sure, most of them headed west to visit the Buddhist shrines in the other countries of Asia. But some traveled east to Japan, where in the sixth century they persuaded the people of that kingdom to embrace the beliefs of their religion.

Question two: Given the small size of the seagoing vessels available to the Chinese in the fifth century—they were little more than open rowboats—could Hoei-shin and his companions have gone from China to Alaska?

They could have. One of the most interesting chapters in Leland's *Fusang* presents comments on this matter by Colonel Barclay Kennon, an American officer familiar with the navigational problems of the North Pacific. According to Colonel Kennon, it would have been easier for Hoei-shin and his friends to sail to America in the fifth century than for the Vikings to sail there in the eleventh century. No matter where the Vikings started from—Europe, Iceland, or Greenland—they would have had to spend several days in the open sea. Hoei-shin and company did not have this problem. They steered

northward along the coasts of Siberia, then eastward across the Bering Sea (the narrow waterway that divides Asia from Alaska), past a string of islands known as the Aleutians. In other words, Hoei-shin and his friends would have been able to keep land in sight for all but a few hours of their journey. They had the shores of Siberia and the Aleutian Islands, a string of islands curving southwestward from the tip of Alaska and dividing Bering Sea from the Pacific, to guide them on their way. As one authority quipped: "Compared with the difficult overland jaunts undertaken by the fifth-century Chinese Buddhists, Hoei-shin's journey to Fusang was a Sunday School excursion."

Well, it did happen long ago. And all we know of it rests on scattered snippets of information, laboriously assembled by curious historians. But one thing we can be quite sure of: Fifteen hundred years ago a handful of devout and daring Buddhist monks stood on the soil of the New World.

Mary Henrietta Kingsley

1862–1900   British explorer, scientist, and writer whose travels in West African regions provided the readers of her books with a greatly enlarged understanding of the African mind.

Mary Kingsley was born on October 17, 1862, in the London borough of Islington, but by early 1864 her parents, George and Mary Bailey Kingsley, had moved the family to Highgate on the northeastern outskirts of London.

Here, in a gloomy box-like house, the Kingsleys lived for sixteen years. Here Mary's brother Charley was born in 1866, and here Mary grew up. It was a strange childhood. As an adult she would become famous as a brilliant lecturer and as the author of books that were both popular and learned. But to this day how she acquired the basis for her learning remains a mystery.

In the England of the Victorian Age, it was customary for an upper-middle-class young lady to be taught a few things (to read and do some sums, for example) either at a school for girls or at home by her mother or a governess. But Mary attended no school, and no governess ever entered the Kingsley home. As for Mary's mother, she'd been a domestic servant prior to her marriage and seems to have been barely literate. Besides, she was a chronic invalid, often bedridden and too concerned with her own symptoms to guide the mental development of her children.

Mary's father, on the other hand, was knowledgeable in half a dozen fields. He was a physician, a scientist, and, like his more famous brothers, the novelists Charles and Henry Kingsley, he had a flare for writing. George Kingsley could have given his daughter a college education. But he didn't. He was a man wholly absorbed in his own interests.

His passion was travel to far and bizarre places. During Mary's growing-up years—first in the Georgian house at Highgate and then in a similar house at Bexley Heath in county Kent—her father's stays at home were brief, often months and sometimes years apart. Perhaps, as Mary's biographer Katherine Frank suggests, Charley taught his sister "the alphabet and a few simple words and sentences and then passed on his primers to her after he began grammar school. Or perhaps Mary, as some gifted children do, taught herself to read." However she began her education, she went through life thinking of herself as dumb. Many self-taught people suffer from this illusion. Mary, for one, continued to regard herself as intellectually lacking even after she had taught herself physics, chemistry, Latin, zoology, some of the mechanical arts, and the elements of ethnography, the scientific study of the various cultural groups of mankind.

At Highgate and at Bexley Heath she seldom ventured beyond the borders of her family's property. In her mind she traveled to the ends of the earth. She idolized her father. She never wearied of hearing of his activities in distant parts. When he did come home, he brought with him voluminous notes on what he had seen and done. It was Mary's job to put them in order for the great book on his travels that he intended to write—but never did. Dr. Kingsley was one of those people who begin many things but finish few.

Mary's ability to produce great quantities of literature with amazing swiftness was not inherited from her father. What she may have inherited from him was her unladylike practice of lacing her speech with swear words. "Where does this child get its language from!" the doctor shouted one evening at his invalid wife. She got it from him, of course. He had a hot temper, and sometimes oaths flew as well as any object that he could put his hands on.

Mary spoke Cockney English, dropping her "h's" like her mother. When a listener at one of her lectures faulted her for dropping "g's," she explained that no doubt she had lost those sounds in her frantic effort to hold on to her "h's." A fine humor flowed through everything Mary said and wrote. It was a gentle humor: She laughed at herself, not at others. It was her way of sparing others the sadness, the sense of being a loner and a misfit, that lay at the core of her being.

When she was not working on her father's notes, she read and reread the books on his library shelves. The works of the eminent explorers of her day received her closest scrutiny. Mentally she walked in the footsteps of Sir Richard Burton and Dr. David Livingstone as those great discoverers penetrated to the heart of Africa. One of her favorite books was *A General History of Robberies and Murders of the Most Notorious Pyrates*. Perhaps it was from the pirates that Mary learned the lingo of the sea. Years later, when an editor altered the nautical terms in one of her books, she protested vehemently. Only in the language of sailors, she scolded, could the arrangement and movement of a ship be described with accuracy.

When she was not reading, she dusted and tidied the house, nursed her ailing mother, and cared for her pet gamecocks and for Mrs. Kingsley's dogs. Such was her life until 1883 when brother Charley enrolled at Cambridge University and the family moved to 7 Mortimer Road in Cambridge to be near him. Dr. Kingsley decided to live at home for awhile. At Cambridge, thanks to her father's high standing in the scholarly world, Mary got about more than in the past. At Cambridge she found people capable of talking about the many things she had taught herself. On the whole, the Cambridge years were happy ones for her.

She was a young woman now: tall, slender, blue-eyed, with golden hair and a high and handsome forehead. Friends noticed that although she was an entertaining talker, she was shy and reserved and ill-at-ease at social affairs. They noticed too that there was no romance in her life. No young men came and went at 7 Mortimer Road. In truth, there was little time for them. Mary continued to be at the beck and call of her demanding and self-centered parents. There were still her father's notes to be handled. Her bedridden mother would eat no food unless Mary cooked it.

Then, in 1892, everything changed. On February 5, quietly and unexpectedly, her father died. Six weeks later her mother died. Suddenly, at the age of thirty, Mary Kingsley was free to do something on her own. Not that all her domestic labors lay behind her. Charley remained on the scene. He was a reasonably bright young man, but he had no sense of direction, no capacity for doing much of anything except some pointless traveling. For the rest of her brief life, Mary would see to it that her brother was comfortable in the London flats they shared after their parents' deaths. She always adjusted her plans to his.

But now, at last, she could make plans. And she did. From the beginning she knew what she wanted to do. She wanted to travel and observe as her father had. She wanted to go exploring like her heroes Richard Burton and David Livingstone.

This portrait of Mary Kingsley appears in her 1901 book, *West African Studies. Neg. 126529, Courtesy of Department Library Services, American Museum of Natural History.*

Her father had loved the tropics. She would go to the tropics. Several European nations, England among them, had established colonies in West Africa. The settlements hugged the coastline. Few Europeans living in them knew anything whatsoever about the dank and wall-like jungle that began only a few miles to the east. It was in this dark and hitherto unexplored region—in this land of gorillas and cannibals—that Mary Kingsley decided to do her work.

Three journeys followed, three "voyages out," as she called them. The first was a practice run. She spent a few months in the Canary Islands. Both aboard the steamers that carried her there and back and on the islands she encountered English people—traders, missionaries and government workers—who lived in West Africa and could tell her the things she needed to know before she went there.

She found what the traders told her especially useful. Indeed, in the course of her subsequent travels she concluded that the traders were the only Englishmen in Africa whose conduct was beneficial to both Africa and England. Later, in the books describing her adventures, she offered many reasons for this conviction.

The traders were in Africa to sell things to the natives. To them, the Africans were customers, and good merchants know the importance of understanding what their customers think and feel. In Mary's opinion, it was otherwise with the government men and the missionaries. Most of them had no idea what the natives were thinking and feeling. The government men, Mary complained, were wasting everybody's time in a futile effort to change the blacks into "imitation Europeans." As for the missionaries, she admired some of them immensely, but their methods struck her as harmful. Like the government men, they were trying to re-create the natives in the image and likeness of themselves. This was wrong, Mary argued, because "people can develop only along the lines of their own development." It was her guess that the missionaries would help neither Africa nor themselves until they began talking to the natives less and listening to them more.

It's worth mentioning that, unlike many of us today, Mary did not condemn colonialism as such. She called herself "an old-fashioned imperialist." England should have colonies, she believed. Every colony was a market for English goods, and each increase in the sale of English goods created jobs for English workers. But her country, she warned—correctly as time has shown—would lose its colonies unless it learned to respect the beliefs and customs of the natives and treat them justly.

Her second voyage out began in August 1893 and ended in January 1894. It took her into the African rain forests along the equator. For weeks on end she lived in the huts of a black tribe known as the Fjorts. She taught herself how to paddle a canoe through dangerous rapids and how to pilot a large ship up West African creeks.

Richard Burton and David Livingstone had financed their explorations with sums provided by scientific societies. Mary asked for no grants. She funded her wanderings out of her own limited income. When this money ran out, she laid in a stock of English goods and supported her investigations by trading with the natives.

Burton and Livingstone traveled with an army of porters, Mary with a few guides and an interpreter. Burton and Livingstone frequently had themselves carried in hammocks slung from the shoulders of husky natives. Mary walked the forest paths. She crossed the crocodile-inhabited streams and swamps the way the natives did: by piling her garments atop her head and swimming.

Friends urged her to don masculine clothes in Africa. She smiled their advice aside. She paced the trails of the jungle exactly as she did the pavements of London, in a long, black silk gown over ample petticoats with a cameo brooch at her throat and a sealskin cap on her head.

One day she fell into a game pit lined at the bottom with tall ivory spikes. Had she been wearing trousers, she might not have emerged alive. The thick folds of her skirt saved her.

The natives, wearing as a rule next to nothing, smiled when they saw her for the first time. One morning, as she roamed the woods, she stepped into a clearing occupied by a group of blacks wearing masks with horns protruding from their foreheads and feathers sticking out. Her first thought was that she had stumbled into an all-male religious ceremony and would be killed if she did not retreat in a hurry. But the men came after her and escorted her back to the clearing.

No, they told her, this was not a religious rite. They were hunting monkeys. Monkeys were curious animals. Sooner or later, seeing these fantastically garbed creatures below, they would come down from the trees for a closer look. Then the men would catch them.

They begged Mary to stay with them. They said her presence would bring the monkeys down fast because she was "much the funniest looking thing" any of them had ever beheld.

She traveled with two goals in mind. One, as she put it, was "to study fish." This was the scientific aspect of her expeditions. With butterfly net and cleft stick in hand, she collected insects and fish and preserved them in bottles. Once back home, she would give these priceless specimens to the zoological department of the British Museum.

Her other goal was to study "fetish," the name students of Africa gave to the religion of its natives. From tribal chiefs and medicine men she acquired a wealth of information about charms and incantations, about witchcraft and funeral rites, about the spirits that the Africans believed to be living in the plants and animals around them.

In time, Mary came to admire the spiritual views of the Africans. "You will often hear this religion of fetish called a religion of terror," she said. "Well, facts are facts; find me a more cheerful set of human beings in this world than the West Africans who believe in fetish; find me a region where crime for private greed is so rare as in West Africa, and then, and not till then, will I say fetish is a horrible thing." Mary admitted that fetish permitted ceremonies during which human beings were slain for religious purposes, "but before you write down the men who do these things as fiends, I ask you to read any respectable book of European history, to face the Inquisition and . . . then go read your London Sunday newspapers."

Her third voyage out began in December 1894. It was during this journey that Mary, accompanied by a few natives, walked from the Ogoue River to the Remboue River—a trek biographer Frank describes as "suicidally risky." There were encounters with leopards and days when Mary and her companions had to struggle through the slime of deep and treacherous bogs.

This was the country of the warlike Fang (pronounced to rhyme with "wrong"). Though the Fang were reputed to be cannibals, Mary not only lived safely in their villages but concluded that she had met one of the most intelligent clans in West Africa. From the land of the Fang she moved on to Mungo Mah Lobeh or "Throne of Thunder," to become the first woman and one of the first Europeans to stand on the sometimes snow-covered peak of a 13,000-foot mountain that today appears on most maps as Cameroon.

When Mary returned to London in November 1895, she found the city unbearably cold, damp, and dreary. For as long as Charley's needs forced her to remain there she thought of her native city as a "place of exile" and of Africa as the "home" to which she longed to return. The newspapers had long since discovered her. She was famous now, and with the publication of her accounts of her adventures, *Travels in Africa* and *West African Studies,* she became even more so.

Soon she was in demand as a lecturer, and much that she had to say from the platform set English tongues to wagging.

Mary defended the African custom called polygamy, the taking by one man of several wives. There was no place in African society, she told her audiences, for an unmarried woman. End polygamy, she said, and thousands of African women would starve to death.

When the British officials in charge of their country's colonies banned the sale of liquor in Africa, Mary exploded. Let those officials now living so comfortably in London go live for awhile in the fever-filled heat of the tropics! How long would they last there without an occasional swig of whisky? Her arguments against Britain's tax on the huts of its African colonials echoed the cry of "No taxation without representation," which had been heard so loudly in America over a hundred years earlier.

In 1899 the Boer War broke out in South Africa—England against the Dutch settlers. Mary volunteered as a nurse, and March 1900 found her tending Boer prisoners of war at the Palace Hospital in Simonstown near the Cape of Good Hope. Enteric fever was everywhere, and a few weeks after her arrival at the hospital she was stricken. Her last request, addressed to her doctor, was that she be buried in the waters off the shores of her "homeland," meaning Africa. Death came on August 3, and on the following day a small torpedo boat put out from the docks of Simonstown. As the teak coffin containing Mary's body was lowered into the ocean, the ship's guns were fired and the members of the crew stood at attention—their way of saying good-bye to a great explorer and a noble lady.

René-Robert Cavelier, Sieur de La Salle

1643–1687 French explorer. Leader of the expedition that traced the Mississippi River to its mouth.

Known to us now as La Salle, a name derived from an estate belonging to his wealthy family, René-Robert Cavelier was born on November 22, 1643, at Rouen, France, the second son of Jean and Catherine Geest Cavelier. Though the Caveliers, La Salle's father and uncle, were untitled merchants, they lived like nobles and numbered among their associates important figures at the court of Louis XIV, king of France.

La Salle received his education at the college of Rouen, an institution run by the Society of Jesus, the Jesuits. On October 16, 1660, he took the first of the vows required of a candidate for the Jesuit priesthood. Six years later, however, he left the Society. We are told that he did this partly because of his dislike of the discipline demanded

of a Jesuit and partly because he was unable to get along well with people—a trait that characterized La Salle's behavior all his life.

In 1667 he sailed for New France, his country's colony in Canada. His destination was Montreal. On his arrival there, the town rulers—members of the religious order known as the Sulpicians, to which his brother, Abbé Jean Cavelier, belonged—gave him a grant of land at La Chine on the western tip of the island in the St. Lawrence River where Montreal stands. Here he erected a village and a fort. From here he carried on, for a few years, a flourishing fur trade with the Indians dwelling in the surrounding wilds.

But a desire for wealth was not La Salle's only reason for having emigrated to the New World. He yearned for the glory that enshrines the explorer who finds new waterways and new lands for his country. There was much talk in Montreal of the existence to the west of a "great water," known to the Indians as the Mississippi. Was this great water the Pacific, the sea believed to lie at the far end of North America? Or was it an enormous river? If it was the Pacific, then cutting a path to it would provide the king with a new commercial route to the riches of China and Japan. If it was a river, then its discovery by the French would discourage the settlers of the British colonies south of Canada from pressing westward across the continent.

In 1669 La Salle began his first journey of exploration, but exactly where he went during the next two years remains in dispute. Some historians think that he located the Ohio River and followed its wanderings at least as far west as the site of present-day Louisville, Kentucky. Others find no evidence to support this contention. To finance his first expedition La Salle sold his holdings at Montreal. On his return he established himself at the northeast corner of Lake Ontario, where he built another palisaded village to be known as Fort Frontenac.

In 1673 he was again pursuing a profitable fur trade with the Indians when an event occurred that was to shape the remainder of his life. Louis Jolliet, a young fur merchant, and Father Jacques Marquette, the engaging Jesuit missionary, found the Mississippi and paddled their slender canoe south, almost to the Arkansas River. Three years later La Salle was in Paris, seeking the permission of King Louis XIV to complete their work by tracing the great water to its mouth on the Gulf of Mexico.

The French were not the first Europeans to explore the Mississippi. A century before Jolliet and Marquette set forth on their 2,500-mile trip on the river, the Spanish conquistadors had discovered it. One of them, Hernando de Soto, died near its banks in 1542 and was buried in its depths. But the Spanish were looking for a cache of gold that they never found, and the sudden appearance of a mighty stream was simply an annoying obstacle. By La Salle's day the finding of the Mississippi by the conquistadors had faded from memory, and the credit for recognizing its importance to the future development of North America must go to La Salle.

The plans he laid before the king of France were those of a man of vision. As the American historian Francis Parkman has written, on the heels of the Jolliet-Marquette journey, La Salle's "imagination took wing over the bound-

King Louis Philippe of France commissioned George Catlin to devote a series of paintings to La Salle, among them "The Expedition Leaving Fort Frontenac on Lake Ontario, November 18, 1678." *Courtesy of the National Gallery of Art, Washington, DC; Paul Mellon Collection.*

less prairies and forests drained by the great river of the west. His ambition had found its field. He would leave barren and frozen Canada behind and lead France and civilization into the valley of the Mississippi."

What he asked from the king was not only permission to track the river to its end, but also the right to build forts and trading centers on the river and its tributaries and to found colonies. To the colonies, the king said no. His Majesty had no desire to see settlements taking form in the dark center of North America, where, due to its remoteness, they might someday slip from his control. But he granted all the other requests, and in the fall of 1678

La Salle, having returned to Canada, began the search that would take him four years to complete.

For La Salle and his second-in-command—Henri de Tonti, a French fur trader and explorer of Italian descent—the long journey was a string of troubles: troubles with some of the Indian tribes and troubles with members of the expedition who chafed under La Salle's high-handed and often harsh leadership.

Near the banks of the Niagara River, La Salle oversaw the construction of the first sailing ship to navigate the Great Lakes. The *Griffin,* as this vessel was named, carried the adventurers to Green Bay on the western shores of

Lake Michigan. But when La Salle sent the *Griffin* north from there with a load of furs to be sold in Canada, it simply disappeared, and he and his followers had to proceed by canoe.

The early weeks of 1680 found them on the southern stretches of the Illinois, one of the tributaries of the Mississippi. At a hastily erected stockade called Fort Crevecoeur, they started to build another sailing ship, only to realize that the tools and material needed to finish it had vanished with the *Griffin*. Leaving Tonti in command of Fort Crevecoeur, La Salle and a few companions trudged the 1,500 miles to Fort Frontenac to collect the necessary materials. By the time they got back, most of the men at Fort Crevecoeur had deserted after destroying the place, and Tonti had retreated northward to Fort Miami, another recently erected stockade near the borders of Lake Michigan.

Meanwhile, war had broken out among the Indians of the region. Traveling from village to village, La Salle undertook to quiet the battling forces so that he and his followers could continue their travels in peace. Even after this difficult goal was attained, there were further delays. La Salle made a business trip to Canada. On his return, he and Tonti established another stockade and trading center on a commanding sandstone hill along the southeastern banks of the Illinois River. They called this

oasis of civilization in the wilderness Fort St. Louis. Some of La Salle's companions remained behind to protect it when, at last, La Salle resumed his hunt for the mouth of the great water.

Not until February 6, 1682, did the canoes of La Salle's expedition glide out of the Illinois into the Mississippi. The descent of the big river was uneventful, and on April 9 La Salle, Tonti, and a little band of Frenchmen stood at its mouth, overlooking the waters of the Gulf of Mexico.

Here La Salle planted a wooden cross, sunk into the ground a leaden plate bearing the arms of his country— and took possession of everything around him for his king. At that moment France became the owner of the vast segment of North America known to history first as the French colony of Louisiana and later, after its purchase for the United States by President Jefferson, as the Louisiana Territory.

La Salle had opened up the American West, and when he reached Paris a few months later Louis XIV was glad to listen to almost any schemes the now famous explorer had on his mind. Indeed, the plan that La Salle laid before his Majesty was so ambitious and daring as to support the charge by some historians that he was given to delusions of grandeur. La Salle asked the king to authorize the establishment at the mouth of the Mississippi of a colony

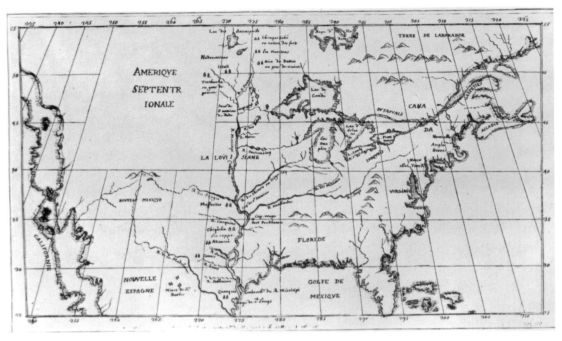

A map of North America shows La Salle's exploration of the Mississippi River from 1681 to 1687. *Courtesy of the New York Public Library, Division of Maps.*

complete with fort to protect France's new lands in North America. He asked for a fleet to carry settlers to the site of this town by way of the Gulf of Mexico. He requested a body of soldiers because France and Spain were at war. Once the colony was in place, the king was assured, he—Robert Cavelier de La Salle—would lead these armed men westward and seize Spain's possessions in the New World.

Years before, La Salle's imagination had taken wing "over the boundless prairies and forests drained by the great river of the west." Now it seems to have winged beyond the borders of reality. To start a colony at the end of the Missis-

sippi was not out of the question, provided the small ships plying the often turbulent waters of the Gulf of Mexico could locate the opening of the river. To propose both the founding of a settlement in the American wilderness, however, and the conquest of powerful Spain's colonies were the dreams of a madman.

But Louis XIV was entranced by these ideas. Four ships and 200 soldiers were provided; settlers were assembled, including carpenters and other artisans to raise the colony's buildings and women to ensure its future citizens.

La Salle wanted to be in charge of everything, but King Louis would not agree to that. La Salle was granted the right to direct the soldiers and the colonists, but Taneguy de Beaujeu, a captain in the royal navy, was put in command of the ships.

With responsibilities split, the expedition began to fall apart. La Salle had left the Jesuits because he could not bring himself to take orders from anyone. His haughty nature rebelled against sharing authority. He and Beaujeu disagreed with one another even before the four ships sailed from Rochelle on July 24, 1684. When Beaujeu suggested a stop at Madeira to replenish the fleet's water supply, La Salle refused, fearing that the captain would tell the Portuguese rulers of the island where his expedition was going. A tendency to have delusions of grandeur was not La Salle's only weakness. He was also paranoid. It is clear from his correspondence that he went through life convinced that most of the people around him were secretly plotting to do him in. In truth, some of them were; but La Salle's morbid suspicions extended even to Henri de Tonti, a consistently loyal friend.

By the time the fleet reached the Gulf of Mexico, La Salle and Beaujeu were barely speaking to each other. The tension generated by their ill will was not lessened by the failure of repeated attempts to find the mouth of the Mississippi. Finally, after almost six miserable months at sea, the members of the expedition landed on the shores of Matagorda Bay in what is now the state of Texas.

Here, on the banks of the Lavaca River, they built a settlement surrounded by wooden walls. La Salle named it Fort St. Louis. Historians now speak of it as Fort St. Louis of Texas to distinguish it from his other Fort St. Louis in Illinois.

One of the ships of the fleet was wrecked during the disembarkation. When Beaujeu sailed away with two of the other ships, the colonists' only lifeline to civilization was a tiny frigate called the *Belle*, which was soon wrecked. They were stranded on a bleak and rolling prairie, framed by a distant forest and peopled by largely unfriendly Indians.

In the beginning La Salle insisted that he had reached the mouth of the Mississippi. Whether he actually believed this or not, one cannot say. It is certain, however, that by the end of 1865 he realized that the great water was many miles to the east and that he must make his way to some settled regions from which he could send a ship to rescue his sick and dying colonists. Twice during the following months he set out in an effort to find the Mississippi and move northward on its waters and on those of its tributaries to Canada. Both times his own failing health forced him back to Fort St. Louis. At last, in the late winter of 1687, he began his final desperate effort to walk to the Mississippi. Awaiting him, as he left the fort with about twenty companions and five pack-horses, was the tragedy that was to end his life.

On March 16, La Salle and his party were encamped within six miles of a place where, on one his previous tramps across Texas, he had left a quantity of Indian corn and beans in *cache*—that is, in some hidden spot such as the hollow of a tree. As provisions were running low, he formed seven of his men into an advance party and ordered them to push forward and find the cache.

Without realizing it, La Salle had signed his own death warrant. All of the individuals he had selected for this mission had reason, or thought they had reason, to despise him. Two of them had put money into the expedition and blamed La Salle for the shambles into which it had fallen. All of the others had their grievances: his cold, aloof, and sometimes insolent manner and the severity with which he punished them for getting drunk and occasionally for indulging in such innocent amusements as singing and dancing—pleasures in which La Salle himself never indulged.

They found the cache of food without difficulty, but its contents had spoiled and they were about to turn back when one of them spotted a herd of buffalo in the near distance. They had shot two of the big animals when a scheme took form among them. They would send one of their number back. He would tell La Salle of their kill and ask him to send forward the horses so that they could drag the meat they had obtained into camp to be cut up and smoked. Sooner or later La Salle himself would come along—and when he did they would be waiting for him in the tall grass of the prairie.

This is exactly what happened. When La Salle arrived two days later on the morning of March 18, 1687, he was shot in the head and killed instantly. There were cries of exultation, historian Parkman tells us, as the assassins gathered around the body of their fallen leader. "With mockery and insult, they stripped it naked, dragged it into the bushes, and left it there, a prey to the buzzards and the wolves."

It was a sad ending to a career marked by one great triumph and an array of misfortunes. Its aftermath was on many counts even sadder. Some of the men who had been traveling with La Salle at the time of his death in his forty-third year did get to the Mississippi, and from there they eventually reached their homes in France. As for the people left at the desolate colony of Fort St. Louis of Texas, in time their plight reached the ears of King Louis XIV, but his Majesty had other matters to attend to and sent no ship to rescue them. When a few years later a band of Spanish soldiers, coming up from Mexico, stumbled upon Fort St. Louis, they found its buildings in ruins and their occupants gone—to what fate, no one will ever know.

Meriwether Lewis

1774–1809   The first American pathfinder, of whom it can be said that he opened the West to the inhabitants of the United States. Commander of the expedition dispatched by President Jefferson to trace a route from the Mississippi River to the Pacific Ocean by way of the Missouri and Columbia rivers.

Born in Virginia on August 18, 1774, precisely a year and a day before the opening skirmishes of the war of the American Revolution, Meriwether Lewis was the second child and first son of William and Lucy Meriwether Lewis.

Locust Hill, the plantation on which he was born, stood so near the hilltop estate of a future president of the United States that in later years, whenever Thomas Jefferson desired the company of his young neighbor, he summoned him to Monticello by jiggling a flashing mirror in the sunlight. These get-togethers started a friendship during which Jefferson came to regard the younger man as the son he never had.

Meriwether Lewis got more than his first name from his mother. When her husband marched off to war, the former Lucy Meriwether was left to defend the plantation and its occupants. For nearly a year the so-called Convention Troops, the British soldiers seized by the Americans in the battle of Saratoga, were bivouacked in the vicinity. Times were hard in war-torn Virginia. Even in Albemarle County, with its productive red-clay soil, hunger was rampant. When one morning some of the captured Redcoats came prowling for food on the Lewis' property, it was Lucy who single-handedly sent them packing.

According to a long-time friend of the family, it was largely from his mother that he gained his attractive traits: intelligence, energy, self-possession in the presence of danger, and loyalty to friends, even though some of them (Jefferson included) proved less than loyal to him.

Lewis was only five when his soldier-father died and his mother, having re-married, moved to a settlement in northeast Georgia with her new husband. As the oldest boy, Meriwether was the master of Locust Hill, but since he was too young to manage the estate of almost one thousand acres, it was left in the care of relatives.

Northeast Georgia was frontier country. Meriwether reveled in its streams busy with beaver and the thick forests of post and blackjack oak. He trapped and hunted. He studied the local animals and plants, acquiring at an early age botanical and geographical lore to which he would continue to add for the rest of his days.

When Lewis was thirteen or fourteen he pronounced himself a man and returned to Virginia to take charge of Locust Hill. He improved the property and acquired additional land in other parts of Virginia and in Kentucky. Eventually he became the owner of so many acres that, as his biographer Richard Dillon has observed, it looked for a time as if Meriwether Lewis might become as "land-poor" as his friend Jefferson. At intervals he attended a small classical school in the neighborhood, but by the age of eighteen he had abandoned his wish to study at the College

of William and Mary and had settled into the life of a gentleman farmer.

Outwardly he appeared content. Inwardly he yearned for activity of a more varied and exciting sort. In 1794, events in the Pennsylvania counties west of the Allegheny Mountains offered him an escape from the humdrum routine of a plantation manager. He leaped at the opportunity. Treasury Secretary Alexander Hamilton had persuaded the United States Congress to impose an excise tax on spirits. The whiskey makers along the Pennsylvania frontier were banding together in an effort to prevent the enforcement of the law. President Washington, determined to quell this threat to the powers of the new federal government, called out 13,000 militiamen, and Meriwether Lewis hastened to join the troops of Virginia. When his regiments reached Pittsburgh in the fall, he was disappointed to discover that the whiskey makers had retreated before the advancing government forces and that the uprising was over.

In a letter to his mother he wrote, "I am quite delighted with a soldier's life." What he most relished about it was the "rambling" it permitted, the chance to see different parts of the country. Instead of returning to Locust Hill, he remained in uniform, shortly becoming an ensign in the regular army. Soon he was serving at a military post in Indian country, where he began his long study of Indian customs and languages. By 1800 he had risen to captain and was "rambling" in the West, moving from post to post as an army paymaster. Then, in the opening months of 1801, he received a letter that was to change the course of his life.

It came from his old Virginia friend and neighbor. Recently elected to the presidency of the United States, Jefferson was seeking a private secretary. He needed someone who was acquainted with the "the Western Country" and with "all the interests of the Army," and especially with its relations with the Indians. In short, he wanted Lewis. The late spring found the captain living at the Executive Mansion, as the White House was then called, in Washington, D.C.

His duties were not exclusively secretarial; he helped Jefferson with his correspondence, but he also supervised the domestic activities of his household. He arranged the formal dinners for foreign diplomats and titled visitors from Europe. On occasion he assisted the President in the conduct of affairs of state.

There is reason to believe that from the beginning Lewis knew that his stay at the Executive Mansion would be short and that another and more de-

manding job was in store for him. This became clear in 1802 when he and the President began poring over maps of North America, planning the exploration that historians would call the Lewis and Clark Expedition. Led by Lewis and his friend, Army Lieutenant William Clark of Kentucky, the "Corps of Discovery"—Jefferson's name for the members of the expedition—were to ascend the 2,475-mile-long Missouri River to its beginnings in the foothills of the Rocky Mountains. From there, they were to cross the mountains and follow the westward-flowing Columbia River to its mouth at the Pacific Ocean.

Behind the desires of the President to learn more about the lands westward of the Mississippi River was his awareness of American feelings and ambitions. In 1802 the United States ended at the Mississippi River, but Jefferson sensed that the day was near when the aggressive and land-hungry Americans would push across the big river, looking for homesteads in the far West. In his inaugural address he had described his country as "a rising nation spread over a wide and fruitful land." At the back of his mind even then, as Lewis's biographer has written, was a determination to "spread the nation wider."

The planning of the Lewis and Clark Expedition required political maneuvering. First Jefferson had to obtain

The prolific C. W. Peale painted this portrait of Meriwether Lewis, who, with William Clark, led the first Westerners to cross North America by land. *Courtesy of the Independence National Historic Park Collection [Missouri].*

funds for the undertaking from Congress. He did this by pointing out to the legislators that British traders, slipping into the Far West from Canada, were making money by purchasing furs from the Indians and selling them in the markets of the world. Surely the time had come for the federal government to establish friendly contacts with the tribes of the area so that the citizens of American could share in this profitable commerce.

Another problem was that the territory into which Lewis and his team were going belonged to the France of Napoleon Bonaparte. Still in the future lay the Louisiana Purchase, that amazing agreement by Napoleon to sell to the new American government the whole of Louisiana. This million or more square miles of land stretching westward from the shores of the Mississippi more than doubled the size of the United States. Would the foreign rulers of these wide-ranging areas consent to the intrusion of a band of wandering Americans? In the hope of persuading them to do so, Jefferson let it be understood that the goals of the impending expedition were "purely literary," meaning purely scientific. In addition, he let the members of his administration leak a lie to the public, saying that Lewis and his Corps of Discovery were not interested in exploring the "big

Muddy," meaning the Missouri River, and intended to confine their attention to the Mississippi.

Whether these ploys would work was still unknown when, on July 4, 1803, Lewis left Washington to move by way of the Ohio River to the vicinity of St. Louis on the western banks of the Mississippi. By this time, Napoleon had signed the Treaty of Cession, making all of Louisiana, St. Louis included, a part of the United States. However, the actual title to the territory had not yet passed, and soon after Lewis's arrival at the Mississippi he learned that until the title did, he could not begin his planned ascent of the Big Muddy.

He and his followers passed the winter of 1803–1804 at a camp on the American side of the Mississippi, eighteen miles from St. Louis and directly opposite the mouth of the Missouri River. At this point, the Corps of Discovery consisted of Lewis and Clark and about fifty so-called *engagés* (volunteers), of whom thirty-one would remain with the expedition from start to finish. Most came from the army. Lewis had chosen some because of their skills as woodsmen, others because of their knowledge of the Indians. Many had been chosen for their hunting ability, for the travelers would have to live off the land.

On April 30, 1803, Louisiana became American property and on May 14 the

Corps of Discovery, traveling in canoes accompanied by a baggage-carrying keelboat, headed up the Missouri.

It was the start of a 4,000-mile trek that was in many ways remarkable. For one thing, it was a great success. Clawing their way up a difficult stream and over difficult mountains, the members of the expedition showed the way to the thousands of Americans who, pouring across the Mississippi in the years to come, would create homesteads, towns, and finally cities and states in the Far West. In the 1840s, when an argument arose over who owned what are now the states of Oregon and Washington, the United States or Great Britain, the United States carried the day by pointing to the passage of Jefferson's Corps of Discovery through those parts of the continent some twenty years before. Indeed, for $18,722, the cost to the government of the Lewis and Clark Expedition, the American people got a lot.

For another thing, the expedition was an amazingly smooth operation. Friction among the *engagés* or friction between them and their leaders—troubles of this sort, so common to long and tiring enterprises—were few and far between. Weak and pliable men are of no value on a long journey over unknown terrain, and it is a measure of Meriwether Lewis's eye for character that few of the strong-willed individuals he selected as his companions ever questioned his authority or disobeyed his instructions.

Jefferson was under the impression that his fellow Virginian was prone to spells of depression, and the brooding blue eyes that gaze at us from the portraits of Lewis suggest as much. But if the people who accompanied him to the Pacific perceived this weakness in him, they said nothing of it, neither then or later. One of the most useful of his attributes was his patient and knowing way with the Indians. More often than not he won the trust of those who at first were less than friendly, and even of those who in the beginning were actively hostile.

From first to last, to be sure, he was fortunate in having a fine man at his side, but it is worthy of note that it was Lewis himself who selected William Clark to be the second in command. Invariably, relations between the two were as cordial as they were correct. Tall, lean Lewis, his oddly soft-looking features rescued from prettiness by a prominent nose, made the decisions and issued the orders. Sprightly, red-haired Clark saw to it that they were carried out.

Since Clark was trained in the art of navigation, he spent much of his time on the boats. He directed the oarsmen, shouting commands and warnings when hazardous narrows or suddenly rushing currents compelled the men to wade waist-deep in the icy waters of the river, pulling the vessels with ropes. Striding along rapidly and purposefully on his bowed legs, Lewis spent much of his time ashore, observing the surroundings and recording his observations in a journal.

In late October the coming of cold weather prompted the travelers to winter in the country of the Mandan Indians, near what is now Bismarck, North Dakota. It was here that they were joined by the Shoshone Indian squaw Sacajawea. Destined to become known to readers of the American press as the Bird Woman, Sacajawea would accompany the expedition to its destination, serving as a guide and, among her own people, as a go-between and an interpreter.

When the members of the Corps resumed their travels on April 7, 1805, they learned quickly why the Indians called the Missouri the "troubled waters." There were frustrating shallows and menacing rapids. In May, windstorms shredded the sails of their boats and drove them to take refuge among the barren brown hills flanking the Big Muddy. When they went ashore to encamp, or hunt, or attend Indian powwows, there were encounters with the grizzly bear, a mean and powerful animal, able and willing to make a meal of a man.

Soon they were passing through plains dark with grazing buffalo. These animals had seen few human beings before. They tended to be friendly to the point of being dangerous. One night a full-grown bull romped through the camp. Its mammoth hooves stomped the earth close to the heads of sleeping men. Mayhem would have followed had not Scammon, Lewis's square-muzzled Newfoundland dog, barked the playful beast away from the area. For several days a buffalo calf took to following Lewis around like a dog.

On May 26, 1805, Lewis sighted in the distance the snow-capped peaks of the Rocky Mountains. At that moment, he wrote in his journal, "I felt a secret pleasure in finding myself so near the head of the heretofore-conceived boundless Missouri. . . . But when I reflected on the difficulties which this snowy barrier would most probably throw in my way to the Pacific it in some measure counterbalanced the joy. . . . But as I have always held it a crime to anticipate evils, I will believe it a good, comfortable road until I am compelled to believe differently."

But it was not to be a comfortable road, as Lewis discovered a week later. Back in the Mandan Country the Indians had drawn in the sand a map showing the course of the Big Muddy to the west of their villages. The map showed all the tributaries that flowed into the Missouri, but now suddenly— off to the right—the members of the expedition confronted a tributary that none remembered seeing on the map.

But was it a tributary? Which stream should they follow? Which stream was the Missouri, the one to the north or the one to the south?

The question had to be answered quickly. Two months of the summer were already gone. They must hurry if they were to reach the Pacific before another winter stopped them. Clark and some of the men went up the southern branch to see what it was like. Lewis took another group up the northern branch.

When a few days later the groups rejoined at the confluence of the two streams, an argument ensued. Clark, his men, and all of Lewis's men believed the southern stream was the Missouri. Only Lewis thought otherwise. No, he said, we'll follow the northern stream; and a few days later the echoing roar of the Falls of the Missouri ahead told the members of the expedition that their leader had guessed right. They carried their boats around the falls, a portage totaling eighteen miles, and moved on.

On July 23, 1805, they reached the Three Forks, the three little rivers in southern Montana that together constitute the source of the Big Muddy. Using Indian horses and Indian guides, they crossed the mountains. October found them floating down the Columbia in canoes, and on November 15 they reached the mouth of the river to find the rolling breakers of the Pacific Ocean stretching out before them.

Winter had arrived, and for the next few months the members of the expedition lived in a hastily built compound named Fort Clatsop after the Indians of the area. With the coming of spring, they began their homeward march, reaching St. Louis at noon on September 23, 1806. From there Lewis hastened east to report to Jefferson, taking with him a number of Indians, the vocabularies of nine different Indian languages, and the skeletons of four bighorn sheep, an animal unknown in the settled parts of the nation.

For months the newspapers teemed with stories of the expedition. Lewis was showered with honors, and on March 3, 1807, Jefferson named him to the governorship of the upper half of the Louisiana Territory.

At this point, Lewis did a strange thing. Instead of hurrying to St. Louis to take up his new duties, he dallied for almost twelve months in Washing-

In Edgar Paxson's painting, the Indian Sacajawea points out the country of her childhood to Lewis and Clark at Three Forks, western Montana. *Courtesy of the Montana Historical Society, Helena.*

ton and in other parts of the East. It was not like him to neglect his work. His biographer describes his behavior at this time as "unaccountable," but it is clear that some of the blame for it lay with Jefferson.

The President liked having his young friend around. He sent Meriwether on errands to Philadelphia. He sent him to Richmond, Virginia, with instructions to watch the trial of Aaron Burr for treason and to report his impressions. The winter of 1808 had passed when Lewis finally arrived in St. Louis on March 8. A morass of problems engulfed him: trouble with the Indians, trouble with the British fur-traders working in the area, trouble with those older inhabitants of the newly Americanized territory, who would have preferred to continue to live under their one-time European masters.

Lewis's health faltered under the strain. He began drinking heavily. He suffered from time to time from what appeared to be nervous breakdowns.

In the spring of 1807, word reached him that a story was making the rounds in Washington, saying that in the fashion of Aaron Burr he was helping to organize a military expedition against the colonies of Spain in the New World. This was a wholly unfounded rumor that prompted Lewis to write to the Secretary of War, "Be assured, Sir, that my country can never make 'a Burr' out of me."

By this time Jefferson had retired from the presidency, and when the new administration refused to honor some of the bills submitted by Lewis as governor of upper Louisiana, Lewis let it be known that he intended to travel to Washington and demand a "fair investigation" of his official acts.

He left St. Louis on September 4. His original plan was to sail down the Mississippi to New Orleans and from there board an oceangoing vessel to go across the Gulf of Mexico and up the Atlantic to the nation's capital. En route downriver, however, he changed his mind. His luggage contained numerous public and private papers, including the sixteen red, morocco-bound volumes of his journal of the Lewis and Clark Expedition. Suddenly, during what seems to have been a spell of mental derangement, he got it into his head that were he to journey all the way by water, these precious papers would be lost or fall into the hands of the British. At once, he decided to proceed overland instead. Accordingly, on the morning of September 29, he set out from a fort on the eastern banks of the Mississippi and began moving north along the Natchez Trace in the direction of Nashville, Tennessee. Ahead of him awaited the ingredients of one of the great unsolved mysteries of American history.

A number of men accompanied him. Among them were Major James Neelly, an Indian agent, a Creole servant named Pernia, and a black servant named Tom. At a place called Dogwood Mudhole, just north of the Tennessee River, two of their horses strayed during the night. When Neelly went in search of them, Governor Lewis rode on by himself. Toward evening he sighted a couple of log cabins and other buildings in a clearing alongside the Natchez Trace. From the woman who greeted him he learned that this was Grinder's Stand and that she was the wife of Robert Grinder, who was some twenty miles away, helping with a harvest.

The governor had told Major Neelly that he would stop at the first white habitation and wait for him there. Could Mrs. Grinder put him up for the night? She agreed and pointed to one of the cabins.

"Do you come alone?" she asked. The

governor said he had not, that his servants Pernia and Tom would be coming along. A short time later they did.

Lewis carried his saddle, pistols, and the portfolio holding his papers into the cabin. When Mrs. Grinder came in to make the bed, he told her not to bother, that his servants would spread a buffalo robe on the puncheon floor and he would rest there.

Later, at a coroner's inquest, Mrs. Grinder described the governor's conduct at this time as puzzling. He ate little of the supper she put before him. Afterward, he requested a glass of whiskey, but when she brought it he took only a few sips. For a time he paced back and forth in the yard, angrily muttering to himself. She was able to make out some of his words, and it is plain that he was rehearsing the statements he intended to make to the authorities in Washington.

When darkness came, Mrs. Grinder prepared a bed for herself in the kitchen, having sent Pernia and Tom to sleep in the loft of a barn 200 yards from the cabins.

Unnerved by her guest's curious behavior, Mrs. Grinder lay awake for hours, only to be startled from a light and uneasy sleep by a gunshot followed by the sound of a heavy object hitting the floor of the adjacent cabin. Next, according to one of Mrs. Grinder's varying versions of the incident, she heard a man's voice saying, "Oh Lord!" Then came another gunshot, and a few minutes later Lewis was at the kitchen door that the woman had bolted from the inside. "Oh madam," he called to her in a strangled voice, "give me some water, and heal my wounds."

The terrified woman crawled to the kitchen wall. Peering through the chinks between the logs, she saw Lewis stagger into the shadows. Soon he was at the door again, scratching on it this time but saying nothing. Mrs. Grinder's only response was to return to her bed.

At daybreak she sent two of her children to the barn to fetch Pernia and Tom, both of whom swore later that they had heard nothing during the night. They found Lewis on the bed in his cabin. A pistol ball had sheared off a portion of his forehead, another had left a gaping wound in his side. According to one of Mrs. Grinder's differing stories, he begged Pernia and Tom to get his rifle and blow out his brains. The first rays of the sun were silvering the treetops to the east when he uttered his last words. "I am not a coward," he said, "but I am so strong. It is so hard to die." The day was Monday, October 11, 1809, and Meriwether Lewis was thirty-five.

Suicide or murder? In the careless investigation that ensued, no real evidence either way came to light, and in our own time historians continue to argue the point. Those who believe it was self-destruction cite Lewis's emotionally erratic behavior during the closing weeks of his life. Those who believe it was murder point out, among other things, that except for twenty-five cents, all of the one hundred twenty dollars Lewis was carrying with him had disappeared and that his papers had been ransacked.

Jefferson was at Monticello when a letter arrived from Major Neelly, telling him of the tragedy. Neelly called it a suicide, and Jefferson believed him. His reaction can be likened to that of a father, suddenly informed that a beloved son has done a disgraceful thing. When in 1811 Jefferson was asked to write a preface to the published journals of the Lewis and Clark Expedition, he maligned his old friend by reiterating the never-proved assertions that during much of his life the leader of a singularly difficult exploration was a victim of "hypochondria" and "sensible depressions of mind."

For almost forty years Lewis's grave at Grinder's Stand alongside the Natchez Trace remained unmarked except for an earthen mound. Then, in 1848, the legislators of Tennessee concluded that the time had come to honor the remarkable man buried in the soil of their state, and a memorial stone was erected. Ironically, the tribute to Meriwether Lewis that appears on the stone is a paraphrase of words written about him by Thomas Jefferson.

"His courage was undaunted," it read. "His firmness and perseverance yielded to nothing but impossibilities. A rigid disciplinarian, yet tender as a father to those committed to his charge; honest, disinterested, liberal, with a sound understanding and a scrupulous fidelity to the truth."

David Livingstone

1813–1873   Scottish medical missionary, geographer, astronomer, ethnologist, anthropologist, chemist, and botanist. Discoverer of Victoria Falls, of several central African lakes, and of the source of the Congo River. Author of books and articles credited with helping to end the slave traffic in Africa.

It has been written of David Livingstone that he never knew what it was to play, that he enjoyed no childhood whatsoever.

During most of his early years he, his brothers and sisters, and his parents, Neil and Agnes Hunter Livingston (as his father always spelled his name)—seven persons in all—lived together in a ten by fourteen-foot one-room apartment in a tenement near the cotton mills that dominated the Scottish town of Blantyre near Glasgow where David began life on March 19, 1813.

At the age of ten he went to work in the mills, where for the next twelve years he toiled twelve and a half hours a day, six days a week. His job was to spot those threads on the spinning frames that seemed about to break and

to place them together—a delicate task requiring great nimbleness, for often he had to crawl under the machine or balance himself above it. Children constituted three-fourths of the work force in the Blantyre mills, and this was what most of them did. Some failed to survive the ordeal. Many came out of it broken in body and in spirit.

Not David. When the workday ended he hastened to the evening school sponsored by the owners of the mills. He studied Latin, botany, theology, and mathematics. Most of the shillings he earned went to his mother. With the few that remained, he purchased scientific works. Somehow he found time to wander the countryside, bringing home specimens of rocks and plants to be identified with the aid of his books.

Where this incredible drive came from is impossible to say, though the influence of his father is obvious. Neil Livingston was a traveling tea salesman. The work paid little, but it satisfied a deeply pious nature by enabling him to distribute religious tracts to his far-flung customers. In a hard-drinking society, the older Livingston touched no liquor. Nor were swear words, least of all those that mentioned the Deity, allowed in his home. Wholly self-educated himself, Neil Livingston understood the value of learning and saw to it that his three sons got all the schooling they could.

In David's twenty-first year his eyes fell on a pamphlet describing the need in some parts of the world for a new kind of missionary, one trained in medicine. Fired by this call, he obtained enough money from his father and a brother to enroll at Anderson's College in Glasgow where in 1838 he qualified as a doctor.

By this time he had been accepted for training by the London Missionary Society. His hope was to go to China, but by 1839 England and China were at war and the decision of the Society was to send the young doctor to Africa instead.

There, in the summer of 1841, he began his lifework. He spent two years at Kuruman in what is now the country of Botswana. Here his superior was Robert Moffatt, founder of the Kuruman Mission and at that time the most famous of the missionaries in Africa. From Kuruman, Livingstone moved on to a place a hundred miles to the north called Mabotsa, where he and another Englishman named Roger Edwards established a new mission.

Livingstone was restless in both places—at Kuruman because another person was in charge, at Mabotsa because he had to share the leadership of the mission with Edwards. Wherever he was, whatever he did, Dr. Livingstone had to be the boss.

Great men often have great faults. One of Livingstone's was his habit of criticizing those whose presence diminished his authority or interfered with his plans. During his years at Kuruman his letters home bristled with criticism of Robert Moffatt. Soon after his removal to Mabotsa he was writing a 9,000-word letter to the directors of the London Missionary Society, berating Edwards as an incompetent.

Before the doctor's departure from England, friends had urged him to marry, citing the loneliness of a missionary's life. He brushed the idea aside then, but in 1844 he was looking closely at Robert Moffatt's older daughters, Ann and Mary. Plump, black-haired Mary was his choice. She was neither pretty nor bright, but she had the qualities Livingstone wanted in a wife: She had lived all but four of her twenty-four years in Africa. She knew how to make candles and soap, how to extract teeth in a dentist-less country, and how to rid the house of fleas by smearing the floors with cow dung.

By the time of their marriage on January 2, 1845, Livingstone was working at a different mission and would soon be moving on to others. Although he was on his own at these places, he remained as restless as ever. Years before, in a letter to the directors of the London Missionary Society, he had outlined in a sentence what he wanted to do with his life.

"I hope . . . ," he wrote, "to work as long as I live beyond other men's line of things and plant the seed of the gospel where others have not planted."

Now, as he shifted his mission from place to place, all his thoughts were on the regions to the north of him—on the vast heartland of Africa where so far no Europeans, save a few traveling traders, had ventured. What would one find in those mysterious wilds? What people, what plants and animals, what mountains and valleys, what lakes and rivers?

He was living in the village of Kolobeng when some natives told him of a distant lake called Ngani, which so far

as they knew no white man had seen. Ngani was 300 miles away. On the small salary of a missionary, the doctor could not afford the supplies such a journey would require, to say nothing of the many porters needed to carry them. Fortunately for him, one of his white friends in Africa, a wealthy sportsman, offered to finance the jaunt—and in the late summer of 1849 the two of them stood on the shores of Lake Ngani. Two more trips followed. In the spring and summer of 1850 they returned to study the lake in detail. During the summer of 1851 they pushed 200 miles past Ngani to find themselves on the banks of the Zambezi, a 600-mile river that begins in Angola (then a Portuguese colony in West Africa), and flows across the continent into the waters off the coast of the then Portuguese colony of Mozambique in East Africa.

Not even his later discovery of the Victoria Falls of the Zambezi, one of the most spectacular sights in Africa, would move Livingstone as deeply as his first look at the Zambezi itself. From where he spotted it, the river was almost 500 yards across, a strong and swiftly moving stream. As the doctor stood there with tears in his eyes, an ambitious scheme formed in his mind—a dream that would direct the course of his life for many years.

His recent travels had provided him

with a revelation. Slave trading was rampant throughout south central Africa. The many tribes were frequently at war, and it was the practice of every chief to sell whatever captives he took to the Arab traders coming into the interior from the island of Zanzibar off the eastern shores of the continent. Every month a caravan of cruelly yoked men, women, and children trekked eastward to be shipped to the huge slave market maintained by the Sultan of Zanzibar. Such glimpses as the doctor had gotten of this traffic in human beings prompted him, at a later date, to write that the "great disease [of Africa] is broken-heartedness," the hopelessness of persons suddenly snatched from freedom and put into slavery.

Why did the Africans sell their own people to the traders? They did it for the products of civilization that they received in return: colored beads, guns, and, most desirable of all in their eyes, a coarse cotton cloth called "Merica" because it was made in the United States.

Livingstone thought, as he stood on the banks of the Zambezi for the first time, that there was a way by which this terrible business might be stopped. He must persuade the merchants of England to come to central Africa with the idea of exchanging beads and guns and cloth, not for human beings, but for the ivory and other valuable products available there. But how could he lure his countrymen into this world of dense jungles and fever-breeding swamps? He could do so, he believed, by proving that they could bring their merchant ships far enough up the river he had just discovered to reach the ivory-rich interior of the continent. The Zambezi, as Livingstone's biographer has written, would be the "highway" by which "legitimate trade would chase out slave trade." By the time Livingstone returned to his mission, he knew what he was going to do next. He was going to examine the Zambezi from end to end, thus assuring himself that a substantial stretch of it could be navigated by British vessels.

The expedition that grew out of this decision was one of the most extraordinary overland journeys in history: a three-year and 4,000-mile march that carried the doctor first west to the Atlantic Ocean and then east to the mouth of the Zambezi in Mozambique. Although this transcontinental walk made Livingstone world famous, it was accompanied by a couple of developments that further illuminate the great faults of a great man.

As he began his preparations for the trip, he realized that he would be away from home for years. What then should be done about his black-haired Mary

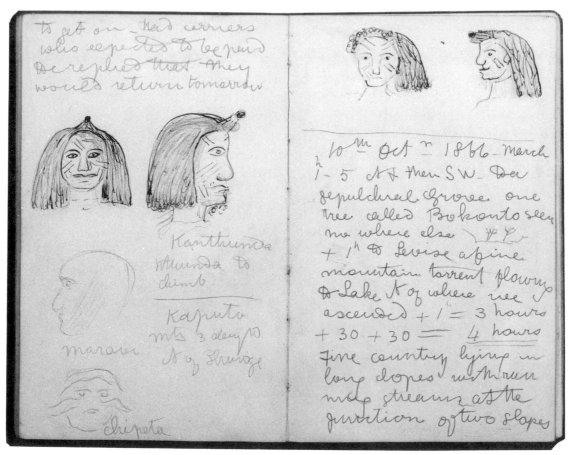

Livingstone sketched the faces of African tribesmen in his journals. *Courtesy of the Scottish National Memorial to David Livingstone Trust, Blantyre.*

and their four young children? His solution to this problem was to send them for a time to England. A different sort of man would have seen to it that his absent family was financially secure, but about such practical matters the high-minded Dr. Livingstone could be insufferably indifferent. In his early years he had overcome terrible hardships, and the experience had left him under the impression that others were equally resourceful and could be depended on to fend for themselves. In England for four and a half years, Mary and her children endured a degree of poverty so profound that Mary took to the bottle and was an alcoholic for the rest of her life.

The other development took the form of a mistake on Livingstone's part, an error he would have reason to regret bitterly. In January 1856 he passed through the town of Zambo, located 500 miles upstream from the mouth of the Zambezi where he was headed. Some seventy miles below Zambo, the Zambezi River takes a wide loop, first to the south and then to the north. Livingstone was tired, worn out from recurrent bouts of malaria. Moreover, he was in a hurry, eager to take ship for England and to inform influential people there that English vessels could move up the Zambezi for at least 800 miles.

Instead of following the course of the river as it turned south and then north, Livingstone decided to shorten the last lap of his journey by walking fifty miles across country to where the Zambezi once more resumed its eastward flow to the sea. As a result of this decision, the doctor arrived at the mouth of the river, unaware of the existence, some 250 miles upstream, of the Kebrabasa Gorge where the Zambezi plunges down a series of cataracts that no vessel larger than a canoe can navigate. In other words, the Zambezi was not, as Livingstone believed, an open highway to the African interior.

His failure to discover this fact is difficult to understand. Granted he himself had not seen the Kebrabasa Gorge, but in the course of his travels he had encountered people who had. Did they tell him about it? If so, did he simply ignore what they had to say out of wishful thinking—out of a determination, during his subsequent stay in England, to spread the word that British merchants could use the Zambezi to trade with the tribesmen of central Africa?

His visit home, the first since becoming a missionary in Africa, was a triumph. Everywhere he was hailed as England's greatest explorer. When his presence in the congregation of a church was revealed, the services stopped while people struggled to shake his hand. He was feted, lavished with honors, and given a private audience with Queen Victoria. When he returned to Africa, it was as the leader of a government-sponsored investigation of the river he had discovered— an undertaking that would go down in history as the Zambezi Expedition of 1858–1863.

It was a disaster. Within weeks it was clear that river steamers could not travel beyond the rapids of the Kebrabasa Gorge. Never one to be deterred by setbacks, Livingstone shifted his attention to a tributary of the Zambezi, but that too turned out to have impassable cataracts. In addition, much of the region it watered was a morass of jungle and mosquito-infested swamp. Several of the people connected with the expedition died.

Among these was Mary Livingstone. Brought by warship to the mouth of

David Livingstone and his family posed for this photograph in 1857. *Courtesy of the Scottish National Memorial to David Livingstone Trust, Blantyre.*

the Zambezi to rejoin her husband, Mary was ill at the time of her arrival in January 1862. During a run of the expedition vessel up the river, her condition worsened, and in April she was taken ashore and died on a mattress supported by packing boxes in a dark waterfront hovel. She was forty-one years old.

In 1864, when Livingstone visited England again, there were no festivities for him, no honors, no invitations from the queen. The people were giving their hearts to another African explorer, a young army officer named John Hanning Speke. Some were saying that Speke had found the answer to a question geographers had been asking for 1,600 years. It had to do with the Nile, the great river that flows through Uganda, the Sudan, and Egypt, and makes the desert bloom. Where in the depths of Africa did that fabulous waterway begin?

In what is now Tanzania, Speke had recently discovered the inland sea known as Lake Victoria, and at a place called Ripon Falls along the upper shores of this huge spread of water was a stream that he contended was the source of the Nile.

But was it? Livingstone thought not. His guess was that the Nile began south of Lake Victoria, that the headstream (its true source) was a river carrying the watery-sounding name of Lualaba. Time would prove that Livingstone was wrong, that the Lualaba was the source, not of the north-moving Nile, but of the west-moving Congo. Time would also prove that Speke was essentially correct, but neither man would live long enough to know of these findings.

By March 1866 Livingstone was back in Africa, beginning what was to be his last exploration. His announced purpose was to show that the Lualaba River contained the headstream of the Nile. He did not achieve this for reasons already mentioned, though this expedition would prove to be the most important of his career by providing the people of the civilized world with their first real knowledge of vast sections of the interior of Africa.

During the Zambezi disaster, numerous Europeans had accompanied the doctor, but on this venture there were none. Except for a few Arabs and natives of India, all the members of his little band were Africans.

This was fine with Livingstone. He did not work well with Europeans; he preferred the company of Africans. He liked the way they did certain things, especially the way every tribal chief acted as a father to his people, seeing to it that no member of the tribe went hungry or homeless. It grieved him that so few of the natives could be induced to embrace the religion in which he had been reared, but unlike many other missionaries, he understood why this was so. The natives, he realized, saw in Christianity a threat to those social customs—polygamy (the taking by one man of several wives), for example— that held their societies together.

Other missionaries said the blacks rejected the Gospel out of stupidity. Not so, said Livingstone. What the Africans knew from everyday experiences, he wrote, showed more intelligence on their part "than was to be met within our own [Britain's] uneducated peasantry."

Moving into the center of the continent, the doctor traveled widely in the vicinity of Lake Tanganyika and along the banks of the Lualaba. As the years went by and no news of his activities reached the outside world, the suspicion arose in England that he was lost. In March 1867 the London press was publishing a report that some of his African followers had killed him. Newspapers ran obituaries, only to wish they had not, for in January 1868 letters written by Livingstone were in the hands of a British official. The dates on them indicated that the doctor was still alive, still someplace in Africa. But where?

In October 1869 James Gordon Bennett, the proprietor of two large New York newspapers, the *Herald Tribune* and the *Evening Telegraph*, ordered his best foreign correspondent, Henry Morton Stanley, to organize a search party. For this purpose Stanley was to have all the money he needed. "Draw a thousand pounds now," Bennett said to him, "and when you have gone through that draw another thousand, and when that is spent draw another thousand, and when you have finished that draw another thousand, and so on; but FIND LIVINGSTONE."

Find him he did, and the meeting in the depths of Africa of the young reporter and the ailing missionary has since received more attention than any other incident of Dr. Livingstone's life. Exactly when it happened remains a matter of dispute, although good evidence dates it November 3, 1871.

In recent months, the doctor had fallen on hard times. His supplies were almost gone. New ones sent by the British authorities had been seized by plunderers before they could reach him. Most of his followers had deserted and he was ill. As he observed in a letter home, his once stalwart frame was reduced by pneumonia to "a ruckle of bones."

Unable to continue his wanderings for the time being, he had retired to Ujiji, a trading center on the eastern shore of Lake Tanganyika. He was living in a small house there, attended by five Africans whom he had befriended in times past and who would never leave his side.

He had not seen another white man for six years when on that autumn morning of 1871 Welsh-born Henry Stanley marched into Ujiji at the head of one of the most abundantly equipped expeditions ever seen in the area. Livingstone was told of the reporter's arrival. He was standing outside the door of his house when Stanley came striding up the street accompanied by a husky native carrying the Stars and Stripes. Stanley was a man of mammoth self-confidence, but as he halted in front of the waiting doctor he was seized with racking uncertainty. Could this sick old man, he wondered, be the great explorer he had been sent to locate?

"Dr. Livingstone, I presume?" he said.

Stanley's theatrical words to Livingstone in Ujiji in 1871 were for years the subject of jokes, of vaudeville skits and newspaper cartoons.

An English official encountered by Stanley on his way to Ujiji had said that Livingstone would not welcome him, that the great explorer had little liking for white men and even less for publicity. On the contrary, to Stanley's great relief, the doctor was delighted to see him, even more so when the reporter arranged to give Livingstone half of the supplies and many of the baggage carriers he had brought along.

The two men spent pleasant and talk-filled months together. At Stanley's suggestion the doctor wrote a couple of articles describing the horrors of the slave trade in Africa that he had witnessed. Their appearance in the *New York Herald* incited an uproar in Europe that a few years later compelled the Sultan of Zanzibar to close down the slave market on that African island.

Stanley urged Livingstone to return with him to civilization. The doctor refused, saying that his work in Africa was not yet finished, and after Stanley's departure on August 1, 1872, he resumed his futile search for the source of the Nile.

This time his travels took him over some of the most difficult terrain he and his attendants had ever encountered. Day after day, mile after mile, they slogged through clinging mud, across broad and sedgy streams. Cold rains pelted them; red ants and blood-sucking leeches attacked them. Though much of the doctor's long-kept journal had departed with Stanley, he continued to record his impressions of everything he saw. Nothing, however trivial, escaped his attention—nothing that might give future readers a picture of the interior of Africa.

"As I sat in the rain," he writes, "a little tree-frog about half an inch long, leaped onto a grassy leaf and began a tune as loud as that of many birds, and

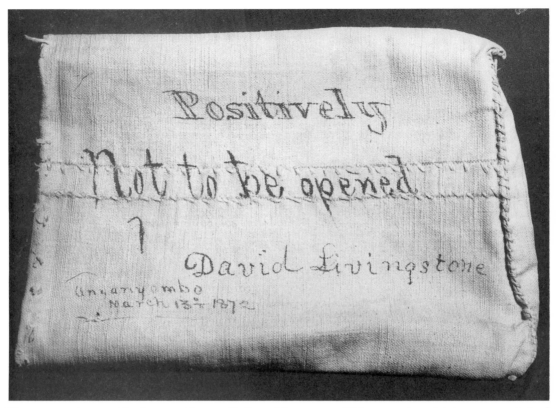

To communicate with the outside world from his remote African station, Livingstone stitched his journals and letters into canvas bags, which he would give to traders heading for the coasts. This package, his last, was given to Henry Stanley. *Courtesy of the Scottish National Memorial to David Livingstone Trust, Blantyre.*

very sweet. . . . I crossed a hundred yards of slush waist deep in mid-channel, and full of holes made by elephants' feet, the path hedged in by reedy grass, often intertwined and very tripping."

His strength was ebbing. It was a fever one day and effusions of blood the next. The nearest thing to a complaint to find its way into his journal was the statement of April 19, 1873: "It is not all pleasure this exploration."

Four days later his legs suddenly gave out. Two of his long-time followers, Susi and Chuma, pieced together a *kitanda* (a stretcher), on which to carry him. They knew he was dying; all the members of the caravan knew it—all, that is, except Livingstone himself. He continued, as he had for twenty-eight years, filling his journal with precise geographical observations: the temperature from day to day, the size of rivers, the direction and speed of their currents. The last observation he ever recorded, the entry in his journal for April 27, was a testament to his incorrigible optimism.

"Knocked up quite, and . . . recover," he wrote, "sent to buy milch goats. We are on the banks of R [the river] Moliambo."

His attendants had brought him to the village of Chitambo, in what is now Zimbabwe, seventy miles south-southeast of Bangweolo, a lake the doctor himself had discovered. Here they built a hut for him and took turns seeing to it that he got his medicine and drank his milk, the only food he could digest. He could no longer move on his own and had to be helped along. On the evening of April 30 he was heard saying to himself, "Oh dear, dear!" Then he fell asleep.

At 4:00 A.M. the boy who had been left at his bedside rushed into the adjoining cabin where Susi was staying. The boy too had fallen asleep, and had just awakened. He was blubbering, saying that something strange had happened. Hurrying next door, Susi was startled to see that somehow Livingstone had dragged himself from his bed. He had assumed a kneeling position on the floor, his head lying on the cot. Susi's first thought was that he was praying, but when he touched the doctor's cheek he found that it was cold. Livingstone had been dead for hours.

* * *

On April 18, 1874, his remains were borne through the streets of London to be buried in Westminster Abbey. It was one of the largest funerals the city had seen. The Prince of Wales was on hand, as was the Prime Minister. Thousands of people lined the thoroughfares as the procession passed.

Few if any of them could have said exactly what it was that Dr. Livingstone had accomplished, either as a missionary or as an explorer. What they did not know was that during his twenty-eight years as a missionary in Africa he had brought only one native to Christianity—and shortly after that conversion, the individual concerned, a tribal leader, had gone back to the beliefs of his forebears. Forgotten by most of them were the tragic disasters connected with his explorations of the Zambezi River. All these silent mourners knew, and these things only vaguely, was that Livingstone had gone to places no white man had trod before; he had done more than any single man to abolish the slave trade in Africa; he had come close to losing his life to an attacking lion, and he had good-naturedly endured a hundred other perils. In their minds, he had conducted himself as a true Briton should, and they were proud of him.

Sir Alexander Mackenzie

1764–1820   Scottish-born fur merchant in Canada. Discoverer of the river that bears his name. Leader of the first expedition to cross North America.

Born in 1764 at the fishing station of Stornoway on the northernmost island of the Scottish Hebrides, Alexander Mackenzie was about ten when he crossed the Atlantic with his widowed mother. They settled briefly in Johnstown, New York, before traveling on to Montreal, Canada. In part, this move seems to have been dictated by Mrs. Mackenzie's belief that her son would get a better education in Great Britain's fourteenth colony in the New World. In part, it revealed her desire to escape the disturbances in upstate New York occasioned by the beginnings of the war that a few years later converted the other thirteen colonies into the independent United States.

Of Alexander's education in Montreal we know nothing. Plainly he had a head

for figures and a flare for business. By his fifteenth year he was working in the countinghouse of a Mr. Gregory. By his nineteenth year he was traveling on his own between Montreal and Detroit as a merchant. And by the age of twenty he had joined with a number of other young merchants to form a fur-trading enterprise called the North West Company.

In the eighteenth century the fur trade was Canada's major industry. Indeed, it was the economic lifeline of the area. This was true back in the days when the little settlements fringing the waterway of the St. Lawrence River were known as New France and belonged to the French kings. It remained true for many years after 1763 when, at the close of the French and Indian

War, New France fell to the British and became Canada.

Mackenzie has left us a written description of how the fur trade operated in his day. On the shores of some of Canada's countless lakes and rivers the managers of a trading company constructed what they called "factories," meaning warehouses. They stocked them with goods manufactured in England "coarse woolen clothes . . . , milled blankets . . . , arms and ammunition; twist and carrot tobacco; kettles of brass and copper; silk and cotton handkerchiefs; hats, shoes, and hose; calicos and printed cottons. . . ." Experienced boatmen, called *coureurs des bois* (runners of the woods), loaded these items onto their birchbark canoes and carried them into the Indian country to be exchanged for the skins of the numerous fur-bearing animals that the natives hunted. From the warehouses, to which the *coureurs des bois* then returned, the skins were shipped to the great marketplaces of Europe, the United States, and China.

The Canadian fur trade was a valuable enterprise, and for over a hundred years "the Great Company"—the famous organization known both as the Governor and Company of Adventurers of England Trading into Hudson's Bay and the Hudson's Bay Company—conducted ninety per cent of the business. Behind

the founding of the North West Company in 1787 was the determination by Mackenzie and his friends to break this old and profitable monopoly.

It was no simple task. From Hudson Bay on the far east of the lower part of what is now the province of Alberta, the trading posts of the Governor and Company of Adventurers of England Trading into Hudson's Bay dominated the Indian trails. To obtain the furs they needed, the Nor'westers, as Mackenzie and his associates came to be known, had to push north and west in search of native hunters living outside the trading area of the Great Company.

Locating Indians willing to provide the new company with furs was one of Mackenzie's main jobs, one that took him on long journeys through previously unknown parts of Canada. The explorer-historian Vilhjalmur Stefansson attributes the ease with which Mackenzie could persuade the natives to his practice of treating them as equals. " 'The only good Indian is a dead Indian,' " writes Stefansson, "is the slogan of the immigrant farmer who wants to dispossess a hunting people . . . [so] that he may raise wheat, corn, and cotton. It was therefore almost exclusively a United States slogan. Canada [with minor exceptions] did not act upon it. . . . The pioneers who opened up for Europeans the continent farther north than the Great Lakes were in the main fur traders, to whom the only good Indian was a live Indian, for only live Indians could bring in furs to trade."

Among the many difficulties confronting the founders of the North West Company was the problem of getting their goods to market. From its ports on the eastern rim of Canada, the Hudson's Bay Company controlled most of the Atlantic sea-lanes. To reach the markets of the world beyond Canada the Nor'westers had to send their products down the winding channels of the St. Lawrence River. This was a long and costly undertaking. No sooner were Mackenzie and his associates organized to do business than they began casting about for a better route.

Soon they were wondering about the Pacific Ocean. It was common knowledge that the Spanish and English had established trading ports on the North American coast of that sea.

Perhaps the Nor'westers could do the same. The problem was how to get there. In 1787 no white man had ventured into the Canadian wilds west of central Alberta. Could a path to the Pacific be cut through those unknown regions?

It was in the hope of answering this question that on June 3, 1789, Mackenzie set out on the first of his two exploratory journeys. For some years he had been making his headquarters at Lake Athabasca in Alberta. During his rambles into what are now Canada's Northwest Territories he had sighted on the upper shores of Great Slave Lake the beginnings of what appeared to be a large river flowing west. It was on this stream that he embarked, only to realize on reaching its mouth on July 12 that the long river which today carries his name flows not west into the Pacific but northwest into the icy waters of the Arctic Ocean.

Back to the Athabasca he went, disappointed but far from ready to give up. Presently he was planning another journey, and this time he knew that none of the streams in the vicinity of his headquarters could take him to the Pacific because the Canadian Rockies were in the way. To reach the Rockies he had to battle the currents of one of the rivers that began in the foothills of those mountains and flowed more or less north. The Rockies had to be traversed on foot. Only on the far side of them could he hope to find streams that ran west to the sea.

When on June 3, 1792, he began his second journey of exploration, he traveled on a broad north-flowing river called the Peace. From time to time rapids or rock-strewn shallows compelled Mackenzie and his crew to disembark and proceed on foot for dis-

Alexander Mackenzie explored the Northwest Territories of Canada. Portrait by Sir Thomas Lawrence, *Courtesy of the National Gallery of Canada*.

tances varying from 75 to 300 paces. The *coureurs des bois* called some of these carrying-places *portages*. Others, they called *décharge*. At a portage both the canoes and their cargoes had to be carried overland. *Décharge* identified a place where only the goods had to be carried and the boats could be left in the water and towed to the end of the carrying-place.

On the first of November the travelers reached Fort Forks, a few miles upstream from where the Smoky River empties into the Peace and near the site of the present town of Peace River. This, in 1792, was the last outpost of European civilization in Canada. Beyond stretched a densely forested country into which no white person had ever stepped.

At Fort Forks, in hastily built log cabins, Mackenzie and his companions passed the winter. Stefansson finds it significant that during these bone-chilling months no member of the party fell ill. Stefansson credits this remarkable fact to the presence of game in the area and to Mackenzie's foresight in having brought along an ample supply of pemmican, a highly condensed food made from jerked and pounded meats soaked in their own fat. Stuffed into easily toted sacks, relatively small amounts of it can feed large numbers of people for long periods. Invented

by the Indians, pemmican is tasty and nutritious; and in all climates it lasts almost indefinitely. Above all it is an antiscorbutic. To people traveling in areas devoid of fresh meat and vegetables it provides protection against scurvy, the dreadful disease caused by a lack of ascorbic acid in the diet. Many years later the explorers Robert E. Peary, discoverer of the North Pole, and Roald Amundsen, discoverer of the South Pole, would be grateful to Alexander Mackenzie for demonstrating the enormous value of pemmican.

On May 2, 1793, Mackenzie resumed his journey, moving southwest on the waters of the Peace. With him this time were four Canadian boatmen, two Canadian women, and a couple of Indians who served as guides and interpreters. The travelers had put a hundred miles behind them when on the afternoon of May 17 they caught their first glimpse of the Rockies.

From this point on, the going became increasingly difficult. As the mountains closed in around them, the Peace narrowed, sometimes to as little as ten yards across. Its currents intensified, occasionally, as Mackenzie noted in his journal, moving with the speed of "an arrow shot from a bow." Rapids and waterfalls slowed them. Portage succeeded portage. So rough was the terrain at one of these carrying places that

J. D. Kelly executed this watercolor representation of Mackenzie's first glimpse of the Pacific. *Courtesy of Art Gallery of Ontario; gift of Ralph Clark Stone Ltd.*

for three days they could advance only by cutting a road through the rocks. Another hundred miles lay behind them when on June 12 they reached the source of the Peace, a mountain lake two-miles square ringed by a forest of spruce and pine.

Crossing the Rockies, they journeyed sometimes by land, sometimes across small lakes or up racing rivulets. Twice the swift currents of these mountain streams smashed their canoe against protruding rocks, compelling them to land and make repairs. When a third such accident threw all of them into the river, calls to some Indians en-

camped on the nearby shore were unavailing. Instead of coming to their rescue, the braves and their squaws seated themselves on the bank, shook their heads sympathetically, and shed some tears.

These were by no means the first natives to be encountered. Coming up the Peace and over the mountains, the members of the expedition had encountered half a dozen tribes. When they finally reached the dark valleys to the west of the Rockies, they encountered others. All were friendly, but getting accurate information out of them proved to be a frustrating endeavor.

How far west was the sea? Mackenzie asked them. Was there some large navigable river up ahead that could carry him and his companions to the coast? So vague and conflicting were the Indians' answers to these inquiries that Mackenzie himself had no choice but to stake out a track as best he could.

The sixteenth of June brought the party to the banks of the 785-mile-long river now known as the Fraser. According to the Indians, this stream emptied into the ocean; but it followed a winding course and was broken by many cataracts. On July 1 Mackenzie and his group left the Fraser to march west on foot. Not until the end of the month did they come to a little stream called the Bella Coola that by July 20 had carried them to the Pacific at a small cape opposite the northern tip of Vancouver Island.

*   *   *

Thus did Alexander Mackenzie, the first man to cross the American continent north of Mexico, open up the Canadian West. Our knowledge of the remaining years of his life consists of the merest bits and pieces. Due in part to his efforts, the fur company he and his friends had founded prospered, and he prospered with it. In 1804 he was elected to the legislative assembly of lower Canada, holding this post until 1808. In 1812 a grateful government knighted him, and during that same year he moved back to Scotland, married a Miss Mackenzie, and purchased an estate at the village of Avoch in Ross-shire. He was on his way to Edinburgh with his wife and children when a sudden illness struck him at Mulnain near Dunkeld, where he died on March 12, 1820.

Ferdinand Magellan

ca. 1480–1521   Portuguese-born mariner who, in the employ of Spain, led the first expedition to circumnavigate the globe.

At Sabrosa, Portugal, where Magellan was born in the spring of 1480, he was known as Fernão de Magalhães. It was not until his thirty-seventh year, after moving to Spain, that he became Fernando Magellanes, the version from which Ferdinand Magellan, the name by which English-speaking people remember him, was derived.

The third child of Roy and Alda Magalhães, he passed his boyhood on a farm in the northern province of Minho. In his twelfth year his father, a member of the local nobility, enrolled him in the royal School for Pages.

Elsewhere in Europe these institutions operated under the eye of the king: Magellan's school was attached to the court of Queen Leonora because plots against the life of King John II

were so commonplace that his court had become an armed camp, endlessly moving from place to place.

At the queen's school, Magellan learned etiquette, swordsmanship, music, dancing, and jousting. These skills were taught in all page schools, but at Leonora's court the students also had to study mapmaking, astronomy, and celestial navigation—the steering of a ship by observing the positions and movements of celestial bodies, the sun by day and the stars by night.

The inclusion of these subjects reflected the intense interest in seamanship and exploration of a country washed by the waters of the Atlantic Ocean. This interest went back to the days of Henry the Navigator, the Portuguese prince who in the 1430s established on the southern shores of his country a school of the maritime arts and sciences. Thanks largely to Prince Henry, Portuguese ship captains were the first Europeans to sail down the coast of Africa, founding trading centers for their king as they went and proving that human beings could live in the tropics, previously regarded as uninhabitable.

By the time Magellan entered page school, the Portuguese navigator Bartolomeu Dias had rounded the bottom of Africa, discovering and naming the Cape of Good Hope. Underway was one of the great eras of exploration. During Ferdinand's first year at court, Christopher Columbus, sailing under the flag of Spain, reached some of the outlying islands of the New World. A few years later Vasco da Gama, flying the flag of Portugal, sailed around Africa and crossed the Indian Ocean to India and the nearby islands known as the Moluccas or the Spice Islands. Da Gama's return home—the holds of his vessels crammed with spices and silks, emeralds and pearls—was a memorable day for Portugal. Overnight one of the poorest nations of Europe became one of the richest.

None of these events went unnoticed at the royal page school. Soon every student was dreaming of the day when as a ship's officer he could sail eastward like Vasco da Gama in search of the riches of the Orient or westward like Columbus in search of new places. No member of the school dreamed more ardently of these things than Magellan. None was more keenly aware of how unreachable they seemed to be.

Supervisor of the page school, when Ferdinand got there, was the handsome brother-in-law of the king, Duke Manuel. And "from the start," writes C. M. Parr, one of Magellan's biographers, "Manuel took a dislike to Ferdinand." Why this was, no one can say. Parr suggests it may have been due to some schoolboy prank. Or perhaps it was because the political views of Ferdinand's parents differed from those of the duke. Whatever the cause, Manuel's "grudge" against Ferdinand was an enduring one. For a page to acquire employment at sea he had to have powerful friends at court, and Magellan's already wavering hopes flickered out altogether in 1495 when King John was assassinated and Duke Manuel succeeded him on the throne.

For Magellan the next nine years were frustrating ones. Though he held a small post at court, his efforts to join one of the ships frequently sailing for the East Indies from the docks of Lisbon fell before the unrelenting enmity of King Manuel. Then in 1504 the king ordered Admiral Francisco Almeida to

Ferdinand Magellan commanded the first circumnavigation of the globe. *Courtesy of The New-York Historical Society.*

India with the largest armada ever to leave Portugal: twenty-two ships of the type known as caravels and almost 2,000 men. Magellan saw his chance. At age twenty-four he had long since learned his way around court. First, he obtained a leave of absence from his trifling job, taking care not to reveal his reasons for requesting it. Then he enlisted as a common sailor aboard one of the caravels of Almeida's fleet.

Arabs still controlled the trade between the lands of the East and Europe, and Almeida's orders were to transfer this flourishing commerce to Portuguese hands by destroying the trading centers the Arabs had founded along the eastern coast of Africa and the western or Malabar Coast of India. For eighteen months the armada operated in the Indian Ocean off the East African seaboard, attacking port after port and chasing their occupants into the jungles beyond. There were blockades and massacres, with Magellan fighting so ably that in December 1505 he was promoted to pilot's assistant and put in charge of an oar-propelled barge equipped with six light cannons. By the time the armada left East Africa for India, he and his small crew had sunk over 200 Arab vessels.

His reward for these devastations was another promotion. He had become second-in-command of a portion of the armada with the rank of captain when in early 1509, in one of the bloodiest ship-to-ship battles on record, Portugal took over the trading centers along the Malabar Coast. During this encounter Magellan, according to an old Portuguese chronicle, was "wounded nigh unto death," to recover only after five months in a hospital.

From India the ship on which he was serving moved on to Malacca, a thriving hub of commerce at the southern end of the Malay Peninsula. Here, in a skirmish with the forces of the sultan of the area, he was wounded again, this time less seriously. Here, too, he acquired a thirteen-year-old slave named Black Henry, who would remain at his side from then on, along with the command of a caravel that Magellan himself had acquired from the enemy.

It was aboard this vessel that he went on a mysterious journey eastward. Most of what we know of this event is contained in a few sentences in one of the old chronicles. In 1511, this source tells us, Magellan sailed "beyond the Spice Islands into seas no Christian man had as yet entered into" and there came upon new lands. But what new lands? Noting Magellan's determination many years later to find and set foot on the Philippines, some of his biographers conclude that those were the islands he discovered on that curious expedition of 1511.

On his return to Malacca, Magellan

got into trouble—an incident that tells us something about his character. He was an honest man. Indeed, in this instance, he was too honest for his own good. He submitted a report of his voyage, saying that he had found some islands but that he could not claim them for Portugal because they belonged to Spain. He based this statement on an agreement known as the Treaty of Tordesillas, signed by the kings of Portugal and Spain years earlier. This document divided the non-Christian world in two by drawing an imaginary line around it from pole to pole. All lands east of this line belonged to Portugal and those west of it to Spain.

Magellan's assertion that the regions he had discovered were the property of another nation so annoyed his superiors at Malacca that they sent him home to be punished by King Manuel. The king was happy to oblige. He demoted Magellan in rank, put him on half-pay, and sent him as a soldier to North Africa, where the Portuguese were warring with their enemies, the Moors.

Again Magellan was wounded. A lance pierced his right knee and left him lame for life. Again he fell into trouble. Charges were brought against him, one of them accusing him of committing treason by doing business with the enemy. Again he was shipped home to be punished.

There was talk of a court martial, but before it could take place, the charges against him were dropped. He might have preferred the rigors of a trial to the situation in which he now found himself. Suddenly he was a master mariner without a ship, an army officer without a command. Worst of all, the little access he once had to the king was gone. Bored and restless, he cast about for some way of reaching the royal ear.

The opportunity came in October 1516 when King Manuel, enthroned in one of the courtyards at the royal palace, permitted the common people to approach him with whatever requests they had in mind. All day a string of favor-seekers, one after another, knelt at the king's feet. The sun was setting when a herald announced the name of the last of them.

"Fernao de Magalhães," he intoned. There was a stir among the attendants. Magellan was still a member of the royal household, albeit in a lowly post. It was a measure of the depth to which he had fallen that now he had to humble himself in public.

Magellan limped forward awkwardly, a short, heavyset man, with a square, weatherbeaten face. Sinking to his knees at the edge of the gold and ebony dais supporting the throne, he began by reciting his record: the battles he'd fought for his country, the wounds he'd suffered. Then he requested a raise in pay and rank. The king said no.

Magellan stayed where he was. He had another request, that he be given command of one of the royal caravels being prepared for a voyage to the Spice Islands. To that too the answer was no.

Still Magellan remained on his knees. "Then, sire," he said, "may I be permitted to seek service under another Lord?"

At this, the king rose, his face dark with anger. "Serve whom you will, Clubfoot," he shouted. "It is a matter of indifference to me!"

A few days later Magellan boarded a merchantman (commerce ship) bound for Oporto, a seaport at the mouth of the Douro River, not far from his childhood home in northern Portugal. Here he took lodgings in a waterfront tavern and here, during the spring of 1517, he was host to a distinguished visitor.

His guest was John of Lisbon, Portugal's foremost navigator. Magellan had served under him in North Africa, and the two had become friends. Still in good standing at court, John of Lisbon had come to Oporto secretly, taking care that no word of his journey came to the attention of King Manuel.

Night after night, in the torchlit barroom of Magellan's inn, the two men conferred. We know now what they talked about. It was during these conversations that Magellan began planning his circumnavigation of the globe. In the last few years Portuguese mariners had been examining the coasts of recently discovered America, hoping to find what they called *El Paso,* a waterway through the huge block of land on which the merchants of their country could travel to the flourishing markets of the Spice Islands of the Orient. During his own exploration of the eastern rim of South America, John of Lisbon had found what he believed to be the opening to a passage to the ocean on the far side of the continent.

He had reported his find to Martin Behaim, the king's mapmaker, and Behaim had shown the supposed *El Paso* on a globe of the world, completed shortly before his death. In the late spring of 1517, when John of Lisbon returned to the Portuguese capital, Magellan went with him. There, one night, they slipped into the royal map room and either snatched Behaim's globe or copied it and smuggled it out.

Back in Oporto, Magellan completed his plans. By this time he had made the acquaintance of two powerful Spaniards, Diogo and Duarte Barbosa. On October 12, when Magellan traveled to Spain, the Barbosa brothers stood ready to help him in every way they could. First they provided him with a wealthy wife, Diogo's daughter Beatriz

Barbosa. Then they arranged an appointment for him with Charles I, king of Spain, better known to us today as Charles V, emperor of the Holy Roman Empire.

We have no written record of Magellan's audience with King Charles, but subsequent events tell us what happened and show that the seventeen-year-old ruler of Spain and the thirty-seven-year-old seadog took to each other at once. Magellan showed the king Behaim's globe and pointed out the break in the coast of South America that John of Lisbon believed to be *El Paso*. He recounted his discovery years earlier of the Philippines. His assertion that those islands belonged to Spain had angered the king of Portugal. It delighted the king of Spain. Charles urged Magellan to rediscover the Philippines, claim them for Spain, and convert their inhabitants to Christianity. Finally, he agreed to give Magellan ships and men for his proposed voyage.

Months of hard work ensued as five tall, square-rigged ships were fitted out and captains, crew, and supplies assembled. As captain-general of the expedition Magellan selected as his flagship the 110-ton *Trinidad*, the second largest ship. To command the other ships— the *San Antonio*, the *Victoria*, the *Concepcion*, and the *Santiago*—he chose one of his Portuguese kinsmen, John

Serrano, and three Spaniards, Juan de Cartagena, Caspar de Quesada, and Luis de Mendoza. At the last minute the *Trinidad* received as a passenger a young Venetian nobleman named Antonio Pigafetta. He came as a spy sent by the rulers of Venice with orders to inform them of any new trade routes to the Orient discovered by the expedition. Spy or no spy, he did all of us a favor by endlessly scribbling in his diary throughout the journey, leaving the only eyewitness account of the first circumnavigation of the globe.

On September 20 the fleet set sail, stopping briefly in the Canary Islands before crossing the Atlantic to the shores of South America. Early January 1520 brought them to the estuary that according to John of Lisbon opened into a strait through the continent, only to learn after an extensive exploration that what they had reached was not *El Paso* but the Rio de la Plata, the broad river along which stand the present-day cities of Montevideo and Buenos Aires.

Magellan was bitterly disappointed but undaunted. Since they had not yet found a waterway across the continent, he told his officers they would move southward along the coast. In time, he assured them, they would find *El Paso*.

Soon they were in the cold and stormy waters in the vicinity of the Antarctic, and on March 31, having anchored in a bay that Magellan dubbed St. Julian, they were making preparations to spend the southern winter on its shores. There was grumbling on all sides. Food was running low, chiefly because before the departure of the fleet from Spain a gang of men from Portugal, perhaps agents of King Manuel, had stolen into the holds of the five ships and removed a third of their contents. Some of the officers urged the captain-general to give up the search for *El Paso* and proceed to the Spice Islands by recrossing the Atlantic and picking up the well-known eastward route to the Orient by way of the Cape of Good Hope and the Indian Ocean.

Magellan refused to so much as listen to these arguments, arresting those who continued to advance them. Well-traveled trade routes did not excite him. He was no trader at heart; he was an explorer consumed with a longing to go where none had gone before.

The grumbles were loudest among the Spanish captains. Cartagena, Quesada, and Mendoza had been a source of trouble from the beginning. They resented taking orders from a Portuguese. During the fleet's short stay in the Canaries they had tried to seize control of the expedition by murdering the captain-general. Told of this scheme in advance, Magellan saved his life by withdrawing his own sailing orders for

a spell and following theirs—only to alter course suddenly and under circumstances which left the Spanish captains no choice but to go his way.

The Spaniards were not the only officers unhappy with Magellan's leadership, but they were the fomenters of the violence that erupted at St. Julian shortly before midnight on Easter Sunday. Some studies of Magellan's life call the events of the next two days a mutiny. Others treat them as a justifiable uprising by men forced to put their lives at risk to satisfy the captain-general's determination to find *El Paso* and explore the unknown waters beyond it.

Leader of the revolt was Cartagena. "On the night of 1–2 April," Pigafetta tells us, Cartagena "boarded the *San Antonio* and forced her ship's company to acknowledge him as their leader." Dawn found the Spanish captain in control of three ships: the *San Antonio*, the *Victoria*, and the *Concepcion*, leaving the captain-general with only the flagship and the *Santiago*. Magellan resorted to a ruse. He put some of his men in a boat and told them to row to the *Victoria* and announce that they wished to join the rebels. Once aboard that vessel, they whipped out concealed weapons and took it over, whereupon Magellan put the three ships he now controlled across the mouth of the harbor.

Magellan's voyages are the subject of this seventeenth-century engraving by Johannes Stradanus. Fear of the unknown is reflected in the presence of monsters and other imaginary creatures. *Courtesy of The New-York Historical Society.*

Outmaneuvered and outnumbered, Cartagena surrendered and a court martial followed. One of the Spanish captains, Mendoza, had been killed during the fighting. Another, Quesada, was executed, and Cartagena was removed to a small uninhabited island in the Atlantic and left to die. As for the members of the crew who had joined the rebellion, until shortly before the expedition put to sea again at the start of the southern summer these men were forced to perform their duties in chains.

The great day came on October 21, 1520, when, having rounded a craggy promontory, the travelers found *El Paso*, the mountain-rimmed waterway lying across the bottom of South America, now known as the Strait of Magellan. On November 27, when the fleet reached the western end of this winding passage, it consisted of only three ships. Gone was the *Santiago*, wrecked on a sandbar; gone too was the *San Antonio*, separated from the other ships in the strait and now on its way back to Spain.

It was storming as the remaining ships put *El Paso* behind them, but at midday the sun emerged and the seas quieted. To mark the occasion, the captain-general assembled the crew of the flagship on deck and signaled the captains of the other ships to do the same. Priests traveling with the expedition led the sailors in prayer and in singing the hymn of thanksgiving known as the *Te Deum*. Then Magellan, climbing to the poop of the *Trinidad*, unfurled the flag of Spain. "We are about to stand into an ocean where no ship has ever sailed before," he shouted. "May the ocean be always as calm and benevolent as it is today. In this hope I name it the Mar Pacifico."

Calm and benevolent the ocean remained, but the voyage that ensued was one of the most grueling in history. For a few weeks Magellan steered north along the coast of Chile. Then he turned west, eventually following a parallel of latitude in the neighborhood of the equator. It was his belief, as he turned away from the shores of South America, that he would reach the outlying islands of Asia in a few days. A few years earlier the geographers of his time had pronounced the only recently discovered Pacific to be nothing more than a large gulf.

A large one, indeed, it turned out to be. Many weeks after the fleet began its westward trek, a sunlit morning found the captain-general standing at the rail of his flagship, tearing up the charts he had brought with him and dropping the pieces into the sea. Obviously the men who had drawn these maps knew nothing about the Pacific. Obviously it was infinitely larger than they thought, which meant that the world itself was much bigger than they believed it to be.

Had Magellan crossed the Pacific fifteen or twenty miles to the south, he would have encountered several islands. But for two months, along the route he selected, the ship's companies did not see so much as a speck of soil. As they sailed deeper into the tropics, what little food remained turned putrid, breeding long white maggots. Scum coated the water in their casks, creating a stench so powerful that the men had to hold their noses to drink it. Dozens of them fell ill, victims of what they called the "plague," what today we call "scurvy," an often fatal dietary deficiency. By the end of the first week of January 1521 almost a third of the men had died.

Not until the end of January did they raise a tiny, uninhabited atoll. There they spent a week, resting, fishing, and collecting fresh water by spreading their sails on the beach when it rained. Two weeks later they spotted another island, but the waters surrounding it were too deep for sixteenth-century ships to anchor in, and they were forced to move on.

By March 4 the food was gone, and it was understood from Magellan on down through the ranks that unless they found a place where they could land within the next forty-eight hours, none of them would be alive. Two days later, in the early morning hours, a seaman posted aloft to watch for reefs, one of the few men aboard the *Trinidad* still strong enough to climb the ratlines, emitted a piercing shout: "Praise God! Land! Land!"

It was the island of Guam. As the ships approached, the bay was suddenly crowded with canoes, loaded with hostile natives brandishing clubs, spears, and oval shields. Magellan ordered the ships' guns fired. The natives, racing back, disembarked and fled into the nearby coconut groves. They remained there long enough to permit the visitors to pass a few hours ashore, feasting on food found in the natives' huts.

That night the three ships slipped away. Nine days later they found themselves in shallow waters, surrounded by a network of lushly wooded islands. On one of these they tarried for a few days, replenishing their supplies before sailing on, past still more well-forested islands. Suddenly, in the early hours

of the morning of March 28, a large canoe carrying eight natives from one of the islands drew alongside the *Trinidad*. The captain-general hastened to the rail, accompanied by Black Henry, the young slave he had acquired years before at Malacca on the Malay Peninsula. Black Henry hailed the occupants of the canoe in Malay. They answered in the same language, and Magellan realized that they had reached the Philippines, the very islands, apparently, that he had encountered during his voyage eastward from Malacca in 1511. "[A]fter 550 days of storm and mutiny, hunger, pestilence and death," writes Ian Cameron, one of Magellan's biographers, "he had circumnavigated the world."

It was a high moment in the history of exploration and the beginning of the tangle of events that would end with Magellan's death. On the following day the Rajah, or ruler of a nearby island, a tall and handsome man named Columbu, boarded the *Trinidad* to speak to the captain-general, with Black Henry acting as their interpreter. Columbu volunteered to direct the three ships to the island of Cebu and there, on April 7, the Spaniards were welcomed ashore by another and more powerful native ruler, whose name Pigafetta fails to provide. All we know of the Rajah of Cebu is that he was a shrewd and calculating man and that he was impressed by the size of the Spanish ships and by the cannon they carried. He permitted the white visitors to establish a market where the iron and other items the Spanish had brought could be exchanged for the gold and precious stones of the Philippines.

"Before long," writes Stefan Zweig, another of Magellan's biographers, "relations of Filipinos and Europeans grew so cordial that the Rajah and many of his followers expressed a desire to become Christians." Magellan made haste to take advantage of this sentiment. On Sunday, April 14, the principal town of Cebu was the scene of an outdoor Mass, witnessed by thousands of natives, during which "the Rajah and his family, kneeling in front of the cross, were baptized." News of this ceremony, Zweig tells us, "spread far and wide. . . . Within a few days almost all the chiefs of the Philippines," having hurried to Cebu from their scattered islands, "had pledged their troth to Spain and been sprinkled with the waters of baptism."

Magellan, elated at this triumph, was seized with a desire to spread the faith still further—a fervor that led him into blunder. Cilapulapa, principal Rajah on the adjoining island of Mactan, had let it be known that he had no intention of bowing to Spain or to Spain's religion. It so happened that for years the Rajah

of Cebu and Cilapulapa had been fighting one another, and the suspicion arises that the ruler of Cebu saw in the situation a chance to use Magellan's ships and Magellan's cannon to overpower a long-time rival. At any rate, he is known to have urged the captain-general to carry the Gospel to Mactan—and Magellan agreed to do so.

His officers objected strenuously. They understood his eagerness to Christianize the Filipinos, but they contended that an attack on Cilapulapa would be an interference in the politics of the area and have the effect of losing for Spain the good will that they had created there. They pointed out that King Charles's orders were to reach the Spice Islands, that these were now only a short distance away, and that the time had come for the fleet to move on.

Magellan brushed their arguments aside and sent his marines to Mactan where they burned villages and killed a number of the inhabitants. But they did not capture Cilapulapa, and Magellan decided to go himself to Mactan. As none of his officers would go along, he called for volunteers.

Pigafetta was among those who accompanied the captain-general. Armed "with helmets and cuirasses" and traveling in longboats, Pigafetta tells us, the sixty members of the raiding party arrived in the waters off Mactan in the dark hours of Saturday morning, April 27. Magellan, however, "did not then begin the attack." Instead, Pigafetta writes:

He sent the Moor [Black Henry] on shore to inform Cilapulapa and his people that if they would acknowledge the sovereignty of the King of Spain [and] obey the Christian Rajah of Cebu . . . they should be looked upon as friends. Otherwise they would experience the strength of our lances.

The islanders . . . replied that they had lances as well as we. . . . They merely requested that they might not be attacked in the night, as they expected reinforcements and should then be better able to cope with us [at daylight]. This they said designedly to induce us to attack them immediately, in the hope that we should fall in the dikes they had dug between the sea and their houses.

We accordingly waited [for] daylight, when we jumped into the water up to our thighs, the boats not being able to approach near enough to land, on account of the rocks and shallows. The number which landed was 49 only, as 11 were left in charge of the boats. . . . We were obliged to wade some distance through the water before we reached the shore.

We found the islanders, 1,500 in number, formed into three battalions, [who] . . . showered on us such clouds of bamboo lances, staves hardened in the fire, stones, and even dirt, that it was with difficulty we defended ourselves. . . . They seemed momently to increase in number and impetuosity. A poisoned arrow struck the Captain on the leg, who on this ordered a retreat in slow and regular order; but the majority of our men took to flight precipitately, so that only 7 or 8 [Pigafetta and Black Henry among them] remained about the Captain. . . .

We retreated gradually . . . and were now at a bowshot from the islanders, and in the water up to our knees, when they renewed their attack with fury, throwing at us the same lance five or six times over as they picked it up on advancing. As they knew our Captain, they chiefly aimed at him. . . .

An islander at length succeeded in thrusting the end of his lance through the bars of [Magellan's] helmet, and wounding the Captain in the forehead, who, irritated . . . , ran the assailant through the body with his lance, the lance remaining in the wound. He now attempted to draw his sword, but was unable, owing to his right arm being grievously wounded. The Indians, who perceived this, pressed in crowds upon him, and one of them having given him a violent cut with a sword on the left leg, he fell on his face. On this they immediately fell upon him.

Thus perished our guide, our light, and our support. On falling and seeing himself surrounded by the enemy, he turned toward us several times, as if to know whether we had been able to save ourselves. As there was not one of us who remained with him but was wounded, and as we were consequently in no condition either to afford him succor or revenge his death, we instantly made for our boats. . . . To our Captain indeed did we owe our deliverance, as the instant he fell, all the islanders rushed toward the spot where he lay.

As Pigafetta makes clear, the survivors of the ill-fated attack made no effort to recover the body of their leader. They fled back to Cebu. There all was chaos. The defeat of the captain-general and his men at the hands of Cilapulapa and his followers rendered the Spaniards contemptible to Filipinos. Before the members of the expedition could escape from the island, several of them had been murdered by the natives.

At the last moment one of the officers of the fleet who had participated in the rebellion against the captain-general in South America put all of Magellan's records—his logs, his charts, even his personal letters—aboard the *Concepcion* and set the ship afire. It is due to the loss of these records, the biographer Cameron believes, "that Magellan is not as well known today as he deserves to be."

Be that as it may, Pigafetta lived to publish his journal of the expedition, and he had kind words for Magellan. "So noble a captain," he wrote of him. ". . . he was more constant than anyone else in adversity. He endured hunger better than all the others, and better than any other man in the world did he understand sea charts and navigation. . . . The best proof of his genius is that he circumnavigated the world, none having preceded him."

The remaining two ships of the fleet reached the Spice Islands in November 1521, but there one of them was wrecked. Only the *Victoria* completed the circumnavigation, sailing across the Indian Ocean, around the Cape of Good Hope, and up the Atlantic to Spain—a journey of 10,000 miles.

It was on a Monday, September 8, 1522, that the *Victoria* reached the docks of Seville. It was from here, three years before, that the expedition had begun the journey—five ships and 277 men. To here it now returned—one ship and eighteen men.

Nils Adolf Erik Nordenskiöld

1832–1901 Finnish-born Swedish geologist and Arctic explorer. Planner and leader of the first expedition to navigate the Northeast Passage.

Born on November 18, 1832, at Helsingfors (Helsinki), the capital of Finland, Nils Adolf Erik Nordenskiöld was one of the seven children of Nils Gustav and Margarete Nordenskiöld, and a descendant on his father's side of a line of Finns notable for their scientific achievements.

A great-great-grandfather, whose given names were Johan Erik, was the chief inspector of the saltpeter factories of one of the states or provinces of Finland. In 1710, when a rat-borne plague overwhelmed the country, Johan Erik protected his family by placing them on a ship and cruising in the open sea until the epidemic subsided. A great-grandfather named Carl Frederik was a charter member of the Swedish Royal Academy of Sciences. A grandfather,

Colonel Adolf Gustav, engaged in scientific research and established at Frugord, the family residence in the forested outskirts of Helsinki, a large museum of the natural sciences. And Adolf Erik's father was a well-known naturalist, whose position as director of the mining department of Finland took him on frequent mineral-hunting forays throughout Europe.

After a few years of private tutoring at Frugord, Adolf Erik enrolled in the gymnasium at Borgo, an academy set up to prepare young men for the University of Helsinki. In an autobiographical sketch, written years later, he wrote of his first year at Borgo, "I distinguished myself . . . by absolute idleness." At the close of the spring term, the authorities pronounced his school

191

work "unsatisfactory" and refused to advance him to the next grade.

Instead of scolding him for these failures, his parents found lodgings for him away from home and gave him to understand that during the remainder of his school years he was free to sink or swim as he saw fit.

He swam. "Self-respect was thus awakened," he wrote later. "I became exceedingly industrious, and was soon one of those then attending the gymnasium who obtained the best reports."

But his independent nature remained intact. When in 1848 the gymnasium suppressed free speech among the students, he expressed his disapproval by leaving the academy to spend a year studying mineralogy with his father before entering the university. There, after receiving the first of several degrees, he was appointed to the faculty of the division of physics and mathematics.

During Nordenskiöld's day, Finland was not yet an independent country. It was a grand duchy of Russia, albeit with its own constitution, its own parliament, its own president, and a devotion to democratic practice at odds with the autocracy prevailing in the other parts of the Russian Empire.

The mid-1850s saw the coming of the Crimean War with the military forces of Turkey, England, France, and Sardinia battling those of Russia. Theoretically Finland was on Russia's side, but among the outspoken Finns sentiments were noticeably mixed—so much so that Count von Berg, the Russian-appointed governor-general of Finland, took the position that as leaders of public opinion the members of the faculty at the university should refrain from political remarks of any sort. Such was the situation when on the night of November 10, 1855, during a lively festival in a tavern near Helsinki, Nordenskiöld delivered a speech containing expressions that Governor-General von Berg promptly announced as "high treason." Two days later Nordenskiöld was confronted with an ultimatum: He must either publicly express regrets for his remarks or leave the country.

He left, crossing into Sweden. There his reputation as a geologist and mineralogist was known, and in the spring of 1858 he was asked to join a Swedish expedition to the Arctic Ocean, led by the scientist Otto Torell, to investigate the group of islands known collectively as Spitsbergen. He had completed this chore and was back in Finland when he received the offer of a responsible position at the Swedish State Museum in Stockholm. Eager to accept this post, Nordenskiöld applied for a passport, an action that brought him into the presence of Governor-General von Berg.

Sharp words ensued. Von Berg began the conversation by charging that the young geologist had gone to Sweden on a passport that had expired. Nordenskiöld pointed out that he knew nothing about passport regulations. If the document on which he traveled was out of date, the officials should have so informed him. Von Berg laid the blame on the lax officials and changed the subject.

He reminded his visitor that he had not apologized for his political remarks at the tavern festival. Nordenskiöld replied that he had suffered enough as a result of that incident and that the time had come for it to be forgotten. But von Berg was not ready to bury the old grievance. "It is not enough for a man to recognize his errors," he said. "He should be sorry he made them." Those words triggered Nordenskiöld's not always firmly controlled temper. "That I shall never be!" he shouted, bringing from von Berg the announcement that "You shall have your pass, but you may say good-bye to Finland. I'll see to that!"

Now in exile from his native land, Nordenskiöld returned to Stockholm to begin his long career in the mineralogy department of the State Museum and to become in time a Swedish citizen. Stockholm would be home to him for the rest of his life, except for occasional stays in Helsinki after Count von Berg's departure from the governor-generalship, one trip for the purpose of celebrating his marriage to Anna Mannerheim, the daughter of a former President of Finland.

In 1861 and again in 1864 he accompanied Otto Torell on scientific inspections of some of the Spitsbergen islands. In 1868, with funds and a vessel supplied by Sweden's Royal Academy of Sciences, he left Stockholm on the first of the several expeditions that he himself would lead. On the first of these he and his shipmates invaded the pack ice of the Arctic to 81° 42′, the highest latitude attained to date. Five years later, having spent the preceding winter on Spitsbergen, he tried to reach the North Pole with teams of reindeer, only to find the ice of the Arctic Ocean too rough to be covered by this means. En route home, he became the first explorer to cross the ice cap of Northeast Land, northernmost of the Spitsbergen Islands. Then in 1875, with six Arctic expeditions behind him, he began preparations for what was to be his crowning achievement—the first navigation of the Northeast Passage.

The effort to sail through the winding channel that connects the Atlantic to the Pacific across the tops of Europe and Asia constitutes a chapter in the history of exploration so old that its beginnings are hidden in the mists of unrecorded time. We can be sure that for centuries before Christ the nomadic tribes living along the coasts of the passage—the Russians, the Lapps, the Nentsis, and Nordenskiöld's Finnish forebears—sailed along portions of it and sighted and perhaps landed on some of its bleak islands. But for us its history begins about the year 870, when a Norwegian Viking named Ottar discovered the Atlantic end of the passage and forged eastward to the White Sea where today stands the city of Archangel, the Soviet Union's major port on these cold waters. Where Ottar left off, other Vikings took over, sailing still farther east, as far as the big island of Novaya Zemlya.

But did this ice-strewn waterway extend to the Pacific? And if it did, could a cargo ship go through it?

These were the questions facing the sea-going traders of Great Britain, when on December 18, 1551 they founded in London a joint stock company called the Merchants Adventurers. By this time the Portuguese had found their way around the southern tip of Africa and across the Indian Ocean to the great silk and spice markets of the Orient. The organizers of the Merchants Adventurers wanted a share of this commerce, and as the Portuguese controlled the sea lanes to the south, they had no choice but to send their fleets in the other direction with instructions to penetrate the Northeast Passage as far as possible.

In 1553 the Merchants Adventurers sent their first fleet northward: three ships and 112 men under the leadership of Sir Hugh Willoughby. Willoughby's attempt to explore the passage and open it to commercial travel was marked, first, by tragic failure and, second, by unexpected success. While wintering north of the Kola Peninsula of Russia, Willoughby and the crews of two of the ships froze to death, but the third vessel, commanded by Richard Chancellor, having been parted from the others by a storm, managed to make a landfall at the mouth of the Divina River, site of present-day Archangel.

From this place Chancellor and his men marched southward, eventually reaching a city called Moscow, capital of the country then interchangeably known as Russia or Muscovy.

Here they were invited to the court of Ivan the Terrible, the first of the Grand Dukes of Russia to receive the title of Tsar. Ivan listened with interest to Chancellor's assertion that the subjects of the King of England would like to establish trade relations with the subjects of the Tsar. When Chancellor returned to England in 1554, he carried to his king a letter from Ivan the Terrible that was to give birth to a long and profitable exchange of goods between Britain and Russia. Happy with this golden windfall, the Merchants Adventurers renamed themselves the Muscovy Company, made two more unsuccessful efforts to conquer the Northeast Passage, and then gave up the effort.

At this time, 1581, the Netherlands took it over. Having just won independence from Spain, Holland and the other Low Countries were looking for trading partners in Cathay, as the people in the European countries along the Atlantic spoke of distant China.

During the next fifteen years the Dutch dispatched a series of expeditions northward in the hope of navigating the passage, thus giving themselves a commercial route to the Orient. Of these ventures the most important were the three voyages commanded by Willem Barents, an accomplished navigator and mapmaker. Although Barents discovered Spitsbergen and Bear Island, and obtained for his country profitable whale, seal, and walrus fisheries, he was unable to prove beyond question that the Northeast Passage ran all the way to the Pacific Ocean. That feat was accomplished in 1728 when Vitus Bering, a Danish navigator in the employ of Russia, sailed through the strait which now bears his name and which separates Asia from Alaska, and found the Pacific end of the Northeast Passage.

Thus was answered one of the questions about the passage. Obviously it ran across the northern coast of Europe and Asia and linked the two oceans together. Now only one question remained: Could the passage be traversed from end to end by a cargo vessel?

Nordenskiöld began his effort to answer this question by undertaking two preliminary voyages, one in 1875 and the other a year later, to test the channels and weather conditions in the Northeast Passage. On these surveys he pushed farther east than any explorer had gone before. Sailing into the Kara Sea, he terminated both journeys at the mouth of the Yenisei River that flows northward across central Siberia to form on the shores of the Kara a well-sheltered haven known in the nineteenth century as Dickson Harbor.

Returning to Stockholm in 1877, he drafted and presented to the king of Sweden his plans for the expedition that would carry himself, five other scientists, two ship's officers, eighteen sailors, and three walrus-hunters across the Northeast Passage. The plans called for the use of two vessels: the *Vega*, a 300-ton steam whaler, equipped with both sails and a sixty-horsepower engine, and

Adolf Nordenskiöld led the first successful navigation of the Northeast Passage. Portrait by Georg von Rosen, *Courtesy of the Swedish National Portrait Gallery*.

the *Lena*, a 100-ton steamer. Under the arrangements approved by the king, the smaller ship was to leave the expedition at the Lena River which enters the waters of the passage eastward of Dickson Harbor. The larger *Vega* was to complete the journey by itself. Funds for the expedition came in part from the king and in part from two wealthy individuals, Baron Otto Dickson of Sweden, and Alexander Sibiriakov, a Russian merchant.

Today we can follow the progress of the expedition in an English translation of *The Voyage of the Vega*, a two-volume work written by Nordenskiöld and first published in his own language in 1881. It is no mere log of a remarkable exploration. It teems with scientific observations of everything the voyagers saw. Pages are devoted to speculation concerning the presence of dust on a piece of drift ice. What was this stuff? Was it ash borne on the wind from the volcanoes of Iceland or particles from outer space? We are treated to the picture of a polar bear trundling rapidly landward when saluted by the cannon aboard the *Vega*, to descriptions of the customs and manners of the Nentsi people living on an island at the western end of the passage and to the Chukchi dwelling on the shores of Siberia along its eastern reaches.

On July 21, 1878, the *Vega* and the *Lena* sailed from the Norwegian port city of Tromsö. The thirty-first found them passing through the Yugor or Pets Strait into the Kara Sea. Here they were joined by two vessels belonging to Sibiriakov, one of which was carrying coal to fuel the engines of the *Vega* and *Lena*. On August 6 they reached Dickson Harbor at the mouth of the Yenisei River, where Sibiriakov's vessels ended their voyage.

At this point Nordenskiöld had traversed those sections of the Northeast Passage that he had reconnoitered in past years. When on August 10 the *Vega* and the *Lena* left Dickson Harbor, it was to sail into unknown waters. Ahead lay the low and slate-colored hills of Cape Chelyuskin, the arrival at which on August 19 was an occasion for rejoicing. As Nordenskiöld wrote later, "We had now reached a great goal, which for centuries had been the object of unsuccessful struggles. For the first time a vessel lay at anchor off the northernmost cape of the Old World. No wonder that the occasion was celebrated by a display of flags and the firing of salutes, and when we returned from our excursion on land, by festivities on board, by wine and toasts." After lingering some twenty-four hours in a cove at the foot of the gently sloping Cape, the two ships pushed on through the mouth of the Lena, where on the night of August 27–28 the smaller vessel left the expedition and the *Vega* steamed on alone.

Its occupants, shaping their course in a northeasterly direction, soon found themselves among the New Siberian Islands. Nordenskiöld noted that these islands were "renowned among the Russian ivory collectors for their extraordinary richness in tusks and portions of skeletons of the extinct [hair-covered elephants] known by the name of mammoth . . . [a species] which, at least during certain seasons of the year, lived under conditions closely resembling those which now prevail in middle and northern Siberia. The widely extended grassy plains and forest of North Asia were the proper homeland of this animal and there it must at one time have wandered about in large herds."

Throughout most of the journey few natives had been spotted, but on September 6, as the *Vega* proceeded east past Cape Shelagski on the northern coast of Siberia, two boats were sighted in the near distance. At once, according to Nordenskiöld:

Every man, with the exception of the cook, who could be induced by no catastrophe to leave his pots and pans and who had circumnavigated Asia and Europe perhaps without having been once

on land, rushed on deck. The boats were of skin, built in the same way as the uniaks or women's boats of the [Greenland] Eskimo. They were laden with laughing and chattering natives, men, women, and children, who indicated by cries and gesticulations that they wished to come on board.

The engine was stopped . . . and a large number of skin-clad, bareheaded beings climbed over the gunwale in a way that clearly indicated that they had seen vessels before . . . a lively talk began, but we soon became aware that none of the crew knew any language common to both. . . . This did not prevent the chatter from going on, and great gladness soon came to prevail, especially when some presents began to be distributed, mainly consisting of tobacco and Dutch clay pipes.

It was remarkable that none of them could speak a single word of Russian, while a boy could count . . . up to ten in English, which shows that the natives here came into closer contact with American whalers than with Russian traders. They acknowledged [to] the name of [Chukchi].

After the natives returned to their tent ashore, the members of the expedition continued eastward. So far they had encountered little ice, a fact that confirmed Nordenskiöld's conviction, later proved to be correct, that the Northeast Passage could be used for commercial shipping during the summer months. But now, with the coming of September, the northern winter was setting in. The days were shortening, and extensive patches of solid ice, difficult to get around, were appearing with increasing frequency.

Aboard the *Vega* a sense of alarm emerged. The goal for which Nordenskiöld and his crew were striving—the Pacific exit of the Northeast Passage—lay one hundred miles in front of them. A few more days would bring them there if they could keep going, but on the night of the twenty-ninth the *Vega* became frozen into Kolyuchin Bay.

Here, a mere seven miles short of the open waters that could have carried them through the Bering Strait into the Pacific, they were forced to stay for the next ten months.

They put the time to good use. A Chukchi village stood on the neighboring coast. Nordenskiöld and the other scientists visited it frequently, taking notes on how the natives lived and on their physical surroundings. The Chukchis were consistently friendly. On the possibility that in time the thick ice would crush the *Vega*, the crew carried portions of its arms and provisions ashore. These stores, Nordenskiöld tells us, "were laid up on the beach without the protection of lock or bolt, covered only with sails and oars, and no watch kept . . . it remained untouched. . . ."

On July 18, 1879, the members of the expedition were having their noon meal in one of the collection rooms of the *Vega* when suddenly the ship began to move beneath them. At 3:30 P.M. they steamed eastward, rounding Cape Deschnev two days later as they sailed into the waters of Bering Strait. Now they could celebrate an achievement that had eluded other seafaring explorers for 326 years—the navigation of the Northeast Passage.

Nordenskiöld was forty-eight years old when he returned to Stockholm in April 1880 to be made a baron by the king of Sweden and to receive other honors. In 1883 he undertook his last polar expedition, taking his ship through the great ice barrier of Greenland, a feat that for 300 years other explorers had attempted without success. He devoted the remaining years of his life to writing, producing not only his account of the conquest of the Northeast Passage but also a two-volume historical geography that would continue to attract readers for many years after his death in Stockholm on August 12, 1901.

Francisco de Orellana

ca. 1490–1546   Spanish conquistador. Leader of the first group of Europeans to navigate the Amazon River and cross the continent of South America.

Born at Trujillo, Spain, in 1490 or thereabouts, Francisco de Orellana crossed the Atlantic while still a boy to soldier in the armies of his country in the New World.

He fought first in Central America, then in South America, where he participated in the Spanish seizure of what are now Peru and Ecuador from the highly civilized Indians known as the Children of the Sun or Incas. In 1536, as a reward for his services, he was granted the right to found and develop a town that he called Santiago de Guajaquil, on the Pacific shores of Ecuador.

He was managing the affairs of the settlement when he learned that his Trujillo-born cousin, Gonzalo Pizarro, had been named governor of the province where Santiago de Guajaquil stood and had established his capital at nearby Quito. What made this information intriguing to Orellana was that the new governor was planning an expedition into the interior of South America to look for cinnamon trees. These trees yield a valuable spice, and according to the Indians a great grove of them stood in the jungle on the far side of the Andes Mountains.

The prospect of going with his cousin Gonzalo to help him find La Canela, the Land of the Cinnamon Trees, delighted Orellana. His long-nurtured ambition was to win for himself the governorship of a province in the New World. What better way to call himself to the attention of the king of Spain, the giver of such appointments, than to help Pizarro find those wealth-producing trees?

Traveling to Quito, he begged Pizarro to let him join the expedition. The governor hesitated at first, but when Orellana offered to bring along additional soldiers, he relented, and Orellana hurried back to Guajaquil. There he procured the services of twenty-three men, but by the time he could return to Quito, Pizarro had already forged eastward at the head of 220 armed Spaniards and 4,000 Indian slaves.

Orellana at once decided to catch up with him. Friends in Quito advised against it. They said the terrain beyond the mountains was too hazardous for a small body of men. They pointed out that the natives could be lying about the existence of La Canela. They had been known to lie about such things. Before the Incas faded into the tropical rain forest to the east, they spread the story that somewhere in the jungle was a city called El Dorado, a place so abounding with gold that the stuff lay on the ground and had to be swept into pools to let the people move about. It had been suggested that the Incas' purpose in disseminating this fairy tale was to lure their greedy conquerors into a jungle where many of them would die, as indeed most of those who had gone looking for El Dorado already had.

But Orellana's mind was made up. Off he went with his twenty-three companions, trudging eastward over the Andes and into the densely forested valleys of the foothills beyond. More than once, roving Indians attacked and were repulsed with difficulty. Food supplies dwindled. In late March, when Orellana and his followers stumbled into Gonzalo Pizarro's camp at a place called Zumaco, they had nothing left but their swords, their shields, and the garments in which they had set out.

Conditions in Pizarro's camp were almost as bad. Many of the Indians, unaccustomed to the hot dampness of the jungle, had died. Most of the 4,000 swine brought along to feed the expeditionary force had been consumed.

Pizarro named Orellana his second-in-command and the two of them conferred. Should they turn back while some food remained? Or should they press on until they located what they were looking for? The choice, both men realized, was between the possibility of starvation if they continued their search and the possibility of acquiring great riches if they found La Canela.

Riches won. The decision was for Pizarro to take eighty of the men and move eastward in search of the cinnamon trees. During his absence, Orellana would take charge of Zumaco.

Pizarro began his journey in the late spring of 1541. The last month of the year had begun before the bad news reached Zumaco. Pizarro had found La Canela, yes; but things were not as the Indians had pictured them. The natives had given the impression that there was a large plantation of the spice-bearing cinnamon trees. In fact, there were only a few of them, and these were so scattered about the jungle as to be useless.

Since making this discovery, Pizarro had wandered aimlessly for a time. Now he and his soldiers were encamped in a region called Quema, a broad open space, sparsely treed, covered with coarse grass, and washed by the waters of a mountain stream called the Coca.

Here, in the opening days of December, Orellana and the other members of the force arrived. Again Pizarro and Orellana conferred. This time there was an even tougher issue to be considered. The members of the expedition were now 400 miles east of Quito. For so large a body to go back there would be exceedingly dangerous because on their way to this place they had stripped both the countryside and the Indian villages of everything edible. The decision, therefore, was to move on in the hopes that somewhere to the east they could find a native settlement flourishing enough to supply them with provisions. Even this plan posed difficulties. The hardships of the recent months had left many of the men sick and disabled. It was when this problem grew acute that Orellana suggested a solution that Pizarro immediately endorsed.

For use on the Coca the Spaniards had constructed a small sailing ship known as a brigantine. Also available for navigating the river were a number of canoes obtained from the Indians living in the area. Orellana's proposal was that he take the brigantine and some of the canoes and move downriver in search of food.

To accompany him on this endeavor he selected sixty-four persons: fifty-nine Spaniards, two Portuguese soldiers, and two blacks, presumably slaves that the conquistadors had brought from Spain to the New World. Attached to this group was a thirty-six-year-old Dominican priest named Gaspar de Carvajal. Father Carvajal's record of the expedition led by Orellana is the only first-hand account we have of a 2,000-mile journey that began on December 26, 1541, on the banks of the Coca and ended eight months later where the Amazon River flows into the Atlantic along the coast of present-day Brazil.

A shadow hangs over this historic adventure. In a letter to the king of Spain, written eight months after Orellana's departure from the camp on the Coca, Gonsalo Pizarro accused his cousin of desertion and treason. Pizarro's story was that prior to leaving camp, Orellana promised that, whether he found provisions or not, he would return in twelve days. Instead, he and his sixty-four companions simply disappeared, leaving Pi-

The Amazon river, explored by Orellana in 1540, takes on the appearance of a snake in this map of South America engraved by Diego Gutiérrez in 1562. *Courtesy of Library of Congress.*

zarro and his starving followers to make their way back to Quito as best they could.

What are we to think of these charges? Did Orellana deliberately abandon his companions? Not at all, according to Father Carvajal. The Dominican's story is that at the start of the journey Orellana had every intention of returning as soon as he found food, only to realize a few days later that going back might be out of the question. By this time the little fleet had put the Coca behind them and was moving down a larger and more swiftly flowing stream called the Napo. So far no Indian settlement or other sources of foodstuffs had been sighted and the travelers, their supplies depleted, were reduced to eating "leather, belts, and soles of shoes cooked with certain herbs." So weak were the men, Father Carvajal tells us, that they "could not remain standing" and some of them "on all fours went into the woods to search for roots . . . and some there were who ate certain herbs with which they were not familiar" whereupon they became "like mad men and did not have sense." To which the priest adds that "Our Lord was pleased that we should continue on our journey [and] no one died [though] a number were quite disheartened [until] the Captain [Orellana] spoke words of cheer, [telling] them

to have confidence in our Lord, for since he had cast us upon that river He would see fit to bring us out to a haven of safety."

On the last day of the year—or perhaps on New Year's day itself, for Father Carvajal is vague about dates—Orellana gathered his companions about him. Thanks to the strong current of the Napo they were already 700 miles from their starting place. Should they now turn back? The answer was no. Every member of the group favored continuing in the direction they were traveling. None believed the brigantine could buck the strong current of the Napo. All were convinced that if they tried to return to camp by land they would perish. That night Father Carvajal "said the Mass as it is said at sea," pointing out that unless they found provisions soon, death would be their common lot. He urged them to prepare their souls accordingly, but on the following day the beating of drums was heard in the distance and on the morning of the ninth day of their journey, January 3, 1542, they encountered a village called Aparia where, after a talk with the local chiefs conducted by Orellana, who knew the language of these Indians, they obtained food.

They spent several days at Aparia where seven of their number died, having become too ill to benefit from the food. Now that the decision was "to go with the rivers," Orellana instructed his followers to cut wood in the forest, manufacture nails from the supply of iron brought along, and build another sailing vessel. When they left Aparia their fleet consisted of two brigantines, to be known henceforth as the *Victoria* and the *San Pedro,* and about fifteen canoes.

On February 1 they reached the mouth of the Napo, to find themselves floating down the main channel of the river most of us now call the Amazon, although the people in the countries through which it flows—Peru and Brazil—apply other names to certain stretches of it.

Orellana cannot be credited with the discovery of it. Forty-two years earlier, a Spanish ship's captain, Vicente Yáñez Pinzón, had chanced on the mouth of the Amazon, named its 200-mile-wide estuary the Sweet Sea, and sailed on (looking for El Dorado, incidentally), unaware that he had sighted the outlet of a river whose beginnings lay almost 4,000 miles to the west in the foothills of the Peruvian Andes.

Second in length to the Nile, the Amazon flows on a line parallel to and a little south of the equator. Seven miles across at its widest and fed by over a thousand tributaries, it dumps three and a half million gallons of water into the Atlantic every minute, a far larger amount than any other river discharges into its sea or ocean. Unlike the great inland waterways of Africa, the Amazon is unimpeded by falls or rapids. Formed near Iquitos, Peru, by the blending of several mountain affluents, it drops eastward so gently that the level of its waters at the Atlantic is less than 100 miles lower than those at its source. Today's largest ocean vessels travel up the Amazon for 600 miles, and ships with drafts of fourteen feet or less can go as far as Iquitos.

Geographically, modern Brazil is the fifth largest country in the world, and the mammoth valley created by the great river constitutes a fifth of Brazil. Filling the valley on both sides of the Amazon is the world's largest jungle, broken at intervals by open spaces called *campos* and at the eastern end of the river by high hills that in spots descend to the water's edge. So extensive are the thick rain forests of the basin of the Amazon that repeated efforts by modern developers to clear patches for the installment of ranches and towns have not yet made a substantial dent in the dark vastness. Naturalists suspect the existence in the steaming depths of the jungle of trees and animals unknown to us and waiting to be identified. Anthropologists speak of the presence in these leafy corridors of isolated tribes of Indians still living in the manner of those seen by Orellana and his friends over 400 years ago.

Father Carvajal's account of the passage of Orellana and his companions down the Amazon concentrates on their encounters with the people living along its banks. At some places the Indians, frightened at the Spaniards' big ships and exploding guns, fled into the forest, leaving the intruders free to plunder their abandoned huts. At other places, they welcomed the newcomers and shared with them the fish they pulled from the river and the turtles they kept in their village pools. At still other places they gave battle, frequently making it impossible for these white creatures from another world to come ashore.

One of Father Carvajal's tales—most of which are more fanciful than informative—has to do with a bird who, whenever it appeared, sat on a tree limb, singing its plaintive, one-note song, "hui," over and over. "Hui," it would seem, is a Spanish word for "hut" and, sure enough, every time the little bird sang to the Spanish adventurers, the huts of an Indian village came into view

Orellana might have used a device like this sixteenth-century compass card as an aid to navigation. He may also have used an astrolabe to measure the altitude of stars; with this information, a navigator could determine latitude and time. *Both, Courtesy of the National Maritime Museum.*

a few miles down stream. "This bird," the Dominican assures us, "was so reliable with its cry . . . that when it was heard our companions . . . cheered . . . particularly if there was a shortage of food."

In June, during one of the many battles with the natives, Father Carvajal was twice wounded, the second injury depriving him of an eye. The enemy forces on this occasion were led by what the Spaniards took to be a band of women. "Very white and tall" they were, according to Father Carvajal, with long hair "braided and wound about the head." Each of them, the imaginative chronicler reports, did "as much fighting as the Indian men," lodging so many arrows in the hulls of the *Victoria* and the *San Pedro* that "our brigantines looked like porcupines."

Astounded at the sight of these armed females, the Spaniards at once remembered the old legend about a tribe of women called the Amazons who allowed no man into their country in Asia Minor and who fought against the Greeks in the Trojan War. It was Father Carvajal's story of the tall, white fighters with the braided hair that a few years later gave the great river of South America its name.

But who were these sharp-eyed warriors? That question remains unanswered to this day although a logical probability, often advanced, is that they were men with long hair.

The great day for the voyagers fell in early August when they saw up ahead the roiling, five-foot waves of a heavy incoming tide, indicating that they were approaching the ocean. By the twenty-sixth their brigantines were in the waters of the Atlantic and by September 11, 1542 they were resting on the little island of Cubagua in the Caribbean Sea north of Venezuela.

From here Orellana hastened to Spain. The conquistador who had gone as a boy to the New World in search of riches and power had not relinquished his longing for such things. But the trip down the Amazon—what Father Carvajal described as a "rambling voyage" that came about "by accident and not by our will"—had given Orellana a taste for exploration. At Valladolid, where the royal court was meeting, he asked permission to return to the Amazon, to establish settlements in that region and to serve as its governor.

Charles I, king of Spain—also known as Charles V, emperor of the Holy Roman Empire—was not a man given to making up his mind quickly. Nor was he ever eager to spend his country's money. Almost two years passed before he authorized Orellana to lead a fleet of ships across the Atlantic, and when in December 1545 Orellana reached the mouth of the Amazon, it was to face many vicissitudes. Although he succeeded in moving 300 miles inland along one of the great river's many channels, he was unable to locate its principal channel. He was supervising the construction of an additional ship on a small island when Indians attacked and killed seventeen of his companions, and Orellana, grief-stricken at this loss and exhausted from his exertions, died.

During his recent stay in Spain he had taken as his wife a young woman named Ana de Ayala. Ana crossed the Atlantic with him, and he had deposited her on the Island of Margarita in the Caribbean before sailing on to the mouth of the Amazon. As for the date of his death, all we can say with certainty is that the news of it reached his wife at Margarita during the opening days of November 1546.

Robert Edwin Peary

1856–1920   American naval officer and Arctic explorer whose expeditions to Greenland established the northern limits of that island. Discoverer of the North Pole.

On an August morning in 1908 a small steamer called the *Roosevelt* put in at Cape York on the western shores of the continentlike island of Greenland. The Eskimos of the area had seen it coming. They were already in the bay, converging on the vessel in their kayaks. They knew the tall, granite-faced American awaiting them in the prow of the *Roosevelt*. He had spent many a sunless winter among them. He and they had traveled together through the thick snows of the Arctic during many a nightless summer.

Six times before he had come north, driven by two burning desires. One was to determine the northern limits of Greenland. That goal he had already achieved. The other was to make his way to the North Pole. That he had

not done yet. The Eskimos, clambering aboard to shake his hand, remembered his telling them at the close of every stay that he would not be coming back.

Yet here he was again. And none of them was surprised, least of all Alakasingwah, the old medicine man. "You are like the sun, Pearyaksoah," Alakasingwah shouted at the fur-framed visitor. "You always come back."

That was the life and career and spirit of Pearyaksoah in a sentence. He was one of those people who, once they resolve to do something, never give up no matter how unrelenting the difficulties.

He was born Robert Edwin Peary in the mountainside town of Cresson, Pennsylvania, on May 6, 1856. His father, Charles Peary, a manufacturer of barrel heads and staves, was of mostly French descent. His mother, Mary Wiley Peary, was wholly English. Both had grown up in Maine, and when in their son's second year Charles Peary died suddenly of double pneumonia, Mary Peary moved back to Maine to be near her relatives.

Here, in a little house at Cape Elizabeth near Portland, Robert Peary grew up. "It is not a strange thing for a boy to live alone with his mother," his biographer, Naval Commander Fitzhugh Green has written. "Yet . . . Robert Peary's living alone with his [mother] . . . probably did more to make him a great explorer than any other single external factor in his life. She it was who moulded the moral character of her son . . . led him into the right books and hobbies. . . . She taught him of his family, holding them up as traditional examples of splendid men. . . . And she did one thing more. Let Robert say it in his own words: 'She made me *feel* there was a God. Other boys there were who believed it. I *felt* it.'"

From the public schools in Portland, Robert went on to Bowdoin College in Brunswick, Maine, graduating in 1877 with a degree in civil engineering and the natural sciences. For a year he worked as a surveyor in a small Maine town. Then, having been named to the Coast and Geodetic Survey, he moved to Washington, D.C., and spent three years at an engineer's drafting board.

In 1881 he joined the navy with the rank of lieutenant and went to work as a civil engineer at the Washington Navy Yard. Twice he was sent to Nicaragua to help plan a canal through that Central American isthmus, a project that was later abandoned.

One of his haunts in Washington was an old bookstore. Here, one day, he stumbled onto a printed description of that amazing natural phenomenon known as the Greenland Ice Cap. More than 8,000 feet thick in spots and beginning a few miles inland of the island's coasts, this glistening dome of ice covers at least three-fourths of Greenland's 840,000 square miles of land. In the fall of 1885, when its existence came to the attention of Robert Peary, no explorer had examined it. Could it be examined? he wondered. Could its secrets be uncovered? Could it be crossed by a human being, on foot perhaps, or on skis, or maybe with the aid of dog-drawn sledges? To a young man hungry for something big to do with his life, here was challenge worth looking into.

He looked deeply. He tracked down everything that had ever been written about the Ice Cap. Like all great explorers, Peary knew the importance of thorough study. Having read every word he could find on the subject, the next step was to go to the Ice Cap, to see it for himself.

But how was that to be done? He learned that the steam whaler *Eagle* was planning a run from Canada to the Arctic whaling grounds in the waters off Greenland. Could he go along as a passenger? For $500, yes, he was told. It was a lot of money to a man earning $100 a month. He borrowed the money from his mother, wangled six-months leave from the navy, and in May 1886 embarked on his first journey to the frozen north.

Then as now, Greenland belonged to Denmark. It was at the Danish trading station of Godhavn on the western fringes of the island that Peary landed on June 6, 1886. He needed a boat that would carry him up the nearby fjord to the tiny town of Ritenbenk, standing in the shadow of the 2,000-foot western wall of the Ice Cap. He knew no Danish. The authorities at Godhavn knew no English. Fortunately, Peary had acquired a little French and a little German. Using a few sentences in these languages and a lot of gestures, he obtained not only a boat but also the services of a young Dane named Christian Maigaard.

Maigaard helped him to sail the boat up the fjord. By late June the young men had climbed to the top of the Ice Cap and were trudging east, dragging their supplies on two tobogganlike sledges.

For several days a fierce storm imprisoned them in their tent. After it passed, they pushed on. There were deep and jagged crevasses to be got around. There were days when the bright Arctic sun melted the surface of the glacier beneath them, forcing them to struggle waist-deep in freezing mush. There were ice-sheeted hills to be climbed. When at last they came to a relatively even area, they were 7,525 feet above sea level. Their provisions ran low. They had traveled 120 miles from their starting point when on July 19 they realized that to go farther was to starve. Now they must return to Godhavn.

But Peary was content. He had seen what he had come north to see: a fraction of the Greenland Ice Cap. He had experienced its winds, its blinding sun, its forbidding hills. By the time he got back to Washington in the late fall, the whole of his future lay mapped out in his mind. He would return to Greenland. Next time he would take enough supplies to let him travel inland from its coasts for hundreds of miles. He would take along a few husky men to assist him. Once in Greenland, he would enlist the help of the Eskimos, the people who really knew the frozen north. Together they could cross the Ice Cap.

No one yet knew how far north Greenland extended. There were those who thought it stretched right to the North Pole. If so, Peary would go there by land; if not, he would try to reach the Pole by traversing the pack ice that covers the Arctic Ocean.

That fall these were not the only matters on his mind. In recent years a woman had entered his life. Josephine Diebitsch was the daughter of a professor at the Smithsonian Institution. She was one of the belles of Washington. She had beauty, charm, and a sense of humor. When he proposed, she turned him away with a bit of banter. She knew him well. "I'm going to be the first man across Greenland," he had told her, not once but many times. That was his dream, and she knew that nothing would ever stop him from realizing it. Such men, she reasoned, are hard to live with. They are also hard to discourage. On August 11, 1888, in the parlor of the Diebitsch home in Washington, they were married.

The navy had shifted Peary to the Brooklyn Navy Yard, so they began their life together in a one-room apartment in downtown New York. They had barely settled in when staggering news broke. One of the greatest explorers of the era, Norway's Fridjof Nansen, had skied across the Greenland Ice Cap.

End of Peary's dream? Not at all. He was downhearted at first, but that passed. Nansen, he explained to Josephine, had crossed the relatively narrow southern part of the island. He would cross the wider northern end. And while he was at it, he would try to locate the northern limits of the island. Soon he was giving lectures and knocking on the doors of scientific societies seeking the funds that in the summer of 1891 carried him northward for his second examination of the interior of Greenland.

This time a few experienced travelers went with him. Among them was Matthew Henson, the black American who from this trip on would accompany Peary on all his Arctic expeditions. Josephine, too, went along, and became the first white woman to winter north of the Danish settlements in South Greenland.

The outward-bound voyage on the steamer *Kite* was not without incident. On July 11 a freak accident left Peary with a broken leg. He was hobbling on crutches when on July 27 he and his party disembarked at Inglefield Gulf, an inlet of Smith Sound in the northwestern corner of Greenland.

Here they made camp. And here it was that Peary began his long and useful friendship with the Eskimos. Earlier

George Rockwood photographed Robert Peary near the turn of the century. *Courtesy of the National Portrait Gallery, Smithsonian Institution.*

polar explorers had shunned these men and women of the north. Peary was the first one to treat them as equals. He was amused by the belief, common in America, that in the eyes of the Eskimos white men were superior beings, gods to be worshipped. His guess was that the "Inuit"—"*The* man," as the Eskimo called himself—was as proud of his way of life as the white man of his. He employed the Eskimos to drive the dog teams that pulled his sledges. He learned from them how to build an igloo, an art no white person before him had mastered. He also learned from the Inuit the right clothes to wear in sub zero temperatures, the importance, during the hunting season, of laying in the stock of fresh meat that protected his American companions from the dreadful disease known as scurvy.

"I have been asked: 'Of what use are Eskimos in the world?'" he once wrote. "They are too far removed to be of any value for commercial enterprizes; and, furthermore, they lack ambition. . . . But let us not forget that these people, trustworthy and hardy, will yet prove their value to mankind. With their help the world shall discover the [North] Pole."

With their help the world, in the person of Robert Peary, would do just that. But this achievement still lay in the future when on the last day of April 1892 Peary left camp to begin the 700-mile trek that took him across the Ice Cap to the northeastern shores of Greenland.

Still unanswered at the close of this remarkable feat was the question of how far north the island extended. Still unfound was what Peary often spoke of as "the imperial highway" to the North Pole. On his return to the United States in the late fall he immediately began preparations for another northward venture with these goals in mind.

Again he went on a lecture tour to raise some of the necessary funds. Again he obtained grants from a variety of scientific bodies and interested individuals. In the spring of 1893 the newspapers were describing the details of his impending trip. Suddenly a new element crept into these reports. The Pearys were expecting their first baby.

As this news spread, biographer Fitzhugh Green tells us, the public split into camps. The women of the country said Peary should call off his expedition and stay home with his pregnant wife. The men pointed out that thousands of dollars had been raised for the venture, that months of labor had gone into the planning of it. Peary, in their opinion, should go.

Josephine Diebitsch Peary resolved the argument quietly. When on June 26, 1893, the steamer *Falcon* bore her husband northward, she was at his side; and on the shores of Bowdoin Bay, another inlet of Whale Sound, Marie Ahnighito Peary became the first white child to begin life in the Arctic Circle. Her father recorded the occasion in his diary. "On September 12th," he noted, "an interesting event occurred at Anniversary Lodge [the shelter erected at the Bowdoin Bay camp] in the arrival of a . . . nine-pound stranger. . . . This little blue-eyed snowflake, born . . . in the heart of the White North far beyond the farthest limits of civilized . . . habitations, saw the cold grey light of the Arctic autumn only once before the great night [of the Arctic winter] settled upon us."

This expedition, Peary's third, was a series of setbacks. Twice he and his followers attempted another crossing of the Ice Cap. Both times unbearable weather sent them back to Bowdoin Bay. "The fates and all hell are against me," Peary told one of his assistants. "But I'll conquer yet!" And before the expedition ended, he could point to at least one accomplishment.

Seventy-five years before, the British Arctic explorer Sir John Ross had sighted on an island along the western coast of Greenland three large meteorites, three hunks of stone that had fallen from space. The Eskimos had given names to these objects. One put them

in mind of a sleeping animal, and they called it "the Dog." Another, because of its resemblance to a seamstress sitting crosslegged, was known as "the Woman," and the third as "the Tent." The Dog weighed about 1,000 pounds, the Woman 6,000, and the Tent nearly 100 tons, or 200,000 pounds. Previous attempts to bring these awesome figures to the United States had failed, but when Peary came home in 1895 he brought with him the Dog and the Woman. The 200,000-pound tent had proved too heavy for the ship he was using, but on his fourth excursion in 1896 he succeeded in loading it aboard a larger vessel. On October 2, 1897, it was placed on the quay wall of the Brooklyn Navy Yard.

Meanwhile, Peary's efforts to organize another Arctic expedition were running into trouble. His superiors in the navy were tired of his repeated requests for the long leaves of absence that his trips required. They needed his services at home. On April 12, 1897, he received an official paper ordering him to report for duty at a naval station in San Francisco, California.

Peary was horrified. He did not want to go to California. He wanted to return to Greenland. He promptly dispatched a letter to the Secretary of the Navy, asking for another leave of absence. The secretary just as promptly refused it.

What to do? Peary was pondering that question when only a day or two before his scheduled departure for the west he was introduced to a prominent New Yorker named Charles E. Moore. Mr. Moore was active in the Republican Party, and in 1897 the Republicans were running the country.

Peary described his difficulties to Moore. "How much leave [from the navy] would you like?" the New Yorker asked. "Five years," said Peary. A few hours later Moore was at the White House in Washington, talking with his friend William McKinley, President of the United States. A few hours after that Peary held in his hand the document that on July 4, 1898, permitted him to sail for the Arctic again.

During the next five years he encamped here and there in the higher reaches of the frozen north. So terrible were some of the dark winters that several of his American associates deserted. At intervals he found himself living under what biographer Green describes as "Stone Age conditions." On one of his tramps across the snowfields an attack of frostbite necessitated the amputation of eight of his toes. For a time thereafter he could travel only by lashing himself to one of the sledges pulled by his Eskimo dogs and driven by his Eskimo friends.

But this expedition, his fifth, was not a total loss. In mid-May 1900, Peary and his companions rounded the upper shores of Greenland. "At last," he noted in his diary, he had found "the Arctic Ultima Thule." At last he knew exactly how far north Greenland extended. He also knew now that to get to the North Pole he must go by sledge 500 miles or more across the ice of the Arctic Ocean. Three times he tried to do so, once coming within 343 miles of his destination before foul weather and a diminishing food supply forced him to turn back. When in the fall of 1903 he reported for duty at the Navy Department in Washington, he was an exhausted and disheartened man. "Trip a failure," he wrote in his diary.

But Robert Peary was not about to give up. True, he had not reached the North Pole. But during the trying years of his fifth expedition he had learned many things about the polar world. Someday this knowledge would enable him to attain that goal. When in July 1904 a group of his supporters handed him a check for $100,000, he began planning a sixth expedition.

For this enterprise he built a special ship with unusually powerful engines. He named it the *Roosevelt* after Theodore Roosevelt, who had succeeded McKinley in the White House. After stopping at Cape York to pick up his Eskimo drivers, he forged northward through a series of waterways to Elles-mere, a large island to the immediate west of Greenland. One of the things he had learned during his fifth expedi-tion was that off Greenland the ice of the Polar Sea tended to develop so-called "leads" or open spaces. To the west of Greenland these dangerous gaps were fewer. Hence Peary's decision to begin his attempt on the Pole from the northern shores of Ellesmere.

On March 2, 1906, the sledges of his party began creaking northward across the "frozen Hades" of the Arctic Ocean. On some days violent winds made the going heartbreakingly slow. On others wildly drifting snow blinded men and dogs alike. Temperatures ranged from 59° to 66°F. below zero; and from time to time some of the travelers, worn out from their exertions, were sent back to Ellesmere. The weaker dogs were weeded out. "Finally," Peary wrote in his diary, "as I looked at the drawn faces of my comrades, the skeleton fig-ures of my few remaining dogs, at my nearly empty sledges I felt that I had cut the margin as narrow as could rea-sonably be expected. I told my men we should turn back from here."

The date was April 21, 1906, and "here" was latitude 87° 6'. Peary had traveled farther north than any other human being, but he was still 174 miles short of the Pole. No sooner was he

back in the United States than he began planning what was to be his seventh, and last, expedition.

This was the triumphant one. On April 6, 1909, he stood at the North Pole. With him were five sledges, thirty-eight dogs, and five men: his longtime American friend Matthew Henson and four Eskimos named Ootah, Eginwah, Seegloo, and Ookeah.

In 1909 Peary was fifty-three, with eleven more years of life ahead of him. After the many years of struggle and hardship, he was happy to retire to the home he and Josephine had built for themselves on Eagle Island in Maine's Casco Bay, happy to spend time with his wife and children, another child, Robert, having been born in 1903.

For a few months his days were trou-bled by a controversy arising from the claim by another American explorer, Dr. Frederick A. Cook, that he had reached the Pole a year in advance of Peary. By October 1909, however, this ordeal was over. A committee of experts named by the National Geographic So-ciety examined the records of both men and unanimously concluded that the honor of discovering the North Pole be-longed to Peary.

Honors of all sorts followed from sci-entific societies in America and Europe, and from the Congress of the United

Peary and his men raised five flags over the North Pole on April 6, 1909. From left to right are the Navy League flag, the D.K.E. fraternity flag, Peary's polar Stars and Stripes, the Daughters of the American Revolution peace flag, and the Red Cross flag. *Neg. 272317, Courtesy of Department Library Services, American Museum of Natural History.*

MARCONI WIRELESS TELEGRAPH COMPANY OF CANADA, Limited.

MONTREAL.

No. 4   Indian Hr STATION   Sept 6th   19 9

Pref. X   Off. H   Word 8 coll   CHARGES TO PAY.

                                        Marconi Charge
Office of Origin   Other Line Charge
Service Instructions: Delivery Charge
                                        TOTAL

                          Station sent to Time sent By whom sent
                               St   8.26 am   B

To: READ THE CONDITIONS PRINTED ON THE BACK OF THE FORM.

PEARY ARCTIC CLUB

NORTH POLAR EXPEDITION

1908

S. S. ROOSEVELT,_____190

ASSOCIATED PRESS
    NEW YORK CITY.

STARS AND STRIPES NAILED

TO NORTH POLE.

                        Peary

A triumphant Peary telegraphed the news of his conquest of the North Pole. *Neg. 272318, Courtesy of Department Library Services, American Museum of Natural History.*

States, which in March 1911 placed Peary on the retired list of the corps of civil engineers with the rank and retirement pay of a rear admiral.

Years after his death in Washington on February 21, 1920, an article in the *Dictionary of American Biography* asserted that Peary's attainment of the North Pole was only one of his many accomplishments. "As a result of his labors," the DAB noted, "a highly efficient method of polar exploration [was] . . . developed—large parties being discarded in favor of the small party, and Eskimo modes of dress and travel being utilized. His Greenland traverses and his later travels . . . completely revised the map of a large region. . . ."

Marco Polo

ca. 1254–1324   Italian merchant whose account of his twenty-four years in Asia revealed the wonders of the Orient to the people of Europe and greatly enlarged their comprehension of the geography of the world.

In the year 1253 two merchants of Venice, the brothers Nicolo and Maffeo Polo, set out on a trading journey to Constantinople. To Nicolo the parting from his wife was not easy, for she was expecting a child. No doubt he assured her that he would soon return. No doubt she smiled knowingly to herself. In the thirteenth century travel was difficult, and commercial ventures such as her husband and his brother were embarking on tended to take a great deal of time. This one was to last almost sixteen years.

During the Polos' sixth year in Constantinople, trouble broke out in that glittering capital of what was then the Byzantine Empire, and the brothers shifted their headquarters to the town of Soldaia on the northern shores of the Black Sea. But business was not good in Soldaia. Few people wished to buy the wooden utensils and wrought iron, the salted fish, the precious stones, and the healthy young slaves that Nicolo and Maffeo were offering. So they moved on again. This time they plunged into those spacious reaches of Asia that a few years earlier the armed hordes of the fierce Mongol leader Genghis Khan had conquered and that his grandson Kublai Khan now ruled from his capital in distant China.

During a stay of several years at a trading city called Bokhara, the Polos received first bad and then good news. The bad news was that the troubles that had driven them from Constantinople had spread southward into the lands bordering the Mediterranean Sea and that the plans they were making to return to Venice must be put off. The good news, brought to Bokhara by an envoy of Kublai Khan, was that should the Polos wish to move their business to China, they could count on a cordial welcome at the court of the powerful ruler of the Mongol Empire.

This was a prospect that the curious and enterprising brothers could not resist. It took them a year to cross Central Asia, but once under the golden domes of the royal palaces in Cathay (China) they knew that their long hard trip had not been in vain. Kublai Khan greeted them warmly. He saw to it that their every need was met. He questioned them at length and on many occasions about the beliefs and practices of Christianity. When the Polos expressed a longing to see their homes and families again, he let them depart, but only after they had made certain promises. One was that they would return to China as soon as possible. Another was that when they did, they would bring along some oil from the lamp kept burning in the Holy Sepulcher, the church standing in Jerusalem over what was believed to be the tomb of Christ. Still another was that they would deliver to "Master the Apostle," Kublai's term for the Pope, a letter that the Khan had written.

What an amazing letter this was! Kublai asked the head of the Roman Catholic Church to send him a hundred men versed in the doctrines of Christianity. If these teachers, Kublai wrote, could demonstrate the superiority of their religion over the various religions practiced by his people, he and all his subjects would become Christians. As one student of these events has observed, had the Church complied with Kublai's request "the history of the Far East and perhaps of the entire world might have been profoundly changed." But as the brothers Polo would learn to their sorrow, circumstances at home were such that the Church was unable to fulfill Kublai's wishes.

By the time the Polos reached Venice in 1270, Pope Clement IV had died. With no one to whom they could deliver the Khan's letter, the brothers could only wait impatiently until the Cardinals of the Church got around to electing another man to the throne of Peter at the Vatican in Rome.

For Nicolo Polo the return home was an occasion for both sorrow and rejoicing. His wife had died, but the child born in his absence and named Marco after an uncle had grown into a strapping youth.

We can assume that Marco lived with relatives after the death of his mother. We can also assume that he was pleased now to find himself again in a home

Marco Polo's colorful tales enthralled centuries of European readers. A French version of the *Description of the World* is illustrated with a scene of the great Kublai Khan engaged in a hunt. *Manuscript from Bibliothèque Nationale, Paris, Courtesy of Giraudon/Art Resource, NY.*

he could call his own. Soon after the return of the Polo brothers, Marco's father remarried and the day was near when Marco would have brothers and sisters.

And what sort was he, this Marco Polo, whose far-ranging travels were to reopen between Europe and Asia the doors that had clanged shut in 476 with the fall of Rome and the onset of the so-called Dark Ages? Not that there was no communication at all between West and East during these many years. There was some, but it was very slight and it had no appreciable effect on the lives of the people of Europe. In the

"cultural night" that was the Dark Ages, Marco's biographer Henry H. Hart tells us, "there was no place for interest in faraway lands or people. The very memory of the early voyages to the East and of Asia . . . died out"; and little by little fantastic notions about Asia replaced true geographical knowledge. All this Marco Polo would change.

Like most boys coming of age in the Europe of the Dark Ages, he had little if any formal schooling. But he was far from uneducated. He passed his boyhood playing with his chums along the heavily traveled canals of Venice, on its numerous quays and bridges, and in its busy talk-filled public squares.

These places had much to teach him. Loafing on the Rialto, he picked up the rudiments of commerce, for this was the place where the merchants of the city gathered to buy and sell and dicker with one another. Time spent in the ornate recesses of the handsome church of St. Mark's familiarized him with the great stories of the Bible, for these could be "read" in the gleaming gold of the mosaics on its soaring walls. He learned how ships were built from watching hundreds of them hammered into life in the yards abutting the city's lagoons. He learned how guns and ammunition were manufactured, observing these processes in the mammoth arsenal of Venice.

Plainly his alertness impressed his father and uncle, for when on a summer's day in 1271 they began their return to China, seventeen-year-old Marco was with them. Kublai Khan's letter remained undelivered; but the Polos, bearing in mind their solemn agreement to return to China "as soon as possible," had decided to wait no longer for a new Pope to be elected.

A long and narrow ship with banks of oars on either side and a lateen-rigged sail carried them over the Mediterranean to the port of Acre on the shores of the Holy Land. Here they hastened to the Venetian quarter to talk with their old friend Teobaldo of Piacenza,

the Vatican's representative in this area. From Teobaldo the Polos obtained an official paper for the Great Khan, explaining why they had been unable to convey his letter to the Pope. With Teobaldo's help they got from Jerusalem the holy oil they had promised to bring to Kublai. They had resumed their journey when a horse-borne courier, catching up with them on the road, informed them that Teobaldo himself had been elected Pope and had taken the name of Gregory X. Back to Acre they sped, to congratulate their friend on his elevation to the papacy and to get from him the hundred teachers of the faith that Kublai had demanded.

But the members of Acre's Catholic community were loath to join an expedition certain to be fraught with danger. Only two monks, Brother Nicolas of Vicenza and Brother William of Tripoli, were with the caravan led by the Polos when it began a crossing of Asia that would take three and a half years. Neither of them would be on hand when it ended. As the caravan crawled eastward across Armenia, an armed band of Saracens, longtime enemies of the Christian West, came raiding through the region. Nicolas and William took fright, and nothing the Polos could say could force them to go on.

The three Polos and their entourage moved on: sometimes across the monotonous waste of the steppes; sometimes

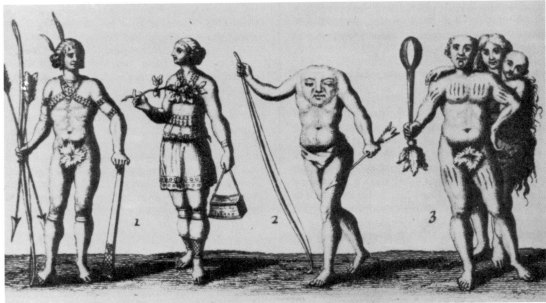

Top: Marco Polo's descriptions of a savage Siberian tribe inspired one artist to depict its members as headless monsters. *Bottom:* Centuries later, the same fear of alien cultures prompted a French author to include headless men in his catalogue of natives of America. *Courtesy of Bibliothèque Nationale, Paris;* from *Moeurs des sauvages ameriquains comparées aux moeurs des premiers temps, I, 1724. The New York Public Library.*

through lush valleys watered by gentle rivers, shaded by date and pomegranate trees, and fragrant with the blooms of exotic flowers; sometimes through the hot and seemingly endless sands of Gobis, the Mongol word for deserts; sometimes through the thick snows of mountains so high that the travelers, speaking to one another in awed voices, expressed the conviction that they had reached the roof of the world.

More than once they circled their top-heavy, two-wheeled carts to protect themselves against the Caraunas, the half-Indian, half-Tartar bandits of Central Asia. On occasion, encamping in a pleasant stand of trees, they relaxed for a day or so, hunting boars and other beasts with bow and arrow. They climbed Mount Ararat where, legend says, the ark of Noah settled after the flood. They lingered at a place called Saba, from whence on a night long ago, as every good Christian of those days knew, the three Wise Men set out on their visit to the Christ Child in the manger at Bethlehem.

In Persia they marveled at the sight of what Marco later described as "a fountain from which oil flows in such abundance that a hundred shiploads of it may be taken from it at one time." What they were seeing was a shallow forerunner of the oil wells that someday would dot this region for miles around.

It was during their passage through Persia that a thought occurred to them. Perhaps they might shorten the time of their journey by going the rest of the way by water. With this possibility in mind, they headed for Hormuz, the port on the Persian Gulf from which ships regularly plied eastward to the cities of China. But once on the docks of Hormuz, looking out over the vessels crowding its harbor, the three Polos shook their heads. After all, they were Venetians. They knew dangerously ill-made ships when they saw them. Back to their caravan they went, to proceed overland as before—always in the direction of the rising sun.

At last, in 1274, they found themselves in Kublai Khan's summer palace at the place so glowingly described by Samuel Taylor Coleridge in the poem beginning

In Xanadu did Kubla Khan
  A stately Pleasure-dome decree:
Where Alph, the sacred river, ran
Through caverns measureless to man
  Down to a sunless sea.

For the next sixteen or seventeen years the three Polos lived and worked within the domains of the Great Khan. What chores they did for him, what offices they held, is not clearly known. There is evidence that the older Polos, Nicolo and Maffeo, served the Mongol emperor as military advisers. As for Marco, he is believed to have traveled much as one of the Khan's envoys and to have spent three years as the governor of a Chinese province on the banks of the Yangtze River.

When in 1291 the Polos asked leave to return to Venice, the Great Khan agreed on the condition that they perform still another errand for him. Recently a lesser Mongol ruler, the Sultan of Persia, had lost his wife. Seeking a new one, he had arranged for Kublai to send him a maiden named Coachin. The young lady was to travel by sea, and the Polos were to see to it that she was safely disembarked at Hormuz on the Persian Gulf.

Thus it came about that when the Polos left China they did so as the guardian of a seventeen-year-old bride and that the Chinese junk on which they traveled was part of a fleet of fourteen royal ships. There were stops at several islands, Java and Ceylon among them, and on the mainland of India. From Hormuz, reached after a voyage of many months, the Polos completed their homeward trek by land.

The Venice at which they arrived in 1295 was at war with its ancient commercial rival, the city of Genoa. Marco was now in his forties, and how he got involved in this fray is another of those questions about him for which no cer-

tain answer is available. We know only that during an obscure naval battle in the Mediterranean Sea in 1296 he was captured and thrown into the dungeon of the Palazzo di San Giorgio in Genoa.

It was here that he encountered, among his prison mates, one Rustichello of Pisa, an author of romantic stories of valiant knights and noble deeds. It was to Rustichello that Marco dictated the account of his Asian adventures that to this day many regard as the greatest travel book ever written. It would appear that the authors of the book called it the *Description of the World*. It would appear, too, that the original manuscript was in French. But when the book was published, soon after Marco's release from prison in 1299, it was almost at once translated into many languages.

Everywhere in Europe people read it. If they were illiterate, as many were, they got someone to read it to them. Everybody loved it. Who could resist Marco Polo's marvelous tales of monsters that were half human and half animal, of acres of diamonds and pearls on the tables of the great bazaars of Asia, of palaces in China so large a man striding fast needed a couple of days to walk around them?

Thrilling these tales were, but of course nobody believed them. Book dealers advertised the work, not as the factual report Marco insisted it was, but as a novel, a romance, a piece of fiction. Walking the streets of Venice, Marco grew accustomed to the shrill voices of children who tagged after him, shouting, "Messer Marco, oh, Messer Marco, tell us another lie." According to his book, the people of China bought things with what today we call paper money. Europeans versed in the ways of commerce knew very well that no tradesman was going to give you his goods for bits of pressed bark from a mulberry tree with some numbers written on them.

Learned Europeans, those who knew the geography of the world, scoffed at Marco Polo's assertion that in the ocean east of China lay a large and fabulously rich island called Zipangu. These gentlemen had read the works of Ptolemy, the great second-century mathematician and astronomer. It was agreed among them that if Ptolemy mentioned a place, that place existed; and if he did not, it did not; and nowhere in the works of Ptolemy was there so much as a word about a place called Zipangu or Japan.

Was Marco Polo disturbed by these criticisms of his book? One gathers that he took them in stride. After all, he had gone everywhere and seen everything. At any rate, he had seen enough to understand the reluctance of human beings to accept as true statements for which they could find no sanction in the tiny corner of the world they knew.

He married, whether before or after his seizure and imprisonment by the Genoese is not known. His wife was a Venetian aristocrat named Donata Badoer, and there were three children, all girls, and in time, six grandchildren, four boys and two girls. He pursued a second mercantile career, dealing in furs from Russia and in tin from England.

He lived in a mansion in Venice and people called him "Il Milione" or "Marco Polo Millions." But in truth he was not all that rich. He was a capable merchant, but buying and selling were not his first interests. Like his father, who died some time before 1300, and like his Uncle Maffeo, he was first of all an explorer. And his most prized possessions, other than his children and grandchildren, were the memories he had of distant places and strange people. His death on January 8, 1324, at the age of seventy, a ripe age for those days, was the quiet departure of a man at peace with himself.

In the centuries that followed, his book enjoyed increasingly more respectful readers. People following his tracks across Asia discovered that ninety per cent of what he had said in his book was accurate. And others, venturing into the Pacific, discovered that a place called Japan was very much there. Indeed, it was in the hope of reaching Marco Polo's Zipangu that a man named Christopher Columbus sailed westward from the shores of Spain in 1492, carrying in his luggage a well-thumbed copy in Latin of the *Description of the World*.

Pytheas

Fourth century B.C.   Greek mathematician and astronomer. Thought to be the discoverer of the British Isles and the first European—and probably the first human being—to invade the waters of the Arctic Ocean.

With Pytheas we go back to the days of Aristotle and Alexander the Great—back, that is, to the fourth century B.C. We also go back to what is called the "Dawn of History"—to that era, beginning about 600 B.C., when people living on the shores of the Mediterranean Sea began writing the story of man's past in an organized way. Coming along on the heels of this development, Pytheas became the first great explorer to be included in the written record of mankind.

He was a citizen of Massilia, a Greek colony on the northern shores of the Mediterranean where stands today the French port city of Marseilles. He was what the Greeks called a philosopher, meaning a mathematician and an as-tronomer. And he is remembered for three accomplishments.

He was the scientist who discovered that it is the pull or gravity of the moon that controls the tides of the ocean.

He invented a method for using the sun and the stars to determine the whereabouts of places, a procedure without which no accurate map of any place on earth can be drawn.

And, in the words of the twentieth-century explorer and historian Vilhjamur Stefansson, he made "the greatest voyage of all time."

Pytheas wrote a book about his journey. He called it *The Ocean*. But in his day there were no printing presses. Books circulated as handwritten manuscripts, and well before the beginning of the Christian Era all copies of *The Ocean* were gone. What we know of Pytheas comes to us thirdhand, from ancient works written by historians who never laid eyes on Pytheas's book and who based their information on quotations from it—quotations which like the book itself have disappeared so that we have no way of checking the accuracy of those who gave them to us.

In Pytheas's day a people called the Phoenicians controlled the trade routes of the Mediterranean. Sailing out from their home cities on the coast of Lebanon at the eastern end of the great inland sea, they established a string of city-states on the northern shores of Africa and on the southern shores of Spain. Some of them even pushed out into the then unknown waters of the Atlantic.

Apparently the Phoenicians found these oceangoing expeditions both commercially and militarily advantageous. At any rate, they went out of their way to discourage the Greeks from following them into the Atlantic. That ocean, according to the Phoenicians, was a maelstrom of dangerous whirlpools. Incredible monsters lurked in its depths, huge serpentlike creatures that were capable of gobbling up a whole ship and everyone on it.

Our skimpy knowledge of Pytheas suggests that, as a scientist, he laughed at these horror tales. Still, whenever it was he began dreaming of taking a ship and exploring the Atlantic, he realized that this would be difficult—perhaps even impossible. To get from Massilia to the ocean, he would have to pass through the Strait of Gibraltar, and it was common knowledge that heavily armed ships belonging to the Phoenicians guarded that narrow passageway.

So Pytheas did the only thing he could. He bided his time. He knew the world around him. He knew that terrible things could happen in it. Someday perhaps a war or some other calamity would compel the Phoenicians to withdraw their warships from Gibraltar. If such was his guess, he guessed correctly.

It happened in 333 B.C., when Alexander the Great marched down the shores of Lebanon and laid seige to Tyre, greatest of the Phoenician cities. Soon every Phoenician ship's captain in the Mediterranean was spreading sail and hastening eastward to help defend his homeland. Did this mean that no Phoenician warships remained at Gibraltar?

Pytheas could not be sure. In 331 or 330 B.C., when he set out from Massilia on his brave and wonderful journey, he could only hope for the best. He took no chances. When he reached the Strait of Gibraltar, he moved at a crawl.

Could the ancient Pytheas have braved the ocean in a vessel like those depicted on this classical Greek vase? *Courtesy of The British Museum; photo courtesy of the Science Museum.*

It took him five days to cross a waterway that the average vessel of his time covered in three at the most. But Alexander the Great had done well by him. No sharp wooden spears, no iron-tipped arrows rained upon him. And one morning he stood on the vast emptiness of the Atlantic.

Mind you, this was 2,400 years ago, a fact that raises an interesting question. What sort of ship did Pytheas command? A very seaworthy vessel indeed, for the Greeks, like the Phoenicians, were master shipbuilders. Pytheas's ship was between 150 and 170 feet long, about 37 feet wide at the beam, with a hold of some 26 feet deep, a very high poop, and a very high prow. Its tonnage was about 500, making it larger

and more serviceable than the clumsy *Santa Maria* that 1,800 years later carried Christopher Columbus to the New World.

Pytheas proceeded north, skirting the western shores of Spain, then turned east into the Bay of Biscay and northward along the coast of France into the English Channel. He made his first extended landfall on the southern coast of County Kent. From here, marching at the head of his crew, he crossed England to County Cornwall.

This was a perilous journey, for most of southern Britain was still in a state of nature. "The valleys," wrote the English polar explorer Sir Clements Markham, "were covered with primeval forest." Swamps gurgled in their declivities, and "only on the downs and hill ranges" were there "*gwents*, or open spaces."

Pytheas and his followers were not the first human beings to disturb these wilds. As the Greeks struggled westward, they encountered members of what Pytheas called "the Keltic tribes." These people, he learned, had occupied this part of England for generations. They lived on cultivated farms, kept domestic animals, and grew wheat and other cereals. They had iron tools and weapons, wooden chariots with iron fittings, and ornaments of bronze and gold. In this wooded world, sunny days were scarce. As rains were common, the natives threshed their corn in large barns rather than on open threshing floors. They stored the ears in underground pits, daily bringing out the portions that had been there longest to be prepared for food. They brewed a fermented liquor from barley. This they called *curmi*. "As Columbus was the discoverer of tobacco," writes Markham, "so his great predecessor Pytheas discovered beer." According to the fragmentary remains of Pytheas's own description of these people, they also made a drink from honey. This no doubt was the mead that we read of in connection with the festivities at King Arthur's court and in the mountaintop haunts of the Greek and Roman gods.

At the conclusion of his long trek Pytheas found himself in what he called the "country of the tin." Here, in Cornwall, were widespreading underground mines complete with shafts and galleries. Pytheas was not surprised at this discovery. He had heard of these diggings; he had seen the products of them in his own city on the shores of the Mediterranean.

The natives of Cornwall carried the metal taken from these mines to an island in the English Channel. There traders from continental Europe picked it up and conveyed it to France and down the Rhone River to Massilia.

Having returned to his ship off the shores of Kent, Pytheas steered north along the western coasts of England and Scotland. His next landfall appears to have been at Unst, the most northerly of the Shetland Islands. It was here, talking with the natives, that he heard of the existence of a place called Thule, some 600 miles to the northwest.

Today we call this place Iceland. Pytheas, reaching Iceland, continued northward until stopped by the drifting pack ice of the Polar sea. He thus became the first European to cross the Arctic Circle, the first to see the midnight sun, the first to travel in those far northern regions where during a portion of the summer months the daylight lasts for twenty-four hours. His explorations did not end at this point. We know that he ventured for a considerable distance into the Baltic Sea and that he examined the Atlantic shores of Ireland before setting his course for home.

Back in Massilia he recorded his adventures in the book he called *The Ocean.* The scientists of his time and place read and praised it, and even a century later it was being quoted from approvingly.

Then, with the appearance in about 200 B.C. of the first professional geographers, a strange shift of opinion occurred. By the opening years of the Christian Era these scholars were teaching that north of Scotland the ocean was a solid block of ice. No ship could penetrate it. It followed, in the opinion of these geographers, that Pytheas never went to a place called Thule or Iceland nor sailed beyond it. Pytheas, they said, had made it all up; he was a liar and a fake.

For more than a thousand years this belief prevailed. Then the Vikings, darting out from the fjords of Norway, found and settled first Iceland and then Greenland. Then Dutch and British seafarers began ramming their little vessels into the pack ice of the Arctic Ocean. Finally, in 1893, Sir Clements Markham, writing as the longtime president of the Royal Geographical Society in London, carefully reconstructed Pytheas's wanderings as Pytheas himself had described them and pronounced his claims correct in every essential respect. Today, according to Stefansson, practically all students of such matters agree.

Amerigo Vespucci

1454–1512   Italian-born businessman, diplomat, and navigator. Discoverer of Brazil, explorer of the Atlantic shores of South America, and member of the first group of Europeans to set foot on the mainland of the New World.

For one destined to make as many voyages as Christopher Columbus, Amerigo Vespucci was born at the right time and in the right place.

The time was the Renaissance, that sudden flowering of art and learning throughout Europe that many historians regard as ending the Middle Ages and ushering in the Modern Era. The place was Florence in central Italy, the "golden city of the Renaissance," where as Amerigo grew up he was in a position to meet and talk with men bearing unforgettable names, Leonardo da Vinci and Michelangelo among them.

The date of his birth, according to the calendar we now use, was March 9, 1454. His parents, Stagio and Elizbetta, belonged to a family so large and so concentrated in the industrial quarter of the golden city that one could not throw a stone there without hitting a Vespucci.

Fifteenth-century Florence was a city-state, a country unto itself. Its rulers, the rich and brilliant Medici, belonged to another large family with whom the Vespucci were closely connected, partly by marriage and partly by mutual intellectual and commercial interests. When in 1479 one of Amerigo's uncles went to Paris as Florence's ambassador to France, his twenty-four-year-old nephew went along as his confidential secretary. For several years after Amerigo had returned home, he supervised the sale of wheat and other business transactions for Lorenzo di Pier Francesco Medici, one of the members of the ruling family of Florence.

In the fall of 1489 one of Amerigo's chores took him to Seville, the great port city of Spain. He liked Seville. For years he had been an ardent student of maps and everything connected with travel on the high seas. Here in Seville he was surrounded by men who shared his passion for these things. It pleased him to notice that unlike Italy, a country divided into many city-states, Spain was united. In Spain a person could go about his business undisturbed by the turmoil created by the endless battles for political supremacy among the little states of his homeland. He noticed, too, that the people of Spain were loyal to their rulers, King Ferdinand and Queen Isabella. Such was not the case in Florence, where outbreaks of discontent with the ruling Medici were commonplace.

On his return to Florence he found it embroiled in one of these disputes. A Dominican monk named Savonarola was preaching in the streets of the city, contending that the Medici were evil and their policies undemocratic. Amerigo was stunned to find the members of his own family involved in this quarrel, some supporting the Medici, some Savonarola. To Amerigo Vespucci all political dissension was a waste of time. In the early months of 1492 he quit his job in Florence and hastened back to Seville.

There, soon after his arrival, he entered into a partnership with Gianetto Berardi, an elderly banker who, like Amerigo, was a native of Florence. Among their customers was another Italian, Christopher Columbus, recently elevated to the post of Admiral of the Ocean Sea by the rulers of Spain. In August, when the new admiral began the first of his four voyages across the Atlantic Ocean, the funds for outfitting one or more of his vessels came from the firm headed by Amerigo and Berardi.

In the spring of 1493 Columbus returned to Spain to find Seville the scene of parades and festivals. Everywhere the talk was of the admiral's discovery of a group of islands lying in what today is known as the Caribbean Sea. Soon Amerigo was dreaming of attempting such a voyage.

In 1496 Columbus returned from his second journey of discovery, but there were no celebrations for him in Seville or anywhere else. This time the word was that King Ferdinand and Queen Isabella were displeased with their admiral. One reason for this was that he had mismanaged the Spanish colony he had founded on the island of Hispaniola, now Haiti. Another was that his enemies were spreading malicious tales. They were pointing out that Columbus had brought home but little gold from the places he had found. Was it possible that in truth he had acquired large amounts of the precious metal but was keeping most of it for himself? Had he reported all the islands he had seen or was he perhaps keeping some of those for himself?

Amerigo was aware of the gossip. He was not surprised when in 1496 he received from the King of Spain a message inviting him to join an expedition that Ferdinand himself was readying for a trip across the Atlantic. Ferdinand was a hardheaded and practical man. He did not believe most of the tales unfavorable to Columbus. Neither did he believe everything that Columbus told him.

According to the admiral, the islands he had discovered were only a few days' sailing distance from the wealthy countries of the Orient: China and Japan, India, and the so-called Spice Islands at the bottom of Asia. But were they indeed a part of the Orient or were they simply isolated little places inhabited by naked savages? At the moment Columbus was asking the Spanish sovereigns to send him on a third voyage, and before saying yes to that, Ferdinand wanted to find out what the situation was in his country's new possessions across the sea. Hence his decision to dispatch a fleet of four ships westward to check on Christopher Columbus.

Ferdinand's wish to send Amerigo Vespucci across the sea as his special observer was dictated by a desire to be fair to his admiral. Amerigo was known to be one of Columbus's admirers. He was also known to be an honest man. He could be counted on to report whatever he saw accurately; he could also be counted on to refrain from fashioning false stories about his friend. As for Amerigo, he was pleased by the king's request. His business partner had died, and the firm they had managed together had been dissolved. He was free to go exploring on his own, and he was eager to do so.

Our knowledge of his first voyage, begun at Cadiz on May 10, 1497, and ended there on October 15, 1498, consists of but a few facts. We know that he and his companions circumnavigated Cuba, thus proving that country to be an island instead of a part of the continent of Asia as Columbus had claimed.

We know that Amerigo and his shipmates reached the waters off Costa Rica and then skirted the shores of Nicaragua, Honduras, and Mexico. Because in his letters home Amerigo described the customs and homes of the inhabitants of these regions, we assume that he and his friends went ashore, to become the first Europeans to stand on the mainland of South America.

We know that when this journey

Amerigo Vespucci clutches one of his own maps. *Courtesy of The New-York Historical Society.*

started, Amerigo had had no practical experience as a seaman, that during the journey he "made the ship his class-room," and that he ended the journey a full-fledged mariner, ready to com-mand a vessel on his own.

We also know that after reading Amerigo's reports, King Ferdinand con-cluded that Columbus was doing well and proceeded to send him on two more voyages of discovery.

Clearly his Majesty was also satisfied with his Italian-born observer, for when Amerigo left Spain on his second voyage in May 1499, he did so as the pilot of one of the three or four caravels consti-tuting the fleet. He accomplished much during this two-year expedition. He ex-amined and mapped long sections of the Atlantic shores of South America. He helped ascertain the extent of the pearl fisheries near the island of Mar-garita north of Venezuela. He devel-oped a way for determining the position of a ship at sea more accurately than any of those previously used. And he discovered the country of Brazil.

Under the terms of a recent treaty, Brazil lay in a portion of the non-Chris-tian world that belonged not to Spain but to Portugal, and the discovery of it brought Amerigo's skills as an ex-plorer to the attention of the Portuguese monarch, Manuel I. In the closing months of 1500 Amerigo returned to

Spain. A few months later, at the urging of King Manuel, he moved to Portugal, and both his third and fourth voyages were conducted under the Portuguese flag.

It was during the first of these expedi-tions for the "Serene King of Portugal" that Amerigo made the most important of his discoveries. Previously, he had believed, as did Columbus, that the strange regions he was examining were part of the continent of Asia. Now, as his ship moved along the coast of South America, south of the equator, he real-ized that he was looking at a separate land mass, another continent.

Columbus had called it an *"Otro Mundo,"* an Other World, still insist-ing, however, that it was connected to Asia. A Spanish historian had called it "a new world." But Amerigo Vespucci was the first to capitalize that phrase and to call this "previously unknown fourth of the globe" exactly what it was—*the* New World.

He conveyed this discovery to the people of Europe in a letter to his old boss in Florence, Lorenzo di Pier Fran-cesco de Medici—a letter that was subsequently published and widely distributed under the title *Mundus No-vus*. The region he was exploring, Amerigo wrote in this letter, was one "which I can licitly call the New World. . . . [It] is not an island, but a conti-

Vespucci is featured prominently on Martin Waldseemüller's sixteenth-century map of the world. *Courtesy of the New York Public Library, Division of Maps.*

nent, because it extends along far-stretching shores that do not encompass it and it is populated by innumerable inhabitants."

Mundus Novus was translated into many languages and read throughout Europe. Soon its author was famous. Soon either a copy of *Mundus Novus* or one of Amerigo's other printed accounts of his explorations was in the hands of Martin Waldseemüller, a German mapmaker living in the ancient monastery of Saint-Die in the moun-

tains of Lorraine. Delighted with this information, Waldseemüller promptly drafted and issued a new map of the known world with his version of Amerigo's first name—AMERICI—printed on that portion of it intended to represent South America. When Waldseemüller published a second edition of his map a few years later, he removed the word AMERICI. But by this time the name had caught on. People liked it. AMERICA the New World was, would be, and still is.

In 1505 Amerigo completed the last of his voyages, said good-bye to King Manuel, and returned to Seville.

It was the city of his heart. He had many friends and relatives there. For years he had been married to a woman named Maria Cerezo. She, too, had friends and relatives in Seville.

King Ferdinand had not forgotten Amerigo. Soon after the latter's return to Spain, Ferdinand named him to the newly created post of Pilot Major, a position roughly equivalent to what Americans call Secretary of the Navy. One of Amerigo's undertakings on this job was the creation of a college where young men could learn the arts of navigation, a naval academy.

Amerigo was very proud of this institution. His biographers tell us that on several occasions during the closing years of a life that ended in Seville on March 22, 1512, he was heard to say that he hoped people would regard the academy as his legacy to the seafarers of the world.

Important Dates in the History of Geographical Exploration

2334–2279.   Dates assigned to the earliest known surviving map. Drafted in the times of one of the early kings of Babylon, it shows portions of two waterways, probably the Tigris River and a tributary, and some surrounding mountains in what is now Iraq.

ca. 600.   Phoenician sailors, dispatched by a king of Egypt and beginning their three-year journey in the Red Sea, circumnavigate Africa and return to Egypt by way of the Strait of Gibraltar and the Mediterranean Sea.

510.   On orders from Darius the Great, King of Persia, Scylax of Caria in Asia Minor explores the Indus River in southwest Asia and the Red Sea, terminating his journey at Arsinoe at the southern end of what is now the Suez Canal.

ca. 500.   Hecataeus, a Greek living in Miletus on the Agean Sea, produces the first book on geography. Herodotus, the so-called "Father of History," prefaces his story of mankind with a description of the then known world—a passage that tells us that by this time the coasts of the Mediterranean and the Black Sea have been explored. Herodotus also describes the journey by five young adventurers of the tribe of Nasamones across the Sahara to a great river, probably the Niger, in Africa. Himlico, a Carthaginian, sails through the Strait of Gibraltar and northward along the coasts of Spain, Brittany, and perhaps England. Hanno, another Carthaginian, carries 30,000 colonists on sixty ships past Gibraltar and down West Africa to an island off Sierra Leone some ten degrees north of the Equator.

ca. 350.   Aristotle formulates six arguments proving that the earth is round.

320–325.   Alexander the Great, in the course of his campaigns of conquest, provides his people with their first knowledge of the region that stretches south from the Caspian Sea to the mountains of the Hindu Kush in Afghanistan and Siberia.

ca. 300.   Pytheas, a Greek scientist living in Massilia (now Marseilles, France), sails

241

through the Strait of Gibraltar, circumnavigates the British Isles, explores the Baltic Sea, and penetrates the waters of the Arctic Ocean above Iceland.

300. Dicaearchus, a disciple of Aristotle, begins to develop the reference-line system whereby future sailors will determine where they are by ascertaining their longitude (degrees east or west of Greenwich, England) and their latitude (degrees north or south of the equator).

200. Hippalus, a Roman sailor, sails from the Gulf of Aden to the coast of India. The southwest monsoon, the wind that permitted him to do this, will for years to come be known as the Hippalus.

100. Returning to his Egyptian home from a voyage to India and blown far to the south of Cape Guardafui at the northeast extremity of Somaliland, Eudoxus finds at his landfall a wooden prow and is told by the Africans that it belongs to a wrecked ship from the west. By this time the coastlines of the Indian Ocean and the China Sea are well known, though during the next two centuries much of this knowledge will fade from the memories of the people of both Africa and Europe.

A.D.

100. Chang Ch'ien, one of China's greatest explorers, opens the eastern end of the so-called Silk Route across Asia to Europe.

138. During the reign of the Roman emperor Hadrian, European traders reach Siam (Thailand), Cambodia, Sumatra, Java, and perhaps even China.

150. Ptolemy (Claudius Ptolemaeus), a Greco-Egyptian mathematician, produces the geography that explorers will follow for the next thirteen centuries. Ptolemy's underestimation of the size of the globe—he thought it about two-thirds as large as it is—will lead Christopher Columbus to believe that his discovery of the New World has brought him to the vicinity of Cathay (China and Japan).

161. The Roman emperor Marcus Aurelius sends envoys, bearing gifts, to the Chinese emperor Huan Ti.

499. Hoei-shin, a Chinese Buddhist monk, discovers "Fusang," a section of land on the western shores of America.

550. St. Brendan, an Irish priest, sails from his homeland to Greenland, Iceland, and Jan Mayen, another island in the Arctic Ocean.

629–645. Hsüan Tsang, a Buddhist monk known as the Master of the Law, crosses the Gobi desert to explore Tibet, India, and other regions westward of his native China.

650. Polynesian chief Ute-te-Rangiora reaches the frozen sea in the vicinity of Antarctica.

890. Ottar of Norway sails around North Cape and eastward along the coast of Lapland to the White Sea, to become probably the first person to enter the Northeast Passage.

982. Norway's Erik the Red discovers and settles Greenland.

1000. Bjarni Herjulsson of Norway, blown off course en route from Iceland to Greenland, sights the mainland of North America.

1001. Leif Erikson explores the coasts of Laborador, Newfoundland, and other areas of North America.

1200. The Polynesians settle Easter Island, probably the most remote speck of land in the world, standing as it does in the Pacific 1,500 miles west of South America and some 1,500 miles distant from the nearest of the many other Pacific islands.

1253. The brothers Nicolo and Maffeo Polo set out from Venice on the sixteen-year trip that will take them to the court of Kublai Khan in distant China.

1270. The Polo brothers begin their second trip to the Orient, taking with them seventeen-year-old Marco Polo.

1300. Marco Polo publishes the famous book describing his travels.

1325–1355. Ibn Battuta, a Moslem lawyer of Tangier, often called the "Arabian Marco Polo," covers over 75,000 miles in thirty years, exploring Arabia, India, other regions of Asia, Africa, and Spain.

1419–1460. Henry the Navigator, a prince of Portugal, organizes and dispatches numerous expeditions down the coast of Africa and into the interior of that continent, thus ushering in the Great Age of Discovery.

1488. Bartholomeu Dias of Portugal rounds the southernmost tip of Africa, discovering that Ptolemy was wrong in linking Africa to Asia and that a sea route to India is possible.

1492. Columbus discovers the New World.

1497. England's John Cabot reaches the mainland of North America.

1498. Portugal's Vasco da Gama rounds the Cape of Good Hope and crosses the Indian Ocean to India, thus creating a sea route to the Orient.

1498. Columbus reaches the mainland of South America.

1499. Italian-born Amerigo Vespucci, sailing first for Spain and then for Portugal, begins his extensive exploration of the coasts of South America, leading to his discovery of Brazil.

1500. Vicente Yáñez Pinzón of Spain discovers the mouth of Brazil's Amazon River.

1500. Pedro Alvarez Cabral of Portugal reaches Brazil and claims it for his country.

Whether the European discoverer of Brazil was Cabral or Pinzón or Vespucci remains to this day an item of dispute.

1507. A map drafted by Martin Waldseemüller at the Saint Die monastery in Lorraine assigns the name "America" to the New World.

1512. Portuguese mariners reach the Moluccas (the Spice Islands) off the southeastern coasts of Asia.

1513. Spanish-born Vasco Nuñez de Balboa discovers the Pacific.

1519. Alonso Alvarez de Pineda of Spain was, according to some authorities, the first European to sight the Mississippi River.

1519–1522. The Spanish expedition organized by Portuguese-born Ferdinand Magellan circumnavigates the globe.

1520–1521. Francisco Hernandez Cordova and Juan de Gryalva of Spain explore the coasts of Yucatan and the Gulf of Mexico.

1534. France's Jacques Cartier explores the Gulf of the St. Lawrence River.

1541. Hernando de Soto of Spain finds and crosses the Mississippi River.

1542. Francisco de Orellana of Spain crosses South America.

1551. English merchants form a trading company—first called the Merchants Adventurers, later the Muscovy Company—to seek the waterway to the Orient destined to be known as the Northeast Passage.

1553. England's Hugh Willoughby commands the first unsuccessful effort to navigate the Northeast Passage.

1567–1568. Alvaro de Mendana de Neira of Spain goes looking for *Terra Australis Incognita*, the enormous and nonexistent continent that, according to the ancient geographers, occupied the lower quadrant of the globe.

1576. English navigator Humphrey

Gilbert argues that China and the Spice Islands can be more easily reached by sailing west than by sailing east, thus putting under way the long search for the Northwest Passage. England's Sir Martin Frobisher, seeking the Northwest Passage, finds at the southeast tip of Baffin Island the bay that bears his name.

1577–1580. Englishmen Sir Francis Drake and Thomas Cavendish circumnavigate the world from west to east.

1586–1588. Drake and Cavendish do it again.

1587. English navigator John Davis, seeking the Northwest Passage, explores Cumberland Sound and the western shores of Greenland to the parallel of latitude at 73°N.

1594–1597. The brilliant Dutch navigator Willem Barents penetrates the Northeast Passage as far as the island of Novya Zemlya.

1606. Portuguese explorer Louis de Torres, sailing through the strait south of the island of New Guinea that now bears his name, sights the northern coastline of the continent of Australia.

1610. England's Henry Hudson discovers the huge Canadian bay that bears his name.

1612–1615. Three English voyagers—Robert Bylot, Thomas Button, and William Baffin—explore Hudson Bay and ascertain that the long sought Northwest Passage does not lead out of it—a finding that shifts interest from a search for the passage to an investigation of the resources of Canada, leading to the establishment in 1670 of England's giant fur-trading enterprise, the Hudson's Bay Company.

1616. Dutch navigator Willem Schouten discovers the southernmost tip of South America and names it Cape Horn.

1618. A Dutch skipper discovers the western coast of Australia and the exploration of this new continent, temporarily known as New Holland, begins. A Portuguese priest named Peaz discovers Lake Tana, the source of the Blue Nile in Africa.

1642. Dutch navigator Abel Tasman discovers the island of Tasmania south of Australia, the southern island of New Zealand, and the Tonga and Fiji islands in the South Pacific.

1682. France's Robert La Salle reaches the mouth of the Mississippi.

1686 or 1687. British buccaneer Edward Davis sights but does not land on Easter Island in the South Pacific.

1699–1701. English buccaneer William Dampier, on what seems to have been the first scientific examination of the South Pacific, explores sections of Australia and New Guinea and discovers and names the island of New Britain. Dampier's lively accounts of his many adventures are believed to have inspired the writing of *Robinson Crusoe* by Daniel Defoe and *Gulliver's Travels* by Jonathan Swift.

1722. Holland's Jacob Roggeveen, seeking the hypothetical *Terra Australis Incognita*, rediscovers and lands on Easter Island.

1734–1743. Denmark's Vitus Bering, sailing for Russia, discovers the sea and strait that bear his name during a series of unsuccessful attempts to enter the Northeast Passage from its Pacific end.

1769. England's Captain James Cook begins the first of the three great voyages that will prove the nonexistence of *Terra Australis Incognita* and reveal most of the mysteries of the Pacific.

1792–1793. Scottish-born Alexander Mackenzie crosses North America.

1796. The Scottish surgeon Mungo Park establishes the true course of the Niger

River in Africa, showing that it is not, as previously thought, a part of the Nile.

1798–1799.   The Englishmen George Bass and Matthew Flinders circumnavigate Tasmania, showing that it is not a part of Australia as previously surmised.

1801–1803.   Matthew Flinders charts the coast of the Great Australian Bight and circumnavigates the continent.

1803–1806.   Meriwether Lewis and William Clark of Virginia explore the American West from St. Louis to the Pacific.

1806.   The English whaler and scientist William Scoresby penetrates the Arctic Ocean to 81° 21′ N., and polar exploration begins.

1813.   Australian Gregory Blaxland becomes the first person to explore portions of the interior of Australia.

1819–1825.   England's Sir William Edward Parry sails westward through much of the Northwest Passage.

1819.   English mariner William Smith discovers the South Shetland Islands, an archipelago near Antarctica in the South Atlantic.

1820.   The New England sealing captain Nathaniel B. Palmer sights the continent of Antarctica, but the British say two of their seafarers, Edward Bransfield and William Smith, discovered it a few months earlier, and Russia also claims an earlier discovery by Fabian G. von Bellinghausen.

1827.   Sir William Edward Parry, on the first attempt to attain the North Pole, reaches 82° 45′ N., the farthest north to date.

1829–1830.   Australian Charles Sturt probes almost to the center of Australia, proving that area to be a desert and not, as had been hoped, a great inland sea.

1831.   England's James Clark Ross discovers the North Magnetic Pole.

1852–1856.   David Livingstone of Scotland, during the first of his many explorations of the interior of Africa, discovers the Victoria Falls.

1858.   Sir Richard Burton and John Hanning Speke of England discover Lake Tanganyika in central Africa.

1858.   Speke discovers the source of the White Nile, the main channel of the great river.

1861.   Robert O'Hara Burke leads the first expedition to cross Australia.

1875.   Welsh-born Henry Morton Stanley explores the Congo to its mouth and makes clear the pattern of the river systems of Africa.

1878–1879.   Erik Nordenskiöld, Finnish-born Swedish scientist, sails through the Northeast Passage.

1888.   Fridjof Nansen of Norway crosses the Greenland Ice Cap from Umvik on the east to Godthaab on the west.

1888–1889.   Belgium's Adrien de Gerlache leads the first expedition to winter in the Antarctic.

1893–1895.   Mary Kingsley of England studies "fish and fetish" in previously unexplored sections of West Africa.

1903–1905.   Norway's Roald Amundsen sails through the Northwest Passage.

1908–1909.   Englishman Sir Ernest Henry Shackleton, during a brilliant exploration of Antarctica, comes close—88° 23′ S.—to the South Pole.

1909.   America's Robert Edwin Peary reaches the North Pole.

1911.   Amundsen reaches the South Pole.

1912.   England's Robert Falcon Scott reaches the South Pole.

1926.   America's Richard E. Byrd and Floyd Bennett make the first flight over the North Pole.

1929.   Byrd makes the first flight over the South Pole.

Further Reading

Titles marked by an asterisk are most suitable for the young reader.

GENERAL

*Jacques Brosse, *The Great Voyages of Discovery: Circumnavigations & Scientists, 1764–1843*. New York: Facts on File Publications 1985.

*Lloyd A. Brown, *The Story of Maps*. New York: Dover 1979.

*Luree Miller, *On Top of the World: Five Women Explorers in Tibet*. Seattle: Mountaineers 1984.

Samuel Eliot Morison, *The European Discovery of America*. 2 vols. New York: Oxford 1971–1974.

Gerhard F. Muller, *Voyages from Asia to America*. Amsterdam: N. Israel, 1967.

Pacific Voyages. New York: Doubleday 1973.

*Gail Roberts, *Atlas of Discovery*. New York: Crown 1973.

R. A. Skelton, *Explorers' Maps: Chapters in the Cartographic Record of Geographical Discovery*. London: Routledge and Kegan Paul 1958.

*Vilhjalmur Stefansson, *Great Adventures and Explorations*. New York: The Dial Press rev. ed. 1947.

Percy Sykes, *A History of Exploration from the Earliest Times to the Present*. Westport, CT: Greenwood Press, repr. 1975.

*Edwin Tunis, *Oars, Sails, and Steam: A Picture book of Ships*. Cleveland: World Publishing Co. 1952.

AMUNDSEN

Roland Huntford, *Scott and Amundsen*. New York: Atheneum 1984.

*J. Gordon Vaeth, *To the Ends of the Earth: the Explorations of Roald Amundsen*. New York: Harper & Row 1962.

BALBOA

Charles L. G. Anderson, *Life and Letters of Vasco Nunez de Balboa*. London: Fleming H. Revell 1912.

*Jeannette Mirsky, *Balboa*. New York: Harper & Row 1961.

BURKE

*Alan Moorehead, *Cooper's Creek: The Opening of Australia.* New York: Atlantic Monthly 1987.

BURTON

Fawn Brodie, *The Devil Drives: A Life of Sir Richard Burton.* New York: Norton 1984.

Michael Hastings, *Sir Richard Burton.* New York: Coward, McCann & Geoghegan 1978.

*Alan Moorehead, *The White Nile.* New York: Harper & Row 1960.

BYRD

*Edwin P. Holt, *The Last Explorer.* New York: John Day 1968.

Richard Montague, *The First Flights over Wide Waters and Desolate Ice.* New York: Random House 1971.

CABOT

Raymond Beazley, *John and Sebastian Cabot.* New York: Burt Franklin edition 1964.

CARTIER

H. P. Biggar, *The Voyages of Jacques Cartier.* Ottawa: F. A. Acland 1924.

*Trudy J. Hammer, *The St. Lawrence.* New York: F. Watts 1984.

COLUMBUS

*Jean Fritz, *Where Do You Think You're Going, Christopher Columbus?* New York: Putnam 1980.

*Samuel Eliot Morison, *Christopher Columbus, Mariner.* Boston: Little Brown 1955.

Morison, *Admiral of the Ocean Sea.* 2 vols. Boston: Little Brown 1942.

COOK

John C. Beaglehole, *The Life of Captain James Cook.* London: Adam and Charles Black 1974.

A. Grenfell Price, ed. *The Explorations of Captain James Cook in the Pacific As Told by Selections of His Own Journals, 1768–1779.* New York: The Heritage Press 1976.

*Ronald Syme. *Captain Cook, Pacific Explorer.* New York: Morrow 1960.

ERIKSON

Gwyn Jones, *The Norse Atlantic Saga: Being the Norse Voyages of Discovery and Settlement to Iceland, Greenland, America.* New York: Oxford University Press 1921.

Donald F. Logan, *The Vikings in History.* New Jersey: Barnes & Noble 1983.

*Magnus Magnusson, *Vikings!* New York: Elsevier Dutton Publishing Co. 1980.

*Jacquelin Simpson, *The Viking World.* New York: St. Martin's Press 1980.

GAMA

Edgar Prestage, *The Portuguese Pioneers.* London: A & C Black 1933.

*Ronald Syme, *Vasco da Gama: Sailor Toward the Sunrise.* New York: Morrow 1960.

HENRY THE NAVIGATOR

Edgar Prestage, *The Portuguese Pioneers.* London: A & C Black 1933.

HOEI-SHIN

Charles G. Leland, *Fusang, the Discovery of America.* New York: Harper & Row 1973.

KINGSLEY

*Katherine Frank, *A Voyager Out: A Life of Mary Kingsley.* Boston: Houghton Mifflin 1986.

Stephen Gwynne, *The Life of Mary Kingsley.* London: Macmillan 1932.

LA SALLE

*Marquis William Childs, *Mighty Mississippi: Biography of a River*. New Haven: Ticknor & Fields 1982.

Francis Parkman, *La Salle and the Discovery of the Great West*. In *France and England in North America, vol. 1*. New York: Viking 1983.

LEWIS

*Robert H. Dillon, *Meriwether Lewis, a Biography*. New York: Coward-McCann 1965.

LIVINGSTONE

Tim Jeal, *Livingstone*. New York: Putnam 1973.

*Alan Moorehead, *The White Nile*. New York: Harper & Row 1960.

MACKENZIE

Alexander Mackenzie, *Voyages from Montreal through the Continent of North America*. 2 vols. New York: AMS Press edition 1973.

MAGELLAN

Ian Cameron, *Magellan and the First Circumnavigation of the World*. New York: Saturday Review Press 1973.

Charles McK. Parr, *Ferdinand Magellan, Circumnavigator*. Reprint. Westport, CT: Greenwood Press 1983.

*George Sunderlin, *First Around the World*. New York: Harper & Row 1964.

NORDENSKIÖLD

Alexander Leslie, *The Arctic Voyages of Adolf Erik Nordenskiold, 1858–1879*. London: Macmillan 1879.

*Helen Orlob, *The Northeast Passage: Black Water, White Ice*. New York: Thomas Nelson 1977.

ORELLANA

Gaspar de Carvajal, *The Discovery of the Amazon*. New York: AMS Press edition 1970.

Brian Kelly and Mark London, *Amazon*. San Diego: Harcourt Brace Jovanovitch 1983.

*Ronald Syme, *The Man Who Discovered the Amazon*. New York: Morrow 1958.

PEARY

*Fitzhugh Green, *Peary: The Man Who Refused to Fail*. New York: Putnam 1926.

*Walter Lord, *Peary to the Pole*. New York: Harper & Row 1964.

POLO

*Henry H. Hart, *Venetian Adventurer: Being an Account of the Life and Times and of the Book of Messer Marco Polo*. Stanford: Stanford University Press 1947.

PYTHEAS

Clements Markham, "Pytheas, the Discoverer of Britain." *Geographical Journal*, June 1893.

VESPUCCI

German Arciniegas, *Amerigo and the New World: the Life and Times of Amerigo Vespucci*. New York: Knopf 1955.

Index